10648265

FIVE SEASONS

Books by A. B. Yehoshua

FIVE SEASONS
A LATE DIVORCE
BETWEEN RIGHT AND RIGHT
THE LOVER
EARLY IN THE SUMMER OF 1970
THREE DAYS AND A CHILD

FIVE SEASONS

A. B. YEHOSHUA

Translated from the Hebrew by
Hillel Halkin

Doubleday

NEW YORK   LONDON   TORONTO
SYDNEY   AUCKLAND

Published by Doubleday, a division of Bantam Doubleday Dell Publishing Group, Inc.,
666 Fifth Avenue, New York, New York 10103.
DOUBLEDAY and the portrayal of an anchor with a dolphin are trademarks of Doubleday,
a division of Bantam Doubleday Dell Publishing Group, Inc.

Library of Congress Cataloging-in-Publication Data
Yehoshua, Abraham B.
Five seasons.
Novel.
Translation of: Molkho.
I. Title.
PJ5054.Y42M5513   1989   892.4'36   88-10900
ISBN 0-385-23130-X

DESIGNED BY CAROL A. MALCOLM

Translation copyright © 1989 by Doubleday, a division of Bantam Doubleday
Dell Publishing Group, Inc., and William Collins Sons & Co. Ltd.
Originally published in Hebrew as *Molkho*. Copyright © 1987 by A. B.
Yehoshua. Publisher: Siman Kriah, Hakibbutz Hameuchad, Tel Aviv, Israel.

All Rights Reserved
Printed in the United States of America
January 1989
First Edition
BG
WAK

FIVE SEASONS

PART I AUTUMN

MOLKHO'S WIFE DIED at 4 A.M., and Molkho did his best to mark the moment forever, because he wished to be able to remember it. And indeed, thinking back on it weeks and even months later, he was convinced that he had managed to refine the instant of her passing (her passing? he wasn't sure the word was right) into something clear and vivid containing not only thought and feeling but also sound and light, such as the maroon glow of the small electric heater, the greenish radiance of the numbers on the digital clock, the yellow shaft of light from the bathroom that cast large shadows in the hallway, and perhaps, too, the color of the sky, a pinkish ivory set off by the deep obscurity around it. He would have liked to think he recalled the dark morning sky because it added a stirring, elemental touch of nature, but he could not be sure of it, any more than he could be of the whisper of the wind and the rain; yet he was certain that there had been music —yes, real music he himself had turned on hesitatingly but convinced that if she wished to hear anything at all as she died, it was the music she had cared for so much in those last months when reading had become such a chore for her. Like the radio operator of a military vehicle heading into battle, she would adjust the small stereo earphones in the dead, painful twilight hours between the visits of her friends, her talks with her children, and her various treatments and pills; choose one of the cassettes by her bedside; and switch on the tape machine. She discussed this music with him and even once hinted that when the end came (so they referred to her death), she would like him to play some of it for her: if he saw it wasn't too much for her, she said, he should let her have music—and he was happy to be able to oblige, for she had trained him well during those last months and he had learned to do exactly as she told him, taking everything with the utmost seriousness. And so now, too, he remembered to flip the switch, though he didn't dare put on the earphones but rather left them dangling by her head as he cranked up the bed, so that from the two pillows came the sound of wind instruments, distant and muffled but assertive, the solemn, aerial flourish of the breathless, staccato hunting horns in the Mahler symphony that he had inserted in the deck three days ago, for though he did not know if its throbbing strains were really the most suitable, he was afraid to surprise her with anything new, no matter how peaceful and simple.

It was thus that he remembered the moment of her death, by its exact bars, the repetition of which could recreate at will that final scene in the silence of the night. He had no way of knowing which of the undulating notes had entered her consciousness as she breathed her last, no way (nor did he seek to find one) of telling if she heard them at all. Never taking his eyes off her, ardent with pity and zeal, he had let himself be led through a black forest in the light of a damp, chill dawn, struggling past heavy branches toward a lit valley or hollow and the soft, tawny doe that stood there, pursued and yet summoned by the throbbing horns.

Just then her breathing had stopped. He didn't touch her, afraid to wake her or hurt her—and yet that was it, the moment she never would know, though of all the moments in the world it was the one most intimately and individually hers, presided over by that invisible hand that tells us thus far and no further. He had never thought much about such things as life after death or reincarnation, had indeed thanked her mentally for shying away from all that mysticism, whose dark unreason would only have been swept away anyhow by her aggressive, bitter intellectuality. It suited him perfectly to be alone with her now, alert, quiet, and wholly concentrated, with no one to distract him or share his thoughts with and, above all, with no doctor or nurse to try some new tube or drug, but rather all by himself, exclusively in control and in charge—alone with the lights, alone with the sounds, alone with Death, the same Death he once had imagined in the form of the black shot put he was made to throw in gym class, the ball of Death that had rolled into her room several days ago and lain silently beneath the furniture or the bed, despite all his efforts to heave it back even a few feet. That Death was now right by him, astonishingly piercing and bursting forth from her at once, while his only thought was to keep her from feeling any pain—. yes, that had been his sole mission in recent months, to ease her pain, so that even now, at the last moment, a whole battery of remedies and devices was available for the task: cranks, handles, crutches, a wheelchair, a washbasin, a fan, medicines, drugs, an oxygen mask, an entire field hospital in one small room, all to lessen her pain, all to help her soul exit gently.

Yes, always, even when sitting at his desk, even when walking in the street, erect, slow, and preoccupied, his head already gray yet his body still youthful, even when eating or sleeping, he had thought all the time of her pain and how to cope with it, had listened continually to her disease-eaten, scalpel-scarred, drug-swollen hulk of a body, which, stewing in the inflorescence of its poisons, had lain for weeks on end in the same giant, ultramodern hospital bed standing like a chariot in the middle of the room, with its jellylike water mattress and its cranks, bars, and wheels, in the hope that her last journey might take place at home and that all those ministering to it —her mother, her children, her family, her friends, and above all, he himself, its general manager—might get her safely past her rampaging illness to the competent quietude of an inevitable death. Lying next to her like a loyal staff officer on the plain, narrow bed that had replaced the old king-size one they had shared since their marriage until the day it was moved out of the room, half beside and half beneath her, he had listened intently, on call to fight her pain, sleeping in snatches, waking up and dozing off so quickly that it seemed to happen automatically, though not without dreams—no, not without dreams. For even on that last, fearful night, he had suddenly dreamed that he was a child again and that someone was whistling for him, looking for him in some street or field, perhaps his wife, perhaps someone like her. At once he awoke as usual, only to realize that the sound, which had frightened him by not stopping and had made him sit up in bed, was simply the wheezing of her breath.

2

THIS TIME, though, he was not mistaken, and in full possession of himself, he acted sensibly and calmly, careful not to repeat his error of three days ago when, awoken by the same wheezing in the middle of the night, he had agitatedly sought to do something and had called out to her, sitting her up in bed when she answered, hugging her and trying to wake her, giving her tea and then wine, even phoning his elder son to come at once from his college dormitory. Together, in the hours before dawn, they had made her put on her glasses and get out of bed to wash her mastectomized body, unthinkingly forcing more life on her by propping her almost upright against the pillows, pale, groggy, and breathing weakly as she listened to the news and the morning jingles on the radio. Only later, when her mother and the doctor dropped by and he told them with pride what had happened, did he understand from their silence and lowered, averted looks that they quite failed to see the point of it.

There followed two excruciating days in which the vestige of the death he had repelled caused her great pain. And yet she had chatted, listened to music, and even laughed when shown old home movies of their youngest son as a chubby little tot rolling in the sand on the beach. Why, her laughter is a gift, Molkho thought, scanning her face greedily: I've raised her from the underworld! Does she have any idea where she's been, any memory or keepsake from there? He even enjoyed it greatly when she argued with him about some trivial matter. It's like quarreling with a ghost, he thought— and indeed, that evening she lost consciousness and then became delirious, so that he gave her a shot of morphine in case the pain started up again. But it didn't. She simply faded rapidly, and he disconnected the telephone by her bed and took her friends' calls in the next room, repeating the same bulletin over and over with infinite patience while her old mother sat with her through the next day, moistening her lips from time to time and trying to get her to talk, though in fact she would not even eat, pushing away the food she had always swallowed heartily until now.

In the evening his mother called from Jerusalem and friends arrived, all walking about on tiptoe—but eyelids fluttering, she heard them and knew who they were, now and then murmuring a word or phrase that assumed for them all an intense and ceremonial significance. At exactly 7 P.M. Death appeared in her hand with a fanning, uncontrollable tremor and they all knew the end was near, that it was imminent; yet, though several people offered to spend the night with him, he stubbornly, firmly refused. "There's time yet," he said, believing his own words. "We have to save our strength." And he sent them all home, even her mother, who didn't want to go, even the student to his dormitory. Later, his daughter arrived from her army base, sat up with the dying woman a while, and then went off to her room, too fatigued to stay awake any longer. His younger son, a high school boy, was in his room too, studying for a history exam, and at ten o'clock Molkho turned off the lights, collected the scattered sections of the newspaper, replaced the books on their shelves, and consulted the calendar, on which the next two days' visits were already written down, purposely staggered to keep too many people from coming at once and exhausting her. At midnight he put on his pajamas and lay down in his bed beneath hers. Soon afterward his son left his room, passed hesitantly by the open doorway, afraid to enter, and asked if he was needed. "No," said Molkho. "Go to bed."

Then he, too, dozed off, only to awaken at 3 A.M. with the knowledge that he would sleep no more that night. He rose, fiddled with the heater, boiled water to sterilize a hypodermic that he knew would not be needed, and drank the last of the cognac from the little bottle they had bought on the airplane two years ago on their last trip to Europe. His wife was restless. "What, what did you say?" he called softly to her when she murmured something, but there was no answer. He went over to her bed, arranged the blankets, and even decided to raise the bars, as though she were a baby who might fall out; then he went to the living room and sat down in the darkness on the couch, inviting Death to come and finish what it had begun. Suddenly, though, remembering the music, he went back and switched on the tape machine. How odd it was, he thought, that after so many years of so many doctors and nurses, now, at the moment of her death, there was no one left but himself—yet he felt sure he had room in him even for Death, and sticking his hands beneath the blankets, he grasped her two feet, which were soft, smooth, and still there. Once again she murmured something that sounded like "Isn't that so?" "What?" he asked gently, bending down to her after a moment. "Isn't what so?"

She didn't answer now either. Slowly she opened her large, heavy, amber eyes, the eyes of a weary animal from which the light had fled, leaving in them neither anger nor pain, but only ultimate defeat. He smiled at her, spoke her name, tried encouraging her as always, but she failed to respond, for the first time not recognizing him, her moist yellow glance spilling out emptily. He had never imagined that Death could be so damp, and when her breathing stopped, he rearranged the blankets and kissed her lightly on the forehead, imbibing her scent. "You're free now," he whispered, switching off the little twenty-four-hour night-light and opening the window, though he did not believe in such freedom at all, only in nothingness. A deep, urgent need to look at the world made him step out on the terrace: this was the moment, this was their last farewell. It was late fall, and the first rains had cooled the earth without sating it. His eye followed the line of the ravine in the darkness below the house, looking for some unfamiliar sign of life, but the night was gray and silent, with a slight, motionless mist hanging over the sea. It was, he thought, his last quiet hour before the bustle of condolence calls began, leaving him no time for himself. Meanwhile, however, the exclusivity of his knowledge made him feel advantageously strong. A car sped along the highway by the coast. Soon he, too, would be free.

3

U PON RETURNING to the room, he realized he should never have turned off the night-light. Suddenly he felt a twinge of fear. The border between Death and Life should be clearer, he thought, the shock of crossing it should be greater: why, if I look at her now in the darkness, I may imagine I see her move. And indeed, he seemed to detect a slight movement as he peered back through the glass door of the terrace, which he vigorously opened, however, refusing to believe in yet another resurrection, striding silently back through the room with his eyes on the floor until, by the hallway door, he turned to look at her again. Now he could see her face clearly, defeat still written on it. For seven years she had fought her illness; four years ago she was actually sure she had triumphed. Yet now the same hand that hours ago had moved with a slow, fanning motion hung lifelessly down from the bed. He glanced at the clock. It was 4:15. All at once he thought with emotion that not only she but her illness, too, that cruel cousin that had moved in with them, was gone.

He walked swiftly out, shut the door behind him, collapsed on the living room couch, and tried to sleep, to rest up for the ordeal ahead, his knowledge like a warm blanket covering him; yet the thought of all the people he was at liberty to wake was too much for him, and rousing himself, he went to phone his mother-in-law, who, perfectly clearheaded, answered at once in her slow, soft, irrepressibly German-flavored Hebrew. "It's all over," he said quietly, tersely, flinging her the death in one throw. For a heartbreaking moment she said nothing. Then, though, she asked, "When?" And now it was he who couldn't speak. With a thickening lump in his throat, he began to sob and shake, the unseen sorrow of the eighty-two-year-old woman stirring up his own grief with unexpected force. The receiver fell in his lap while, with her accustomed restraint, she waited patiently for him to get a grip on himself and answer, "Ten, fifteen minutes ago." "I'll be right over," she said. "Why rush?" he asked. "You may as well wait for it to be light out. You have a long hard day ahead of you." But she wouldn't hear of it. "No, I'll be right over. Are the children still sleeping? Don't wake them. I'll call a cab." And she hung up.

He went to the bathroom and sat doggedly on the toilet until he passed a few drops of urine, washed his hands and face without shaving, and walked down the darkened hallway past the children's rooms. For a second his daughter opened her eyes and saw him, but as he said nothing, she closed them again, while his younger son, deep in sleep, did not stir. They had been bracing themselves for this death, almost angry with it for taking so long.

He opened the front door and turned on the stairway light. It was damp outside. A soft, noiseless rain fell furtively into the world, slicking the front steps with a bright coppery gleam. It occurred to him that in her agitation the old woman might slip coming down the garden stairs. All I need now is for her to take a fall on me, he thought bitterly. His wife had been her only daughter. Throughout her illness she had continued to look after her mother, and now, he thought, all that burden would be his, even if she was a responsible old woman who took good care of herself. Deciding to meet her downstairs, he put on his shoes, an old sweater, and a coat, took an umbrella, and stepped out into the rain, first waiting for her by the entrance, from which he had a view of the street, and then stepping into the garden, treading on the dead leaves that strewed the wet path, all the while thinking of the funeral arrangements. He had already reached the street when the gruesome thought occurred to him that his son or daughter might awake and discover their dead mother, and so he ran worriedly back upstairs, where he locked the bedroom door after a quick glance at her lying in the dark sheen of night flowing through the open window. Relieved to have everything under control again, he stuck the key in his pocket and hurried back down, feeling the light spray of the rain, which, scarcely hitting the ground, seemed to have as its sole mission the cleansing of the air.

The sky had cleared, but the rain, as though coming from elsewhere, kept falling. With an unfamiliar freedom he paced up and down the sidewalk, fingering the key in his pocket, secure in the knowledge that from this moment on, there were no further claims on him. For a moment, as though looking down on her from above, he imagined his wife, utterly alone now, dressed in an old coat among a crowd of dead people in front of some clinic or office that they were waiting to enter, though it was only their first stop. The thought that never again could he help her made him shiver with grief, the hot lump swelling in his throat and sticking there, refusing to overflow, until slowly it dissolved again. By now his mother-in-law should have arrived from her old-age home on the next flank of the mountain—and indeed, approaching the curve in the street, he saw a small light that bobbed in midair like a drunken little star, slowly groping its sinuous way, faltering, flickering, and then flaring up again. Molkho rubbed his eyes. Could she have decided to come by foot? She actually had a small flashlight—he had seen it more than once—yet he was sure this wasn't it. Stopping short to let the Death-propelled world spin on dizzily without him, he suddenly realized that what he saw was the headlight of a bicycle whose rider, a large, cumbersome newsboy, kept dismounting, leaning his vehicle against the curb, disappearing into buildings with his papers, coming out again, and pedaling on. And yet, when he finally rode by, Molkho saw, he was not a boy at all, but rather a heavily dressed woman, her head wrapped in scarves and the cuffs of her pants clipped with clothespins. Though passing quite near him, she failed to notice him; her eyeglasses glinting beneath the streetlights, she rode on as far as his own house, entering it with an armful of newspapers to stuff into the mailboxes. Soon she emerged and straightened her bicycle—but now Molkho saw she was a man after all, varicose and heavyset, who threw him a resentful glance, remounted the sagging bike, and rode off.

But the taxi was coming down the street now too, chuffing and billowing exhaust. Preceded by the cane that for some obscure reason she had taken to carrying in the past month, his mother-in-law stepped briskly out of it, paid the driver, and stood there talking to him. There was something about her that inspired confidence in people, with whom she knew how to get along. Had she told the man where she was going so early in the morning or would she have thought that undignified? The taxi departed, leaving her standing by herself on the opposite curb. Deftly slipping her change into her purse, she glanced in both directions, as if waiting for an invisible flow of traffic to stop, before crossing the street. She was, he noticed, warmly dressed in a raincoat, boots, and gloves, and she was wearing for the first time the red woolen cap they had bought her in Paris two years ago. He stepped toward her, wary of the cane that advanced through the air as if tracking an unseen target, careful not to scare her—and in fact, head bent in sorrow, she took him at first for a stranger and sought to make a detour around him. Gently he blocked her way and held out his hand. Though she had shrunken in recent years, she still held herself upright, and her skin, despite its wrinkled, slightly liverish patina that gave off a faint smell of old scent, had a morning freshness.

"The driver lost his way; he misunderstood," she said in her German accent, which was always strongest in the morning, after a night of German dreams. "I hope you weren't too worried," she added, looking away from him. He stared down without answering, surprised by her matter-of-factness, seeking to help her by the elbow down the garden stairs. But she did not want to be helped. Her ancient body was alive and agile beneath its layers of clothing as she shone her little flashlight on the wet stone stairs of the garden that were strewn with autumn leaves, descending them with her cane hooked over one arm, then transferring it to the other while ascending the house stairs with him hurrying after her, plucking a wet newspaper from the mailbox as he passed it. She all but ran to the bedroom when he opened the front door, her face hard and pale, her lips trembling. "Just a minute," he whispered while she struggled with the doorknob, taking the key from his pocket and trying to explain. But he saw she wasn't listening. Without removing her large coat and hat, and holding her cane and lit flashlight, she burst inside as if she still might not be too late. The room itself had grown quite stuffy, and the face of the limp-handed woman actually seemed flushed. Yet, poignantly, everything was just as he had left it. He remained standing in the doorway, returning his wife of thirty years to her mother, detachedly watching the old woman throw herself without a word on the corpse, fondle it, kiss it, cross its two arms on its chest, lie a while beside it, and emit a piercing sob like the blast of a distant, sinking ship, so that Molkho, whose newspaper was still under his arm, felt the lump in his throat again and wished the strange sound might sweep him away on a wave of wished-for tears, though he knew that it wouldn't, that it was only, after all, a sob.

His mother-in-law was a cultured, educated woman who read books and went to concerts. In Israel, to which she had come shortly before World War II, she had run an orphanage, and during her daughter's illness she and Molkho had become quite close. Despite all the hired nursing help, the real burden of caring for his wife had been shouldered by the two of them, and while they had never talked about Death itself, only about practical things, he felt sure she held the same opinion of it as he did—namely, that it was the absolute end of everything and that the two of them, he and she, were alone by themselves now in this room. And so, going over to her, he laid a light hand on her shoulder, which was something he had never done before, helped her out of her coat, took her hat, and led her to the small armchair in which she had spent so much time in recent days.

She sank into it, her old face deeply creased beneath its shock of gray hair, her heavy glasses misted over, so like and unlike her dead daughter, while he, seeing her stricken and bewildered, began to pace up and down, choking back his emotion. "The end was very peaceful," he said. "I don't think she suffered at all. I'm sure she wasn't in pain, and I know what pain is. I'm quite sure she wasn't," he repeated, carried away by his own conviction as if it were he, rather than she, who had died an hour ago, the old woman hanging on every word and nodding all the time. "Yes, she'll be quiet now," she said, as if the deceased were a troublesome child who had finally fallen asleep, and he felt so touched by her flushed, bewildered face with its glasses halfway down its nose that he burst into tears himself, feeling equally sorry for the two of them, while she regarded him with quiet sympathy until, finishing crying, he went to the bathroom to wash, taking off his shirt and jacket and deciding this time to shave.

When Molkho emerged from the bathroom he found his daughter wide-awake and tearful, her arms around her grandmother, and he nodded to her across the room as if to say, "Yes, now you know too," as though the knowledge were an object that could be passed from hand to hand. Glancing again at the dead body, he felt as overwhelmed by its immobility as if the earth's very orbit had stopped. And yet, the morning paper, lying forgotten at the foot of the bed, reminded him with a pang that it hadn't, and looking out at the sky, he saw a soft white streak that was the dawn.

4

H E PHONED his elder son, the college student, and went to wake the high school boy, which was no easy task in the dark. During the last year the boy had taught himself to sleep soundly, dead to the world, but Molkho forced him out of bed, throwing off the blankets (beneath which his son had slept in his clothes again to save time dressing in the morning) before breaking the news to him. He was prepared for it, had been in fact for quite a while. Over the past month he had detached himself from his mother, so impatient with the slowness of her death that if, asking about her on coming home from school, he was told she had had a good day, he frowned involuntarily. Now his father took him for a last look at her, steering him by the shoulder, though stiff with sleep he stood there so dazed and dry-eyed that Molkho wondered if it wouldn't be better for him to take his exam in school than stay home and get in everyone's way. Meanwhile, pale and haggard, the college student had arrived with the speed of light and was showering kisses on his grandmother while lightly holding his mother's hand. Next he'll start kissing her too, Molkho thought, sensing himself grow more remote, more coldly calculating, from minute to minute.

The telephone rang. It was 5:15. His mother was calling from Jerusalem. Though how was beyond him, she already knew everything; all night long she hadn't slept a wink, thinking about it. She had wanted so badly, she wept, to say good-bye to her. She had loved her so much. Could someone fetch her from Jerusalem? When could they come? Could they keep the body at home until she got there? He heard the distant, muffled sound of her tears and parried her lamely, exhaustedly, ignoring her pleas, for he knew she had always been afraid of her daughter-in-law, whose corpse he preferred she not see in its bed. Finally he hung up and dialed a close friend, the doctor who had treated his wife in recent years. He, too, answered at once and quite lucidly, as if he had been expecting the telephone to ring. Meanwhile, an aroma of coffee filled the house, and Molkho greedily drank the large, hot mug of it poured him by his son, feeling drunk with the sweetness of Death, pacing back and forth in the room, though never too close to the bed, listening to his daughter's endless sobs—she, of all people, who had never gotten along with her mother at all.

His mother-in-law still sat by the bed, guarding it without moving. The doorbell rang. It was the doctor and his wife, both grim-looking. Brushing past Molkho, the doctor went straight to the corpse and examined it thoroughly, as if to make sure it was dead, which made Molkho fear that it wasn't, that maybe it was merely unconscious, while at the same time feeling angry at not being believed. But at last the examination was over; gently the doctor drew the sheet over the dead woman's face, and Molkho told him about the end, imitating her wheezing and the tremor in her hands, though just then the flood of morning light pouring in the window made the two-hour-old death seem something that had happened long ago. The doctor listened and dialed the hospital to order an ambulance, while several neighbors knocked and entered, all of whom—the women, too—had to kiss Molkho. Odder yet, it seemed to him, was how one of them burst out wailing bitterly, starting off the day with a good cry at the corpse's expense, though she and his wife had never done more than say hello on the stairs. Her husband stood by concernedly, conversing with Molkho's mother-in-law, who still sat by the side of the bed as if she were the living half of the dead person and empowered to carry on in her behalf.

Molkho felt exhausted. Desiring to be alone, he went and sat in the living room, from where he listened to the college student telephoning all their friends in his toneless drawl, rousing them from bed without even an apology. No doubt, Molkho thought, they, too, would come running to pay their last respects—an idea that aroused in him such profound resistance that he sat stubbornly brooding in the corner, thinking how much better it would be for no one to see her at all. What did her dead body matter? All along he had taken good care of her, everyone knew that he had, and now all at once he was to blame for her death, for which he was being held accountable.

Time passed as in a waking dream. More and more people, surprisingly quick to arrive, rang the doorbell, all wanting to be with him, just as once, long ago (for so last night already seemed), they had wanted to be with her. Then his mother was on the phone again; but this time, refusing to rise, he asked his son or daughter to take the call. Where, he wondered bitterly, was he to find the strength for it all? He had always imagined that his wife's death would set him free, yet now he felt newly shackled, and when someone removed the sheet from her face, which looked pale and ugly in the strong light, he suddenly had enough and snapped, "What do you think this is, Lenin's tomb?" Just then, though, the ambulance arrived, and two men carried her out of the house. It wasn't even seven; it was like one of those distant days long ago when she left for school ahead of time because her class had an early homeroom.

5

THEY WERE ALL AFRAID that the rain would spoil the funeral, but at noontime, some two hours beforehand, the sky cleared and a warm breeze blew in from the sea. The procession left the funeral parlor on time and covered without incident the short, straight distance to the cemetery, where, the hour being convenient and the news having spread, the crowd turned out to be a large one. All eyes were on him, following him to the grave, and he did his best to look about and remember who was there, asking his children to remember too. A light, delicate mist swirled about them, whitening the tombstones, and they walked in its midst with an unhurried crunching of feet: his mother-in-law, without her cane and surrounded by all her old friends, stepping slowly and supporting each other; his children with their friends; and he himself with his mother in tow, tottering after him in a black fur coat like a cart missing a wheel, stopping in front of all the people she knew to cast them a disconsolate glance. The grave had already been dug that morning in a new section of the cemetery on a low rise of the mountain, and now he stood dutifully beside it, looking down at the fresh earth and observantly up again at the murmuring crowd, pleased to see not only his friends from the office but many secretaries and colleagues too. The woman doctor who had once treated his wife was there also, as were her fellow teachers and many others he couldn't place—teenagers, college students, young soldiers, high school pupils in their uniforms, his children's teachers, even several cousins from Jerusalem, heavy, balding Sephardim of the old school, bundled in scarves, their eyes, unused to the sight of it, fixed on the stormy sea nearby with a look of astonished concern. He had never been such an attraction before, besieged by so many people—who were thinking mainly of her, of course, but no doubt also of him.

The rabbi beside him was an impeccably dressed, distinguished-looking man of German origin who had presided two years ago at his wife's uncle's funeral to the satisfaction of the entire family, at which time her mother had had the presence of mind to jot down his telephone number. Quickly, expertly, he tore the lapel of Molkho's shirt while Molkho looked at him hopefully, trusting him to guide them just as smoothly through the rest of the ceremony. Surrounded by his children, friends, and family, he stood there certain of the acknowledgment in their warm, approving looks, for he knew that they knew how devotedly he had cared for his wife, doing everything he could to nurse her at home until the end—yes, even the rabbi, in brief but eloquent words, was now speaking in his praise. Raising his eyes to the somberly listening circle of women, his wife's friends, now regarding him contemplatively, Molkho wondered if any of them knew things he didn't, intimate secrets she might have shared with them during the long hours they had sat with her, strange fantasies even, the product of her illness, against which he was unable to defend himself. Why, even though she had refused to make love to him since that day seven years ago when her first breast was removed, he had never been unfaithful, had never protested even once!

6

AFTER THE FUNERAL WAS OVER and he had cried a bit, the mourners filed by to shake his hand. He could tell that they wished him to remember their presence, and trying not to sound too doleful, he promised them all that he would. In the last twenty-four hours he had even perfected a sad nod that was at the same time not so grief-stricken or hopeless as to suggest only Death, for as drained of vitality as he felt, he needed to demonstrate that he was someone still worthy of love. The crowd kept filing by, mostly couples, yet sometimes a lone man or even woman who managed to convey her singleness, such as the legal adviser of his office, a senior official who, three years ago, had lost her husband, whose funeral he had attended with some of his friends, even though he was not on close terms with her. In those days he had already begun to practice going to funerals, and indeed, he now remembered that her husband was buried not far from his wife's fresh grave. In recent months he had even thought of her as of a definite postmortem possibility.

7

I T RAINED all during the week of mourning, and the weather turned so cold that everyone began to wonder if an early winter hadn't already set in. The heater was turned on in Molkho's living room, where he sat on the couch with his three children, across from their grandmother, who occupied the large armchair facing them. Molkho's daughter took off her shoes and wrapped her feet in a blanket, and it was warm and cozy sitting there together, watching the rain fall and greeting the constant flow of visitors, with whom they talked about the weather, and the deceased, and the funeral, and who had been there and what they had said, and the distinguished rabbi and his elegy, which was short but to the point, so that he wasn't at all as tiresome as he might have been. They sat like that all morning, lay down to rest after lunch, rose at four o'clock, sat again until supper, and then sat some more into the night. At first, Molkho had thought of excusing his younger son and sending him back to school, of which he had already missed enough in recent months, but the boy insisted on joining them and sat there alertly as though feeling much better now that his mother was dead, curiously regarding the old people who came to visit his grandmother, odd octogenarians whom Molkho had never seen before and who now filled his living room, carrying on long conversations in German, of which he understood not a word, though he made a point of smiling whenever they did. Acquaintances and relations came from all over, and Molkho rose immediately to greet them, kissing even those he hardly knew, even those who hadn't meant to kiss him. Dressed in a soft black turtleneck sweater, unshaven as was the custom, he was perfectly ready to kiss anyone; in fact, all the kissing on sight rather pleased him, and even though most lips did little more than graze his cheek, sometimes a woman from work hugged him tightly, tickling his forehead with her hair and pressing her breasts (or so he assumed them to be) against him. Yet there were some he was wary of touching, such as the young teachers his wife had supervised, the attractive, manicured woman accompanying the fat old lady who came to see his mother-in-law, or the legal adviser from the office, who paid a condolence call with the head of his department and several other colleagues, in whose company she seemed so ill at ease that she even refused to take off her coat, despite the heat in the apartment.

Later at night, at about ten o'clock, after the college student had accompanied his grandmother to her old-age home and returned to his dorm and the two younger children had settled down to watch the late show on television, Molkho would retire to the bedroom— which, in perfect order, still looked like a little hospital waiting for its next patient. True, the large bed was now a bare metal frame, its mattress, for which they had been charged a daily rate, having been returned on the first day; yet everything else, whether borrowed, rented, or bought, was still in place: the intravenous drip, the bath basin, the wheelchair, the oxygen mask, the hypodermics, the drugs, the books she had read, the books she had planned to read, the music she had listened to over and over, his bed lying next to hers. He undressed and got ready for bed while wondering what to keep and what to sell, especially of the drugs, one of which—an expensive medicine called Talwin, which he had bought in bulk months ago, fearing the drugstores might run out, but which was hardly used in the end, because it was contraindicated by something else—lay in stacked boxes on a shelf. Could he find a buyer for it, he wondered, and if so, how? Once in bed, he left the night-light on as he had done for his wife, making a mental note to replace the bulb with a weaker one. He still slept very lightly, rising four or five times in the middle of the night to wander about the apartment or to sit in the living room listening to music with the earphones on, thinking of all kinds of things, such as the big newspaper deliverer who had ridden by that morning as though he were part of her death. Suddenly, as if the man's clothing, his headlight, his newspaper pouch, his bicycle wheels, were the last tidings from Molkho's dead wife, he longed to see him again. He missed her lying beside him, even sick and unconscious, missed even her water mattress, as if it were part of her too. Did she still exist somewhere, was someone else taking care of her now? Soon, however, wrung dry as a sponge by fatigue, he went slowly back to bed, glancing on his way at the pile of unpaid bills on his desk. And he would have to register her death with various government offices too. Although he hoped that having to deal with such practical matters would help put him back on his feet, he still felt too weary to tackle them.

8

O N THE SEVENTH DAY, at the crack of dawn, they went to visit the grave. The rain had stopped, but it was still rather cold. The likable rabbi had set the occasion for 6 A.M., because he had a prior engagement in Tel Aviv the same morning, and though he had offered to find them a substitute, they declined. "It's all right," they told him. "We'll get up at five," which was indeed far better than risking an unknown who might decide to ask all kinds of questions and deliver all kinds of sermons. Yet there were barely the ten men needed for a prayer group and they had trouble finding the grave, though as soon as the rabbi appeared he led them straight to it. By

seven they were back home again, alone for the first time in months.
The college student went off to his classes, the soldier returned to her
base, and the high school boy, after a moment's hesitation, was
persuaded to go back to school too, leaving Molkho by himself to
shave off his beard in the empty house he had been confined to for a
whole week, waiting for the movers to pick up the large hospital bed.

At eight-thirty the morning help arrived. Molkho did not know
the woman well, especially because whenever he had called from the
office, it had always been his wife who had answered the phone. Now
she had come to return the key and be paid; she was, after all, a
practical nurse, not a housekeeper, and she had already found a new
job elsewhere. "Where?" asked Molkho, feeling a twinge of envy.
"Not far from here," she replied. "Just a few blocks away." He
looked at her, a short, dark-haired, presumably divorced woman of
about thirty, reasonably efficient though never overly dedicated to
her job—but his wife had given her exact instructions and she had
carried them out well enough. Perhaps, he suggested after a moment's thought, afraid of being saddled with the housework just
when he had been finally set free, she might remain a while until he
got organized. She had the key, she knew where things were; why
not stay on to cook and do some light cleaning? Perhaps she could
even work at both places, since he didn't need her every day. "Sit
down," he said, feeling her dark eyes on him. Could she possibly
suspect him of some ulterior motive? She looked at him uncertainly
and then said a few feeling words about his wife, whose body she
knew as well as he did and whose death-smell still clung to her too,
so that for a moment he almost believed that she might be a bridge to
something whose nature was unclear to him. Except that again she
repeated, "I'm a practical nurse, not a housekeeper." "Of course,
you are," he said. "It's just that meanwhile the boy should be given
a hot lunch and the house needs cleaning now and then. I can do a
lot myself, but I'm not organized yet." The woman thought it over
and agreed. "But only for the time being," she insisted.

Just then there was a knock on the door, and a brash young
moving man in blue overalls appeared for the bed, grinning at them
both and addressing the woman as Mrs. Molkho, an error that

Molkho was not sure how to correct. Hurriedly he ushered the man into the bedroom, where he first checked the bed from all angles for damage and then produced some papers to sign. The deposit would be returned in a month or two, he told Molkho, who began at once to protest, having assumed that the sizable sum would be refunded right away. "Why, it's not even indexed," he said. "It will just go on losing its value!" The mover did not disagree. Still, he said, those were the rules, it wasn't up to him, and in any case, Molkho didn't stand to lose much; there were people who had kept such beds for years and had their deposits wiped out by inflation. Molkho barely argued for a minute before feeling too tired to go on. Why quarrel over money with someone who had no say about it anyway? All that mattered was getting rid of the bed, in fact, of everything in the room. But unfortunately the moving man was in no hurry, he was a garrulous type who seemed eager to stage a colloquium, and worse yet, he had come by himself and in a small car, so that the bed had to be disassembled and carried out piece by piece.

Meanwhile, before going to wash the dishes piled high in the sink, the new housekeeper had changed into an old smock hanging by Molkho's towel in the bathroom, which—though he could have sworn it was his wife's—she had apparently decided to expropriate. As for the moving man, he was now in the bathroom, where he remained for quite some time, leaving Molkho anxious and impatient. "What should I cook?" asked the housekeeper. "What would you suggest?" parried Molkho, opening the refrigerator and peering into it. But instead of one suggestion, she made several, forcing Molkho, whose wife had always dealt with such things, to decide. "I could make a chicken with olives and tomato sauce," she proposed, "but it's a bit on the spicy side." "Let it be on the spicy side," said Molkho. "I like hot food myself." The moving man, having finished washing up, now came to the kitchen to ask a question that had been evidently bothering him on the toilet: "Who," he wanted to know, "was the bed for, your father or your mother?" "For neither," hissed Molkho angrily. "It was for my wife." The moving man nodded. Without batting an eyelash, he asked the housekeeper for some tea for his sore throat and then sat down at the table and began to banter with her. Molkho left the room quickly, as though in search of something. Why indeed stay with them? He told the woman to lock up when she was done, went to the bedroom, seized the wheelchair, the oxygen mask, and the intravenous drip, and dragged them downstairs to his car.

9

H E RETURNED ALL THREE ITEMS, received his deposits back, and barely had time to get to the bank and withdraw his wife's last monthly paycheck. It was the first time all week he'd been out of the house by himself, and though he'd hoped to accomplish a lot and even enjoy it, there were long lines everywhere and nothing went smoothly. Moreover, hardly anyone seemed to know his wife had just died. The silent, empty house was depressing to return to, yet there was also something promising about it, for the kitchen was spotless, the bathroom was clean, and several pots stood on the table with their lids on. The little hospital had a new look too: the large sickbed was gone and in its place stood his own bed, which for some reason had been moved against the wall, leaving an odd vacuum in the room. Suddenly he had the feeling that the two of them had made love on it. The moving man had had a roving eye, . . . and indeed, it rather pleased Molkho to think that sex, even that of two strangers, had returned to his house and left its imprint. Sitting down on the bed, he sniffed its linen. Was that tobacco he smelled? Perhaps, though he couldn't be sure.

He went to take lunch in the kitchen. The chicken was good, if full of strange tastes, and there was another dish made with some unfamiliar purple vegetable. Checking the refrigerator, he found more pots there too. Had he really told her to cook that much or had she gone and done it on her own? It was three o'clock. He dialed his mother-in-law to see how she was and to ask if she knew the whereabouts of the high school boy, who still wasn't home from school and sometimes went straight to the old-age home to lunch with her, but there was no answer in her room. Nor was there any at the college student's dormitory. The end of the week of mourning, so it seemed, had been taken by them all as a signal to kick over the traces. There was a deep, strange silence in the house. Molkho drew the bedroom blinds and lay down to take a nap, as he had done regularly when his wife was sick and he had had to get up at all hours; yet, though awake since dawn, he couldn't fall asleep, for all at once he felt worried about his son. He rose, switched on some classical music on the radio, and began to go through the medicines, of which there was a great pile, throwing some out, returning others to the cabinet, and leaving the twenty boxes of Talwin on the shelf, where he built a colorful wall of them. It was madness, he thought, to throw out anything so new and expensive. Next, turning to the room itself, he slowly began restoring it to its former state, before its paramedical conversion. Dragging back the chairs and table that had been moved out of it, he tried them in different places, pausing to decide where they looked best and were most sensible. Arranging the furniture had always been his wife's job. The double bed alone still remained on the terrace, covered with a large sheet of plastic, its mattress hopelesly rotted. Picking up the special bath basin he had bought, he leaned it against the doorway: it was brand-new and could surely be sold, perhaps even to his mother-in-law's old-age home. It was best not to involve her in it, though, because she might expect him to donate it and he was not about to lose all that money.

His son was still not home, and Molkho realized that he didn't know the name or even the telephone number of a single one of the boy's friends. He went downstairs to wait for him, but a cold, dull wind drove him back up to the apartment, where he made the boy some coffee and put a plate of cookies by the cup. Then, sitting down at his desk, he began going over the bank statements that had lain neglected since his wife's death. He had already drawn up a list of the sums still owed her by the Department of Education.

H IS SON TURNED UP at half past five, without a key naturally, since he had grown accustomed in the last half-year to someone always being at home. "We're under new management," Molkho told him. "From now on you better take a key; I'm not going to sit around all day waiting for you like a nursemaid!" He set the table for supper, and they sat down to eat the new dishes, whose spiciness the boy did not like. Molkho, too, had no appetite. A new worry on his mind, he dutifully dialed the old-age home; yet again there was no answer, and inquiring about his mother-in-law at the switchboard, he was told she had gone out at noontime and not returned. Since he could feel himself coming down with a cold, which he must have caught in the cemetery, he decided to go to bed. Meanwhile, his son had sat down in front of the television. "Don't you have another history exam tomorrow?" Molkho asked him. The boy wasn't concerned: the later at night he studied for it, the better he would remember in the morning. "Well, then," said Molkho, "I'm going to bed. If your grandmother calls, tell her I'm sleeping." Reflecting on the events of recent days, which seemed to have happened not close together but rather at great intervals of nebulous time, he went to the bedroom, now its old self again. Turning off the night-light, he was plunged at once into unfamiliar darkness and fell asleep; yet shortly after midnight he sat up in a fright, for he had suddenly heard wheezing close by. Quickly he jumped out of bed. The light was on in the kitchen, and the kettle was steaming on the stove. At first, he thought it must be morning and that the housekeeper was back; it was, however, still night, and fully dressed, his son strolled casually into the kitchen to make himself a cup of coffee, his hair falling over his face. "Are you crazy?" asked Molkho. "What are you doing up at this hour?" The boy, it seemed, was still studying. Molkho sat down beside him, made himself a cup of tea to soothe his aching throat, and leafed through the last week's newspapers, which he had barely had a chance to glance at. Among the condolence notices he was touched to find a large one addressed to him by the Ministry of the Interior, one that he had overlooked before.

The next day he went back to the office. Whoever hadn't been to the funeral or paid a call on him at home now came by to express his sympathy. Yet the hours dragged and the prickle in Molkho's throat grew so bad that he decided to quit ahead of time. On his way down the stairs he spied the legal adviser, looking quite elegant in a brown knit dress and unaware that he was behind her, which enabled him to study her at leisure. Around her pale neck she wore a metal chain that was rather heavy and crude for his taste. Was she in good health? The odd thought occurred to him that she, too, might be incubating some illness. And yet she seemed robust enough, her heels clicking gaily as she quickly descended the stairs. Though his job in the office rarely brought him into contact with her, she was considered, he knew, to have a first-class legal mind. Suddenly, as though sensing his presence, she turned and halted in a fluster, blushing at his sad nod, her cheeks reddening in curious blotches. Molkho, who was wearing a rather old sweater and whose sore throat and cold were getting worse, was not at all eager to encounter her, but already she was hurrying back up the stairs and pressing his hand warmly. "Is the week of mourning over? I also went back to work right away. It's good that you did."

Y ET HE DID NOT GO TO WORK the next day, which was rainy
and dreary, his cold having gotten even worse. Feeling he had a
fever, he phoned his mother in Jerusalem, hoping to be told by her to
stay home, as indeed he was. "Don't go out," she pleaded. "Take the
day off." Shortly before nine, which was the hour the housekeeper
came, he dressed and sat down in the living room, loath to have her
think he was ambushing her in bed. But she was late, and after
poking about the house for an hour, tired and runny-nosed, he left a
note in the kitchen with instructions for cooking and cleaning, added
the postscript that he was sick, and returned to the bedroom, where
he shut the door behind him and began to doze off. At eleven he
heard her come in. Evidently she hadn't found the note, because at
once she turned the radio on full blast to an Arab station, listening to
its trilled music while rattling about with the pots. Not that he had
anything against Arab music. It was melodic enough, and lately, he
had noticed, the accompaniments had improved and become more
sophisticated. Still, it was too loud—though afraid to frighten her by
a sudden appearance in his pajamas, especially since she was now
singing lustily herself, he remained lying in bed, pretending to sleep
while waiting to be discovered, or at least for his note to be found.
And in the end it was. At once she switched off the radio and opened
the door to his room in amazement. "I have a bad cold," he nodded
to her from his pillow. "I didn't go to work today." "It's good you
didn't," she answered. "Would you like a cup of tea?" "If it isn't too
much trouble," smiled Molkho. Oddly misaligned, her bottom too
heavy for her girlishly thin arms, she walked out of the room. House-
hold help had never lasted long with his wife, who was very critical,

and this one—who was it who had told him she was divorced?—had only been with them a few months. When she brought him the tea, along with some cookies he hadn't asked for, he coughed a few times to let her know his cold was real; yet even after he had thanked her, she remained standing by his side, as if waiting to see if he would drink. And he did, sitting up in bed. "If you'd like," he said, "I'll get up so you can clean the room." But she had cleaned it just two days ago, she explained, looking at him with a new freedom and confidence, and there was no need to clean it again. "Would you like me to bring you a glass of brandy?" "Later," said Molkho softly, anxious not to hurt her feelings. Yet, as though mesmerized by the thought of what else she could do for him, she didn't budge or take her eyes off him. The nursing instinct was clearly strong in her. Smiling uncomfortably, he swallowed the burning tea in little sips. "You can turn the radio back on," he said. "Just make it a little lower. And I really don't mind the music. You can listen to whatever you want. You can sing too. Please, I like it." She reddened but said nothing, and immediately he regretted the remark, afraid she had taken it amiss.

And yet, Molkho realized all at once, from now on, whatever he said to a woman could be misconstrued, for it would be like a little box in which anything you wanted could be put. The thought of it made him feel foolish and undignified. "I can do without music," said the housekeeper, still scrutinizing him. "You need to rest. If you want any more tea, let me know." And she left the door open behind her, the better to keep an eye on him.

Molkho finished his tea, put down the cup, and lay looking up at the ceiling and then out into the hallway, catching glimpses of the furniture, the rug, the lit floor of the kitchen, the slippered feet of the housekeeper by the sink, and thinking how this was the view his wife had had during the last months of her life. Once again he felt pride at having managed her death at home. "Here," said the house-keeper, coming back with a small glass of brandy, "this is just what the doctor ordered." Though he wasn't at all in the mood for it, he sat up again, drank it, and thanked her. This time she shut the door when she left. Was he about to become a sexual object, he wondered, even though sex itself was but a dim and distant memory of a bond-age cast aside for a more compassionate love, for the greater subtle-ties of affection, for the finer complexities of human relationships? Must he struggle now to rearouse himself? Certainly this woman of dubious status would be glad to help him out. And yet he wished to prolong the truce a little longer, without knowing exactly with whom. It was quiet in the house. A gray drizzle fell silently outside. He had to go to the bathroom, yet while he did not wish to be seen in his pajamas, getting dressed for no other purpose seemed oddly unneces-sary. Finally, he rose and padded noiselessly off to the toilet, notic-ing the many new pots on the table as he passed the kitchen. And still more was cooking on the stove. Alarmed to think they were being inundated with food, he went irritably off in his pajamas to look for the woman and, finding her mopping the floor in the room of the high school boy, to ask her not to cook so much, because it was more than he knew what to do with. Huffily she muttered something back, but he was already off to the bathroom and thence to his room, locking its door and falling asleep at once. When he awoke, she was gone. On the back of his note she had written that he should buy more spices, because they were almost all out.

12

WHENEVER HIS WIFE HAD RAISED THE POSSIBILITY of his remarrying one day, he had put her off with some joke or sarcastic remark that denied her approaching death. One Saturday in summer, however, when they had awakened from their afternoon nap and were still lying in the double bed beneath light blankets, the dim Sabbath light agreeably striped by the warm, sweet rays of the sun creeping through the slats of the blinds, she brought up the subject without warning, calmly making him face up to it, despite his attempt to play dumb. "You won't stay a widower all your life," she had said. "Why not?" he had asked. "Who would want me?" "Believe it or not," she had answered, "someone might want even you" —to which, hurt and baffled, he had made no reply. "Just don't have any more children," she cautioned. "Don't marry too young a woman, because she'll want babies and you'll regret it." His heart skipped a frightened beat; yet making a joke of it, he had said, "But why should I? Babying is my specialty." Now it was she who fell silent, as if no more words were necessary. He looked at her; her face was hard and gloomy. "I don't want to hear any more about death," he said petulantly, afraid of her ire. "Tomorrow I can get run over in the street and die too." "But why should you get run over?" she asked logically. "You only have to be careful." Taken aback, he burst out laughing. He imagined her death as a sudden burst of light but also as the threat of solitary confinement hanging over him in this house.

13

SOMETIMES HE HAD THE FEELING that, without bothering to pack her things, she had set out before him for some destination, where she had arrived and was truly at peace, leaving him behind in the empty house to care for the children, worry about meals, and look after her old mother. As if his only attractive feature had been his proximity to illness and Death, he rarely heard anymore from old friends, and his children, too, had become distant and apathetic, no longer hastening to do his bidding or seek the reassurance of his glance. And yet the first Sabbath after the week of mourning, when his daughter came home on leave and the college student was there too, and they all set the table together, and he asked her to light the candles and she did, tears came to his eyes, as was so often the case, he had noticed, in the wake of unexpected little things. Afterward, he wished his mother in Jerusalem a good Sabbath on the telephone and drove to the old-age home to pick up his mother-in-law.

She was not yet downstairs when he came, and so, opening the large glass door with its flowery curtain, he waited for her in the spotless, elegant lobby, studying the old German books on the shelves of the mahogany cases donated by one of the residents. Each time he visited the home he was impressed again by its order and cleanliness. In easy chairs sat several old men, washed and combed for the Sabbath, in distinguished three-piece suits, chatting politely in German, still sipping pleasure from Life as if they had made their private peace with it and all the hard times they had lived through had softened into sweet pablum. Several of them had skullcaps on their heads and were waiting for Sabbath services to begin in the small, curtained-off chapel, where Arab help ran back and forth arranging the ark, the lectern, and the chairs. Though not all of them were aware that he was Frau Starkman's son-in-law, they followed his every movement, their watchful, age-burnished eyes shining like black olives. Furtively he entered the darkened dining room, which, set for the festive meal, had about it something almost sacramental. Fresh slices of artfully cut hallah lay so lusciously white in their straw baskets that it was all he could do to keep from taking one. It was odd, though, that his mother-in-law wasn't down yet, because he had called to say he was on his way. Some of the old men had begun to enter the chapel, parting with a nod from their less-observant companions, who chose to stay in the lobby. Molkho liked everything about the place, its flowers, its greenery, even the shiny red emergency buttons in the corners. At last his mother-in-law stepped out of the elevator, apologizing for being late, erect, energetic, and all there, despite her eighty-two years. An old friend she had known in Germany before the war, she told Molkho, had recently arrived from the Soviet Union with her daughter and they had spent a long time talking on the telephone. The other old people, Molkho noticed, were looking at her with sympathy and respect; her bereavement, so it seemed, had enhanced her stature in their eyes, as though, having managed to deflect onto her daughter the death intended for herself, she had joined the ranks of the immortals. He was already holding the front door for her when she stopped and turned back, remembering that she had forgotten her cane. "Never mind," he reassured her. "You have me, and there's a cane at home too, the one I bought her." She wavered for a moment, but then gave in. In the car, he told her about the children and the new housekeeper, whose cooking, he confided worriedly, might not be to her liking.

And indeed, it wasn't. Not that she said anything, but he could see the food was too hot for her. Though his wife's chair still stood at the table, the plates were spaced differently now. At first, they discussed the new housekeeper, after which the college student told some story that made the high school boy burst into laughter. Good-humoredly, for their political views were alike (only those of his wife, who saw everything through dark glasses, had been different), they discussed the events of the week. After dinner Molkho's mother-in-law asked to see the refurbished bedroom, and he showed it to her, wondering as she squinted brightly at it through her thick lenses what she would think of his remarrying. Before leaving she reminded him that the concert season was starting next week. She had asked the office of the old-age home to find someone to take her ticket, though most of the residents had subscriptions of their own. "Would you like them to find someone for yours too?" she asked. But Molkho knew this meant giving the tickets away and was loath to lose the money. "No," he lied, "I already promised them to two friends at the office."

On the night of the concert a cold, jarring wind blew on the mountain, sweeping dead leaves across the pavement. He arrived fifteen minutes early, parked his car on a sidewalk near the concert hall, and hurried coatlessly to the entrance to sell his tickets. For some reason, however, there were no buyers. The audience entered quickly, among them many old folks bundled up in warm clothes, helping each other into a lobby of pulsing light. Spying a couple that had been at the funeral and paid a condolence call on him at home, he edged away beneath the marquee and turned his back on them, hoping not to be seen. The crowd in front of the building did not linger there long. A musician in tails, a small black case in one hand,

scurried roachlike through a back door of the building. The only
people still outside were trying to get rid of their tickets too. He
would have parted with his own for nothing by now, but there were
no takers even for that. The warning bell rang in muffled tones and
ushers in khaki urged the audience to take its seats. Within minutes
the lobby was deserted. He stood by the entrance reading the program, which began with some piece by an unfamiliar composer, followed by Mahler's Fifth Symphony, which he could not recall ever
having heard either. All at once he felt a longing for live music.
What harm would it do? he wondered, thinking of his two empty
seats while glancing up at the sky, where faint stars were fleeing an
onslaught of racing clouds. In the end, he decided to enter, assuring
the ticket taker, who cautioned him to stay outside the hall until the
intermission, that he knew the rules. "You may as well take both
tickets," he added, but the man took only one. Climbing the stairs,
Molkho halted outside the closed door of the auditorium, his heart
quickening as he heard the horns and drums. It was a complex
modern piece, yet not without its haunting, melodic parts. Through
the shut doors he heard only the music; not a stir came from the
audience, so that for a moment he imagined that it was somewhere
else, that behind the orchestra was a further space in which people
were promenading or dancing, his wife too—yes, she had arrived
and was waiting for him, she had entered from an entirely different
direction while he stood forlornly outside. Meanwhile, all out of
breath, a pretty young woman in a short fur wrap, her car keys still
clutched in one hand, joined him with a smile by the door and stood
listening too. As soon as a solemn wave of applause announced that
the piece was over, she darted inside, but Molkho, who suddenly
realized that he was not properly dressed for the occasion, stayed
behind: some old person in the audience was bound to tell his
mother-in-law, and he did not wish to cause her more sorrow. Walking quickly back to his car, he found a traffic policeman writing out
an expensive parking ticket. A bitter sense of humiliation welled up
in him. "At night too?" he cried, losing his temper. "But why?
Whose way am I in? Why can't a person be allowed to live? Why

can't a person . . ." But the policeman, in his slicker with the yellow glow-stripes down the back, was not in the least impressed and quietly but firmly asked Molkho for his license.

14

NOT THAT MONEY WAS A PROBLEM. True, the illness had set him back a large sum, but there were benefits too, such as life insurance policies, some savings accounts that had accrued in his wife's name, and various pension plans that were now explained to him. One day he sat with two accountants from the school system who tallied up in hushed tones, flushed with the drama of it, the funds released by her death, as though it were a secret investment that had yielded a handsome dividend or some rare achievement on her part that deserved a special prize. Slowly he went over their figures; carefully he double-checked them; obsessively, exhaustively, he reviewed them a third time, jotting down sums, rereading clauses, checking tables, photographing documents to take home. It was, after all, his profession; he was an auditor himself. For a while, transferring the money to his name, consulting how best to invest it, and giving the bank instructions what to do with it were all he thought about. "It's for the children," he told himself. "They've been through so much, and I'm only thinking of their future."

There was also a remittance of German marks, not a particularly large sum, to be sure, but one that had arrived in her name every month. Both she and her mother received this money as reparations for the property abandoned by them when they left Germany before World War II, after her father's suicide; and indeed, when Molkho's mother-in-law came to dinner that Friday evening with a gift of strudel for the children, she asked if he had informed the German embassy that the payments should be stopped. "I haven't gotten around to it yet," he replied. "I'm swamped with things to do;

I never imagined there was so much to take care of after a person's death. If it was me who had died, she would never have managed to cope with all the paperwork." "Would you like me to do it for you?" asked his mother-in-law. "I'll call the lawyer who arranged it and he'll have it stopped." "You needn't bother," said Molkho. "I'll see to it myself. I just have to make a few inquiries." Yet stubbornly, as if suspecting him of defrauding the German government, she insisted on knowing what inquiries there could be, forcing him to explain that he wished to find out if there wasn't a last, lump sum to close the account. "After all," he said, "she could have gone on living for years, and they would have had to pay her for each one of them. If she saved them all that money by dying, maybe there's a special grant for the children." "There's no such thing," declared his mother-in-law adamantly, and so he dialed his own mother in Jerusalem to wish her a good Sabbath, calling the children to the phone. Then they chatted with their grandmother, who seemed to enjoy their confidence, while complaining in unison about the food. Why did it have be so spicy? After the meal they watched the news on television. The old woman joined them, but when an entertainment program followed, she rose to go. "There's something I wanted to ask you," Molkho told her, taking her to the bedroom and showing her his wife's clothes. "I'll see if anyone wants them," she said. "And how about all this medicine?" he continued, pointing to the expensive boxes of Talwin, now stacked in the form of a high tower, and slipping one into her hand. "Do you know anyone who might want them at half price? They cost twenty dollars apiece, and it's a shame to lose the money. How about someone on the medical staff?" he persisted when she didn't answer. Yet (rather surprisingly, he thought, for someone who was always so polite) she merely glanced at her watch as if late and walked slowly out of the room, helped by him into her coat, from whose pocket she took out the red woolen cap she had last worn on the night of the death. "I'll see what I can do about the clothes," she announced at the top of the stairs, and then they climbed down them and up the garden stairs to the street, where it was drizzling, while Molkho recalled how she was the first person he had phoned on the night his wife died. Though she now seemed preoccupied and in a hurry, a bond had formed between them in the three weeks that had passed since then. "You needn't bother," she told him when he stepped out of the car to walk her to the entrance of the home, and so he watched from a distance as she walked down the street cloaked in greenery and slowly opened the large glass door to the lobby, in which a little old lady, who appeared to have been waiting for her, rose quickly with an odd sort of bow.

The television was off when Molkho came home, the dishes in the sink were washed, and the children were preparing to leave. "Why didn't you say you were going out?" he asked them. "You could have taken your grandmother with you." The silence in the house enveloped him like a soft cocoon. Opening a window, he peered into the dark ravine, down which he sometimes primitively imagined his wife to have vanished that night. The rain had stopped, and he felt a sudden thirst for human company. How quickly I've been abandoned, he thought. Granted, in recent years their social circle had grown less active, but the last months had seen such a steady flow of visitors that they had had to be booked in advance. Head propped high and cheeks feverish, his wife had lain in her hospital bed talking openly, almost avidly, about her death with a black irony that extended to things in general, to the whole country, for which she prophesied gloom and doom, while he bustled about her like an impresario, occasionally uttering a few soothing words to keep her mockery from becoming too aggressive.

He switched on the television, turned it off again, put on some music, and immediately toned down the volume, feeling at loose ends. Should he try phoning someone in the hope of being invited out? Unfortunately, he had napped that afternoon and now was wide awake—so much so, in fact, that he could feel his wakefulness like a lump in his chest. During the first year of his wife's illness, he had had such feelings often. Several times he was sure he had found some malignancy of his own, and once or twice he had even rushed to the doctor, making it difficult to determine who the real patient was, until her illness finally gathered such momentum that it devoured his own complaints too.

Deciding to go for a walk, he put on his coat and went down-

stairs, where it was calm but cold. He glanced at the windows, the
terraces, the doorways of the houses, and followed a woman walking
a dog while the moon rose above the rooftops into a cleared, pacific
sky, returning to his unlit apartment with a feeling of wonder that
soon changed to pleasure at his freedom. For months, even at night,
the apartment had not been this dark, and so, curious to see how it
looked from the ravine, he descended to the backyard, turning by its
mesh fence to look up at the house suspended above him on columns. When they had bought the apartment four years ago, it was
already with this green gully in mind—that is, with the thought of
the view she would have from her deathbed. Now, staring into its
blackness, which was only heightened by the luminous sky, he
walked carefully along the path he knew well and had followed often
to the bottom. The ground was very wet. Puddles of water lay about,
and broken branches and building debris obstructed his progress.
Once again he pictured her leaving this way—yes, this was the direction she had gone in that night—and absconding with part of him.

All at once the telephone rang loudly in his apartment. Was it
some friends calling to ask him over for a drink? He started back up,
refusing, however, to run, while the phone kept ringing stubbornly,
only to fall silent as he reached the door of the apartment. Now, he
thought, everyone will say that I'm never home at night! There were
no doubt people who envied him his new freedom without realizing
how lonely it could be. And yet he was glad his wife's death was
behind him. A year ago the thought of it had terrified him, but it had
gone easily enough in the end.

He poured himself a glass of brandy, opened the clothes closet,
and surveyed his wife's wardrobe, which was hanging there. Just
then the telephone rang again. It was a woman who introduced herself as Ruth, a friend of his wife's who never had met him, though
she knew all about him and kept tabs on him even now. Her voice
was warm and cheery, like a self-assured schoolteacher's. Did he
mind having a personal chat with her? "No," Molkho said. Was he
sure? "Yes," Molkho said. Well, then, she wanted him to know how
sorry she was and how full of admiration for him. "For me?" he
asked, knowing perfectly well what she meant. "For taking such

good care of her," explained the woman. Was he really sure she wasn't intruding? Perhaps he would rather she called some other time. "No, go ahead," replied Molkho, his heart suddenly beating faster. "Please don't misunderstand me," said the woman . . . although, on the other hand, no one could possibly suspect her of . . . and especially since it had dragged on so much longer than . . . "Than what?" Molkho asked. Than it usually did: that's why she had decided not to wait any longer. Though he wished she would stop beating about the bush, he was startled by her boldness. The idea of her dialing him just like that! "What are you getting at?" he asked, regretting the question at once, because now he heard the hesitation in her voice, as if it were about to beat a retreat. But it didn't. "What I'm getting at," it plunged on, "is that I know someone you might want to meet, a lovely woman who's just your type"— although if he thought the subject was premature, he only need say so. Secretly thrilled, he did his best to sound casual. Was it anyone he knew? No, she didn't think so, though, of course, she couldn't mention any names; the person in question had not been consulted and didn't know Molkho herself. For the moment, it was just a thought in the minds of some well-wishers. Were those their voices that he heard in the background? Molkho wondered. Could she actually be speaking to him with all of them right there? Suddenly it occurred to him that it was perhaps she herself who wished to meet him. "I bet it's you," he said jokingly into the phone. She laughed. "I thought you'd say that, but no, it isn't. I'm just trying to be helpful, to do what I can." Was she a professional matchmaker? he inquired appreciatively. No, it was more of a hobby with her, replied the woman with a friendly chuckle. Receiver in hand (they had bought a cordless telephone when his wife became bed-ridden), Molkho walked about the apartment, gazing out the windows at the moon-bright sky. "How old is she?" "Six years younger than you. You're fifty-three, aren't you?" "What? I'm only fifty-one!" He felt injured, a vague fear forming inside him, as if a graying, overweight, infirm woman was about to move in with him. "I'm afraid that it's a little too early for this," he said curtly, sounding offended. "It's not even a month yet. You can't just expect me to . . . why, it's a matter of simple decency!" In the silence at the other end of the line, he thought he could hear people talking, although perhaps it was only a television. "What, not even a month yet?" they were saying in shocked whispers. Oh dear, she was terribly sorry. She had been misinformed. "Oh dear, please excuse me," said the woman and hung up.

He hadn't expected her to ring off so quickly. Flushed and excited he kept walking about the apartment, the telephone still in his hand. The idea! Who could it have been? And yet it touched him that someone was thinking of him, that he was already on somebody's list. Why let it upset him? She had meant well; her warm, reliable voice still echoed in his ears as though it were now his own. He went over to the television, but didn't touch it, having watched enough of it in the past year, and went instead to the bathroom, in which there were still more things to sort out—lotions, salves, and all kinds of bottles and tubes that had had nothing to do with her illness. It was ages since he had last sat in the bathtub, which had become her exclusive domain, her own private little sanatorium, in which, all alone, she could look without fear at her body, talk to it, soothe it, cry over it, comfort it under suds, her scarred and tortured body whose ruins he was a witness to, at first the only one, later joined by the nurses who bathed her and once a week by his elder son, who had helped lift and lower her into the greenish water. Only during the last month of her life, when this body already had turned into another creature, into some fossil of a species that had become extinct long ago or would perhaps not evolve for another million years, did she not want to see it anymore (nor did he let her, wrapping her in a huge bath towel before his son could fish her out of the tub in the special rig that she sat in), not even in the small hand mirror by her bed, which she abandoned in favor of the glass strip in her compact that reflected only her eyes, the one part of herself she could bear to look at toward the end.

He turned on the faucet and started to undress, yet noticed that the water was a brownish color, and was trying to decide whether to wash or not when the doorbell rang. Quickly donning a bathrobe and going to see who it was, he found his friends, the doctor and his wife, all dressed up on their way to a party. They had decided to drop by without warning, they explained, because his telephone was always busy; they hoped it wasn't too late and apologized for having been out of touch. "Thank you for coming," said Molkho, genuinely happy to see them. "It's just for a minute," they cautioned. "Then, thank you for coming for a minute," he replied. They entered and headed automatically for the bedroom, realizing their error only by the door and halting there awkwardly, uncertain whether to sit down. But he made them, only then answering their questions, telling them a bit about the children and a little more about his mother-in-law, who was managing very well. "Rather too well," he added with a smile, describing how healthy and independent she was: why, even her cane was just for show! They seemed to listen with interest, like the good and loyal, if somewhat dull, friends that they were. Despite his overoptimistic diagnoses, the doctor had been a great help to them in dealing with the hospital staff. Though Molkho had an urge to tell them about the phone call and to ask if they knew the woman who made it, he changed his mind at the last minute, not wanting them to think it gave him pleasure. When the two of them rose to go, he could feel the doctor's wife being drawn back to the bedroom, as if she had a need to see it. It was dark and untidy, and his clothes were lying all over. "Why, it's completely different," she whispered in amazement after silently regarding it. "Yes," sighed Molkho. "Even the bed is gone," she added sadly, as if the least he could have done was continue sleeping in it himself. The doctor put an arm around him. "If you need any help," he said, "just ask." "I'm fine, really I am," said Molkho, the thought crossing his mind that the man might want to buy the Talwin. Though something warned him it would make a bad impression, he wanted to be rid of the tablets so badly that he couldn't restrain himself. "Just a minute," he said, running to bring a box of them; he had thrown out all kinds of drugs, but this was brand-new, it had cost twenty dollars a box, perhaps the hospital might like to buy it at half price. The doctor weighed it in his hand, holding it at arm's length while giving his wife a look that plainly said that Molkho had made a mistake. Hospitals, he explained politely, were not allowed to buy secondhand medicines, even if unopened, but if Molkho would give him a box as a sample, perhaps a private buyer could be found. "Never mind," said Molkho, reaching out for the Talwin, which he knew he never would see again once the doctor took it. "Never mind. I'll find a buyer myself."

He walked them to the street. A flood of light, as if the moon had been turned up to full amplitude, poured down from the cloudless sky. A solemn beauty filled the world. Now that they, dressed in their best, were about to vanish into the wonderful darkness and leave him all by himself, it was hard to part with them. And yet it irked him to be pitied. His unhappiness, he feared, would only alienate them more, and so on the spur of the moment, he told them about the phone call, concluding with a wry smile, "So you see, I'm already an eligible bachelor." They didn't smile back, though. The woman was aghast: "But how could she? How awful!" The doctor said nothing, regarding Molkho with curiosity. "And not even a month gone by!" added his wife bitterly. Wrathful and incredulous, she made him regret having mentioned it. Why, you would think he had secretly arranged that telephone call himself! Suddenly all the years of devotion to his wife meant nothing anymore, and he was being stared at as though he were her murderer.

15

THE NIGHT GREW BRIGHTER and colder, and he slept fitfully, turning from side to side and waking up every two hours as though to boil water, to give an injection, to check the intravenous, to fetch pills or tea, to say something comforting—instead of which he went to the bathroom and then plunged back into his bed, over which loomed the triumphal moon while fresh, enormous stars drifted upward from the horizon. In the middle of the night, he turned the bed to the window to get a better view of the spectacular sky. His two youngest children were not yet home, and he decided to wait up for them. The first to arrive was his daughter; he chatted with her for a while until she went to bed and then talked with the high school boy, who had meanwhile come home too, while the moon sank into the ravine. At last, after the boy had gone to sleep also, Molkho retired himself, waking the next morning to find a bright sun shining in. It was, he decided, the perfect day to wash the car, which had not been cleaned in months, and he scrubbed and waxed it for a long time while talking to his neighbor, who had come down with the same idea. The weather, though chilly, was crisp and clear, and remembering last night's message that there were people thinking of him, planning for him, Molkho felt suddenly happy. Not, of course, that he needed their help. He could manage quite well by himself, he was sure, but meanwhile they could point him in the right direction, provide him with warmth, restore his faith in the lost power of desire.

The old clothes he had on made it seem a good time for the walk in the ravine he'd been thinking of, and so he headed some hundred paces down the path until he found himself standing on a large, smooth boulder and looking into the branch-entangled gully, over whose trees and bushes played a milky light, as if the moon that had vanished there during the night were still slowly in the process of dissolving. Back in the house, he set about vigorously organizing a wash of dirty linen, waking the children and pulling the sheets out from under them, after which he started cleaning up in the kitchen. When the dishes were done, he tried persuading his son and daughter to pitch in and make lunch with him: "if you don't like the housekeeper's cooking," he told them, "let's try to do better ourselves." The children, however, were unresponsive, his daughter getting involved in a long phone conversation, while his son went off to tinker with his bicycle. When the girl hung up at last, Molkho phoned the college student to invite him over too, and though at first he tried begging off, the disappointment in his father's voice made him promise to come. True to his word, he appeared before noon, and the meal they cooked up was a good one; they sat talking intimately about this and that while looking at the calendar to choose a day for the unveiling. Gradually the children began reminiscing about their mother as they never had done before. Even the youngest, who kept silent at first, spoke up in the end, his wet eyes glistening, and it made them all glad to see him cry a bit. It's the end of another chapter in our lives, thought Molkho, feeling strong.

But he also felt his lack of sleep now. "At least wash the dishes," he told them. "I've done everything else." And shutting the bedroom blinds, he lay down with the Friday papers and soon fell into a short but delicious sleep. When he awoke the house was quiet. The dimming, brackish light made him realize how short the days had grown. The kitchen and the table were just as he had left them, with dirty dishes lying all about. The college student was reading in the living room, the soldier was embroidering in her bedroom, and the high school boy was contentedly doing his homework. Irritably Molkho went from room to room. "How could you have left the dishes like that when that was the one thing I asked you to do?" he asked, but they barely glanced up at him, as if he were a ghost. Why, it had all begun on just such an afternoon seven years ago, in early spring, when he and she had gone together to the doctor, who wrote them out an urgent referral for a biopsy. There was no hiding the grim truth from themselves, and he remembered how, on emerging from the office into the soft, balmy air that contrasted sharply with the sudden terror they were gripped by, he had felt less frightened by the illness than by his wife's fear of it, or perhaps by her anger. He had talked on and on while she walked silently beside him, trying to be logical, to point out all their options, to find comfort in the doctor's words, each one of which he had parsed like Holy Writ, though all the time, numbed and ashen, she said nothing. "Even if they have to remove a breast," he said, "even if they do, we've caught it in time, it's still not the end of the world, it's not as if you were a fashion model. You can get along without it, and I can too, without them both in fact. It will just leave me more love for the rest of you." That's what he had told her, calling on reserves of humor and imagination that he never knew existed, even though, absorbed in her own slow plodding, she was only half-listening and not even looking at him. It was only when they were already in the entrance of their old building and he paused by the mailbox to take out the letters and quickly tear open their envelopes that she looked at him angrily in the warm, enveloping dusk and said, breaking her silence, "Just remember, whatever happens I'm dying at home, nowhere else." He smiled at her, a shiver running down him at what he knew was only her first salvo. Why, he started to protest, she shouldn't even think about dying! "No, promise me," she interrupted earnestly, a look of desperation on her face, "promise me you'll pay whatever it costs, because I'm not dying anywhere else." Again he tried humoring her, but this time she turned on him with her full, fearful strength, so that he said at once, "I promise; of course, I do. How could you even imagine . . ."—a promise he would have to repeat a thousand times right up to the moment of her death. Grimly she climbed the stairs and waited for him to open the door for her. It was almost dark in the house. All three children were still in grade school. Quiet and strangely peaceful, they sat doing their homework together, knowing nothing but already guessing all.

16

A MONTH AFTER HIS WIFE'S DEATH, they all gathered again for the unveiling, the family and its many friends, some of whom had missed the funeral. Though it was a rainy day and they all had umbrellas, not a drop fell during the short ceremony. The mood was calm and peaceful; several of his wife's fellow schoolteachers spoke briefly but movingly, and there was a feeling of closeness among them all. The new tombstone stood in its place. Molkho was rather sorry that it had only his wife's name and the dates of her birth and death, but the children had said that anything else would be false and sentimental. To his surprise, the legal adviser from the office was there too, along with one of her coworkers, dressed in a smart suit and blue raincoat, an umbrella in one hand and a wreath of flowers in the other. He caught his breath, feeling himself turn red: she must have come to look over his family, he thought, and her appearance with the wreath—she, who hadn't known his wife and hardly even knew him—seemed to him as daring as a striptease. When the ceremony was over, he watched in amazement as she laid the wreath on the grave, and afterward, stopping to shake the hands of those present and say a few words to them with his tottering mother hanging on to him, he paused to thank her warmly too. "We're here on behalf of the whole office," she said a bit uncomfortably, though looking straight at him, which touched Molkho, so that he almost choked with gratitude, unable to find the right words. "The office couldn't have chosen a better representative," he said at last. "I thank you, I really do." "Who was that?" his mother-in-law inquired in the car, nodding when he told her and saying, "Oh, yes. That widow from work."

17

H E KNEW THEN that it was only a matter of time before they struck up a relationship. Was it perhaps too soon? he wondered. Was he ready for it? What would she expect of him physically? He hadn't made love to a woman in years. Might she be in too much of a rush? He made a few discreet inquiries, yet though his informants spoke freely and willingly, there was little new they had to tell him apart from the matter of her rank, for whereas he had always believed her to be a single civil service grade above him, he was now shocked to discover she was three. How, and by whom, had she managed to be promoted so quickly? Late one night, while out walking, he stopped by her house on the West Carmel, an unassuming building with only four apartments of a type built in the early 1960s. Noiselessly he stepped inside and scanned the names on the mailboxes to see who her neighbors were; none of them was familiar, though the fact that one was a doctor rather pleased him. Stepping back outside, he circled the building, noticing the old garbage cans and the neglected little garden and lawn; the house committee, it was evident, had been falling down on the job.

And yet he wished to put off seeing her again, which, as they worked in different departments, could easily be accomplished by his not venturing into the hallway or downstairs to the cafeteria, something he rarely would have done anyway, because ever since his wife's death the daily loaf of bread from the grocery was too much for them to finish at home, so that he had begun taking two large sandwiches to work, washing them down with coffee from a thermos. After all, he told himself, it's not as if I were in any hurry.

18

ONLY NOW that he had time on his hands did he realize how busy his wife's illness had kept him; how many hours he had put in every week talking to her or her visitors and dealing with all the endless problems, how on guard he had been day and night, how many difficult decisions had been left to him, how tense he had been made all the time by the Unknown that awaited him, mornings, evenings, at work, on the telephone, in his long talks with the doctors and the nurses. He was the male lead in a drama, strutting about on a stage with a big hospital bed in the center, whispering, shouting, crying, for she had reduced him to tears—yes, she had done that too. Wistful for those lost days, he thought of them with nostalgia. Now it was over with, the audience departed, the sets disassembled, the stage itself a pile of old boards; and bathed in a yellowing glow, time stretched out endlessly and wearily before him like a flat road. He came home from work each day, napped for a while, shopped at the little supermarket nearby, stopped in at the bank to check on his stocks or transfer funds from one account to another, and then took a short walk and came home to listen to music, the sound of which on his records and tapes seemed suddenly flat to him. One day his daughter brought home a Hebrew translation of *Pride and Prejudice,* and slowly he began to read about the adventures of the five Bennet sisters and to think, Why, I'm like Lizzy and Jane: it's time I was married off too. First, though, there had to be a way of arousing his lost desire, of assuring he would not be found wanting when the day arrived. Perhaps he should buy some pornographic magazines. Meanwhile, he leafed through them in the bookstores, staring with cold revulsion at the perfect, pinkish bodies they displayed.

19

I N THE END, when he began to look for her in the cafeteria, she was nowhere to be found; indeed, she had as much as vanished from the building. He would have to find a professional pretext to meet with her, he thought, since he needed a closer look to decide if she was or wasn't his type. Yet he mustn't let it seem unnatural. And he would have liked to obtain her personal file, too, if only to find out how old she was. True, women sometimes lied about their age, but such fibs were usually not great. Though he guessed she was in her forties, she might also be pushing fifty, might conceivably already have passed it. Even assuming that a young woman was not for him, that didn't mean he wanted an old one. I'm in no hurry, he told himself. Yet he kept returning to the cafeteria, where one day he spied her surrounded by some members of her staff. From behind, he felt sure that her short, straight auburn hair was dyed, for he had seen its coppery tint before, had even helped his wife mix a solution of it in the days before she wore a wig. A gray sky was visible through the window. She was saying something assertively, gesturing firmly with both hands, her face well chiseled despite its lines, her small, almost oriental eyes giving her a squirrelish look. Though he nodded as he passed her, she did not respond or seem to know who he was, which made him wonder whether she was nearsighted. It was odd, he thought, sipping his strong black coffee, that she should be too busy talking to recognize him. Just then, though, she caught sight of him and flashed him a smile . . . and yet she went on talking. If she's been a widow for three years and has time, he thought, so do I. He could feel the strong coffee perking him up and worried that it might spoil his nap.

20

FOR THERE WERE HABITS from before his wife's death that were hard to break, such as his afternoon nap. Was it really worth the effort of taking it? Once he had needed that hour of sleep to be fresh for the sleepless night ahead, and his wife had made sure he had gotten it; in fact, it had been his favorite hour of the day, one in which, lying curled beneath a blanket in the quiet apartment, the afternoon light filtered by the blinds, even his wife's illness had seemed to him remote and unmenacing. Now, however, he sought in vain to recapture its sweet sensation; his naps grew progressively shorter, losing their inner tang, and after fifteen or twenty minutes of them he would wake up feeling cross. Not even leaving work early, at one o'clock, when he was at his most tired, could restore those lost sleeps to him.

The arrangement made with his department head that he could leave the office early by taking work home was still in force. Even after his wife's death, he had kept it up, for he had wanted to give the high school boy his lunch, the preparation of which was no easy matter, in light of the quantities of food in the refrigerator. The new housekeeper was hyperactive; no matter how clear his instructions, she simply kept cooking more and more. Besides, the boy was beginning to follow in her footsteps; opening all kinds of cans when he came home, he had taken to concocting private dishes of his own while ignoring the leftovers that were crying to be eaten and filling up the house in pots and pans. Sometimes, thinking while at work about the overflowing icebox at home, Molkho fell into a rage; reaching for the phone, he would shout at the housekeeper to stop her cooking at once and would hang up, leaving her out of sorts and hurt. Worse yet, his daughter was away at an officers' course and no longer came home from her base, making them one mouth less. Only now did Molkho realize how voraciously his wife had eaten, despite her illness. The refrigerator had never been too full while she was alive.

But it was his younger son who was the problem. If only he would stop his solo experiments! It was impossible to get the housekeeper to make what he liked, because the boy kept changing his tastes; yesterday's favorite was today's bugaboo, and so Molkho made a point of getting home in time to be in charge of promoting the leftovers. "Just tell me what you like," he would plead for the tenth time with the long-haired boy in his blue uniform, who, besides being totally uncommunicative, was having a hard time at school, though Molkho hoped it was only a phase. "We have to finish what we started yesterday. I can't be expected to eat this for a whole week by myself," he would say, dumping the cold potatoes back in the frying pan and trying to resuscitate the dry rice with a slab of margarine and some tomato sauce. Once his son brought home a lanky friend, and Molkho invited him to stay for lunch. The youngster wolfed down everything on his plate and even asked for seconds, and Molkho, who was waiting on both boys with an apron, was encouraged to see that his son ate more too. He asked the guest for his name and inquired about his parents, who, he was told, were often away. "Then why not have lunch with us more often," he said.

H IS YOUNGER SON had always worried him. Several times in recent years he had barely escaped being left back a grade, and it was only because of the illness of his mother, who taught in the same school, that he had been given the benefit of the doubt. Often he answered his parents impatiently, even rudely and with unprovoked anger, getting up and stalking out into the rain in a short-sleeved shirt without a sweater. While he had always been more hostile to his mother and closer to his father, his antagonism now seemed transferred to Molkho, who had even thought of sending him to a psychologist, though his friends had counseled waiting until the boy was older. Moreover, now that they spent long hours alone together, Molkho discovered that his son was a heavy masturbator; sometimes, opening the door to his darkened room, he found him in bed on his stomach, his face buried in the pillow, pretending to be asleep. Poking through the laundry bin, Molkho came across wet underpants whose young, animal smell assailed him, and once, rummaging in his son's bed, he found beneath the mattress a photo of a nude, ripe-breasted, no longer young woman. His first reaction was to tear it up, yet on second thought he reflected, So what?

TWO MONTHS HAD PASSED since his wife's death, the second of which, Molkho noticed, went by particularly slowly. The days turned warm and clear, and the cold, rainy weather of the premature winter was forgotten. Though each time the telephone rang he still ran excitedly to get it, he had no idea whom he hoped it would be. Sometimes the call was from distant acquaintances who had only now heard the news, either because they didn't read the obituaries or because they had been abroad, and he enjoyed being able to describe his wife's last weeks again and to hear their sincere expressions of regret. Gradually, though, there was less of this. And galloping inflation notwithstanding, his own telephone bill had shrunk too, quite extraordinarily so; his wife, he realized, must have been on the phone constantly during her last, bedridden months. Calling whom, though? Out-of-town friends, no doubt, perhaps even her cousin in Paris. In any event, he himself used the phone sparingly, though he still called his mother in Jerusalem every morning with news of the children and himself. Slyly she would ask him how he felt and whom he was seeing, always with the same advice: "Don't go to the movies yet, don't go to any concerts. It's too early for that. Just see a lot of people, keep in touch with your old friends before they forget you, and find new ones," she would warn him again. "But don't go to the movies. You have a TV at home; that's enough for you. When your father died, I didn't even have that, and I had to stay home a whole year doing nothing." Grumbling, he would try to hang up, but it was impossible to get a word in edgewise; she simply repeated over and over, "Don't go to any concerts. You know what people will think.

You've done the right thing until now. Just have patience a little longer. Isn't that what her mother says too?"

Nevertheless, when it was time for the next concert, he decided that enough was enough, though he did not, of course, say so to his mother-in-law over dinner that Friday. As usual, having arrived early at the old-age home, which he found himself liking more with each visit, he wandered about it. With sympathy he regarded its clean, bald German Jews who sat in their Sabbath best in the lobby, talking politely and looking at him affably, a stoutish man with curly gray hair and dark Levantine eyes that scanned the bulletin board with wary tedium, reading up on the cultural programs being offered that week. Perhaps, Molkho mused, he should put up a notice about the Talwin. Sometimes, his heart beating faster, he rode the elevator up to the fifth floor, curious to see the dying patients in the medical ward and the apparatus by their sides; yet each time, intercepted at the door by an elderly nurse who asked him where he was going, he stammered an excuse and rode back down.

He spoke in praise of the home to everyone, jocularly adding that the only thing wrong with it was its being exclusively for German Jews. "I can become a Christian," he protested, a note of seriousness creeping into his voice, "even a Moslem, but there's no way I can become a German Jew and get in there one day myself." His mother-in-law liked the place too, though she had resisted moving into it for years, being used to her apartment near her daughter's in which she had continued to lead an independent life, even after turning eighty. It was only when the illness took a turn for the worse that Molkho's wife insisted that she move. "What will we do if anything happens to you?" she asked her mother. "Who will take care of you?" And even then the old woman put up a fight: she had two rooms in her apartment and would have only one in the home, and besides, she was in perfect health, there wasn't anything wrong with her. But his wife refused to back down. "We can't be responsible if anything happens to you," she persisted. "What can happen?" asked the old woman with a quiet smile. "Suppose you fall and break something," suggested Molkho. "But why should I fall?" asked his mother-in-law, amused by the thought. Then his wife said in desperation, "But can't you see, you're not letting me die in peace," and her mother's resistance crumbled. The old woman moved into the home while her daughter was still well enough to visit her there in her small but dignified room, and in fact, she got on famously with everyone, a little old, lucid, 100 percent German Jewess who could read Hebrew and had even once run an orphanage, so that she was soon elected to the social committee—which gave Molkho, now waiting impatiently for her in the lobby filled with potted plants, a feeling of having a personal stake in the place. Recently she had begun to remind him more and more of his wife. Smiling at him as she emerged from the elevator, her cane hooked over one arm, she looked as chipper as ever and carried the usual box of strudel that was her contribution to the Sabbath meal, whose chef he now was, though he refused to run any risks, playing it safe with a salad, french fries, and some frozen, codlike fish on which he had practiced all week, even burning it once or twice in the frying pan before getting the hang of it. And indeed, at first it was a great success with everyone, though after a while it, too, began to pall.

Their meals were not talkative. His wife had been the conversationalist in the family. "Without me," she used to say to them, "you'd just gobble your food like animals," and in fact, though it did not make them feel particularly bestial, that was how they now ate. Sometimes one of them would groan in despair over the political situation, but fatalistically, as one despairs of the incurably ill; and sometimes Molkho's mother-in-law would tell the children about their dead mother, relating some childhood story about her from the age of ten or eleven. None of them had ever heard these anecdotes, which the old woman evidently rehearsed during the week; but though Molkho would listen to them with interest, feeling a bittersweet pain, the children would sit through them bored and fidgety. Soon the college student would return to his dorm (he had fallen behind in his studies and had a lot to make up), the soldier would pick up the telephone and began dialing her friends, and the high school boy would slip off to his room, leaving Molkho and his mother-in-law to watch the news by themselves until, as soon as the entertainment programs started, she would rise from her chair and put on her coat and scarf. Sometimes, driven by habit, she first went to her daughter's bedroom and stood looking at it from the doorway, casting Molkho a kindly glance. Though she had never thought particularly highly of him, he knew that she felt a subtle affection for him, which had grown stronger in recent months. "Is there anything I can do for you?" she asked. "Perhaps you'd like me to invite the boy for a meal now and then."

He would have liked to ask if she was going to Tuesday's concert, but he thought better of it. Driving her back to the home, he parked near the entrance and watched her step out of the car, her feet groping weakly for the sidewalk, then quickly recovering and striding firmly down the path between flowerbeds and bushes surrounding a small pool until she reached the large glass door, on the other side of which the postprandial light was an almost blackish violet. He waited to make sure she passed safely through it, watching her gaily say hello to the old folks chewing their cud in the lobby and the little old lady who greeted her, rising quickly from her corner with an old-fashioned bow.

23

T HAT TUESDAY NIGHT he went to the concert. The program featured Haydn's *Creation* and rumor had it that the performance was a good one, Sunday's and Monday's audiences having only the highest praise for it. Though at first the college student had promised to join him, Molkho found a note from him that afternoon saying that he couldn't make it, and so he asked the high school boy instead. "What's there to lose," he cajoled him. "Try it one time. It's wonderful music. You can always leave in the intermission if you don't like it." "Ho, ho, ho," said the boy, rejecting the offer disdainfully. Molkho did not make a point of it. This time he was sure his wife's ticket could be sold. His last Philharmonic concert had been over half a year ago, in early summer, before his wife, who had come leaning on a cane, took to bed for the last time; later on in the season, when he had wanted to bring her again, she had asked him, practically begged him, to go by himself, and he almost did, until suddenly she began to throw up and he was forced to stay home with her.

He washed, put on a dark suit, and arrived earlier than he had meant to. Yet the mall was already crowded, and its festive mood was infectious. There were numerous people he knew, many of whom came over to shake his hand earnestly, and he wished the college student were with him so that the blame, such as it was, could be shared. The concert was sold out; quite a few youngsters circulated among the crowd in search of extra tickets, but none were to be had. He himself was approached in a friendly manner by an attractive young lady in glasses; she seemed to be alone, perhaps even available, and seeing her bright, beaming face, he thought, Why not, who knows what may come of it? Yet he wavered, afraid how it might look, and then feebly shook his head. Soon after a young man in jeans came up to him too. No, said Molkho decisively after starting to take a step toward him, making up his mind to forfeit the price of the ticket. Entering the auditorium, he took his customary seat. The two old men on his right, who were partners in an optometrist's shop, greeted him diffidently, not quite sure it was he, while quickly he sought out his mother-in-law's seat a few rows ahead of him and saw it was empty. The musicians began coming onstage, taking their places and warming up deftly on bars of the opening piece. The hall hummed with people, more of whom kept streaming in, though it looked almost full already. Students were sitting in the aisles. Now and then, someone stopped to ask Molkho if the seat beside him was taken, to which he testily replied, "Yes, it is." Still tuning up, the orchestra was now wildly improvising on all kinds of themes. He kept staring at the empty seat ahead of him, hoping to see his mother-in-law appear, but instead, an usher arrived with a little old lady in an old velvet dress who, anxious and flustered, bowed to her neighbors with a timid smile and sat in Frau Starkman's place. Just as he recognized her, a hand on his shoulder made him jump. It was some old friends from Jerusalem, who helped him to his feet and sorrowfully embraced him. "We heard about it," they said in low voices. "We're so sorry. We wanted so much to come see you. Was it very hard in the end? Did she suffer much?" They wanted some preconcert consolation, and he gave it to them warmly. "No, she didn't suffer at all. Not a bit. I know, because it happened at home." "At home?" they asked astonishedly, their arms still around him. "Yes," he said proudly, "at home. She hardly suffered at all." The old men on his right listened open-eyed, regarding him sympathetically when he sat down again. No doubt they had suspected as much, from the moment they saw her last summer with the cane, and now they put two and two together. Still, they didn't seem to mind his being there. They even seemed about to speak to him, but just then the conductor made his entrance.

The first piece was Vivaldi's *Four Seasons,* which was new to him. In general, Molkho's knowledge of classical music, which had come to him via his wife, was sketchy. Both his parents had been born into Orthodox families in the old walled city of Jerusalem, and what little musical education he possessed was the result of his wife's patient efforts. He still preferred compositions with plenty of trumpets and drums, although he couldn't deny that the strains of the first violin now washing over him tugged at his heartstrings too. Suddenly, glancing at the empty seat beside him, he missed his wife acutely, as if he had left her at home and was now needed by her there, hobbling about on crutches in the dark apartment. Why did he have to say she hadn't suffered, what made him need to be so comforting? A light cough from somewhere behind him sounded like hers. Reassuringly he laid a hand on the soft plush of the open seat beside him.

During the intermission the two of them used to join her mother in the lobby, where they would arrange to meet after the performance. Now, elbowing his way through the resplendent crowd past elegant women whose bare, perfumed flesh-scent he inhaled, he craned his neck to get a better look at the old lady. She was still seated in her place, her big, clear eyes wide with wonder. Tiny, dressed in old clothes, her gloved hands in her lap and her white hair streaked with dull gold, she looked like someone out of the pages of a fairy tale, shyly smiling at her surroundings with an aura of faraway lands, at him, too, although she did not appear to recognize him. Returning from the lobby, he found the seat next to him occupied by an aloof young man and made him change places, giving him his own and moving over to sit in his wife's. Meanwhile, a choir had filled the stage. Surprising him with a beauty that struck a chord deep within him, the music began on a powerful note.

24

H E STILL HAD NOT FOUND the meaning of his new life, its deeper rationale. During the illness, each day had been a recurrent test whose ultimate goal was Death itself. His task, he had known, was to prevent, or at least to forestall, suffering, while at the same time hastening it along. As evening jelled outside the windows and he finished his last preparations for the night's vigil, having already given her a shot of morphine, or sometimes even before that, he felt that he had vanquished the day and that this victory had not only a physical but also a spiritual dimension, so that Death, which he sometimes imagined as a distant and soon-to-appear relative dressed in black, regarded him from afar with approval, the hidden observer of his resourcefulness; whereas now, his lunch already eaten, the dishes washed, and nothing left to do around the house, the day still stretched half unfinished before him with no apparent reason for its being there.

He still hadn't disposed of the Talwin, which was beginning to weigh on him. It was worth some four hundred dollars all in all, and it was a crime to throw the money away, especially as he had broken a fixed-time deposit at the bank for it. He had known even then that he was overpurchasing, but the lady pharmacist had warned him that her stock was low and his wife had made him buy it all. In fact, the drug hadn't even been prescribed by her regular doctor, who was abroad at the time, but by an elderly stand-in whose promise that it would relieve her pain she had believed implicitly, though in fact it turned out to be contraindicated by another, more crucial drug and had to be discontinued. Who, he wondered, would take it off his hands now? Standing on the shelf across from his bed, the white boxes with their neat blue stripes were the first thing he saw on getting up in the morning and the last thing he saw at night. There were drugstores that hadn't even heard of it, and though by now he was almost willing to give it away, he knew of no one who needed it. Finally, one night, he called the old doctor who had prescribed it. The doctor, it so happened, was sick himself; when asked by the man's wife what he wanted, Molkho's first inclination was to hang up, but before he knew it, he was telling her the whole story. What was the drug called? she inquired. Apparently she had heard of it, because she asked how much he had, and when told twenty boxes, she said, "Bring them over. We'll see what we can do." "When?" asked Molkho. "Right now if you'd like," the woman told him. And so, stuffing the medicine into a plastic bag, he set out for the doctor's house, a small stone building on top of the Carmel.

The doctor's wife met him at the door, a small, sprightly woman in a smock who led him down a hallway lined with books and bric-a-brac. Charmed by the old-world ambience, his wife, Molkho remembered, had believed in the man from the start. Now he lay with a bad cold on a leather couch in his office covered by a plaid woolen blanket and surrounded by a disorderly pile of papers, folders, instruments, books, and medicines. Indeed, there were drugs everywhere, glutting the shelves and filling the spaces between and above the books. Pointing at Molkho, who suddenly regretted coming, the wife said something in German to her husband. "I hope I'm not intruding," Molkho apologized, observing the old man's pale face and bloodshot eyes as he stepped into the overheated room whose blinds were lowered halfway. The doctor simply nodded. "When did it happen?" he asked, questioning Molkho about the last stages of the illness, listening morosely to his answers and nodding again, this

time with annoyance, as if, despite the inevitability of it all, he felt
let down by the outcome.

All at once he asked Molkho about his own health. Throwing
off his blanket and sticking his thin, sinewy feet into a pair of slippers, he began, cold, pajamas, and all, to give the visitor a checkup,
taking his blood pressure and peering into his eyes with a little
flashlight, his dry, hot hands giving Molkho such a fright that he felt
his heart skip a beat; quickly, however, the old man lost patience,
spoke to his wife again in German, picked up the boxes of Talwin,
and held them up to the light. They had stopped using the drug,
Molkho stammered, because it was contraindicated by something
else whose name he felt he was mispronouncing, though the doctor
said nothing to correct him but merely ran a hand over the boxes. At
last he said crossly, "There was no contraindication," and turned
again to his wife. "I hope it's still in use. Lots of drugstores have
never heard of it," said Molkho, shifting the blame back to the
doctor. "Of course it is," replied the old man, his feathers ruffled
now. "It's the best painkiller there is." "And can a normal person
take it too?" asked Molkho. "What do you call normal?" asked the
doctor. "Someone healthy," Molkho replied. "Why should someone
healthy need medicine?" smirked the doctor. "I mean someone
healthy who's in pain," explained Molkho. "Of course," said the
doctor, consulting his wife again in German and mentioning several
names, apparently of patients who might need the Talwin. "Well, all
right," he said to Molkho, as if doing him a special favor. "You may
as well leave it all here." By now, though, Molkho was having second
thoughts: suppose the medicine disappeared among the many piles
on the shelves and he never got a cent for it? Perhaps the old man
and his wife were illegally trafficking in pharmaceuticals. "Are you
sure you can find a buyer?" he asked. "I might," shrugged the
doctor. "In that case," said Molkho, "why don't I leave you my
address and you can give it to whoever is interested." Getting only
hurt silence for an answer, he wrote down his address, took the
Talwin, and left. Back home, having returned it to its place, he
wondered if he had done the right thing.

25

Mornings he rose early. By six he was already out of bed and in the bathroom, where he sat drowsily on the toilet for a long time, tearing off the day's page from the memo pad and making lists of shopping, of things to do around the house, and of people to be phoned. Then he checked his stool for blood. Sometimes he even talked to it. "What's with you," he might ask it, or else, "What do you want from me?" When it was finally flushed down the drain, he washed, shaved, and studied himself in the mirror, a fifty-one-year-old man with gray but still thick curly hair and dark, deeply set eyes, at loose ends in a freedom whose nature was not yet clear to him. Sometimes, shutting those eyes, he would think of her. "Where are you?" he asked wonderingly, picturing her for a moment in the ravine by the house, whose stone path he had followed that night not long ago until forced to turn back by the slippery mud. Then he would turn on the heater, put a kettle up to boil, think of what to have for breakfast, and wake up the high school boy, something that was easier said than done, especially on days when school started early, so that he had to raise the blinds, turn on the radio, and wait for these measures to take effect while glancing at his son's school things. Next there was breakfast to prepare and sandwiches for work and school, after which Molkho made the beds and gathered the scattered sections of the newspaper. At times, recalling the rules laid down by his wife, he followed his son around the house to make sure he combed his hair and brushed his teeth. "Do it for your mother," he would beg the boy, who always seemed most estranged from him in the morning. Then he washed the dishes, shut the windows and blinds, picked out a tie that he was never sure matched his jacket, and left for the office. There, striving to snap him out of his slump and up his output, which had dropped sharply in the last year, his superiors handed him files and summoned him to conferences about the budgets of several small northern municipalities that were on the verge of financial collapse. At ten he went to the cafeteria for coffee, on the lookout for the legal adviser, whom he occasionally ran into. Sometimes they chatted a bit or exchanged smiles on the stairs. He knew she was waiting for a sign from him; yet, afraid to do anything impulsive that he might later regret, he preferred to bide his time. Perhaps, he thought, the best time would be in early spring, with the fifth or sixth concert in the series, which he had already marked down on his calendar. He would ask her to come with him: it would be a good way to begin, because he was sure she liked classical music. Meanwhile, he'd have a chance to look her over and decide if he liked her tailored wardrobe, whose different outfits he already was familiar with. She can wait a bit, he thought; if she hasn't found a man in the three years her husband has been dead, another month or two won't hurt her. It wasn't as if she had been waiting just for him. True, he had informed the office of his wife's illness several years ago, at which time she might have been consulted about his request for a flexible schedule that would allow him more time at home, but she could scarcely have had her sights on him then, especially as the illness was not yet clearly fatal and his devotion to his wife was public knowledge. Even now, what did she see in him? He thought of himself as a gnarled old tree, so unlike this vivacious woman with her clipped hair and small, brown oriental eyes, whose look was that of an intelligent pointer or, better yet, of a sagacious squirrel. Could she be harboring a fatal illness herself that she wished him to nurse for her? Her husband, a travel or insurance agent, had died of a sudden heart attack—hence her buoyancy, Death having gone easy on her, making no demands and teaching no hard lessons. That much he knew about her, even if he rarely saw her, just as he knew her perfume, which had a special, subtle fragrance. His wife's illness had sharpened his sense of smell too.

He would wait. He had time. Setting the pace, he thought plea-surably, was a male prerogative. Meanwhile, he went for long walks about town, and one day he took off from work, packed a suitcase with his wife's clothes, and drove to Jerusalem, where he accompanied his mother to the cemetery on the tenth anniversary of his father's death. Amid the old, crumbling tombstones of the ancient graveyard he stood with her and the other members of the family, aristocratic old Sephardim who shook his hand gently and commiserated with him on the loss of his wife. He had not been in Jerusalem for half a year, and the city he grew up in now seemed to him excessively wintry and religious. He brought his mother home, attended to some business in town, and returned to eat the large lunch she had cooked for him, which consisted of his favorite greasy foods. Then, cozily sleepy, sitting with his shoes off on the old couch in the heart of the city's dilapidated downtown, he listened to her talk on and on. What, she kept asking him, did he think? "Think about what?" he parried innocently. "About what?" she echoed, sitting there large and multicolored like a big cockatoo and peering at him intently as if for the first time. "About your future." "I really haven't thought about it yet," he answered lamely, stretched out comfortably on the couch. "I feel too drained." Ever since his wife had taken ill, his mother's presence in their life had become far less intrusive; the illness frightened her, so that her visits with them grew more subdued and were marked by a reluctance to interfere. "Don't be in any hurry," she cautioned him now. "Have a good look around. Just remember, though, that you're not a young man anymore. Don't be caught napping." The house was ill heated and cold. Through the glass door of the terrace he watched the sun shoot apocalyptically out of a black tunnel of clouds. His mother refused to drop the subject. "Maybe you should think of coming back to live in Jerusalem. You have plenty of friends here who can help you find the right woman, the kind that you're used to. Maybe even someone from your old high school class. There must be some divorcées and widows among them." He opened his eyes wide, staring fondly at this woman who never failed to surprise him, silently shoveling peanuts into his mouth from a bowl and chewing them vigorously. The thought of marrying someone from his graduating class of thirty-five years ago struck him as being so wildly original that for a moment he pictured the classroom, with its four rows of seats, many occupied by young girls in black dresses. "How am I supposed to find them?" he asked in a feeble attempt at a joke. "If you came back here, you'd find all your old friends. You're the only one who ever left. Ask for a transfer." "I can't," he whispered exhaustedly. "I can't leave her." "Leave whom?" his mother demanded. "Her mother," he said. "It wouldn't be fair."

He went to nap in his old bedroom, yet even wrapped in a large woolen blanket he was unable to keep himself warm. The roar of the city, which was the sound of his childhood, and the cold beneath the high ceiling kept him awake, his thoughts wandering from his children to the legal adviser, and then to his mother-in-law. Lately, the old woman had been hard to reach on the phone; it was as if she no longer needed him, as if she, too, had been set free by Death. And then, too, she was busy with her little friend from Russia who had arrived in Israel with her daughter, having taken them under her wing and made herself not only their counselor but their handyman; just the other day, for example, while stuck in a traffic jam, he had seen her dart out of a hardware store with a long metal pipe in one hand.

At last he fell into a troubled sleep, hearing his mother opening the suitcase he had brought and making bundles of his wife's clothing for some woman's charity, while he dreamt he was standing in the yard of his old high school among a pack of Boy Scouts, though his tie was not Scout blue or green but rather bright red, as were the ties of the smaller boys lined up on either side of him. He lay in his old bed listening to the city rhythmically pound and churn, as if he were inside the drum of a big washing machine that kept filling and draining, spinning, stopping, and filling again. From time to time, his mother tiptoed in to see if he was awake and tiptoed out again, annoyed at him for sleeping away his visit with her. Shivering with cold, he watched her through slit eyes until she gave up and returned to her pots in the kitchen, bursting with maternal compassion and impatience to talk with him.

Finally, she came and woke him, unable to keep her latest idea to herself any longer: he should take off his wedding ring; that way, at least, no one would get the wrong idea. "What difference does it make?" he asked, still flat on his back, enjoying her concern for him. "I'll be dead soon myself." He could feel her protest ripple through her. "How can you say such a thing! You have children!" "They don't need me any more," he answered, getting up to eat the early supper that was lavishly laid out for him on the dining room table. His wife's clothes were already sorted, folded, and neatly tied with string. A purplish green light glinted off the plates and silverware. He went over to the window to gaze at the sky, which had grown dark and frothy, as though it were being brought to a boil. "Just look at that sky," he told his mother, who suggested that he spend the night with her and return to Haifa in the morning. Molkho, however, declined. As soon as supper was over, he began gathering his things, hoping to beat the storm, his mood so improved that when she mentioned the wedding ring again, he answered, "Why not?" and tried pulling it off his finger. He did not succeed, however, for the finger had grown thicker, and his mother had to bring a bar of soap and slowly, painfully, work it off. With a glance at its grimy inner curve he stuck it in his wallet. "We'll see," he said, bending to kiss her good-bye.

A strong wind was blowing as he drove out of Jerusalem in a ghostly yellow light, its sudden gusts making the car swerve. He slowed down by the line of hitchhikers waiting at the city's edge and stopped by a cluster of soldiers, some of them still wet with rain they had brought with them from elsewhere. On the spur of the moment he made up his mind to take only women. The soldiers crowded around him like bees on a honeycomb, but slowly, determinedly, he winnowed out four north-bound girls, who all removed their army berets as soon as they got in the car, filling it with the scent of their hair. Gingerly he fastened the seat belt of the passenger beside him and then smiled in the rearview mirror to the three girls in the back. All this young femaleness will do me good, he thought, carefully taking the sharp curves of the road that ran westward toward the setting sun, which glowed like a hot coal through a tattered curtain of sky and fog. Within minutes, however, it was gone from sight and was followed by a furious cloudburst, through which the car chuted downhill between two vast sheets of rain. He slowed down, turning on the windshield wipers, the heater, and the radio all at once, hunched tensely over the wheel in the torrential downpour while trying to make out, above the music and the sound of the motor, the soft, childish chatter in the rear. From time to time, he scanned the mirror for the pretty eyes and smooth, youthful faces behind him, waiting for some expression of feminine interest, for some sign; but the rain kept up, flooding the sides of the road, and he had to concentrate on the fogged-up windshield, turning the defroster on and off and opening the window a crack to let in cold air. It grew dark out. Soon the headlights of the oncoming cars were all he could see; the girls behind him fell silent, and the music on the radio faded away into a fuzzy drone, leaving him on edge with a coalescing blob of passengers, their faces obscured in the mirror by the encroaching darkness. With his fingers he felt the white circle left on his skin by the missing ring. It was a long, nerve-racking drive; the traffic lights took forever to change, the tense motor threatened to overheat, and the silence deepened with the night. Once on the coastal highway, he thought of stopping at a diner, but the car plunged on of its own accord and the head of the soldier next to him fell back in deep slumber. He felt as if he were transporting a single, giant woman, a sleeping, shallowly breathing, tetracephalous female pudding whose separate heads kept banging against the windows, opening and shutting pairs of eyes until Haifa, when suddenly it awoke and squirted off in four thin tentacles that quickly vanished beneath the streetlights into the wet night.

He arrived home at eight o'clock, retrieved from the rear seat the crushed morning paper, which was still warm from female flesh, and dashed through the rain to his house. As soon as he entered he noticed that the living room door was closed. His youngest son came accusingly out of his room. "Someone's here to buy medicine," he said. "He's been waiting for an hour and wouldn't go away. He even threw up in the bathroom." Molkho opened the door to the living room. The man was still in his wet coat, a tall, thin fellow who jumped to his feet as if seeing a ghost. The symptoms of his condition were obvious: the puffy face, the unnatural redness, the thin, limp hair like the bristles of an old brush, the eyes bulging with the effort of his struggle. Why, it's like a family reunion, thought Molkho, who hadn't realized until now how he had missed all these things. But the man was impatient, self-involved in his illness; sent by the old doctor, he wanted to pay for the medicine and go, so that Molkho quickly took the boxes from their shelf, showed him they hadn't been opened, and told him the price. "Exactly half what they cost in the drugstore," he said, removing his coat while describing the rain to the visitor, who, however, had not the slightest interest in either the weather or Molkho's adventures. I wonder what's been carved out of him beneath that coat and what's rotted away by itself, wondered Molkho, smelling vomit as he approached him, trying to befriend him a bit, to tell him about the Talwin. But the stranger did not need to have the drug explained, for he had been taking it for years, and hurriedly counting the boxes, he did a mental sum and wrote out a check. And still Molkho clung to him. The man, something told him, was at the climax of his drama. Did he have a wife? Children? Yet already he was on his way, the blue-and-white boxes stuffed into the pockets of his coat. "It's raining out," Molkho warned, making one last effort to detain him. "Don't you have an umbrella?" But he was already gone.

In the bathroom Molkho thought he could still smell the man's puke. He took a look at the day's mail and, feeling suddenly fatigued, lay down in bed, where he could not find a comfortable position. All at once he felt sorry he had sold the medicine. He had parted with it too cheaply; he should have asked for more. And besides, he was used to seeing the colored boxes before going to sleep; he should at least have left himself one. He glanced at the check to see who had written it, but it was the old-fashioned kind, without a name at the top, and he couldn't make out the signature. Getting up, he poured himself a nip of brandy and then, though he was exhausted, paced restlessly around the house, feeling the four girl soldiers' sleep instead, which had rubbed off slimily on him. He had a moment of panic and even after dozing off kept waking up again, as in the days when his wife was ill. It was after midnight when he suddenly felt the presence of a stranger in the house. It was a woman. A light was on, and in it he saw a girl soldier stepping out of the kitchen—but it was only his daughter, whose officers' course had just ended. He called her name. She looked just like her mother. He held her hand.

26

AND THEN THE INVITATION CAME. The legal adviser was tired of waiting. There had indeed been prior indications, but he had read them wrong, had not been at all sure she had anything to do with them or with the sudden flurry of activity in the office that seemed meant to wake him from his trance. Suddenly he had been bombarded with documents and memos about the state comptroller's report on the finances of townships in the north and his department head's insistence that these be more closely audited, several cases of corruption having already been uncovered. Long meetings were held, and of all times, on Fridays, when all he could think of was planning a nice Sabbath meal. During one such conference a note was slipped into his hand. "I'm having a few people over tonight," it said. "If you feel up to it, you're invited. It's not RSVP." Underneath was written her address. Turning around, he spied her behind him, study-ing him quietly with her oriental eyes. Blushing, he nodded his agreement, pleased to feel everyone looking at him understandingly.

After lunch that day he tried to nap, but within ten minutes he awoke and took a bath. Then he called his mother-in-law to arrange to pick her up for dinner, noticing a hesitancy in her voice. "No," he replied when she inquired if he had a cold. "What makes you think I do?" "You just sound like it," she said. "Well, I don't," he repeated, asking, "Why not?" when she wondered aloud whether he should come for her on such a rainy night. In the end, she broke down and confessed that she had forgotten to bake her strudel. "Don't even think of it," said Molkho, insisting that she come, especially since his daughter would be there too. He set a time and arrived early as usual to watch the Arab help arrange the chapel, read the menu in the dimly lit dining room, and look at the old folks, scrubbed clean for the Sabbath and glad it was storming outside, lounging with their German magazines. Once again he thought of ways to visit the fifth floor, where the terminal cases lay dying.

The down elevator arrived, and his mother-in-law stepped out of it, bundled up in a large, old fur coat. "You really didn't have to come for me on a night like this," she said, which made him answer in protest, "but when would we see you if I didn't?" She smiled at him. The secrets they had shared during the illness belonged to them both, and they were aware of an unspoken bond between them, although sometimes he still had to dispel her suspicion that he was only being nice for his wife's sake. The old people in the lobby rose to greet her, saying something in German (perhaps to dissuade her from venturing out into the rain), but his umbrella was already open and his arm was gripping hers. "Why don't I carry your cane for you," he suggested. "There's no need to," she replied—and there wasn't, because it remained hooked on her arm while he led her between puddles to the car. "How was the concert?" she asked as they drove off. "Wonderful," he said, feeling a hot flush. "Haydn's *Creation* was magnificent, and Vivaldi's *Four Seasons* was perfect too." "Who went with you," she asked, "the boy?" "No," he answered, "no one." The old folks who told on him, so it seemed, had mistaken the young man sitting next to him for his son. "Won't you go to any concerts at all this season?" he asked. "Most likely not," she replied.

For dinner, he served a new dish he had made from a package of frozen food, couscous with vegetables and gravy, which seemed a great success until he noticed that no one wanted a second portion. His mother-in-law asked him for the recipe, listening to his explanation with a rather pitying look and chiding his daughter for not helping him. As soon as the television news was over, she rose to go. "Stay a while," said Molkho. "I'm going out soon, and I'll drop you on my way. I was invited by the legal adviser at the office," he went on, curious to test her reaction, which turned out to be one of perfect calm. "She's a widow," he added, letting her see that he was keeping nothing back, but she simply sat unperturbedly down again. For the second time that evening he shaved and changed clothes, taking his time because he did not wish to be early. In the car his mother-in-law gently pointed out that he had some soap behind his ear, and he wiped it away. The rain had stopped, and he let her off in front of the home without waiting to see if her little friend was there to bow to her.

It was already late. He drove to the West Carmel, losing his way but finally finding the house. As he climbed the poorly lit stairs he felt a pressure on his bladder and realized he had neglected to relieve himself. For a moment he considered using the backyard, but afraid he might be mistaken from a window for a pervert, he quickly dismissed the idea. Outside the slightly peeling door of the legal adviser's apartment, he paused in a vain attempt to hear voices, and then rang the bell, whose sound was followed by a laugh and a woman's quick footsteps. Her hair looked more rumpled than it did at work and her heels were not as high; indeed, he thought, there was something childlike about the way she stood in the doorway, staring at him with her crinkly, oriental eyes as if trying to make out who he was. Behind her, at the end of a hallway, was a living room clouded by cigarette smoke in which stood several men. Two women, he saw when he entered it, were there too; yet it was the men, of whom there were five, whose warm camaraderie set the tone. In one corner of the smallish room, which was furnished in a modern, minimalist style, a fireplace burned with an exquisitely pure orange flame.

His hostess introduced him to her guests, all but one of whom were members of her family: her father, a straight-backed, sturdy-looking man; her younger brother, whose small, narrow eyes were like hers; the two brothers of her late husband; and an elderly lawyer from abroad whose relation to the others was unclear. They were all friendly, cultured Haifaites of Central European origin, balding and a bit on the thin side, lawyers and travel agents—in short, people whom Molkho's own wife might have dismissed as superficial and beneath her. Though at first it made him nervous to be so unexpectedly put to the test of the family's approval, they did their best to set him at ease, and the legal adviser, far from clinging to him, soon left him to his own devices. With perfect naturalness she led him to a seat by the fireplace beside the two women, who professed surprise that he had come coatless in such cold weather, and brought him a whiskey and a tray of hors d'oeuvres, from which he chose some vividly candied fruit peels.

The conversation rambled intimately. Though he had prepared a few subjects to talk about, especially several of a legal nature, he saw at once that he needn't make the effort, for everyone appeared harmoniously acquainted and he, it seemed, was passed back and forth among them in a discreet and unaffected fashion. Afraid of being suspected of some organic problem if he went to the toilet too soon, he sat with his legs together to ease the pressure on his bladder while one by one the men came up to him, introducing themselves once again and steering the talk to safe topics that all could agree on without seeming overly bland. One of the brother-in-laws' wives, who had met Mrs. Molkho in a teachers' course, spoke about her warmly and sincerely, moving him with her appreciation of the devotion he had shown in nursing his wife at home while comparing it with other cases, in Haifa and elsewhere, some of which he knew about too. Then one of the brother-in-laws mentioned seeing Molkho at the last concert and asked him what he thought of it. The man himself, so it seemed, was highly critical of the performance, especially of the soloists, who, he claimed, were often flat and left out whole bars of the score. Molkho was shocked; he had no idea that whole bars could be skipped in a concert—and in such a well-known work! Who would have thought that there was fraud even here, he reflected resentfully. Meanwhile, the conversation was getting heated. The names of orchestras, conductors, choirs, soloists, were bandied about, one after another, making him realize with amazement how highly musical and well traveled the legal adviser's family was. They spoke of hotels and restaurants all over Europe, but especially of operas and concerts; it seemed that there wasn't an opera house they hadn't been in, even behind the Iron Curtain. And, to his surprise, they apparently considered him their equal, because they spared him none of the details and fell respectfully quiet when, after listening attentively, he expressed an opinion of his own. Until twenty years ago, he confessed, he had never been abroad at all. "I'm a fifth-generation Sephardi in this country," he told them, "and Europe is another world to us." The five generations impressed them. "In that case," joked someone to the laughter of them all, "your family has served its time here and is free to live where it wants!" The legal adviser, Molkho noticed, let her family do the talking while she served the food and drinks, after which she sank down on an embroidered leather hassock, where she sat like a well-trained dog. And yet whatever she said met with general approval, so that Molkho, struck by her keen intelligence, wondered again what she saw in him. Was it simply his good looks, his curly hair and fair eyes, or perhaps, too, his being a concertgoer whom her family could talk music with? Already nettled by her outranking him, he felt a pang of envy when, half just to him and half to them all, she mentioned being sent next month to a legal conference in Germany. No one, he asserted aggrievedly, had ever sent him abroad at the taxpayers' expense! "Nor us, and it's her third such trip too. How she gets them to foot the bill is beyond us," chimed in everyone fondly. When, they asked Molkho, had he last been in Germany himself? "Never," he answered, although his wife was born in Berlin and spent her childhood there. She and her mother had managed to leave just in time, after her father, a pediatrician, had taken his own life, and she had refused on principle to go back. He and she had been in Europe several times, especially in Paris, where she had a favorite cousin, but never in Germany.

Suddenly—it was no doubt the fault of the cup of tea he'd just drunk—the pressure on his bladder grew worse, yet he still did not wish to be the first to use the bathroom. There was a momentary silence in the room, though by no means a disapproving one. They could understand his late wife's feelings; they themselves, however, looked at it differently, and in any case, he was now free to travel there himself. It was well worth it if he loved music. Paris was Paris, of course, but for music there was no place like Germany. And there were special opera flights now too, with the price of the tickets included in the airfare; in fact, it was the rage all over Europe, where opera was back in fashion. "You say there are flights like that all over Europe?" Molkho asked. "Of course." "From Paris too?" From Paris too—but why did he ask? Because, he told them, suddenly inspired, he had been thinking of going there next month. "When next month?" asked the legal adviser's family with great interest. He wasn't sure yet, he said. Perhaps he would wait a little longer, because Europe in the winter rather scared him. But why should it scare him? they asked. It was at its best then! Who was his travel agent? He mentioned an agency that, of course, they all knew of, adding with a knowing smile, because he expected them to pooh-pooh it, "I hope you don't think too poorly of it." They smiled back sympathetically. "It's not fair to ask us," they said, "because we can't be objective." "But I'd like to know anyway," he persisted. "Well," they smiled, "it's not such a bad agency; it's just a very simple one, a bit unsophisticated. A man like you, of your age, deserves something more cosmopolitan." Of course, he thought, listening good-naturedly, they were out for his business; they were simply waiting for a hint—but he was not about to drop one. From across the room the legal adviser flashed him a smile. "You have a nice place here," he said appreciatively, rising from his chair with an air of freedom, because he had to go to the bathroom at once. Yet attracted to the fireplace, he approached it instead and exclaimed, "What a lovely fire. And it draws so well—there's no smell of smoke at all!" The guests exchanged embarrassed glances while the legal adviser explained that the fire wasn't real but electric. "Electric?" he marveled, grinning foolishly at his ignorance. "It certainly had me fooled!" Red-faced, he asked her in a whisper for the toilet. She rose from her hassock to show him, and he slipped away at once, cursing himself for not having gone at home.

Molkho shut the bathroom door behind him, quietly slid home the bolt, and inspected the little room, which, compared to the rest of the house, had a rather neglected look, a strict and nonaesthetic functionality: the paint was peeling above the toilet and in a web in one corner hung a large spider, which he felt he should kill. His own bathroom, which boasted a shelf with some books, an illustrated calendar received each year from the bank, and a large poster of three monkeys wearing clothing, was much livelier. Sighing with relief, he carefully aimed a silent jet of urine at the side of the toilet bowl and waited for the last concluding dribble while straining to hear the voices in the living room. Yet when he tried flushing as quietly as he could, the water burst from the tank with a roar. Quickly he switched off the light and went to the separate washroom, which was equally Spartan but clean. He soaped his hands thoroughly, musing about Death and whether some part of the legal adviser's late husband was not still grappling with it on these walls, and then peeked at the medicine cabinet, hoping for some insight into her condition. It was, however, poorly stocked: a few tubes of makeup, some old aspirins, a box of Band-Aids, the usual antacid preparation, and a paper bag from the drugstore with some little red pills that he could have sworn he had seen before. Slowly he inspected himself—his Levantine curls, his handsome eyes—in the mirror. If he was not just a guest in this house, if he was really an official suitor, he had the right to take his time.

The conversation in the living room was still flowing naturally, no advantage having been taken of his absence to discuss him behind his back. Slowly he walked back up the hallway, peering into a darkened bedroom whose faded wallpaper needed to be changed. Outside the window were the dotted lights of houses and a dark ravine. Did it merge with his own somewhere? A pair of kicked-off pink slippers lay by a bed. There was an awkward lull in the living room: so they were following his progress after all. Yet he did not rejoin them but rather glanced into a lit room to his right in which, on a junior-sized bed, lay a girl of about thirteen who looked like her mother, having the same straight, smooth hair and slanted eyes. She was reading a book, and suddenly, Molkho felt a great pity for her. Why, she's an orphan too, he told himself, thinking of his own children and stepping with unforeseen boldness into the room. There was a hush behind him in the living room. He introduced himself to the girl—who, her head on a pillow, might have been either sick or just resting—and struck up a friendly conversation, sitting on the edge of her bed and looking around while asking her about herself and the book, reassured at being able to make out through the window the tall building of his mother-in-law's old-age home on the opposite flank of the mountain. The girl struck him as bright but rather sad, and returning to the living room with his eyes cast somberly down, he felt a new warmth directed toward him and even made out tears in the eyes of her grandfather. Indeed, the whole family spoke of her lovingly, after which he told them a bit about his own children. And so the evening passed pleasantly until it was time to go home and he left in the company of a brother-in-law and his wife. Still chatting, the two walked him to his car, surprised all over again that he wasn't wearing a coat. "It must be my Asiatic blood," he said, watching them in the mirror as they turned around and walked back to the legal adviser's apartment, no doubt to take part in the postmortem.

27

T HE WIND HAD DIED DOWN and the sky was clearing. Dark, fallen leaves lay in the street. He felt pleased with himself, even joyful, at having passed the test, whatever it was for. Most of all, he was proud of his initiative with the girl. That's what really won their hearts, he told himself. How odd it was that barely two and a half months after his wife's death he was already on the matrimonial circuit! He did not go straight back to his apartment but rather drove past the sleeping old-age home, from which he strove to make out the legal adviser's house, but the night proved too dark and at last he gave up and went home. It was after midnight. Suddenly parched, as if by his own inner excitement, he opened the refrigerator to look for a drink, settling in the end on a big dish of strawberry ice cream. Then, remembering how as a boy in Jerusalem he had never been allowed to eat ice cream in winter, he went to bed.

In the morning he awoke in a triumphant yet anxious mood.

The next move was up to him, and not only she but her whole family would expect him to make it; the smallest gesture on his part would have all kinds of meanings read into it. It had happened too quickly, before he was ready, before he had even heard again from the matchmaker who had phoned him two weeks ago. It was unimaginable that he should already be permanently linked with this woman. Why, his children, to say nothing of his mother-in-law, would be sure she'd been there all along, that he had simply waited for his wife to die to bring her out of the woodwork! The whole next day, even while hanging out the wash and hoeing the little garden that he kept behind the house, he thought of nothing else. In the afternoon the college student came for lunch, and he and his sister decided to make a feast for all their friends. At first, Molkho hovered over them to make sure they didn't cook too much, not wanting to eat leftovers again all week long; but in the end, laughing merrily, they threw him out of the kitchen, and he went for a walk in the neighborhood, thinking of his wife while glancing up at the sky in which a new storm was brewing. What, deep in earth, was still left of her? Her body must have rotted completely by now, its vanished outlines surviving only in his own frail mind and memory. He tried imagining its weight, lifted and carried by him so many times, now lighter than the flight of dust. And then a strong wind blew up, and he returned home to a kitchen full of steaming pots and bowls heaped high with food to say, "Take it easy, kids, don't overdo it," but they were all in a fabulous mood, and soon friends came, and everyone let down his hair, and he saw how quickly they had forgotten her. That's how they'll forget me too, he thought quietly. The party lasted all afternoon. More and more youngsters kept coming, and in the evening they all decided to go to the movies, where a new comedy was playing, and he felt like going too and said jokingly, "Maybe you'll take me along," but he saw at once how upset they were, as if certain he would spoil all the fun. Why, they don't even feel sorry for me, he marveled, and indeed, they saw no reason to. "Never mind," he said out loud, "it doesn't matter. Go without me. I'm too tired anyway."

28

H E KNEW THE NEXT MOVE with the legal adviser was his, yet he kept putting it off. What move can I make. It's too early. Why can't she wait. For two days he deliberately avoided her at the office, keeping to his room, but that Tuesday afternoon, as luck would have it, he met her in the street, practically running right into her. For a moment he hardly recognized her, for she was wearing a short, broad-shouldered fur coat of a yellowish, leopard color and her face glowed ruddily from the cold. "I'm so glad to see you," he said warmly, his hand lightly grazing the soft fur. "I've been looking for you. I wanted to thank you for a lovely evening. I enjoyed it so much. And what a darling your daughter is!" "Everyone liked you too," she said—which set him off on a blue streak, especially about her daughter, as if it were the girl he were thinking of marrying, after which he asked if she was really going to Germany. "Of course," she replied, thus leading him to inquire, as though seeking his good offices, about her brother-in-law the travel agent and where he worked. She gave him the information at once, writing down the address and several telephone numbers while standing in the street. "You'll find him useful," she confided. "I'm sure he'll be glad to help." Though Molkho would have been happy to end the conversation right there, he could feel her impatience, her expectation of something more. Three years had passed since her husband's death, and she wasn't getting any younger. He glanced at her small, almost miniature face, her darting, Tatar eyes, and her body, the sharp angles of which stirred his anxious compassion. Just then, though, an acquaintance of hers happened by, and Molkho was given a chance to excuse himself.

That evening he ached all over and his eyes began to smart. Soon he noticed shooting pains in his back, and when the television news was over, he climbed into bed and took his temperature, surprised to see it was high. Along with a small flash of pleasure, this produced a shiver of fear, for he had not run a fever in years, whereas now, as though he were a small boy again, he suddenly had one. Although he waited for the symptoms of a cold to appear, there were none; the trouble, he reasoned, must be something else, as yet unidentified, as if a last squall of the tropical storm that had raged in this room were now brewing inside him. The next morning his son was alarmed to find him in bed with the lights off, unshaven and listless. Aspirin had not brought down the fever. "What's wrong?" asked the boy, who never had had to worry about his father before. "Just a little temperature," Molkho reassured him. "It's nothing. Go to school." He tried phoning his mother-in-law, but she was out. And though he was sure the fever would pass during the day, it did not; on the contrary, it knocked him out totally, dropping each time for an hour or two only to return as though bubbling up from some mysterious source deep within him. Still, capped by a pleasurable stupor, he felt it was under control. For hours on end, he lay fetally beneath the blankets in a darkness real or delusory, rising only to go to the bathroom, and though his urine seemed to have turned a greenish color, this, too, may have been only imagined. He was too weak to make lunch, yet when his son, who had meanwhile come home from school, wanted to call the doctor, Molkho refused. "It's nothing," he said. "Just bring me some tea and crackers and make something for yourself. And don't forget to do the dishes." From under the blankets he watched the boy move about, enjoying a bed's-eye view of the house, his glance sweeping over the floors and the bottoms of doors and furniture.

After the boy had eaten he went off to do his homework, the radio playing softly in his room, from which he emerged now and then to look in on his father and ask how he was feeling. "Don't worry, I'll be fine," said Molkho. "Just don't come too close—I don't want you to catch it," though he had no idea what precisely there was to be caught.

When evening came, he asked the boy to call his grandmother and tell her that he was sick. "What did she say?" he asked him when he came back from the phone. "Nothing," said his son. "She hopes you'll feel better." In the middle of the night he awoke as if on fire; his temperature was nearly one hundred and four and he felt as dry as a desert, though still not unpleasantly so. Now it's me who's dying, he told himself with a smile, contemplating, as he put on the earphones to listen to music, a brief expiration followed by a more lasting resurrection.

It was late when he awoke the next morning. The house was empty, the high school boy's room neat and orderly. At noon the concerned college student arrived, and Molkho, speaking feebly from under the blankets, dictated a shopping list. Perhaps, suggested the student before going out with it, he should ask his grandmother to come. "What for?" Molkho asked. "She'll just catch it from me." But the student called her anyway, talking in hushed tones on the telephone. "What did she say?" "That you should call a doctor." "And what else?" "Nothing." But Molkho did not want a doctor; deep down he wanted his mother-in-law to come sit by his side, as she had sat by the side of his wife. However, no one came at all, and the telephone was silent all day; his temperature stayed as high as if an internal combustion engine were working away inside him. The old woman, he told himself, must be angry.

The hours went by indistinguishably. The reddish, wintry light of a cloudless sunset poured through the west, seaward window. Another night passed and then another morning, and still his mother-in-law did not come or even call to ask how he was. His fever was down a bit, yet he kept to his bed, unwashed and unshaven between the crumpled sheets, enjoying a detached convalescence, his main link with the world the soft music that he played on the tape machine. Though he phoned his mother each morning as usual, he did not inform her of his illness, keeping the conversation to a minimum to prevent her from becoming suspicious.

When he awoke early on the morning of the fourth day, the fever was gone. Pale, weak, and slightly thinner, he opened all the windows to air out the house, made himself two eggs, and was leafing through the newspapers in bed when suddenly he heard his mother-in-law opening the front door with the key she still had in her possession. She had come to see him at last, and now she sat facing him in the armchair from which she had watched her dying daughter, her cane between her legs and her coat still on as if already eager to depart, regarding him more severely than worriedly through her thick lenses with a look that was, except for its slight squint, genetically coded just like his wife's. And yet, as they talked—and not at all about his illness—it struck him again how close they had grown, how much they had in common. He had been thinking, he told her, of visiting their cousin in Paris, but now, having just read in the newspaper about the latest economic decrees, including a new travel tax, he had his doubts. The new taxes, for some reason, interested her; she wanted to know all about them. One might think, Molkho thought, that she were planning a trip herself—and indeed, why shouldn't she? She certainly could afford one: there were new sums all the time from Germany, where her husband's suicide must have put her in a lucrative category. Two years ago, in fact, upon turning eighty, she had astonished everyone by going on an archaeological tour of Turkey sponsored by the Geographical Society. Soon, though, the talk shifted to more practical concerns, such as the high school boy, who should perhaps eat lunch with his grandmother at the home and sleep at a friend's house until Molkho recovered. The idea seemed a good one; he even envied the boy for being able to dine with all the old folks. Outside the sun was shining. His mother-in-law rose, made a quick tour of the apartment with her cane, and was already on her way out, apologizing for having an appointment. He put on his bathrobe to walk her to the street. "I see you're all better already," she said, as if realizing she had wasted her time on him. Forced to confess that he was, he opened the front door of the building and was blinded by the sudden winter light. It was a cold morning, scrubbed clean by the rain. Slowly he walked her to the street, where, sitting in an ancient fur coat at the bus stop like a peasant in an old painting, was the little old woman from the concert. She rose smiling to greet them, as round-cheeked and rosy as if fed on a diet of potatoes, bowing genially to them from afar. "Who is that?"

Molkho asked. "Stasya," said his mother-in-law. "She's the friend from Russia I told you about, the one who arrived a few months ago." Molkho smiled back at her. "Why didn't you bring her up to the apartment?" he asked, already on his way to introduce himself in his bathrobe and floppy slippers, lured onward by the crisp morning. "No, don't," his mother-in-law warned him. "It's too cold for you. You have to take care of yourself." "So I do," Molkho said, turning to go back upstairs.

❄ PART II WINTER

1

MOLKHO'S WIFE DIED in early autumn, toward the end of September, and at the beginning of January he left for Paris. They had been together in that city three times, each time reconfirming their special love for it. Now, the fourth time, he arrived by himself. His wife's cousin, who was ten years her junior, and her husband, a non-Jewish doctor, hugged him hard at the airport and bundled him off to their home, where they so insisted he stay with them that he abandoned his original plan of putting up at his old hotel. As if feeling guilty for merely sending him a telegram instead of coming to the funeral, they showered him with warmth. On the first night they did not go out at all. Once more Molkho told the story of his wife's death, describing the days before and after it, enjoying sharing all its details with his two eager listeners. The doctor asked professional questions and Molkho did his best to answer them, though he did not know many of the medical terms in French or how to pronounce the names of the drugs. It was late when they turned in. His hosts lived in four small rooms, one of which belonged to their eight-year-old daughter and year-old son, and though at first they had planned to put him up in it, the mess there was so great that over his loud protests they gave him their own room and spent the night in the living room. After sleeping for a year in a single bed, it was hard to get used to the width of a double one.

It was still dark out when, crawling into bed with him and babbling in French, the baby woke Molkho in the morning. Though the little fellow seemed not at all disturbed to find a stranger in his parents' place, his mother soon appeared in a flimsy nightgown and gathered him up with an apologetic smile. Molkho, however, saw no need to apologize. After months of waking up to silence, he was greatly pleased by the morning bustle of the French family. They all left the apartment together, and after driving the girl to school and the baby to his nursery, the doctor and his wife dropped Molkho off in the Latin Quarter, where beneath a gray sky he walked the long boulevards past places he already knew and loved. As soon as the department stores opened he began to go from floor to floor, checking prices and looking for gifts.

That evening the three of them had dinner at a little neighborhood restaurant, during which the doctor and his wife questioned Molkho about Israel and its prospects. "Are you trying to commit national suicide?" the doctor kept asking with an anger of obscure origin, forcing Molkho, who explained things as best he could, onto the defensive. "I really don't know much about politics," Molkho confessed at last.

The next day was windy; the temperature dropped sharply and the weather forecasts on the radio had a menacing tone. Molkho joined a small bus tour to Versailles, listening to the guide's pedantic descriptions while slowly traipsing with the other sightseers from one coldly ornate room to another. Rigidly symmetrical, the elaborate gardens of Louis XIV could be glimpsed through the windows.

Once back in Paris, he huddled in a café to warm up, waiting for his wife's cousin, who worked as a technician in a research institute. Lively discussions of the weather went on at the surrounding tables. When the cousin arrived, they drove to pick up her daughter from school and then her son from his nursery. The children took a liking to Molkho, who was playfully physical with them. Clearly, though it did not spend much time together, the family was a boisterous one that lived in great disorder, even filth. Beneath his bed Molkho discovered some underpants and socks of ancient vintage, while, half-crawling on all fours and half-tottering on two, the baby took his food everywhere, smearing and dropping it in secret places. And yet Molkho felt at home, and his hosts did their best to feed him well and keep him in good spirits. Indeed, he ate a great deal, the cold weather doing wonders for his appetite.

On the third night of his visit they had planned to go to a small theater, but the doctor came home late from the hospital and they ended up watching television instead. Much of the news program was devoted to the weather. The announcers showed maps and diagrams, even satellite photographs, and predicted snow for the next day. Afterward, his wife's cousin decided to call Molkho's mother-in-law in Israel. She spoke to her in German, and at first, the old woman kept confusedly talking the same language when Molkho got on the phone. He inquired about his children, told her about Paris and the snow, and asked about the weather in Israel. His mother-in-law, however, had trouble following his questions and answered him a bit crossly, her voice slow and groping, as if his trip abroad had caused a sudden deterioration in her condition. Then he and his hosts discussed the next day, and Molkho suggested they all go to the opera; he had never been to one, he said, and had heard it was all the rage. Though the doctor and his wife, who felt bad about the missed night of theater, seemed to welcome the idea, Molkho noticed a hesitation in their voices. Opera tickets, apparently, were very expensive, and for tomorrow only the best seats would be left. Well, then, he insisted, let them be his guests! Hadn't they saved him the cost of a hotel?

The next morning it was a few degrees colder and and the city was cloaked in a chill white mist, though the promised snowstorm had not yet arrived. For three hours he stood in front of the box office, kept there only by the stubborn enthusiasm of those on line with him, some of them tourists like himself. Apparently that night's production, which was of Mozart's *Magic Flute*, was supposed to be especially good. When he finally reached the window, he saw that the prices were indeed outrageous, but he did not have the heart to walk away. The first snowflakes had begun falling outside. It was getting still colder. He thought of buying the children their presents, but the blow to his pocket was so great that he resolved to go straight back to the apartment to recuperate.

That evening they ate early and prepared the children for bed.

The doctor arrived at the last minute, straight from a difficult operation, and barely had time to change his clothes. At seven the baby-sitter, a gorgeous teenager, arrived. It was snowing heavily, and in a gay and animated mood they decided to take the metro instead of their car.

2

T HE OPERA WAS VERY LONG, lasting for some three hours. Parts of it were tiresome and difficult to follow, but there were others so superb and moving that he felt as if long-dead cells within him were thawing out and coming back to life. Whenever Papagano and Papagana appeared, a fresh, burgeoning breeze seemed to blow from onstage. The doctor, however, was too exhausted to sit through it; as early as the first act he began to doze, while eventually, seated between the two of them, he fell into a deep sleep, his head alternately falling on his wife's and Molkho's shoulders. Smiling, gently whispering, "How can you waste all that money," they tried in vain to wake him.

It was almost midnight when they left the opera house. Unexpectedly, the sky was clear and the city was covered with a thick, white blanket of glistening snow, the public statues, the iron banisters, and the gargoyles of the houses all artfully draped with festive white bunting. Molkho had never seen Paris in the snow; suddenly he felt an inexplicable fear, worried by the thought that the flight he was scheduled to leave on in two days' time might be canceled. From all around them came the merry shouts of surprised Parisians unable to find a cab. The metro was as crowded as during rush hour, but the snow had put everyone in a good mood. Arriving home, they found the children wide awake and excited, and after briefly debating whether it was possible to take the baby-sitter home, they decided to put her up in the children's room for the night. A great commotion of blankets and linens ensued, and it was 2 A.M. before they were all in bed. Molkho could not fall asleep. Initially aroused by the nearby presence of the beautiful French girl, he soon found himself obsessed by the music of the opera. As on the night of his wife's death, he turned from side to side, unable to get the themes, already confused with others, out of his head, the music of Mozart now fused with that of Mahler, so that, hearing the throbbing horns, he rose from his broad bed and tormentedly lit the small lamp. His anguish must have been felt by his wife's cousin, who, appearing by his side with a sleeping pill and a glass of water, offered them to him with a tenderness that, he felt, he had been deprived of for many long years.

He slept late the next morning and awoke to find the house empty and an indecipherable note in French on the table. Last night's snow shone through the window with a purplish gray gleam. He had no key to the apartment and so took his time about leaving, knowing he could not return until evening, walking aimlessly about the rooms and then leafing through magazines and picture albums until he found an old photograph of his mother-in-law, standing in a strange European city with a small baby in her arms who did not at all look like his wife. Perhaps it was his wife's cousin, perhaps someone else. He kept on poking through closets and inspected the medicine cabinet, surprised by the paucity of its contents, which included only a few bottles of cough syrup and some agent against hemorrhoids.

Finally, he put on his coat and made up his mind to go out. His first stop was a travel agency whose address he had, where he confirmed his flight to West Berlin. The agency was on the second floor of a large office building, next door to a ticket office for shows and tours that was filled with sightseers from all over the world, especially from India and the Far East. After confirming his flight he asked what the weather was like in Berlin, but no one was able to tell him, and so he went back outside and walked about the city, among drifts of snow that grew slushier as the clearing blue sky grew brighter. In the side streets behind the opera house, he sternly eyed some women in large fur coats whom he took to be prostitutes intent on his business, but none of them made a move in his direction. All at once he felt anxious about Berlin. Should he perhaps call the trip off and fly straight back to Israel? His left arm, he thought, was beginning to hurt, and more depressing yet were the huge throngs of shoppers who burst out of the department stores at noontime, congesting the streets. The air was warming, filling the gutters with rivulets of melted snow. He bought a few presents and sat down to wait for his wife's cousin in a little café opposite the nursery. For some reason, she was late, and so he decided on his own to pick up the tot, who went with him quite willingly with no questions asked, standing on the street in his winter clothes like a little red bear until his mother came running, all out of breath and wearing a most becoming shawl. She gave Molkho a grateful kiss, and noting for the first time that she looked like his wife, he felt a twinge in his heart.

When the doctor came home, they ate a delicious hot dinner while Molkho told them about his flight to Berlin, to which, he said, his office in Israel was sending him, and about his return flight via Paris, where he would only be changing planes at the airport. They seemed genuinely sorry that he would be leaving. "We've gotten used to you. The children are wild about you. Couldn't you stop over for a few days on your way back?" "I've put you out enough as it is," he replied, thanking them with emotion.

It was not without sorrow that he said good-bye in the morning to the comfortable bed that he had spent the last five nights in. His wife's cousin, who had grown attached to him during the visit and found their parting difficult, insisted on taking him to the airport. She drove slowly, carelessly, in the heavy traffic, talking about his wife and about her own problems and worries. At the airport, instead of simply dropping him off at his terminal, she parked in the underground lot and came with him. At first, they had trouble finding the check-in counter. No one at the information desk had heard of the line he was flying. The two of them ran from one wing of the building to the other until at last, in the charter-flights section, they found a small counter with the airline's name and a piece of colored cardboard on which was handwritten *Voles Opera*. His wife's cousin was first amused, then angered, and finally shocked. "Why, how could they have stuck you on a flight like this? It's meant for operagoers!

Did you sign up for an opera too?'' Caught red-handed, he turned pale under questioning. It must have come with the ticket, he stammered, pretending to know nothing about it. But when he checked his suitcase and received a boarding pass made to look like a sheet of music with a violin drawn on it, she regarded him with sudden suspicion. Overcome with guilt, he went to the cafeteria and bought a large bar of chocolate for her children.

3

T HE PLANE WAS A SMALL FIFTY-SEATER that belonged to an airline he had never heard of before. Its passengers were mostly middle-aged Indians, Japanese, and Koreans, with a smattering of Italians and South Americans. Some of them, having apparently flown together to Paris, were already acquainted, and a number passed the time on the flight studying musical scores. It was an oddity, Molkho thought, that such a plane and flight should exist at all. Soon after takeoff they climbed above the clouds into a deep blue sky and the stewardesses served peanuts and wine. After about half an hour, as they were descending again into a cloud bank, stormy music that everyone identified at once was broadcast over the sound system. "Wagner!" several passengers cried out, immediately beginning to argue among themselves about what opera it came from. In the front seat a flushed and tipsy passenger rose to his feet and began ardently singing the words to the music while everyone broke into laughter and applause. The plane was pitching slightly, immersed in a milky fog that pinkened now and then while droplets of water streamed down the windows. As if his wife's death had only now become final, Molkho was stricken by a frightening feeling of freedom. If the plane should crash, he thought as it battled the wind and the strains of Wagner grew fainter, no one would even know what had happened to him; he should never have kept this part of his trip

a secret. But at last they emerged from the clouds and stopped jounc-
ing, flying over a flat brown terrain checked with fields, villages, and
a surprising number of graveyards. Although the ground looked
damp, there were no traces of snow on it. It's insane to be traveling
so far to meet when we live two kilometers apart, he thought—but
somehow, beginning like this in a distant and neutral place seemed
the right thing to do. Soon they landed in a small airport and were
immediately driven in a quiet bus to a downtown terminal. Hearing
Hebrew, he spun around instinctively, but it only turned out to be a
rather noisy Israeli family burdened with many suitcases and trunks.
Were they émigrés? he wondered, glancing at them idly while chatting with two women standing next to him by the conveyor belt that
would be bringing their luggage. They were Romanians from Bucha-
rest, they told him, opera singers themselves, who had come for the
opera in Berlin. Could it be as good as all that? marveled Molkho.

His brown valise arrived, and he took a taxi to his hotel, whose
address was clipped to a page of his passport. Considering the early
evening hour, the streets of the city appeared civilized and tame.
Never, he calculated, looking up at the reddish sky, which glowed as
though stoked from afar, had he been so far north. The thought that
his wife was born and spent the first six years of her life in this city
made him smile. He should have asked his mother-in-law for their
old address, but that would only have made her inquire about the
reason for his trip, and what could he possibly have told her? The
taxi was now jolting over cobblestones, threading its way through
narrow streets that clearly belonged to some old neighborhood. At
last, it stopped in front of a small hotel that appeared to have only a
few rooms.

The lobby, though small, was clean and uncluttered, its walls
paneled with reddish wood and decorated with pictures and prints of
the Nibelungs, ancient nautical maps, and glass cabinets with old
swords and daggers. And yet, though it had a style of its own,
Molkho suddenly found himself missing Paris, his wife's cousin, the
baby, the snow, the crowded streets. Would he have to make love to
the legal adviser in one of these German rooms, he wondered, putting down his valise and reaching for his passport, or would they be

content to develop their relationship through a few hugs and kisses? And yet how ludicrous for people of their age and experience to neck like teenagers! The catch was that he didn't feel at all sexy. Not even Paris had awakened that side of him. Why, how could he even kiss her when he had no clear notion of her body yet? Not that the lines in her face were a problem—they were light and not deeply etched—but how did he know where they led when her waistline was unlocatable and the shape of her legs still a riddle? If only it were summer, he thought, there wouldn't be so many question marks. He would have known where he stood and what he was capable of, and he would not have had to put her through all this or to fear that, if disappointed, she might take her revenge in the office. Meanwhile, the female receptionist, whose English was exceedingly primitive, had given him some forms to fill out, after which she handed him a large copper key attached to a leather holder in the shape of a dove that had the number 6 on it. *"Sechs,"* she said to him, and he repeated it easily after her. When he inquired about the legal adviser, however, asking if he and she were the only Israelis registered, he was astonished to be told that he was the only guest in the hotel so far. And, indeed, all the other keys were hanging in front of their cubbyholes, eleven little doves minding their nests. The thought that she planned on sharing a room with him alarmed him. It can't be, he told himself, asking the receptionist to check again—and indeed, this time she found the legal adviser's name, booked for another room. Taking his key with relief, he started for the elevator, as conscious of the adventure getting under way as if watching himself in a movie. He was glad, at least, that she was no longer young, because he couldn't count on an erection; no, if they could think of this simply as a first step, like warming up a motor, it would be a good beginning. Could he have imagined several months ago that he would soon be so free and so far north? On the walls of the small but modern elevator were more old maritime maps and another little dagger in an elegant case. Berlin must be a safe place, mused Molkho, if the management needn't worry that some drunk might grab a weapon and start using it.

His room, like the lobby, was small but clean, smelling of soap and starch. It had neither a television nor a telephone, and only two stations could be gotten on the radio, one with Germans singing and one with Germans talking. He went to the bathroom, not having relieved himself since Paris, but surprisingly, all he produced was a thin dribble, as if all the coffee, tea, and wine that had gone into him that morning, on the ground and in the air, had vanished somewhere in his bloodstream; then he opened his valise and hung all his shirts and jackets in the narrow closet. The last item was a book, Volume II of *Anna Karenina.* It was a novel he had never read, and seeing how Jane Austen had him stymied, his daughter had given it to him with a warm recommendation. "At least try it," she said—but now he saw she had given him the wrong volume. He took a long shower, put on fresh underwear, and lay down on the bed with his head on the pillow, beneath which he felt something hard. It was another book, the New Testament, and he opened it, feeling that room service expected no less of him. It was in English, and the simple, homey story of Jesus and his disciples in Jerusalem made Molkho think of the Jerusalem he had known long ago, before the 1948 war, a summery city full of tension and fear, yet also of great promise and activity, with its Jewish Agency officials in dark suits, the very embodiments of Integrity and Justice, standing by the chiseled stone walls of the Terra Sancta Building and planning the Jewish State. He turned the pages, now and then stopping to read the unfamiliar tales: they may not always have been likable or logical, he thought, all those people who ran after Jesus, but they knew enough to ditch the Jews in time and cover their tracks by vanishing among the Gentiles. Shutting the book, he went downstairs, where the receptionist now was an older man with a mustache like Hitler's, only white. The legal adviser, he told Molkho, had called just a minute ago to say she was delayed because her conference wasn't over yet. She would be there no later than four.

4

HER LATENESS ANNOYED HIM, as if it was her way of saying
that, unlike him, her sybaritic companion, she was here for a
practical purpose. Though the hotel's rates, which he now inquired
about at the desk, were not high, he was sure she would find some
way of putting them on her expense account. Not that he could do
anything about it, but he had gone over enough bills at the office
handed in by junketing officials to know all the tricks. In any case,
he would not wait to lunch with her, as he would no doubt have to
treat her to dinner and might as well have his main meal now alone;
that way, they could order less later, and anyway, she was no doubt
being fed at the conference. He drank coffee and ate an order of
french fries with two frankfurters while jotting down some things to
talk to her about in the days ahead, for he felt rather intimidated by
her intelligence. Then he strolled down a long, narrow street, making
sure not to lose his way while peering into clothing stores and groceries.

It was three-thirty when he returned to the hotel. This time the
receptionist was a man his own age who told him in excellent English
that madame had called fifteen minutes ago and was on her way to
the hotel. He decided to wait for her in the lobby, by a column next
to the elevator that was festooned with old maps and swords, from
where he saw her rush in anxiously, followed by a cab driver carrying two suitcases. His first reaction—for he had expected her to be
dressed differently—was surprise at seeing her in her familiar
clothes, over which she wore her short leopard-skin coat. The receptionist, to whom she spoke in fluent German, seemed to know her
well; perhaps she brings all her lovers here, thought Molkho, decid-

ing she was definitely a complicated woman whom three years of widowhood had not simplified. With whom, he wondered, had she left her daughter? Though the receptionist was pointing in Molkho's direction, the legal adviser was still too busy filling out forms to look up; finally, just as someone in an apron appeared from a side door, bowed, and took her luggage, she finished the last of them and glanced around. For a moment he thought of getting even by hiding behind the column; but she knew he was there, and so, with a dancerlike grace, he stepped forward, putting on his best, warmest smile and gently embracing her in the gloomy light of the short winter afternoon. The soft fur of her coat made him think of a cold dog.

She was heavily made up and had on a new perfume. "I just couldn't get away from the conference," she apologized. "I was elected to chair a committee and had no choice." For the last two hours she had been on pins and needles; twice she had called the hotel to leave a message. Yes, he had received it, Molkho reassured her, but anyhow, it didn't matter; the main thing now was for her to rest and be ready for the evening. "Rest?" she protested. Her luggage was already in her room, and she was all set to go out; perhaps she would come back to change before the opera, but she would take the tickets with her just in case. "You mean you'll go as you are?" he asked in astonishment. "Of course," she replied, "why not?" The opera in Berlin wasn't formal. People came for the music, not to show off; he would see as much for himself.

There was an easy matter-of-factness about her. One could certainly learn to like her, thought Molkho, one could even learn to live with her wrinkles. "Who is your daughter staying with?" he asked. But the girl, it seemed, was independent and had preferred to stay by herself. "She even does her own cooking," said her mother, "and it's not the first time I've left her alone like this either, although she does have an uncle two blocks away." Even if she did, replied Molkho, he was impressed by such maturity.

Once they were out in the street, she began telling him about Berlin, in which she had been before. Tomorrow, of course, they would tour the city; she already had it all planned. She was looking forward to it herself, having been cooped up at the conference for three whole days, and indeed, Molkho saw, she was window-shopping avidly, stopping every few steps to look at some new display. Once again, he felt a pang: his wife's last dresses had been made at home by a seamstress and he hadn't looked with a woman at a shop window for over a year. And this particular woman, with her waistline that was too low and her body that seemed rather hastily thrown together, was not even as attractive as his wife. Still, did she not have her redeeming features—a certain intellectual animation, indeed an almost feverish intensity? And she was certainly high up on the bureaucratic ladder, he thought, listening to her tell him about the conference. Was her car paid for by the office or was she not as senior as all that? He made a mental note to ask her, inquiring in the meantime about the Berlin Wall. "Would you like to see it?" she asked, stopping to look at him. "Come, I'll show it to you now." And turning to the right, she led him into a broad, empty thoroughfare.

A frigid wind lashed at them, laced with driving rain. "It's damn cold," said Molkho. "We're almost there," she assured him, though the wall was nowhere in sight. On the contrary, though they had entered a rather desolate area, in front of them, like a purplish gash on the horizon, were nothing but factory chimneys. And yet when he suggested asking directions, she told him she knew the way. "It can't be far," she said, "the wall runs everywhere," and they plodded on block after block, the rain whipping them crosswise, Molkho, loath to be thought finicky about getting wet, saying nothing more. At last, however, she stopped to ask two passersby, who pointed in the opposite direction, and after challenging them briefly, she confessed, "I'm afraid I lost my way." Suddenly he pitied her. After all, she had meant well, had wanted to make him a gift of the wall. And so, gripping her lightly by the elbow, he said, "Never mind," and put his arm around her, the sidewalk being quite slippery. At once, as if she had been waiting for that, she leaned her weight against him. What an old squirrel she is, he thought, amused by his own image, for he had hardly seen a squirrel in his life. Thus, he told himself, steering her by the shoulder, the grand betrayal begins.

And perhaps his wife wasn't born here after all, but rather in East Berlin, though of course it was a single city then. The rain was falling harder now, sleety and sharp, and they took shelter from it in a clothing store, where he could finally release the legal adviser from his grip. It was a large, nearly empty establishment, on whose listless young salesgirls their entrance made no visible impression. Aimlessly they walked past rows of pants and jackets and shelves of sweaters and knitwear, all equally sexless, until they reached a large straw basket full of hats and began to rummage through it. He watched her try on hat after hat, each pert toss of her head in the mirror a drop of refreshment on his parched heart. One, a red woolen one, was particularly becoming. "Why not buy it?" he urged, helping her translate the price from marks into shekels while thinking so hard of his wife and her lost breasts that the tears came to his eyes, for here, snugly out of the rain with him before stepping out to the opera, another woman was by his side. Though he would gladly have bought her the hat himself, especially as it was cheap, he feared this being taken for a promise he would not be able to keep. We'll see, he thought; if all goes well, I'll buy her something tomorrow—and anyhow, I'm treating for dinner. Meanwhile, having moved on from the hat basket, she was now browsing in the pants department. Something was pressing on Molkho's bladder. "Just a minute, I'll be right back," he said, remembering how he had gone to the bathroom that night in her house. Now she was sure to think he had some disease! Well, let her, he thought; it will cool her off a bit. But if he ever really were sick, who would take care of him?

While the store was modern enough, the bathroom appeared to date from a different era: its large copper faucets were tarnished with verdigris, its toilet seats were high, narrow, and stern, its rough bars of gray soap smelled of antiseptic, and an icy draft blew through it. Urinating quickly, he returned to find the legal adviser trying on a pair of sleek black pants. Now he had a better view of her waistline and rear, which were indeed low and flabby-looking—unless it was just the cut of the pants, a new style from India. At last, without making a purchase, she promised the salesgirl she would return, though no one particularly seemed to care whether she did or not.

They walked on through the gathering dusk. It was time to eat, and after considering a few spots, they picked a modest restaurant, where they sat in a cozy corner apart from everyone, as if in a bubble all their own. He was glad their first date was not taking place in Haifa, where someone was sure to have recognized them. She ordered quickly, and her choices, he noticed, were not particularly expensive. Though she was eager to tell him about the conference, he preferred to turn the talk to her late husband, refusing to change the subject, despite the reluctance with which she answered his questions. "Very suddenly," she said when asked how he had died. He never complained of a thing. One minute he was washing dishes in the kitchen and the next he was dead on the floor. "At first we thought it was just some pot that had fallen." "Did he like puttering in the kitchen?" Molkho asked. "No," she said, "not especially. He just happened to be there when it happened. And his death left a terrible vacuum." For a whole year afterward, she hardly slept a wink, so shocked had she been. Perhaps he, who had had so much time to prepare himself, found that difficult to imagine. Yes, he had been ready for Death, admitted Molkho, struck by how, though she was doing most of the talking, her plate was empty before his. Though her table manners were impeccable, she ate much faster than he did.

Afterward, they discussed the office and politics, for which she, like his wife, had a passion. His opinions, when she pressed him for them, made her look slightly incredulous, and he could see that his mind worked too slowly and banally for her, disappointing her with its simplicity. I'd better sharpen my brain, he told himself; it's time I thought about something besides medicines, hospital beds, orthopedic mattresses, therapeutic baths, changing linens, and playing doctor. And yet they talked for a long while until, despite her repeated assurances that he looked perfectly respectable and that no one dressed for the opera anymore, because all that mattered was the music, they hurried back to the hotel for him to change. He went to his room, turned on the light, turned it off again as though someone were watching him, and quickly began to undress. Deciding to change underpants, too, he paused to examine his penis by the reddish glow of the streetlight streaming through the thin lace curtains. "So, old man," he whispered, morosely observing how small and scrotal it looked, like a tired gray mouse. He hurriedly put on a tie and descended to the lobby, where, freshly made up but still wearing the same dress, she was waiting; he felt annoyed that she didn't attach the same value to clothing that he did.

It had gotten colder, and the drops of icy sleet jabbed at them like little javelins. "The snow's following me from Paris," he said, and she answered impishly, "I wish it would catch you already. I love it." In the taxi she took out the German program of the opera from her handbag. "It looks like a modern piece," she informed him. "I hope we'll like it." "Modern?" he asked, feeling vaguely anxious. "Yes. Experimental. My brother-in-law says he's heard it's good. Let's hope we'll think so too. Tomorrow we'll see something more classical." "You'll have to explain everything to me," he warned her, looking out at the widening streets, "because I don't know a word of German. I'm at your mercy." "I know," she replied, smiling gaily while slipping a warm hand into his that sent a shiver down his spine.

His first thought upon reaching the opera house and stepping out of the cab beneath the large marquee was that they had stumbled on some college demonstration. Though he had expected to see the passengers he had flown with from Paris that morning, none were visible in the crowd, which seemed composed for the most part of young Berliners, a throng of whom surrounded them at once, asking for extra tickets. So many youngsters were unheard of at the orchestral performances in Haifa, whose elderly concertgoers seemed rejuvenated now in Berlin, quiet and well-mannered in their steel-rimmed glasses and clipped beards, so that the occasional oldster, like the tall woman leaning on her walking stick in the midst of a circle of reverently listening youths, stood out in contrast. The legal adviser, Molkho now realized, had been right, for most of those present had on jeans, army jackets, and windbreakers.

5

I T WAS AN OPERA from the 1930s. The overture struck up, muted
but urgent, and the curtain rose on a bare canyon of a stage.
Slowly, by means of a hidden effect, long strips of yellow fabric
swirled across it like a sandstorm, and groups of performers, all
dressed in identical black—some of them, to Molkho's surprise,
quite old—entered from the wings, dancing, singing, and even shouting, while old-fashioned street and shop signs descended from the
cavernous ceiling on radiant wires. Molkho found it rather exciting,
and indeed, it was very different from the opera he had seen in Paris:
serious, even somber, yet electrifying the young audience, which
seemed mesmerized. He did his best to concentrate, trying to banish
the last twenty-four hours from his mind, yet unable to do so: the
morning in Paris, the slow drive to the airport, the search for the
unknown airline, his wife's cousin's annoyance at the sign saying
Voles Opera. His eyes moved back and forth across the stage, from
whose pit came music that was softly melodic and wildly discordant
by turns. Had the high school boy, he wondered, remembered to shut
the gas cock at night? Now the protagonists were left onstage by
themselves, two men and three women who soon became involved in
a tortuous operatic argument, quarreling passionately, almost mur-
derously, and then making up again before somersaulting down a
kind of manhole in the middle of the stage and popping up unexpectedly somewhere else. Gently Molkho covered his mouth with one
hand, smelling his breath and reproaching himself for not brushing
his teeth in the hotel, suddenly recalling that endless night a year
ago when, riddled with tubes after major surgery, his wife amusedly
told him that she could no longer distinguish the orifices of her body

or tell what entered or exited from which, and he had listened attentively, eagerly trying to imagine the feeling, convinced that he was on the verge of a new insight, carefully probing her with questions until she fell silent and said no more. Dully he now strove to follow the performance, whose cacophonous score was giving him a headache, though the legal adviser, sitting bright-eyed beside him, seemed quite taken by it. Beneath her blouse he made out the outline of her breasts; what, he wondered, were they really like? Would he have to fondle them later that night or would a good-night kiss be enough, leaving the next uncertain installment for tomorrow? Again he regretted having failed to brush his teeth. Feeling her eyes on him, he smiled at her dolefully. "Tell me if you understand anything," he whispered. "It's symbolic," she told him. "It's really very symbolic." "Yes, I can see that myself," he replied, "but of what?" Yet, though she tried explaining, he doubted she understood more than he did, and besides, they were already being shushed by the German audience, which was, it appeared, very sensitive. Considering the price of the ticket, it was odd there was no program in English. Not that it matters, he thought, shutting his eyes defensively against the violent music, which barreled on as if squeezing the life out of him, though what I need, he told himself, is some life squeezed into me, only not too quickly, for the weird clangor, he felt, shutting his eyes still tighter, was wringing him dry. He managed to drowse a bit, there being no intermission, but not for long, because suddenly the legal adviser poked him sharply and he awoke to find a floodlit stage growing still brighter and a gorgeously costumed cast breaking into an unexpectedly melodious ensemble that made him, sitting in the overflow crowd, decide it was a splendid opera after all and that, even if he didn't understand it, that was no reason not to like it, so that he joined in wholeheartedly when the applause broke out, even rising for the standing ovation as if to make up for his catnap. "It's true that a lot of it was over my head," he said with a smile to the legal adviser, who, her narrow eyes appraising him, seemed baffled by his enthusiasm, "but something did get through to me in the end. I'm not sure what, but I'm certainly glad we came."

It took a while to find the checkroom where his coat was, because they kept getting lost in the rapidly emptying corridors. Outside they discovered that the driving sleet had gotten worse. Though it was not especially late, barely half past ten, the streets were already deserted, the young audience having vanished as though into thin air, leaving only a ragged line of older people standing at the top of the steps, at whose bottom an even older footman in a black uniform and a smartly brimmed cap, a red armband on his sleeve, was trying to flag down cabs with an ancient and ineffective whistle. Feeling his companion pressing against him, Molkho allowed himself a gentle response. Did she really have the secret hots for him? But, unless he had disappointed her by falling asleep or by being such an uninspired conversationalist, the opera must have exhausted her too, for she seemed pensive and uncommunicative. Taxis were scarce and the wait was a long one. "Perhaps we should walk," she suggested. "The hotel isn't far, and I'm sure I can find it." For a minute he wavered. But his faith in her sense of direction had been shaken, and the little spears of icy rain kept jabbing down. "No," he answered, "I think we should wait for a cab," and so they joined the long queue, which was slowly inching along.

Indeed, the flow of taxis increased, and soon they were next in line. Just then, two more cabs pulled up and the two old ladies in front of them started down the slippery steps. Though they had not exchanged a word, Molkho was sure they were together and prepared to follow them down; the legal adviser, however, held back. Sure enough, the two women climbed into a single cab and the car behind it honked softly. "Quick, it's our turn," he exclaimed, breaking free of his companion's grip and darting down the rainy stairs to catch the taxi. Hurriedly, as if searching for his missing arm or afraid he wouldn't wait, she started after him, her fur coat flapping around her. "Watch out," he warned, seeing her stumble and then, losing her balance, pitch forward and tumble down the broad steps, stopping after three or four of them because, agile squirrel that she was, she caught herself and sat up, her face twisted in pain, one shoe on the ground behind her. Frightened, he ran back toward her, reaching her ahead of the Germans who came to the rescue too, even though he paused on his way to pick up her shoe, which looked more worn from use than scuffed. He held her arm, bending over her while she tried first telling him in Hebrew, and then the Germans in German, that she was all right. Above her ankle, where her stocking was torn, were a few drops of blood, which stirred him sadly as with an old passion. Kneeling beside her on the cold stairs, he tried helping her on with her shoe. "I'm fine, I'm fine," she said crimsonly, snatching the shoe from him and getting to her feet. Then, holding it in one hand, she hobbled down the stairs and disappeared through the open door of the taxi to the relief of the bystanders, who appeared to be genuinely concerned.

Inside the taxicab, cursing under her breath, she bent down to feel her ankle. Her face looked gray and old. Although eager to remind her that he had warned her, Molkho said nothing, remembering how his wife had always hated such I-told-you-so's. The taxi was still standing there, its driver awaiting instructions. Slowly the legal adviser got a grip on herself. "We have to give him the address," said Molkho and she did.

He insisted, of course, on helping her up to her room. "Lie down, let's have a look at you," he said as she pulled off her stocking, catching a glimpse when he removed the two suitcases from her bed of an unlikely pair of red panties and an old-fashioned girdle that resembled those worn by his mother. At last, he could get a good look at her foot in the light. The bruise above her ankle, for which she let him make a compress from a washcloth, was superficial and no longer bleeding, but the ankle itself was swollen and painful, though when he tried to turn it gently, they both agreed it wasn't broken.

6

S HE SMILED AT HIM and he smiled back, feeling fully awake
now, his tiredness forgotten. Now she'll see what I'm made of,
thought Molkho. As she hopped to the bathroom on one small foot,
he rose to have a look around the room, which was slightly larger
than his own but, except for the double bed, furnished in the same
Spartan style. His glance fell on familiar items in her open suitcases,
such as the pink slippers she had worn that evening in her home.
How strange to see them here in Berlin! He laid them neatly on the
floor, took out several other things she was likely to need, put them
on the table, and hung her cold, wet fur coat in the closet. He heard
the toilet being flushed in the bathroom, and when she returned to
the room, still hobbling but freshly combed and made up, he hurried
to help her lie down, examined her foot again, and asked if she had
medical insurance. Of course she did, she replied, though she had no
intention of calling a doctor. "It's nothing," she smiled with a grimace. The puffy redness around the ankle looked edematous; he
knew the symptoms, had become an expert on them during the past
year. Lightly touching her foot, he searched for the point where the
natural irregularity of the bone yielded to the actual swelling. He
should make her a splint or ligature, something at least for the night,
though it wasn't the swelling that bothered her but the pain. Could
he look to see if she had any pills? she asked, still badly flustered,
especially as her back hurt now too. He poked through her toilet kit
and found nothing but a few crumbly aspirins. "Here, let's have a
look," he said, thinking how odd it was to be turning a strange
woman over on her stomach. "I've become half a doctor this past

year." There was a faint blue contusion on her back, but when he pressed it gingerly, they agreed it was no cause for concern.

The opera seemed far away now, a forgotten figment of the imagination. Giving her two aspirins—just one would do no good— he suggested finding a drugstore and buying an athletic bandage to bind her foot for the night. "That's hardly necessary," she said, so clearly pleased by his solicitude that he had to warn himself not to overdo it, afraid to be trapped in a relationship that might not be at all what he wanted. At first, he proposed taking her key to let himself back in with, but she preferred to leave the door unlocked. Downstairs the hotel was quiet. The ten other keys were in their cubbyholes, a mute sign that they were still alone in the hotel.

Once again there was a new clerk at the reception desk, this time a young student, who looked up from his heavy book to give Molkho directions in excellent English, as if helping guests find drugstores in the middle of the night were routine, even drawing a map of how to get to one that was only five minutes away. Molkho took several of the hotel's cards from a box on the counter, stuck one in each pocket in case he got lost, and, quite proud of himself for venturing out in this city behind the Iron Curtain guided by only a slip of paper, strode jauntily into the narrow streets, whose shroud of desolate fog was pierced by the lights of bars and restaurants. Before long he arrived at the drugstore, which was visible from a distance; large and well lit, it was located in what seemed to be an old church or fortress or, at any rate, an artfully renovated old building, though the giant containers of brightly colored liquids on its shelves and the large straw hampers filled with tubes and boxes gave it more the appearance of a supermarket, over which presided the druggist, a stout, jovial man in a black cravat who seemed greatly to amuse his young assistants. Indeed, every sentence he uttered aroused peals of laughter, the cause of which, Molkho concluded, could not possibly be the man's wit but simply his buffoonish manner. Slowly Molkho walked down the aisles, enjoying the special night mood of the place, examining the rows of medicines while looking for an athletic bandage. Poking about a bit in the hampers, where he noticed several over-the-counter drugs that in Israel were sold only by prescription, he suddenly came across the most familiar of them all lying inno-cently in its blue-and-white box. Talwin! Lovingly he turned it in his hand, feeling all the excitement of a chance meeting with an old friend whom he had never expected to see again. He consulted the price, figuring it in shekels, and was so angered by the enormousness of the Israeli markup that he went on calculating its precise, scandal-ous percentage all the way to the checkout counter, only to discover upon arrival that the elderly druggist, who bore a striking resem-blance to Doctor Doolittle, didn't understand a word of English, which not only failed to prevent him from making jokes that were translated for Molkho by an assistant but inspired him, to the merri-ment of all, to mimic the translation too. At last, producing several athletic bandages, he laid them on the counter, and Molkho bought the next to the cheapest, having already decided that he would not let the legal adviser reimburse him. As he started to pay, the druggist inquired with a wink about the box of Talwin, which was still firmly gripped in Molkho's hand. "Ask him if it's good for pain," Molkho requested of the English-speaking assistant. The druggist regarded him with his merry blue eyes. *Jawohl*, he declared, it was *wunderbar*. "Then I'll take it," declared Molkho, already plotting his revenge on the drugstore in Haifa that had overcharged him.

7

THERE WASN'T A SOUND in the hotel. Most of the lamps were turned off and the shades of the lit ones cast reddish brown patches in the corners of the lobby. Molkho took the elevator up to the room, knocked lightly, and gently opened the door. Still fully clothed, the legal adviser lay in misery on her bed, the night's music having fled and left her with a sprained ankle, at which she stared in despair. Tearing its wrapper, Molkho took out the athletic bandage and vigorously bound her foot, which now looked like a fat little fish, informed by her cry that her threshold of pain was nothing like his wife's, which had reached truly supreme heights toward the end. Indeed, what did she know about suffering? Her husband had dropped dead on the floor like a pot cover, her whole family pampered her, and intellectuals like herself had no powers of endurance anyway. Now she was gazing at him contemplatively, her close-cropped hair on the pillow, looking just like her daughter that night in her room. The aspirins, it seemed, hadn't helped. He had suspected as much when he saw them, small, old, and crumbly; it was amazing how people didn't realize that no drug was immortal. She was terribly sorry, said the legal adviser; she was afraid their whole trip would be ruined now. "I told you to watch out," replied Molkho, unable to restrain himself. "I had a feeling you were going to slip," he added, realizing too late that she might be blaming him for just that, for letting go of her in a hurry at the wrong time. Yet, how long was he expected to hold onto a woman he hardly knew—and one three whole civil service ranks ahead of him, not to mention car expenses, a subject that still bore looking into?

Still, he felt for her. The best thing, he told her, was to get a good night's sleep and wake up feeling better in the morning. Gently he took a few things from her suitcases and stood there wondering whether to help her undress, only to decide it might embarrass her; and so, too much attention being as bad as too little, he left her room. It was 12:15 and as the elevator didn't seem to be working, he descended the narrow, padded stairs. Clearly, there were still no other guests. What, apart from its low rates and cleanliness, had made her choose this place? Had she already stayed here with someone before him? Strangely, as if all the events of the day had never happened, he didn't feel at all tired. Not ready for sleep, he sat in the armchair reading about Jesus in Jerusalem until suddenly it struck him that it was Friday night and he hadn't even thought of his children. "How could I have forgotten them," he reproached himself, trying to go back to his book. Yet, when he tried picturing Jerusalem, all he could think of was his mother sitting grumpily in their big, old house.

Finally he undressed, put on his pajamas, got into bed, and

turned off the night-light. It was after one. Just as he was dozing off, however, he heard someone hobble down the hallway. He rose and went to the door, through which the legal adviser asked in her brisk manner if he had anything stronger than the aspirin, which wasn't doing any good. "I'll be right there," said Molkho. Dressing quickly, he took the box of Talwin and went upstairs.

Her fully lit room looked a mess, its window wide open as though she were about to throw herself out of it, though she was in fact limping anxiously about in a flowery nightgown and light bathrobe while the radio played soft German songs. Her back pains, she told Molkho, were gone, but her foot was in agony. He nodded sympathetically, amazed how frightened she was of pain, showed her the box of Talwin, opened it, and pulled out a chain of little pills. Over the past year, he explained, telling her about his wife's experience, he had become an expert anesthesiologist.

The legal adviser listened eagerly to Molkho's stories of his wife, who had suddenly turned into a role model. But why, she wanted to know, had he brought all those pills with him to Europe in the first place? He hadn't, he explained; he had bought them just now at the drugstore, over-the-counter and cut-rate. She took a blue pill from him, swallowed it obediently, and suggested taking another. "Absolutely not," he declared, slipping the box back into his pocket while feebly stifling an astonished yawn at the sight of her breasts bobbing up and down beneath her nightgown. "They're very strong," he said. "One is enough." Regretfully she watched the box vanish. "Maybe you should leave them with me," she said. "If one doesn't work, I'll take another during the night." "One is enough," he repeated, "you'll see." Yet, not wanting her to think he didn't trust her, he left her the box anyway. Reassured, she hobbled back to bed, where he helped cover her with a blanket and was rewarded at last with a smile. "Now you'll sleep well," he promised, wondering whether he shouldn't crawl in beside her, though he was more used to having the patient prone beneath him. The main thing was for her to rest her foot—the thought of which made him lift the blanket and decide to undo the bandage for another, last look. The ankle was good and swollen now. Expertly he rewound the elastic, feeling the flabby warmth of her flesh around the bruise, in which the blood had jelled like rubies, reminding him again of a fat, white, blind, stranded little fish. "I'm afraid I've ruined this trip of yours," she said for the second time. There was something touching about the no-longer-fresh bloom of hopelessness on her face. "You haven't ruined anything," he answered quietly. "Tomorrow you'll feel better. Just let me take care of you." Overcome by fatigue at last, she fell back against the pillow, and he felt a faint stirring in his loins, as if the gray mouse had turned over in its sleep. He closed the window, drawing the blinds. "To let you sleep late in the morning," he explained, offering to lock the door after him to keep the chambermaid out. "Never mind," she said resignedly from her pillow, "you can leave it unlocked. No one's about to burgle or rape me here." Once again he considered sedating her with his body warmth, but her eyes were already shut, and so he switched off the light and descended to his room.

8

H E AWOKE AT 6:30 A.M. Outside the window the darkness and silence seemed total, infinite, as if the night were just reaching its peak. The thought of the woman in bed a floor above him and of the bond he had formed with her last night, as though she now were part of him, made him feel an inner glow. Soon, however, he fell back asleep. Upon awakening a second time, he rose, washed, dressed, and even made the bed, after which he gazed at the rooftops and strips of gray sky that ran between them, and then on the toilet, read about the crucifixion of Jesus. He descended to the lobby, hoping that the legal adviser was feeling better and might be already downstairs. But she was nowhere to be seen. The student on night duty was gone, his place taken by a plump girl of about eighteen who was feather-dusting the old swords. Reddening at the sight of him, she murmured, "Good morning," in German. Through a narrow, half-open door behind the counter, next to the cubbyholes of keys, he caught a glimpse of a kitchen, dinette, and hallway in which a schoolbag was lying on a chair. It was, it seemed, a family hotel—but where was the family?

Breakfast was already waiting in the dining room: several varieties of sliced bread, little baskets of sausages and cheeses, and a hot plate with a canister of coffee and a bowl of hard-boiled eggs. He regarded the food with satisfaction and went up to the legal adviser's room. At first, he knocked lightly, gently trying the doorknob only when there was no response. True to her word, she hadn't locked the door. A thin shaft of light accompanied him into the darkened room and fell on her bed, where she lay soundly sleeping like a baby. Possessed by an old feeling of well-being, he went downstairs again.

The plump girl was still dusting the swords. "Madame is asleep," he informed her when she glanced at him curiously; then, seeing she failed to understand, he pointed to the ceiling, laid a cheek on two folded hands, and went off to have breakfast in the dining room, making sure to take no more than his share, which he piled high on his plate. He poured himself a cup of coffee and began to eat, thinking as he chewed of his wife, who had refused to visit Germany, and of what she might have thought of the odd circumstances that had brought him here. Not that he hadn't respected her principles, of which her death had freed him, but the fact of the matter was that, had she not been so principled, so critical, so brutally judgmental that he never knew what would annoy her next, she could have enjoyed being here with him. Well, she had had her say, and now he was recuperating from her with a big breakfast in Berlin, of all the places in the world.

He finished eating, even appropriating a slice of bread and a wedge of yellow cheese from the legal adviser's share of the food, and wrote her a note that said, "Good morning, I hope you're feeling better and slept well. I didn't want to wake you, so I ate and went out for a walk. I should be back by nine." Then he went upstairs, slipped the note beneath her door, descended to his room, donned his coat, and continued on down to the lobby, where he handed his key to the girl with the feather duster, took two more of the hotel's cards, stuck one in each pocket, and sallied forth. To his amazement, the snow from Paris had arrived silently during the night, thinly blanketing the city. The sidewalks, the fire hydrants, and the housefronts were all daubed a streaky white, amid which he carefully made his way, heading in a hitherto unexplored direction, along a path already trodden by early risers that soon led him through a maze of little side streets. Thinking of the opera, he recalled how the bare proscenium had suddenly filled with performers, and he imagined faint music playing again while he—only an extra, of course, but an indispensable one nonetheless—took the stage himself, watched by an audience beneath the distant, white trees. He strode on energetically, climbing a little rise until he came to an old church with a golden rooster on its belfry and pausing there for a while, breathing in the frozen air and straining to hear the far-off drums, which were followed by a short flourish of trumpets. Then, as the violins struck up, he walked back down again, surrounded now by schoolchildren who, as though at an agreed-upon signal, had burst from all the houses at once with their bags. Crossing streets and sidewalks, he maneuvered past housewives with their shopping baskets and waited at frozen red lights with men on their way to work while the soft, light, now-familiar snow squished underfoot and the music played stubbornly on. "Just keep going, just keep going," an invisible director was telling him, and indeed, in the distance, where a golden light had begun to glow in the east, the audience was watching him, transfixed by the new opera in which he was taking part.

It was only when he found himself back on the street of the hotel and heard the church bells strike nine that the dreamlike vision vanished. The girl with the feather duster was no longer in the lobby and had been replaced by an old lady in a black woolen shawl, who sat behind the counter knitting. He smiled at her. "*Sechs,*" he said in German, taking the key and adding an English comment about the snow. The old lady, however, did not know English. The legal adviser's breakfast was still untouched.

He hurried upstairs and knocked on the door of her room. Again there was no answer. Silently he opened the door, once more admitting a narrow shaft of pink light that lapped at the foot of the bed. His note was still on the floor and for a moment he experienced a delicious feeling of apprehension. Could she have overdosed on the pills, or did she always sleep late on vacations? Boldly he tiptoed into the room. She was sleeping too soundly to hear him, her face, from which the makeup had rubbed off, pale but peaceful. Standing above her and gazing down on the dry white roots of her dyed hair, he felt an urge to lift the blanket and see if the athletic bandage was still in place. Yet, fearful she might wake and think she had caught him in an obscene act, he turned soundlessly and fled. Descending the staircase thoughtfully, he returned to his room, changed into warmer, more comfortable clothes, and stepped back outside.

The street was full of life now. Workers armed with hoses of hot air were melting the snow with German thoroughness, and vans were unloading large trays of fresh rolls and pastries. He walked around the block for fifteen minutes, fretting over his strange love affair. Could she, he wondered suspiciously, have gone and taken a second pill without asking him? He hurried back to the hotel and opened her unlocked door. Nothing had changed. Quite clearly the drug had knocked her out. He examined the box of Talwin, cursing himself for leaving it in her room. Sure now that she had taken a second pill, he called her name. She stirred slightly, and leaning down, he called again, doing his best not to sound worried. Slowly she gave signs of hearing, struggling to open her eyes and momentarily even succeeding, "What is it?" she asked. "It's past nine," he said. "That's some sleep you had! I just want to know how you are." Her eyelids drooped again, as if to give her time to think behind them; there was something poignant, almost adorable, in the effort of her once quick legal mind to extract an answer from the depths of her sleep. "I'm fine," she said slowly and weakly at last, turning over to go back to sleep again, but he was determined not to let her. "Does your foot hurt?" he asked. The silence before she shook her head was so long that it was not at all clear whether she remembered having a foot at all. "Do you want to sleep some more?" he persisted anxiously. "Then go ahead," he finally added as if giving her permission, despairing of an answer to this too, glancing about the room on his way

out to look for something else to do. He was already at the door when
the thought occurred to him that perhaps she didn't recognize him.
Could she be brain-damaged? He went back and shook her lightly,
his hand on her frail shoulder. "Do you know who I am?" he asked.
This time, when her oval eyes opened, he was relieved to see a gleam
of understanding in them. "Of course," she said, not especially enthusiastically—or at least so it seemed to him, and indeed, he was
perhaps fatiguing her with his worry and should go away and leave
her alone. "Then sleep all you want," he counseled. "I won't bother
you anymore." And quickly, his duty done, he walked toward the
door. It was, he reflected, a Saturday morning, and perhaps she was
used to sleeping late then.

He found a small sign that said "Please Do Not Disturb" in
several languages, including Arabic, hung it on the outside door
handle, and went back downstairs, feeling he had earned the right to
go off and see Berlin on his own, especially as she already knew the
city and he didn't. For a moment he considered eating her breakfast,
which was going to waste in the dining room, yet how would it look if
he did? And so he stepped outside and into a nearby café, where he
ordered a second breakfast of coffee and a small frankfurter to help
brace himself against the cold. Their main meal, he assumed, would
again be in the evening, when she would have her strength and
appetite back. The question of the Talwin, however, still bothered
him: he would have to find the drugstore and count the number of
pills in a box to know how many she had taken.

Outside the day was in full swing and on the steamy sidewalks
the shopkeepers were busily sweeping away the snow and polishing
the brass handles of their doors. The entire area seemed to be under-
going renovation, for beside slummy old grocery and junk stores
there were other, quite fashionable shops, all kinds of boutiques and
art galleries. He soon reached the drugstore, but the funny old man
with the cravat wasn't there. In his place stood two slender, stern-
looking pharmacists defending their locked cabinets of drugs, the
open straw hampers, apparently a private promotional device of the
night shift, having vanished too, so that, after a brief debate with
himself, Molkho decided to forgo the Talwin and walk on, treading

adventurously on the snow past the high wall of the old fortress, though perhaps it had been a factory or school. The street ran downhill now, curving left, then right, and soon grew quieter and less crowded. The snow beneath his feet was thicker too. Passing an apparently abandoned building and stopping by a concrete wall between two houses, he noticed a rusty skein of barbed wire protruding from the snow. Dimly he had a sense of déjà vu: there was no way of passing the barrier or seeing what lay beyond it, and so he tried to outflank it to his left, only to encounter it again, slightly taller than a man and scribbled over with graffiti. Only now did he realize that it was the Berlin Wall itself, which he had never imagined being so low and so gray. He stepped back, looking for a vantage point from which to see the other side. A few deserted houses were visible there, and something that looked like a frozen pond. Suddenly, with a surge of pleasure, he knew what he was reminded of: it was of that other divided city, the Jerusalem of his youth. At first, half-afraid of some Communist body snatcher, he walked parallel to the wall at a distance. But the cold grew harsher, snowflakes swirled around him, and afraid of slipping, he followed it more closely, making his way slowly alongside it. Once in all his childhood it had snowed in Jerusalem; his mother had been so afraid of his catching pneumonia that she refused to let him out of the house and—it still made him laugh to think of it—sent his father up to the roof with a wash basin to bring him down some snow to play with. If only she could see him now!

Nevertheless, not wanting to take any chances with the storm, which was getting fiercer, he turned and walked back to the hotel, deciding when he reached it, however, not to go inside just yet. Let her sleep a while longer, he thought. In fact, it was beginning to seem likely that she might sleep for another day or two and force him to extend his stay. It was lucky his children were grown and could get along without him, he told himself, passing the hotel entrance and disappearing down some more side streets, which soon emptied into a large square. Yes, it was an oversight not to have asked his mother-in-law for the name of her old street, which he pictured being like one of these. Why, right here might be where his wife had played as a child, unless it was further on, in what was now a no-man's-land between East and West. He could hardly believe that just four months after her death he was touring the city she had refused to come back to. But the storm was still gathering strength, and he resolved to return to the hotel for his fur cap, which he had had the good sense to pack.

In the lobby he wondered why the old lady at the reception desk had changed clothes; then, coming closer, he saw that a different and even older old lady, who smiled at him blankly, had replaced her. *"Sechs,"* he said in what he felt sure was a much-improved accent while raising six fingers, and she gave him the key at once, responding in German to an English remark about the snow, so that they stood talking for several minutes in perfect agreement until he nodded one last time and went up to his room, where he found a swarthy young chambermaid changing the soap in the bathroom. Excusing himself, he rummaged through his suitcase until he found the hat. The windows of the room were frosted over. For a minute he debated going upstairs to lock the legal adviser's door against the chambermaid, but in the end he thought better of it. His fur hat on his head, he descended the stairs again, nodded to the old woman, returned the key, and strode gaily out into the snowstorm, whose soft, giant flakes now whirled round and round in the viridescent light of a sun reflected back from the battered old sidewalk.

A church bell rang in the white fog, which seemed to issue from some vast darkness and through which, brushing by him as bulky as bears, pedestrians made their way. He paused by the window of a small, empty barbershop in which an old, white-smocked barber sat reading a newspaper in a big, multilevered leather chair, the tools of his trade set out gleaming before him—razors, scissors, old clippers, a stack of spotlessly laundered white towels—as though in a cozy little operating room. A fireplace was burning in one corner, beside which stood a potted plant. On the walls hung pictures of clean-cut, smooth-shaven men, and there was something so confidence-inspiring about the whole place that Molkho nearly stepped inside for a haircut. In the end, however, he continued on his way, once again regretting the lack of his mother-in-law's old address, since tracking down his wife's childhood could have given this aimless morning a profound purpose of its own. Should he step into a post office and call her long distance? But he knew that by the time she understood him and remembered how to spell the German name, the call would have cost him a fortune, and so, rejecting the idea, he entered a large department store full of shoppers seeking shelter from the storm.

Fingering the clothes, he went from floor to floor and even bought a sweater for his daughter, a double-barreled canteen for his younger son, and, for his mother-in-law, a collapsible cane with four jointed sections that made him think of Mozart's magic flute. In the furniture department he opened closets, slid drawers back and forth in their grooves, and passed through a huge area divided up into living rooms, going from one to another and sitting with his legs crossed in sofas and easy chairs while pretending to be a welcome guest in each. And yet, thinking of the woman asleep in her hotel room, his pleasure was mingled with guilt, as it had been in those not so distant days in Haifa when he had sometimes done shopping while his wife lay in her large bed, the prow of which breasted the waves of a different existential sea.

Through the windows of the store he could see that the sun was back out and that the snowstorm was over. The morning was getting on. Most likely the legal adviser was up by now and wondering where he was. He hurried back, proud of his perfect sense of direction in the little streets of the pleasant neighborhood, entering the hotel on a carpet of fresh white snow played on by squealing children. Though the lobby was as silent as ever, breakfast was gone from the table. Had they finally given up on her or had she actually come down to eat? He *sechs*ed the old lady at the reception desk, was given his key, and went first to his room, which had been tidied up, took off his hat and coat, and shoved the gifts into a suitcase before bounding upstairs. Apprehensively he entered her room. She was still lying motionless, though it was already after eleven. The Germans, so it seemed, had let her sleep. At once he cheered up again, feeling as if all that snowy morning he had been burrowing toward this strange woman down some hidden tunnel. And yet the guilt and the fear were still there. Suppose something had really happened to her? The room was dark, pungent with the sour smell of sleep. He decided to wake her, no matter what.

"Get up," he said, "get up. Those pills really knocked you out. It's almost lunchtime and you haven't eaten yet. I'm worried about you." She opened her eyes, and he helped her sit up weakly in bed. "There, you had me worried!" he said. "I told you not to take a second pill, it was really unnecessary." She sat listening dreamily, her eyelids poised to shut again, the dry skin of her face deeply creased, an aging woman he had slipped a powder to. "The first was unnecessary also," she said at last, perfectly distinctly. He smiled anxiously. "Maybe it was," he confessed, "I didn't know you were so sensitive." In the ensuing silence he thought he was losing her again, but suddenly she exclaimed, "Just to these," and said no more. And in fact, he now recalled with a glow that his wife, too, though she was used to all kinds of medicines, had slept a great deal when first put on the Talwin in late spring. Every new drug had been an adventure then, her reactions to which they had vigilantly lived through together. Sometimes, curious to know how she felt, he had even been tempted to try it himself, deterred only by his reluctance to gamble with his health, on which the entire family depended, for if at first he had sought to be sick together with her, gradually he had had to relent and let her illness serve for the two of them. Now, observing the legal adviser's stupor, he remembered his wife's reaction to the Talwin, the "philosophy pill," as they had called it, for it had caused her mind to feel separated from her body, and her thoughts to be uncommonly clear. The long conversations they had had then were carried on as if from opposite ends of the earth, and yet, though even her quickest responses seemed to travel across far continents, they were unfailingly sharp on arrival. The memory of it made him miss her. Where are you now? he wondered. Are you really gone forever? And when would he join her there?

He let out a laugh. So did the legal adviser. Her eyes were shut again as though with the pleasure of her involuntary slumber, over which he presided worriedly. I'll bet the old squirrel doesn't do this often, he thought; it isn't every day that a high-strung career woman like her gets such a good night's sleep. Her breathing grew slow and regular, as if, glued to the rumpled sheets, she once more wished to drift off, but he refused to let her and was even about to turn her over in bed when suddenly he remembered her foot. "How's your ankle?" he asked. She didn't answer, still drugged by the potion in her veins, and so he pushed aside the blanket and groped for her bandaged foot, which seemed to have shrunk to a child's size during the night. He lifted it and expertly undid the elastic like a crack surgeon treating a minor infection. "It's much better," he announced happily, as if discovering that it presented a different and less worrisome case than that of its owner. The legal adviser said nothing; no doubt he could have her other foot, too, if only he would let her sleep. Swiftly he replaced the bandage, talking out loud to himself as he had done in his wife's final months. "This can't go on. You have to eat. You've already missed breakfast, but I'll go get you something, at least some coffee and rolls." And indeed, off he went to ask the old lady at the reception desk, in a combination of sign language and English contrived to sound like German, for a canister of coffee, after which he dashed out into the street to buy some rolls and pastries, bringing it all back up on a tray, only to find the patient fast asleep again. He drew the curtain, pulled up the blinds, even opened the window to let in a blast of cold air, determined to make her wake up.

And she did, wearily and unwillingly. He helped her out of bed, amazed at how light she was, hurrying to check the sheets as soon as she shut the bathroom door behind her. Sure enough, they were sticky and slightly damp. Deftly he shook them out, reversed them, and spread them again on the mattress; so proficient a sheet-changer had he become that he could even do it while his wife lay in bed. Then he tidied up as best he could with one ear cocked toward the bathroom, afraid that the silence there might spell a new and dangerous relapse. At last, though, she emerged, washed and even wearing makeup, causing him to marvel at the quiet intimacy that had sprung up between them, as though they were an old married couple. Perhaps, it occurred to him as he served her from the tray, her hibernation was simply a way of getting attention. She ate and drank, laughing at being so weak that she could scarcely swallow her food, while

he poured himself a cup of coffee and ate another roll. "Where have
you been all morning?" she asked, regarding him for the first time as
if he were more than just a bedside shade. "Oh, around," he replied.
He had even run into the Berlin Wall not far from the hotel and been
disappointed. "But that isn't the place for it," she explained. "Go to
the Brandenburg Gate. It's much more impressive there. It cuts right
through the heart of the city." He told her about the storm, too, of
which she had been unaware. "Berlin's white all over," he said.
"The snow's caught up with me from Paris, though the Germans
seem to be taking it more calmly than the French." Maybe I should
bring her a bowl of it, he thought when she expressed regret at
missing it. Yet, as funny as that seemed, he only answered, "You
should rest up for the opera tonight. There's no need to overdo it."
He watched her lie flushed on the pillow, hypnotized by the to-and-
fro movement of her earrings—something his wife had never worn—
while she looked quizzically back at him, trying dutifully to listen
and pecking at her roll like a child who has no appetite, evidently
unused to such loving care, even from her doting family.

　　He wondered whether to take her temperature. Could her sleep-
iness be a symptom of some deeper disorder? Outside the window
the snow was flying grayly again, and the rumble of the radiator
broke the silence like an airplane. The daylight grew faint, turned to
a milky grime by the storm, and he sat in the armchair feeling logy
himself, trying to get her to talk about something, her childhood, for
instance, or even her reasons for choosing this hotel. Had she been
here with someone, perhaps her late husband, on a previous opera
tour? She was not up to answering, though; her replies were short
and drowsy, as if a new attack of sleep were imminent, and so he
switched the subject to himself, or rather to his wife, who, though
born in this city, had never wanted to return to it. The legal adviser,
however, seemed to know all about it, for she dozed off in the middle
of a sentence. She must have been a pharmaceutical virgin if two
little pills could do this to her, Molkho thought, carefully removing
the tray with its half-eaten roll and nearly full cup of coffee from her
limp hands, which made her sit up with a start and then slump to a
prone position in the bed. "I suppose it's partly my fault," he whis-

pered, hoping for a little sympathy. At first, lying mutely on the pillow, she didn't react, yet all at once she smiled bitterly. "Just partly?" she asked, which was more than enough to alarm him. "I never thought," he stammered, "that you would be affected like this. Why, they weren't even prescription pills. I bought them over the counter. My wife . . ." But sleep had carried her off again, and her breath came in slow, heavy waves. How, he asked himself worriedly, could he fly back to Israel tomorrow if she didn't break the habit by then? He had no choice but to stay by her side and wait for her to sleep off the poison in her system. Meanwhile, not even the snowstorm seemed able to rouse her.

He stretched out in the armchair and watched the snowflakes, which, caught in an updraft, seemed to blow skyward from the earth; they did not look to him like crystals of frozen vapor but like the torn whites of an egg or some scrambled, primeval matter. Well, then, he told himself, I'll just sit here like I used to do in Haifa. In fact, it was even quieter here because of the storm windows. He thought of that final month, in which so much time had sometimes elapsed without talking that at last his wife would beg, "Say something, anything, tell me what's new in the world." "Nothing is new," he would answer. "All I care about is you, nothing else interests me"—which happened to be true enough. Now he was sitting by another bed, trusting once more in his patience to compensate for the intellectual superiority of its occupant, yet harassed by a feeling of fatigue. Groping for a pick-me-up, he noticed a copy of the Bible here too. This one—perhaps because the bed was a double one—had the Old Testament in it as well, but unfortunately only in German. He tried mouthing the first line of Genesis, but then shut the volume and put it down.

He could feel his tiredness flowing through him. Should he take off his shoes and lie down beside her? After all, his coming and going all morning had exhausted him too. And yet he stayed where he was. In the first place, it might frighten her; and in the second, even if it didn't, as soon as she realized he only wanted to sleep, she would suspect him of being a pervert. The best tactic was to get some shut-eye in the chair while she slept. Was she someone he could marry? And if so, where would they live—in his house or hers?

Perhaps they would have to sell both apartments and buy a single larger one with room for all their children. He was beginning to doze off himself now, lulled by the rhythm of his breath, but suddenly, still curled beneath her blanket, she woke him by saying quietly, "You really needn't sit here all day. Why don't you have a look at the city? You're flying home tomorrow, and who knows when you'll be back. There's an expressionist museum not far from here with some important early twentieth-century paintings. Go out and enjoy yourself. I'll feel better soon, I promise."

He sensed a note of rejection in her voice. "All right," he said, getting up, "I'll take another walk." He collected the coffee cups and unfinished roll and asked if there was anything else she wanted, a thermometer perhaps. "No thanks," she replied, leaving him to exit quietly with the tray, though he could just as well have left it behind. As he waited for the elevator he heard her patter across the floor and turn the key in her lock, and felt sure, cut to the quick, that their brief affair was over.

He finished the roll in the elevator and laid the tray on the reception desk, behind which sat a schoolgirl doing homework. She took his key with thin fingers and hung it up. The door of the apartment was wide open now, and inside the family was eating its lunch from steaming bowls of crockery; indeed, every one of the receptionists of the last twenty-four hours was gathered around the table, at the head of which sat the paterfamilias, a hefty man of about Molkho's age dressed in overalls. Seeing the guest, he came out to greet him, asking in broken English whether everything was all right and even half-inviting him to join them. Politely, with words of praise for the hotel, especially for its old swords and daggers, Molkho declined. He would have liked to say something about the woman upstairs, who was no doubt causing concern, at least to assure them that she was being cared for, but in the end he made do with inquiring about a thermometer, which he would perhaps have need of later. At first, he failed to get his meaning across; he did not give up, however, but continued popping an imaginary thermometer in and out of his mouth until the worried German understood and promised to bring him one after lunch.

9

A GAIN HE STEPPED OUTSIDE, where he now saw that the storm had died down to reveal a strip of blue, Israeli-looking sky amid the clouds overhead. The snow-carpeted street hummed with people. Workers in caps and overalls and elegant women in high leather boots strolled on the crispy surface, against which a golden sun dashed its rays. Church bells rang. The restaurants and cafés were crowded. Should he eat something now or keep walking to build up an appetite? In the end, he chose to grab a bite, since who knew if he would find another place as cheap as the one near the hotel. Joining the throng inside, he squeezed in at a table beside some jolly young workers and ordered sausages, potatoes, and beer, all reasonably priced. Then, full and slightly groggy from the ice-cold lager, he asked directions to the expressionist museum; yet arriving at the gloomy old building and spying the long line in front of it, he thought, Who needs all those morbid German paintings; I'm getting enough culture as it is. And turning left, he continued downhill on the street that led to the wall, which, he now realized, mysteriously attracted him. Soon he reached it and struck out alongside it, noticing the delicate white, vinelike pattern traced on it by the newly fallen snow. Yes, there was something about it that he liked. It serves them right, he thought, though it did not particularly seem to bother the Germans at all. On the contrary, because of the wall the busy city had a chain of peaceful nooks right in its center.

He kept walking until he reached a broad boulevard that appeared to lead onward to some central spot, and indeed, surrounded by lawns and gardens, he soon found himself at the Reichstag Building, where he joined a trickle of tourists climbing the stairs of an observatory with a view of the eastern half of the city and the Brandenburg Gate, which, ringed by wide, shopperless streets, looked dreary and deserted. Even the snow seemed heavier and deeper there. Two sentries with fur coats and submachine guns trundled back and forth like baby bears. It was freezing, but the storm (now that it's found me, thought Molkho with a smile) seemed to be over. Starting back for the hotel, he made his way down busy streets and came to a large building whose familiar look puzzled him until he realized that it was the opera house seen from behind. On the clean white steps—newly washed by the melted snow—that the legal adviser had tumbled down, fair-haired youngsters sat, eagerly taking in the brightening afternoon sun.

He carefully climbed the steps, trying to see just where and why she had fallen and what had stopped her when she did. It was only a matter of luck, he concluded, that the accident hadn't been worse. Inside the building he scanned pictures of the somber performance they had seen, studying the faces of the singers, who looked different close up, and glancing at the advance billings for *Don Giovanni*, which they were to see that night. The sets, costumes, and performers seemed quite splendid and promising, and for a long time he stood gazing at a photograph of someone done up as a statue, advancing from the depths of the stage with his arm out to seize the frightened Don Giovanni.

By the box office were stacks of colored fliers, with which Molkho stuffed his pockets, even though they were in German, intending to present them to his Sleeping Beauty. Tonight, he thought happily, we'll see something calming and human for a change; indeed, he felt as though the Mozart opera were meant especially for him, as if it were the final act of the Drama of Death, whose uncomplaining hero he had been for months.

He stepped outside, where the clearing weather had grown remarkably, audaciously warmer. Tonight he would make sure to hold her tightly on the stairs. Should he walk back to the hotel? Afraid of losing his way, though, he hailed a taxi, taking one of the cards from his pocket and thrusting it at the driver. A warm glow of homecoming came over him as they pulled into the street. If only she hadn't locked her door. Could she really be angry at him? But what had he done to her? At most he had helped her to a good sleep; brain damage was out of the question. Getting out of the taxi by the little barbershop, he noticed the proprietor and his wife sitting idly in their white smocks and stopped to check the price list in the window. Then, convinced he would be in good hands, he stepped inside.

A little bell tinkled softly, and the old couple hurried courteously toward him; the fact that a foreigner had chosen to patronize their shop, and one from Israel, as it turned out, seemed to make them inordinately proud. Not that they weren't probably Nazis like the rest of them, thought Molkho, but what difference does it make? Now they're just two doddering old people who may as well wait on me before they die. And they did, hand and foot, first tying a large white bib around his neck and then leading him to a big sink in a dark corner, at which, he realized with alarm, the old woman meant to wash his hair. There was no choice, however, but to present her with his head, lowering it into the sink, where her expert fingers massaged and tickled it, working steamy water and shampoo into his scalp. She repeated the treatment a second time, dried him with a towel, wrang it out, and led him wrapped in it to a large chair, where the barber was waiting with his scissors and instruments. It was all done quite slowly and methodically, with frequent pauses for whispered consultations, and the barber's tools, though old, looked shiny and reliable. Between them, the old couple clipped and cut and swept and combed and powdered and clipped some more, and though Molkho tried lamely to warn them that he didn't want his hair too short, the stubborn Prussian had his own ideas and gave him a military crew cut that met with the definite approval of another old Berliner who dropped in just then to pay a friendly visit.

10

I T WAS ALREADY LATE. The haircut had taken longer than he had expected, and he was sure that the legal adviser was up by now and perhaps already out of the hotel. At the reception desk he was handed his key and a black leather case like the one he had kept his compass in as a schoolboy; in it was a thermometer, gleaming in its bed of red velvet. Though he was so impatient to use it that he bounded up the stairs without waiting for the elevator, once standing outside her door he had an attack of cold feet. Nevertheless, he knocked lightly, and then, when there was no answer, more insistently, calling out in a voice that was tinged with desperation. "It's me, it's just me." The jilted lover, he thought ironically, but at last he heard her footsteps and she opened the door, still sleepy and disheveled but awake. Cautiously he followed her into the dimly lit, overheated room, eyeing it, as he used to eye his wife's sickroom, to see what was new in his absence. And indeed, as if afraid that the light might keep her up, she had lowered the blinds he had raised. Why, she's on a real jag! he told himself in astonishment, her existence having as though split in two, one half of it, such as her slip, her scuffed pink sandals, and her toothbrush sticking out from a glass on the bathroom shelf, remaining familiar and even intimate, while the other was now a mystery, such as the odd smell he detected, which made him think of exotic mosses growing deep in a subterranean cave.

Feeling a new wave of worried compassion for this temperamental, loose-boundaried woman now flopping limply back onto the sheets, and determined to get close to her, he sat down on her warm, rumpled bed and began talking intimately in the slightly scolding, humorous tone he had sometimes employed with his wife when nothing else seemed to work. "Now look here. This has got to stop. You're just using the pills as an excuse. It's not them anymore, because I know all about them, and they can't put anyone to sleep like this. Maybe you're exhausted from your conference, but you can't just go on like this without eating or drinking. I'm good and worried about you." He laid a familiar hand on her arm and then moved it up to her head, gently palpating medical areas. "Maybe it's too hot for you in here. Or else you're coming down with something. Here, I brought you a thermometer. We'll start by taking your temperature." "My temperature?" she wondered. "Yes, why not?" he replied. "Do it for my sake." But when he reached out to switch on the bed lamp, she begged him not to. "Please don't turn on the light yet," she said, opening her eyes to a snakelike slit, through whose faint flutter of an aperture he felt her studying him. He complied, keeping a fatherly hand on her while taking out the thermometer, which he then went to the bathroom to wash, not knowing what German germs might be on it. Peering anxiously in the mirror at his new crew cut, which made him look like a Wehrmacht officer at the siege of Stalingrad, he soaped, rinsed, and wiped the long pipette and carefully handed it to her, gently helping to slip it under her tongue. Surprisingly, she offered no resistance, and he timed three minutes on his watch, pacing up and down while entertaining her with an account of his morning, telling her about the wall, which seemed so peaceful, about the melting snow and slowly clearing skies, about coming across the opera house, and about the fliers he had brought so she could read up on that night's performance. She lay in wizened silence, her mouth slightly twisted in protest, the elastic bandage from her foot rebelliously tossed on the chair. "Well, at least you don't have any fever," he declared, having put on his glasses and swiveled around to hold the thermometer up to the reddish, crepuscular light that filtered through the slats of the blinds. "And that means there's no reason to sleep so much. Why, you'll be up all night now!" But this, too, elicited no response, though an inner smile of sorts shone through the slit of her eyes.

Baffled, he scratched his head and persisted. "Look here. At least let me bring you something to eat. You'll need your strength back for tonight. Do you want me to be blamed for not taking proper care of you?" Yet still she refused to budge, stubbornly clinging to her bed, though he felt sure she was wide awake now, probing him with her flickering laser beam, so that suddenly he felt a wave of panic in the dark room gloomy with twilight. "Come on!" he said, his voice cracking. "Get up! I'll wait for you downstairs and we'll go out. You'll see—the snow and the cold will wake you and we'll have a bowl of hot soup somewhere." Though not a muscle stirred, he felt her make an effort to talk. And suddenly she did. "Did you get a haircut?" she asked. He grinned at her. "Yes, I did," he answered, standing up and patting his head. "Down below on the street. They really clipped me, but it will grow back." She ignored this, however, sitting up and turning on the light. "Don't be angry with me," she said quietly, "but I'm not going to the opera tonight. I don't feel up to it. I'd better rest and keep off my foot. The last thing I need is to trip and fall again. You needn't feel bad for me. I've seen enough operas in my life. Why, they even took us to one at the conference. Why don't you go by yourself? It's awkward, I know, but you'll enjoy it. *Don Giovanni* is too good to miss."

Though he did his best to seem disappointed, he felt a surge of relief. Indeed, with an almost hysterical adamance she insisted that he go without her, even asking for her purse and handing him his ticket like a mother sending her son to the movies, assuring him, as she lay propped up by the pillow with her eyes wide open now, that he needn't worry and that she would soon get out of bed and have a meal sent up. It was her first day of real rest in ages; God knew how long her fatigue had been building up! She would, she promised, wait up for him and meanwhile read a book or listen to music on the radio. "Good, I'll try it," she said when told about Volume II of *Anna Karenina* that his daughter had given him by mistake. "The second half is fine because I read the book long ago and still remember a bit." And so, having gone through the motions of protesting, he went downstairs to fetch the book, which she hurriedly took from him at the door as if anxious to be rid of him. It was all he could do to persuade her to bring him her ticket too, since perhaps he could manage to sell it.

11

T OWARD EVENING the hotel came festively alive. Previously con-cealed light bulbs helped brighten the little lobby, so that the swords gleamed in their glass cases and the blue seas reddened on the old nautical maps. The desk was now staffed by the grandfather of the family, a genial, immaculately dressed man who sat reading a newspaper while now and then helping his grandchildren in the apartment with their homework. In one corner stood several valises, sure proof of fresh guests. Self-conscious of his new crew cut, Molkho checked his key and stepped out into the street, which, too, was lit by numerous lamps whose warm, bubbly glow created a holi-day feeling. People were doing their last-minute shopping and crowd-ing into the bars, and the night, with its clear skies above and last patches of snow on the sidewalk, had a special magic. Entering his little working-class restaurant, which was nearly empty at this hour, Molkho ordered the usual, substituting coffee for beer. But after-ward, looking for a taxi while glancing up at the still-reddish sky, he cursed his loneliness under his breath. How could you have left me all alone like this? he asked, picturing his wife back in Haifa, mak-ing supper for their daughter while he wandered, a stranger in a strange land.

The crowd in front of the opera house was unexpectedly small. Indeed, it was clear from the outset that he stood no chance of selling his extra ticket, for even before he began climbing the steps, tickets were being offered to him. The audience was different too: instead of the intense-looking young people of the night before, he was now surrounded by the most bourgeois of audiences. Over the posters by the entrance, large red stickers announcing some change in the program had been affixed diagonally. Could the performance have been canceled? Sure enough, inquiring of a couple standing there, he was told that the man who was to play Don Giovanni was sick and that, to his astonishment, the opera tonight would be Gluck's *Orpheus and Eurydice*. How could they go and change operas just like that? And who was this Gluck, whom he had never even heard of? The thought that he was to be deprived of *Don Giovanni* after all he had been through was thoroughly unacceptable. "Who ever heard of changing operas?" he asked the couple loudly. "Why, I came a long way to see *Don Giovanni!*" "You did? Where from?" "From Israel." "From Israel? Just to see an opera?" "Yes," he said, telling them about the special *Voles Opera* while they listened in amazement. "Why isn't there an understudy?" he asked. "I can't believe no one else can sing the part!" But the sympathetic couple merely shrugged and went inside, not knowing the answer themselves, leaving Molkho debating whether he shouldn't perhaps go to the movies or a nightclub instead. In the end, however, the ticket being paid for, he decided to see *Orpheus and Eurydice* and let himself be swept by the crowd into the familiar lobby, which now seemed to him dreary and plain. And there was nowhere even to lodge a complaint, for every single office was locked! That's the sort of people they are, he thought bitterly, going off to relieve himself in the men's room, whose four huge white walls seemed one big urinal. Just look where I've landed, he told himself, choking on his loneliness, as if his wife's death were a spring whose action had flung him to the far ends of the earth.

He was one of the first to take his seat, which was in the center of a front row. The audience kept drifting in, but the hall was still far from full. He felt indescribably weary, and the people around him looked gray and listless too. A row in front of him sat a couple that drew his attention, especially the man, who sat with his head hunched between his shoulders: tall and fortyish, he had a pocked red face whose sad, suspicious eyes darted nervously and a shabby black suit over which was thrown a dirty white scarf. The seat on Molkho's right, on the other hand, was occupied by a well-dressed, elderly German holding a large, fancy program that was partly in

English. Yet though Molkho asked to borrow it, he was feeling too tired and dispirited to make head or tails of it, even of the cast, which listed a female alto in the role of Orpheus. Bewildered, he asked his neighbor if it wasn't a misprint, to which the man replied in broken English that he hadn't the slightest idea, since he came from a small provincial town where they didn't have opera at all.

The orchestra began tuning up, and as if he were accompanying it, the man in the next row grew suddenly tense and emitted a series of small grunts that made his wife look worriedly about. Slowly the huge overhead lights were dimmed, the conductor strode forward, and the overture struck up, quick and forceful, while the pock-marked man swayed back and forth in time to it. Evidently he knew the score well, in fact, by heart, for he paused slightly before each transition, as if anticipating a new theme, so that Molkho wondered if he was perhaps an unemployed musician, possibly even a down-and-out conductor. Even when the music reached a crescendo, with new instruments joining in all the time, the man did not look up; head down, he kept listening intensely, conducting with his hands, springing up with the horns and kettledrums, and swaying rhythmi-cally again with the strings in preparation for the next bars, which he telegraphed with his body as if convinced that the orchestra was following him, only suddenly to freeze and cast such a haughty glance around him that the audience began to whisper. His wife alone remained perfectly quiet, her hand resting soothingly on his knee as though to keep him under control.

All at once the music stopped. The curtain rose, revealing a minimal, almost symbolic set that Molkho stared at resentfully. It seemed ugly to him, and as the music resumed again, dusky and constrained, he grieved inwardly for his lost *Don Giovanni*. The stage was apparently meant to represent a large hall, or perhaps something else, a street, city, or even world, through which a coffin was being carried by a singing entourage. Soon it was laid down, however, and a woman leaped out of it and fled like the wind. Next Orpheus appeared; he was indeed a heavyset young woman with a small harp in one hand, at which Molkho stared with profound hostility. The whole opera seemed to him a punishment. No, it isn't a misprint after all, he whispered to the fat German sitting next to him, who nodded back smilingly. Their tones clear and pure, the voices of the singers rose and clashed; what little action there was took place almost in slow motion to an excruciatingly slow poetic aria. Though he would have liked to doze off, Molkho felt it was out of the question. Ahead of him the man in black began to tremble, shaking his head so violently that his neighbors, roused from their theatrical spell, began to stare at him with mirth and revulsion, or even, like the middle-aged woman sitting next to him, with open horror. Yet the man seemed quite used to all this, which he dealt with by growing perfectly still for a while and glancing innocently around him. Before long, however, the music got the better of him again, and clenching his fists, he ordered the obedient orchestra to play on. The elderly German on Molkho's right seemed transfixed by the spectacle too, yet apparently not unpleasurably, for he stared at the man with a good-natured smile. Meanwhile, onstage, Orpheus was searching for Eurydice in her thick alto voice, which clashed with the other singers in long, complicated arpeggios that seemed inscrutably modern and harmonically elementary at once, making Molkho borrow the program again to see when the piece had been written. Unable to find the information anywhere, he felt more indignant than ever.

Act I was drawing to a close: Orpheus was told he could set forth for Hades, while the orchestra, faultlessly led by the man in the next row, broke into a strong, sweeping melody. The applause that broke out as the curtain fell was prolonged and patient, though not particularly loud, causing the man in black to bow his head modestly. He did not seem to notice the irate looks of his neighbors, who rose in protest as soon as the lights came on; rather, his head still bowed, he busily blew his nose while conversing quietly with his wife. Something about the couple, especially the deep serenity of the woman, made Molkho like them both. Was the man mentally ill? Or perhaps a concentration camp survivor who now haunted operas? But no, he looked too young for that.

Molkho went to the buffet, where he ate a piece of chocolate cake and drank a small glass of juice. From somewhere came the sound of voices speaking Hebrew, and he spun around to look for them, yet already they had vanished into thin air. Could it have been simply his homesick imagination? Tomorrow night he would be back in Haifa with his children; the countdown had already begun. On his way back to his seat, he met the couple from the lobby, who inquired how he was enjoying the performance. "It's not bad, not bad at all," he replied, wanting to ask them if they knew when Gluck lived. Quite a few people, he noticed, had changed places to get away from the man in black. Not his elderly neighbor, though, who collapsed heavily into his seat; bored though he was, he appeared to be highly pleased with the culture it took to spend the evening at an opera rather than a brothel.

The lights dimmed slowly, casting a bluish white pallor over the audience. The music began again, and the man in the next row braced himself and clenched his fists. He signaled to the wind section, cautioned the violins, grunted, and swayed; but this time, determined to stop him, his wife scolded him savagely until hushed by a chorus of furious hisses from around her. The man winced like a stricken animal, and Molkho, feeling a deep sorrow, cast a sympathetic glance in his direction just as Orpheus and Eurydice began their slow ascent from Hades. Molkho knew that Orpheus musn't look back as he led Eurydice after him, but he also knew, anxiously waiting for it to happen, that Orpheus would forget. And so he did, in Act III: with a loud cry, Eurydice disappeared down an opening while Orpheus, or rather the fat woman playing him, burst into a lovely, truly moving aria. The audience adored it, breaking into stormy applause, and the man in black, still waving his fists, threw his head back uncontrollably and stared slack-jawed into space as if swallowing the music, tears running down his cheeks. A green spotlight lit the stage, a little Greek temple, columns and all, descended from the ceiling, and Molkho knew with an inner pang that the man was crying for him too. Even the German on his right was sitting on the edge of his seat.

12

O**N HIS WAY BACK** from the opera, he felt the full weight of the long day, which lay in his chest like a sleeping giant that kept pulling him down. And yet he felt stirred, the music, the performers, the orchestra, the audience, all churning wildly inside him. At first, he thought he had entered the wrong hotel, for the lobby was full of people, mostly tall, elegant Scandinavians gathered in a corner where the paterfamilias and his wife stood pouring drinks in full evening dress. Surprised, Molkho made his way through the crowd, took his key off its hook, and hurried up to the legal adviser's room, determined to do something for their romance, which was still stalled at the starting line, even if it took a little foreplay (though a kiss on her sprained ankle, after removing the bandage, might be enough), after which he could crawl into bed and sleep next to her—a noncommittal move in itself, to be sure, but one sufficient to keep her hopes alive. Yet, no matter how loudly he knocked on her door, almost shouting her name, there was no answer from within.

As he was returning to his room, however, the elevator door opened and a chambermaid handed him a note with the address of a restaurant at which the legal adviser was dining and a request to join her there. Though so tired he could barely stand, he stepped back out into the cold night air, following the chambermaid through the slushy remains of the snow and down deserted little streets beneath a star-strewn sky until they arrived at a huge, crowded, smoke-filled establishment with old green velvet wall-hangings and loud music; there, he wove his way down to a cellar that was twice the size of the upstairs, an immense, poorly lit, barnlike place with big barrels of beer along the walls and endless tables of noisy customers. He noticed her at once, sitting by herself in her short fur coat, squeezed in at a little table covered with a checked cloth on which were an empty half-bottle of wine and a plate of several well-gnawed bones. She was lively and bright-eyed, despite the great crush, puffing on a cigarette and chatting with three men at the next table. There was no doubt about it, he told himself, feeling his spirits flag at once: she had been resurrected. Yet, though he wanted only to get away, she had already spied him and was nodding to him casually, quite indifferent to his attempts to fight his way through the boisterous crowd. At last, he reached her table and stood there wordlessly, feeling tired and bewildered, while she regarded him with wide-open eyes beneath her heavy mascara, not a trace left of her great sleep. There was not even a chair for him to sit on. The three men at the next table bowed to him, appraised him with a glance, said something to or about him in German, and broke out laughing, to which he replied with a feeble grin while a red-vested waiter with a witty, intellectual air deftly emptied the plate and ashtray and produced a small stool, on which he sat Molkho, who huddled there uncomfortably, a head shorter than everyone, the butt of a spate of jokes that seemed part of the general atmosphere. But somehow he did not mind his low perch, which at least made him feel out of harm's way.

The waiter stood to take his order. "No, thank you," Molkho said, "nothing for me," but the legal adviser insisted. "Come now, you have to have something. The beer here is first-rate. I won't let you pass it up." "All right," he said, "just a small glass of beer, but nothing to eat; really, I'm not hungry," because if he ate anything he would have to pay for her meal too, which had obviously been a large one. "But you must be hungry. Please, eat something," she repeated —rather oddly, he thought, so that, wondering whether she was concerned for him or merely exhibiting a new truculence, he gave in again, looking for inspiration at the diners around him until his eyes fell on a pungent-looking plate of blood-red sausage, and he asked the waiter for the same. Immediately, though, he regretted it. "But not such a big portion," he said in Hebrew to the legal adviser. "One sausage is enough; tell him one's enough," and signaling to the waiter, he called out, *"Eins,"* while she stifled an embarrassed smile.

Suddenly she seemed her old self again, the self-assured senior official attending international conferences at the public's expense. No
longer were they just two lonely people making contact on neutral
territory, and so, seeking to recoup his position, he said, first of all,
"Tell me how your ankle is." The question appeared to surprise her.
"It's fine," she murmured with a sharp glance at him, sounding
rather irritated, perhaps because she sensed that he would have liked
to bend down and examine it beneath the table. "I was worried about
you," he continued quietly, though slightly indignantly, realizing
that she and the errant foot were again on good terms. "I really
was." "Yes, I know," she said, her eyes zeroing in on him, "I could
feel it." There was a sudden distance between them, as though all
that had happened that day had happened to someone else.

"So how was *Don Giovanni?*" she asked, wanting, he felt un-
easily, to smoke him out. "It wasn't," he replied, managing to stay
calm and keep smiling, perhaps because she still sounded tentative,
as he told her about the last-minute switch to *Orpheus and Eurydice.*
Had she ever heard of it or of a composer named Gluck? Without
waiting for an answer, he handed her a program that he had found
on one of the seats after the curtain calls. She took it with an air of
bemusement and absently leafed through it while he reached into his
pocket for her ticket and explained at great length why he hadn't
sold it, there having been no demand and the box office having been
closed, though he was sure she could get a refund through her brother's travel agency, since it wasn't her fault that the opera was
changed. Yet, far from being interested in a refund, she only seemed
annoyed by his advice. "It's really of no importance," she murmured
rather formally, tearing up the ticket and dumping the pieces in the
ashtray. "You still haven't told me about the opera." None too exactly, he began to describe it for her, aggrievedly expressing his
amazement that Orpheus had been played by a woman. "But why
should that bother you?" she asked. Because, he explained, it annoyed him to see a big fat woman with a little harp singing about her
love for Eurydice. True, he got used to it after a while, but why bring
in a woman in the first place? Was it just someone's idea of being
contemporary and feminist? She looked at him pityingly. "I sup-

pose," she said, still turning the pages of the program, "that the part was originally written for an alto and that you can't find men with such high voices anymore."

The waiter arrived with a stein of beer and a single sausage so grotesquely huge that it made Molkho shudder. "That's not what I had in mind," he smiled. "I wanted one of those smaller ones." "Never mind," said the legal adviser. "They won't take it back, so you might as well eat it—it looks quite juicy. This is a famous beer cellar." Rising to bring him a jar of mustard from the next table while ordering coffee and cake for herself, she deftly arranged his napkin and handed him his knife and fork, seeking perhaps to repay him for all his care. Meanwhile, the men at the next table broke off their loud talk to crack some joke about the steaming knockwurst, their coarse laughter making him regret having ordered it even more, especially as he wasn't even hungry, just tired and slightly cowed, or perhaps simply sorry that she wasn't still silently sleeping in her soft hotel bed, with the snow blowing against the window. Why, what a magical time that was, he thought longingly, remembering the feeling of tunneling toward her, though it now seemed rather doubtful whether he had gotten anywhere.

Listlessly, in the orange gloom of the barnlike space, with its walls of dirty green velvet, amid the noise and the raucous music, he began cutting his sausage, eating it with the sleepy self-discipline learned long ago as a child when his mother had always made sure he left his plate clean. The reassuring little stool now felt like an interrogation seat, and her beady eyes, like a squirrel's catching sight of a nut, bored steadily into him, the target verified and ready to be pounced on. Running a hand through her short, girlish hair, she began to question him about the day, as if to ascertain whether there had really been such a thing or whether they simply had gone from night to night. Who, she asked, suddenly catching him off guard, had changed her sheet? He flushed, playing for time by pretending to think, only to break down and confess: the sheet had been sweaty and damp, and she had been too weak to change it herself. He was sorry if it had been indiscreet of him.

For a moment she said nothing, concentrating on her cigarette;

then, as if the time had come to talk frankly, she asked to be told about his wife, about the kind of woman she was. "My wife?" said Molkho, at a loss. "Why my wife?" "But why not?" asked the legal adviser. "I'm terribly curious." "I would have thought that by now you'd have heard all about her," he said. "Yes," she replied, "I have. But now I want to hear it from you." But he felt this was not the place to discuss his dead wife, this huge barn into which more and more people kept pouring as the movies and theaters let out, apparently because it was known for its capacity, which was, however, fast becoming exhausted.

"She was an intellectual," said Molkho, seizing on the first word that came to mind while looking at the legal adviser, who returned his gaze steadily. "She was very honest . . . I mean, very critical . . . of herself too. An intellectual. Nothing was ever good enough for her. She never felt fulfilled or happy. And maybe she never even wanted to be. Although . . ."

He stopped in midsentence because just then there came a sound of thumping from upstairs, followed by such loud singing that he couldn't hear himself think. "And I'm not an intellectual at all," he concluded, though it wasn't what he'd started out to say. "Yes, I've noticed that," she said gently, regarding him with a newborn affection that only made him feel more certain that the coup de grace was imminent. Despairingly he glanced toward the entrance, through which new customers were still elbowing, checking their coats and plunging into the crowd. Suddenly he missed his wife so badly that it hurt. The legal adviser bent toward him, leaning so far across the table that he felt her hair brush his face, in her eyes a cold, intellectual glitter. "And so," she whispered, "you killed her little by little —I only realized that today. . . ." For a second he felt his blood curdle; yet at once, as if a soft quilt were thrown over him, he felt a warm, rich happiness in his veins. Slowly his eyes met hers. The thought was not new. "You're killing me," his wife used to say to him, although it was odd that the two women should think the same thing when they had never met. Wearily he smiled, feeling his near-naked scalp beneath his crew cut. What else, faced with such a verdict, could he do? He had no wish or way to defend himself and was tired of arguing. Indeed, he had stopped arguing completely during the past year. "You should know," he said brightly, "that I did my best to take care of her." "Yes, I do know," she answered with compassion. "I know everything. I want you to try to understand . . ."

The waiter deftly slipped two checks, his and hers, under their plates and disappeared. Molkho made up his mind to pay only his; she would get her share back from the office anyhow. "Try to understand," she persisted, not wanting to hurt him yet intent on pursuing her insight. "I don't mean that you did it consciously, but I felt today that you were trying to kill me too." He blinked happily, deliciously drunk; the German beer had gone to his Levantine head, and the juicy sausage, seemingly reconstituted there, was now crawling through his stomach. Feeling slightly seasick, as though he were on board a big, throbbing ship pitching in the waves, he struggled to stay calm and take his time answering. And she, too, was silent now, perhaps shocked by her own words. "To kill you too?" His big brown eyes opened wide. "But why?" "That's what I'd like to know," she said. Slowly he drained the last drops of beer from his glass. The men at the next table had suddenly stopped talking, as though aware that something significant was going on between the two foreigners.

But Molkho was tired of arguments and would have gladly postponed this one, too, until they were home, if ever they met there again. It's a lucky thing we're not on the same flight tomorrow, he told himself, looking at her eyes, whose feverish glitter repelled him, the gleeful, intellectual glitter of her clever, twist-all mind. "In that case, you must have killed your husband too," he said with a curt laugh. "Perhaps I did," she answered candidly, "though not in the same way as you." He shivered, wanting to put an end to it. The noise level was unbearable and he had been on his feet since six o'clock that morning. "Shall we?" he asked, laying a warm hand on hers, which let itself be held like an old bird.

He followed her quietly to the entrance, glancing over her shoulder at her wristwatch, whose hands said almost midnight, before planting a light kiss on her dry forehead, which had a slightly sweetish taste. Mechanically he apologized for his tiredness and for having to catch a plane in the morning, and she urged him to go to bed, though she herself, she said, was not ready to turn in yet. And so they parted, and he stepped out into the frigid night, thinking of the shabby man at the opera, from whose strange, contorted movements the music had seemed to flow. Still, I enjoyed it, he thought, that's one opera I'll never forget, even if I can't sing a note of it. In the hotel, which he found unaided, all the lights were already out; the bar in the corner was shut, and the only keys still in their cubbyholes were his and hers. *"Sechs,"* said Molkho with the last of his strength, his hand held out as though to salute the student with the book, who was on the night shift again; then, recalling that the young man spoke English, he asked to be awakened at five. The student wrote it down, though just to be on the safe side, he gave Molkho an alarm clock as well.

PART III SPRING

1

D URING THE THREE-HOUR WAIT at Orly for his flight to
Tel Aviv, Molkho bought some perfume for his mother-
in-law and a large bar of chocolate for his mother while
trying every half-hour to phone his cousin, whose home didn't answer. Once in the air, above the Alps, dinner having already been
served, he took out a large sheet of paper, wrote "Paris" on one side
and "Berlin" on the other, extracted the receipts he had saved from
his wallet, and began to calculate his expenses, racking his memory
for every cup of coffee, piece of cake, gift, or taxi he had paid for
while thinking of his days abroad, which now seemed to have passed
with a sort of muddled intensity. Yet though the Berlin figures tallied
to the mark, he was unable to account for three hundred and thirty
francs spent in Paris. No matter how hard he shut his eyes and tried
reliving every moment in the French capital, the missing sum continued to elude him, until finally, somewhere over the Aegean, he gave
it up and went for a stroll in the aisles to see if there were any
passengers he knew.

In Israel, stepping out of the terminal, he was assailed at once
by a hot, dry wind that heralded the onset of spring, and noticed that
the rows of oleanders were already in bloom. The winter, he saw, was
gone for good, though the harassed-looking Israelis running back
and forth seemed not to have realized it yet and might take several
weeks to do so. He telephoned his mother to inform her of his arrival
and then looked around for a cab, half-hoping that the college student would be there to meet him, although he had expressly told him
not to bother. And indeed, the young man did not.

At the taxi stand Molkho was approached by a woman who

asked if he wished to share a cab to Haifa, and he agreed. The woman, who had just returned from a shopping spree in London, was in the best of spirits, having managed to slip through customs without paying a cent of duty. Unabashedly she told Molkho about all the money she had saved and about the weakness of the British pound, and all the while, their driver, who had never been abroad at all, listened to her recite the bargain prices in London with resentful amazement, all but ready to set out for there himself. Molkho listened sleepily, glancing now and then at his vivacious fellow passenger surrounded by her bundles and feeling thankful he hadn't surrendered his single status in Berlin. Halfway to Haifa, after they had heard the 11 P.M. news, he made a few discreet inquiries about her own status, only to find out that she had a husband who was very much alive, a Sephardi from Jerusalem, like him. "There's no place like Jerusalem," she exclaimed, telling him how she and her husband missed it. "Don't you?" she asked. "Not especially," answered Molkho. And whenever he did, a single visit was enough to cure him.

The taxi let him off by his house. The street was deserted, and he felt as though a hundred years had passed since he had waited in it for his mother-in-law on the night of his wife's death. The apartment was dark. Oddly, though, the double bed, piled high with blankets, was back in his bedroom, the single one having been pushed aside to make way for it. The high school boy was asleep in his room, and Molkho woke him and kissed him. "Who moved the double bed in from the terrace?" he demanded. "Some friends who slept over," answered the boy. "And how is grandma?" asked Molkho worriedly. "She's fine," his son said, recoiling a bit when caressed. In fact, he had had several meals with her in the old-age home, and last Friday night his brother and sister had joined them. "I missed you," said Molkho, a lump in his throat, suddenly thinking of the shabby man drunk on the music of the opera. He wanted to talk, to tell about his trip, but the boy was too sleepy and had an early class in the morning.

2

E ARLY THE NEXT MORNING Molkho called his mother-in-law to
say that he was back. He told her about her niece in Paris, but
only briefly because he wished to save the rest for a visit that afternoon, even though she did not seem too keen on it. "Why bother?"
she asked. "You must have lots to do, and you'll see me on Friday
anyway; you can tell me everything then." But Molkho was not to be
dissuaded. "I have some gifts for you," he informed her happily.
"Gifts?" she asked, a note of worry in her voice.

He went the next afternoon. It was a warm, bright day. The
teacups, sugar, and the crackers were already set out in a corner of
her spic-and-span room. As usual, she seemed in good health, although a trifle thinner, and her squint had gotten slightly worse
beneath her heavy glasses. Without further ado, he took the gifts
from a plastic bag: a white nightgown with a lace collar and the
collapsible cane that folded in four like a magic flute. "It's perfect for
you," he told her, "because you don't generally need it, so you can
take it out of your bag when you do." She seemed quite bewildered,
even slightly distressed, and had no end of trouble opening and
shutting it, despite all his efforts to show her how simple it was.
Finally she thanked him, laid the cane aside, and promised with a
smile to practice. That was the moment for the last present, a bottle
of perfume from Orly—the same scent, explained Molkho, that she
had liked so much when brought some from Paris on his last visit
there with his wife.

The old woman blushed, took off her glasses, and gripped the
vial of perfume in her veiny hands, staring at the label. She seemed
to want to say something but, with that deep inner control of hers,

refrained; instead, putting down the bottle, she thanked him perfunctorily, and he turned to his tea and crackers, telling her about Paris and her niece, who seemed so contented and full of life, not at all bitter or hypercritical like his wife. The old woman nodded understandingly, her stiff white hair falling forward. He told her about the snow too—in fact, about each single day, even the visit to the opera —while she did her best to follow, glancing from time to time out the window at the sun setting into the clear, mild evening above the bushes turning red at their branch tips. "To think that winter is already over here and that there I ran into a blizzard!" he exclaimed. "Don't be so quick to bury the winter," retorted his mother-in-law; and so, changing the subject, he asked her about the high school boy, how he had been and what he had eaten, and about her old-age home. Had anything happened there in his absence? Yet though he inquired about several residents whose names he had heard mentioned by his wife, all were still alive and well.

Perhaps, Molkho found himself hoping, the old lady would invite him to have dinner with her at the home. But she gave no indication of it, and if anything, seemed eager for him to depart— something, however, that he was not in any hurry to do. The two of them, after all, had shared the same adventure, and even if it was over now, the deep bond between them remained. Sinking deeper into his armchair, he watched the dusk fall on her wrinkled old face and suddenly confessed, as if he had done it just for her sake, "I was in that Berlin of yours too." "In Berlin?" she asked, astonished, perhaps even upset. "Yes," he said. His wife never wanted to go there with him, so now he had seized the opportunity. "All those countries are so close anyway," he added breezily, as though to prove that he was free now and that the rules had changed. "You went by yourself?" she queried. "Yes," he said, not wanting to distress her, "by myself," and he told her about the travel agency that arranged opera tours of Europe. The idea of his becoming an opera buff clearly seemed bizarre, if not perverse, to her, for at once he felt her hostile reaction, though controlling herself she held her peace and waited for him to go on; but instead, he asked about her memories of Berlin, and especially about the house she had lived in, which she was not at all eager to recall, mentioning only that it had had an elevator, the only one on the street. Producing from his pocket the hotel map of Berlin, Molkho asked her to show him where it was. "You mean the street?" she asked with an unsure laugh, holding the map upside down, still unable to fathom his being there. She turned the map around, tried taking off her glasses, complained about the small print, went to bring her reading glasses, and announced that they were no better, while Molkho patiently sought to help her, pointing out his hotel, which was circled in red, and the Berlin Wall, though he could see she wasn't really listening. "Nothing is left of it anyway," she said to him. "It's all been destroyed and rebuilt." At last, she laid the map on the table and compromised by promising to ask one of her friends and perhaps even to try remembering herself.

Out in the street the last rays of daylight lingered on. The hot spring wind grew stronger, oblivious of the rain clouds still drifting slowly in the west, and Molkho thought, Here I am free to choose any woman I want, even two, and all I lack is the desire. He stared at the sexy model in an illuminated bus-station ad and recalled with a smile how the little old squirrel had said to him, all excited by her discovery, "You killed her little by little." Did his mother-in-law think so too? And yet she had been his faithful partner, even if lately she had been acting rather coolly toward him. He remembered how, eight or nine years ago, his wife had wanted to leave him, how she even had run away for a few days, only to return in the end, and how, knowing that she would, he had managed not to panic. The children were small then. Once again he felt how much he missed her. He pictured her lying gloomily in bed, listening to music and reading. "What's left of her now?" he mused, clenching his fists, imagining her rotting like the binding of an old book.

He noticed a brand-new supermarket and went in to have a look at it, having no end of time at his disposal; but returning to his car, he spied his mother-in-law sitting by herself at the bus stop in her winter coat and red cap, her glasses glinting in the sun and her old cane gripped in one hand. Why, he wondered indignantly, hadn't she asked him for a ride? He stood staring at her hypnotically, listening to her bus climb the hill until it appeared and stopped.

Quickly, erectly, as if she intended to live forever, her ticket in her other hand, she boarded it and disappeared. I should see a little less of her, thought Molkho. Maybe I scare her. It wasn't as if his wife had asked him to take special care of her.

3

AFTER THE SABBATH DINNER that Friday night, when the table had been cleared, his mother-in-law reached for her reading glasses and handed Molkho the map of Berlin, on which the conjectured location of her house had been marked beside the name of the street, written in an unfamiliar hand. Her recently arrived friend from Russia, who had been her neighbor back in the prewar days when her husband had worked in the Soviet embassy in Berlin, had helped find it for her. It was far from Molkho's hotel—in fact, in the eastern part of the city. So much for his sixth sense of being near it! But why, asked the old woman, did it matter? Did he intend to go back? Of course not, he replied, he was simply curious. In fact, the whole thing was unimportant; he just thought she would be happy to know he had been near his wife's birthplace. She looked at him suspiciously, her eyes a dark velvet. Since his return from abroad, she seemed to harbor some resentment against him, and so he placatingly asked about the new friend from Russia she had been spending so much time with. The fact of the matter was that there seemed something strange, even slightly absurd, in the intensity of this relationship, which had resumed after a break of close to fifty years. Could it simply be a way for his mother-in-law to distance herself from him, or even from her grandchildren, for whom she also seemed lately to have so little patience? Why, tonight she had not even wanted to watch the news with them, rushing home as quickly as she could when the meal was over.

4

T HE NEXT MORNING he set out to visit his mother in Jerusalem, almost stopping on the way to pick a branch of regal white almond blossoms. He went to see some old friends first, arriving at his mother's in time for lunch, which was already waiting on the table. Though she scolded him for his lateness, his German crew cut pleased her greatly. "It's very becoming," she declared while refusing to accept the scarf he had brought as a gift. "I told you not to bring me anything!" She even declined the bar of Swiss chocolate he had bought her until he finally prevailed on her to take it. He ate the peppers she had stuffed for him, listening to her stories, complaints, and opinions, while praying—in vain, as it happened—that she would not refill his plate. Afterward, he tried napping in his childhood bed, but no sooner had he dozed off than he became aware of her lurking behind the door. At last, he rose and went out to sit lethargically on the dusty terrace, looking down on decrepit old Jaffa Road below and breathing the heavily accented Jerusalem air. He drank the coffee he was served, munching almonds and walnuts while his mother, a corpulent woman whose fallen face was painted like a savage's, questioned him about his trip, how much it had cost and whom had he met, crudely trying to ferret out everything, especially if there had been a woman. "Yes and no," he replied. "How yes and how no?" "Just for part of it." "For which part?" "The opera part, in Berlin." "Which opera?" "I suppose you'd know if I told you," he laughed. "Why, I'd never even heard of it myself!" "Then why go so far for it?" "To see what it was like." "And where's this woman now?" "Out of my life," he answered patiently. "But who was she?" probed his mother. "Someone from the office," he answered, refusing to name names. "All right then," she said, "just don't be in any hurry." "I'm not," replied Molkho. "You mean it's just sex?" she inquired. "Why, I don't believe you know what that is any more!" Flabbergasted, he laughed, popping nuts into his mouth so fast that they seemed to fly into it, stealing a glance at this berserk woman while doing his best to keep his temper. "I suppose you know all about that too," he said, trying to keep calm. "Well then, tell me if I'm wrong," she persisted, "tell me if you feel like having sex." "What on earth are you talking about?" he snapped, turning red. "Forget it, it doesn't matter," said his mother. "For my part, you can have all the sex you want. Just don't be in any hurry. Take a good look around. You suffered enough these past years. You cared for her enough, it's time someone cared for you. You'll see, you'll have women running after you, they'll be knocking on your door. Your children are grown up and you're financially secure. Just don't get involved too quickly. Try them out first. Try out a whole lot of them before you make up your mind."

He listened in silence, amused by her unself-conscious brutality, gazing down the hallway that led to the twilit rooms of the apartment and imagining a woman reclining in each, waiting to be tried out. Gazing down at the triangle formed by the three old streets of King George, Ben-Yehudah, and Jaffa and at a group of children off to some activity in the blue shirts and ties of a youth movement, he recalled the British policeman who had directed traffic there and the green tie he himself had dutifully worn when he had gone to such activities too. "There aren't as many women as you think," he said with sudden bitterness. "There's no one out there but desperate divorcées, psychotic spinsters, and widows who've murdered their husbands." "What kind of crazy thing is that to say?" she asked, shocked by his attitude, her anxiety only increasing when he wouldn't answer. If only he would come back to live in Jerusalem, he would be sure to find someone—someone from his old class or school, for example, whom he had grown up with and who would be more like him, perhaps even a cousin of theirs. After all, all of Jerusalem remembered him and asked about him. "Who?" he challenged. Her friends, said his mother. "They're always interested when I tell them about you." "What, those old biddies of yours?" The idea was so daft that he laughed out loud with sheer delight. "A penny for your thoughts," coaxed his mother. "I have no thoughts," he retorted. "She's only been dead for half a year, and I still need time to get over it." But his mother was relentless. He should visit her more often, once every two months was not enough; did he think she could find him a new wife over the telephone? "The gas alone costs a fortune," he said gently, looking back down at the deserted Sabbath streets; in fact, he had neglected her in recent years, for his wife had sapped all his strength. "And no one pays my car expenses, either." "Then take a bus on Friday and stay over. You can sleep in your old bed and go home on Saturday night." The idea, however, did not appeal to him: taking buses was not his idea of travel, especially as he was planning to buy a new car. Naturally, his mother was against this too. She rose, went to fetch a brown paper bag, and refilled the empty plate of nuts against his protests. "That's enough," he begged. "Don't give me any more. I can't stop eating and lately I've been putting on weight." "That's from your trip," said his mother. "People don't notice, but they put on weight abroad."

5

NIGHT CAME and Molkho seemed in no hurry to leave Jerusalem. After rejecting the idea of calling several old school friends, fearful of the disinterest he might hear in their voices, he agreed to go over some recent bank statements of his mother's to make sure there were no mistakes in them. Down below, the ugly old shopping district began filling up with people, many of them fresh from the Saturday soccer match. A desert chill was in the air. Feeling his meal burble inside him, he padded off to the bathroom for relief. It was a room that he liked, generously proportioned and high-ceilinged in the old style, with a tall bathtub, its elaborate feet of reddish iron resembling the claws of a peacock. He kept the light off, preferring to sit in the dark room, which was faintly lit by a purplish glow trickling through the window. From here the view was different, more cheeringly picturesque, with its red roofs of the old quarters of Jerusalem and its distant, partly wooded hills. Visible too were the backyards of the buildings on the street, which had mostly been converted into offices and banks. Breathing in the clean night air with a sigh of pleasure, Molkho peeked into the tall straw laundry basket that was covered with a cracked enamel bowl, the same bowl that had been the steering wheel of bus number 9 when, sitting on the toilet as a child, he had driven it all around town, handing the passengers tickets of torn toilet paper. He finished, rose, and bent down to peer into the still fizzing bowl for signs of blood; then, yanking the long chain that reminded him of the emergency brake of a railroad car, he watched the water gush from the tank, smiling with pleasure at the train wreck once again averted in the nick of time. He still did not pull up his pants, however. Bare-bottomed he leaned out the window, ravenously drinking in the night, eyes combing first the aging old neighborhood and then the sky for three stars, which meant he could run tell his father that the Sabbath was over and that he was permitted to smoke. Below, in the white glare of a streetlight, he made out his old car, dry and dusty-looking; yet as sorry as he felt for it, he knew he did not want it anymore. His pants still down around his ankles, he was a little fat boy again, his parents' only child, his thirty years of married life vanished like a dream. Had she, he wondered, been taken by, or given to, someone else by now? Was her spirit finally at peace, quiet and resting somewhere, her compulsive criticizing over at last? Or was she still carrying on in the heavenly spheres, going from one to another and finding fault with each? Was the universe not good enough for her even now? Did she remember him?

6

B ECAUSE SUDDENLY THERE WAS NO ONE to criticize him anymore, it had stopped all at once, though he woke up in the
morning and went to bed at night still expecting it: "Just look at
yourself! How can you eat like that? Stand straight! Don't twist your
hair! The idea, stop being ridiculous!" Her voice lived on in him, and
he listened all the time, so that—"You must shower at least once a
day!"—if he sometimes forgot to, or was so tired at night that he
skipped it, he felt guilty and positively unwashed. The days came at
him out of nowhere, one after another, blanketing him in a spongy
morass through which he had to burrow his way to freedom. As if
sated by his trip to Europe, he hardly listened to music any more,
nor were there any concerts, for the Philharmonic was on a foreign
tour. He passed the days by reading *Anna Karenina,* starting this
time with Volume I, the old library copy giving him the odd feeling
that he would be tested on it. As for Volume II, it arrived in the mail
two days after his return in a brown office envelope bearing the motto
"Pay Your Taxes on Time." Though in it was a thank-you note
expressing the hope that his flight had been a pleasant one, its
sender was not to be seen in the office, neither in the cafeteria nor on
the stairs; she must have been avoiding him while reporting on her
conference in Berlin, not to mention itemizing her expenses, which
no doubt included the opera tickets. What had she told her family
about him? A dud. The sooner forgotten, the better. He even tried
killing me there. *Killing* you? Yes, killing me. The thought of it
made Molkho smile. I'd better be more careful, he told himself. True,
I'm in no hurry. I'm only fifty-two, but I'd better do a little research
and find out what my type is. And I'd better take off a few pounds

too. He even resumed his evening walk, remembering how he had forced himself to go out each night for a slow, short turn around the block during the last months of his wife's illness.

Like most intellectuals, she had never cared for Nature, which had bored her. Now he again walked by himself, sometimes still flicked by the damp, raw tail of winter, whose fog drifting in from the sea shrouded the mountain and sprayed him with drops of fragrant rain. He roamed the streets of different neighborhoods, sometimes stopping in front of a window lit by the ghostly glare of a television and listening to the laughing voices of the women within, or else sitting down on the bench of a deserted bus stop beside its illuminated ad, stared at by German shepherds selling dog food, huge boxes of detergent, or the faces and bodies of shapely women, against which he would occasionally lean his head, feeling their chill incorporeity. Mainly, though, he kept an eye on the new cars, pausing to peer at their interiors and dashboards while trying to guess what each knob and button was for. His own car, when he came home to it, seemed gray and tired-looking; and though his trip to Europe had eaten into his savings, the high school boy was a prodigal spender, and the German reparations had stopped coming, he was still determined to buy a new one, especially as the market was jittery and there were rumors of fresh automobile taxes. He had to act fast, he admonished himself, choosing a Citroën. "It's a more feminine car than my old one," he told the salesman with a grin, finally signing the order form after circling the floor model for several hours. The salesman took offense. "What do you mean 'feminine'? Just because it's French?" "Feminine *and* French," insisted Molkho. "Just look at those curves, how she bellies down below, the flare of that rear of hers . . ."

7

G ETTING RID OF HIS OLD CAR, however, was far from easy.
There were no buyers at the price he was asking; mechanical
problems kept turning up that he had no idea existed; and in the end
he began to fear that he would not be able to sell it. Finally, after
bringing it back a few times to the garage for repairs and bodywork,
he lowered the price and found a buyer at once, only to discover that
his new car had not arrived from France yet. Forced to travel by bus,
he began coming late to work, so that, though he still had special
status as a widower, he was summoned one day to the office of the
director, an affable man who had both been to the funeral and paid a
condolence call on Molkho at home. He shook Molkho's hand, asked
how he was, and inquired about his children and mother-in-law. "Is
that old lady still alive? How is she getting along? And how are your
kids coping? You have to let them let it all out!" He seemed relieved
to hear that Molkho had not five children but only three and that the
youngest was a junior in high school. Well, then, it wasn't so bad; he
himself had an aunt who spent a whole year of her life attending to
practical arrangements after her husband passed away. Though at
first Molkho thought that the purpose of the summons was to fix him
up with the director's aunt, this roundabout opening was simply a
way of popping a different question—namely, was he prepared to
resume a full work load, since the director had a special job for him?
The deadline for the state comptroller's report was rapidly approaching, and it was imperative to check the books of certain small northern townships that were being run by inexperienced officials, several
of whom were suspected of fraud. Most suspicious was a village
called Zeru'a, the council manager of which, a young semistudent,

had recently filed an annual statement of such irregular character that it was impossible to know which he was—hopelessly naive or cunningly corrupt. Both he and the village treasurer would have to appear before the comptroller, but perhaps Molkho should pay them a visit first and spot any malfeasances before they could be covered up. Naturally, the office would pay his expenses, and the work was sure to be interesting. How about it? Did he feel up to it, or was he still too busy with personal matters in consequence of his wife's death?

At first, Molkho balked; psychologically he did not yet feel ready for the task, especially as the responsibility was great; yet the more the director pressed him with bureaucratic geniality, the more he began to reconsider. After all, why not? The office had gone out of its way, in recent years, to be nice to him. In fact, his wife had been shocked to hear that upon discovery of her illness he had gone at once to ask his boss for special consideration. Was he already, she had wanted to know, feeling as desperate as that? So that now, seeing the file waiting for him on the director's desk, or rather several files banded together, he took them and left. Passing the legal adviser's door, he decided to stop in and say hello. She was sitting behind her desk in her large, sunny office with a pair of glasses perched on her nose, talking on the phone; yet she smiled at him and he smiled back, waited for her to hang up, and said, "I was just passing by and thought of you. How was your trip back? How's your ankle?" Holding a pencil, she rose amusedly to greet him, her squirrel eyes squinting in the sunlight looking slantier than ever. Her hair, too, Molkho saw, had been cropped even shorter and more girlishly. They stood there for a while chatting like old acquaintances, paring down their shared adventure into little particles of nothing. His heart aching for his lost wife and his own empty solitude, Molkho clutched the files to his chest.

8

CURIOUS AND APPREHENSIVE, he took the files home with him. At once, he saw they were a mess. Though the documentation of government budgets and loans, adding up to millions of shekels, seemed in order, the village's records of how the money had been disbursed were pitifully inadequate. Most of them were handwritten and had pinned to them a small number of unacceptable receipts scribbled on loose notebook paper and signed with illegible scrawls. Despite his initial reaction that it was a clear case for the police, he tried going over the material, even attempting to telephone the council manager in Zeru'a the next morning. But it was impossible to get through; either there was no answer or for long periods the phone rang busy. Finally, it was picked up by a boy who said something incomprehensible in a gruff accent. "Let me talk to Ben-Ya'ish," Molkho said, but he was left waiting for a long time on the line, over which he heard the voices of playing children and something that sounded like a schoolbell. Then there was silence, and after waiting in vain for the boy to return, he hung up.

An hour later he called again; once more the line was busy. At two o'clock, before quitting work, he tried a last time; now the phone was answered by a girl who spoke clearly. "Tell me," Molkho asked her, "is the phone you're speaking from in a school?" "Yes," she said. "Then let me talk with the principal or one of the teachers," he requested. "They've all gone home," said the girl, "but the janitor's here." "Then give me the janitor," said Molkho. But the janitor was hard of hearing and apparently none too bright. "No Ben-Ya'ish," was all he kept saying, eager to hang up. "Then let me talk to the girl again," said Molkho, loath to give up after having gotten this far, but the janitor had no idea whom he meant.

The next morning he phoned again and got through to a secretary, who was apparently also a teacher. "Ya'ir Ben-Ya'ish isn't here today," she said in a pleasantly husky voice. "He's in Tel Aviv." Molkho explained who he was and that it was urgent, and the woman promised to tell the council manager, who would be sure to call back the next day. "What about the treasurer?" asked Molkho. The treasurer, however, was indisposed and had no home telephone.

The next day there was no call from the village, so Molkho phoned again. Once more it took forever to get the secretary, who, though sounding more suspicious, promised that Mr. Ben-Ya'ish would be in the next morning and would return the call. Outside the window a warm spring shower fell briefly, evoking a pungent smell of blossoms from the gray streets. The director's office called to see what progress Molkho had made. "Then drive up there yourself," he was told when he mumbled an inconclusive answer. "What, in my own car?" he asked, thinking of his new Citroën. "Yes, don't worry," was the answer. "We'll cover all your expenses."

9

T HAT EVENING he consulted a map to see exactly where Zeru'a was and discovered that it was way up in the Galilee, surrounded by Arab villages. In the morning he rose to find the streets wet, as if a heavy but silent rain had fallen all night. The northbound roads were packed with huge army trucks bringing tanks, prefabs, and other equipment back from Lebanon, where the Israeli pullout was in full swing. Once again, Molkho thought of his wife. She had been bitterly opposed to the Lebanese war and now it was ending.

On the highway to Acre the traffic was backed up. A prefab had fallen from a truck and blocked the road, and soon after there was an accident; by an overturned car, surrounded by police, a large, disheveled woman sat screaming on a stretcher. When Molkho slowed down to get a look at her, the policemen waved him on. "Step on it, step on it," they shouted angrily at the passing vehicles, "this isn't a sideshow here." And so he drove on, not turning on the radio, so as to listen to the motor, which was still being broken in, and even passing up a female hitchhiker so as not to overload the car in the hills ahead. The light drizzle stopped, a fierce sun emerged cocksurely from behind the tattered clouds, and the asphalt was suddenly dry.

At Karmiel he stopped, took off his jacket, and entered a diner for a second breakfast. Through the window of the restaurant a chain of limestone hills formed an unbroken wall leading north. He could see the same mountains from his own house in Haifa, yet only as an abstract blue line; now, however, they loomed solidly and massively before him. When he rose to pay, he made sure to ask for a receipt. Fancy me an investigator with an expense account.

Several kilometers out of Karmiel, after consulting his map, he left the highway and headed north on a narrow old road that began an abrupt climb into the mountains. He drove slowly on the steep curves, sticking to second gear and keeping an eye on the RPMs, which appeared on a special indicator; but the road seemed endless, pressing on past forests and tangled gullies along the narrow, rutted asphalt, on which the only traffic was an occasional army vehicle or Arab tractor that forced Molkho, afraid for his new car, onto the shoulder before continuing his steady ascent to dizzying heights. Halfway to his destination he stopped at the top of a rise to rest the engine, which was air-cooled and had no heat gauge. This car is too sophisticated for me, he thought, although perhaps he would appreciate it more on the easier drive to Jerusalem. Meanwhile, he parked it beneath a big pine tree and went to relieve himself in the bushes, examining his penis, which here, in the clear, pure air, amid the murmur of leaves and the flowers and rocks of the Galilee, resembled a dark little animal, rather comic in the loyal arching of its spume onto the thick carpet of dry pine needles that absorbed it without a sound or trace. She was the first and only woman I ever slept with, he thought. It would be easier if there had been others, but I was too faithful. He shook the last drops, which looked rather greenish to him, into the air, regretting not having urinated on one of the stones, against whose light background the color would have stood out. Zipping his fly, he turned to face the wind, reminded of the country near Jerusalem: the same light asphalt dating back to British times, the same black curbstones, the same pine and cypress trees—just fresher and moister, not powdered with desert aridity like the Judean Hills. A sharp feeling of déjà vu told him he had been here before, yes, on this very hilltop, where he had perhaps stopped to rest or even spend the night, for he had been here on foot, on a Scout or army hike many years ago, brought to see one of the scenic ravines of the Galilee, and the memory flowed sharply through him, the adventure of a sheltered boy from Jerusalem whose parents never ventured beyond Tel Aviv. Once he could depend on his wife, who was better at it than he was, to remember times and places, but now he was on his own.

But when, soon after, he reached the village, which was little more than an overgrown farming cooperative of the type established for new immigrants in the 1950s, the feeling of familiarity faded quickly, yielding to a dreary sense of desolation. It was a place in which nothing seemed to have changed in thirty years: the same peeling little houses on the same concrete columns, with here or there a new story or wing; the same little orchards on the same rocky, rust-colored earth; the same chicken runs and sheds, with the same untended fields between them dotted by the same scraggly trees; the same narrow approach road passing through an antiterrorist perimeter fence and suddenly, for no apparent reason, turning into a broad thoroughfare that led to a center boasting several shops and a deserted bus stop. Molkho stopped by a tall electric pole to which was nailed a bulletin board plastered with posters from the last elections, one of them bearing the repeated picture of a smiling, stubbly young man. A heavy silence hung over the place, as if it were abandoned, though somewhere in the distance the chug of a tractor was drowned out by the clunk of a water pump.

A woman leading a fat sheep on a rope showed him the way to

the school, and Molkho, taking out his files and locking the car, headed toward it into the wind, noticing the snowy peak of Mount Hermon between two houses, so big and near that his heart leapt. Crossing a playground and passing a water fountain, where again he had the sensation of someplace revisited, he climbed a short flight of stairs to the school, hearing schoolchildren singing old Passover songs with the same gruff accent as the boy's on the phone. A passing teacher pointed out the council manager's office at the end of a hallway. The room itself, however, was empty and dark; its blinds were lowered, an obsolete map of the country hung on a wall beside photographs of long-dead presidents and prime ministers, an accordion case leaned against a chairless desk, and several baskets of vegetables stood by a table on which lay an electric heating fork. There was no file cabinet or evidence of an office in sight, and Molkho felt instantly depressed. What am I doing here? he asked himself.

Just then the bell rang, and the children rushed out of their classes with a war whoop. Footsteps approached; no doubt word of his arrival had spread, and perhaps the children had been let out early because of it. But it was only the overweight and out-of-breath secretary, who, it seemed, was also the music teacher, for a bright red accordion was strapped like a baby sling to her chest. Standing on ceremony, he introduced himself with glum formality. "So you came after all," she said. "But Ben-Ya'ish isn't here yet. He must be on his way." "Didn't you tell him I was coming?" asked Molkho. "Of course," said the secretary, "and he suggested that meanwhile you go over the books with the treasurer." "Then the treasurer is feeling better?" asked Molkho. "More or less," said the secretary. "I'll find someone to take you to his home." She hurried back out of the room, the accordion still strapped to her chest, and returned a minute later with a dark-skinned girl, who—such, later on, was Molkho's first memory of her—stood in the unlit hallway surrounded by a crowd of children. She was so thin and straight, as though delicately carved out of ebony, with such painfully large steel-rimmed glasses that at first he mistook her for a boy, even though she was wearing a black leotard. "Take this man to your father," the secretary told her. She stared seriously up at him with her dark, exotic eyes and turned at once to guide him with the pack of children on her heels.

Outside the soft wind licked at their faces, and the afternoon light stretched tautly over the mountains. "I wouldn't advise it," said the secretary as he started to lead the girl to his car. "It's not a long way, but it's muddy and rocky. Why not just follow the girl."

The girl, however, had come to a halt and was arguing with the other children, who wanted to come with her. "She said just me," she stated firmly. "He's here to see my father. She said just me." But the secretary was no longer there and the children were so adamant that, after trying briefly to fend them off, the girl turned to Molkho and said, "Let's go." They left the schoolyard through an opening in the fence and walked quickly along a muddy path, Molkho following behind her with his files, stepping on new tufts of bluish grass while watching her spindly legs and little buttocks, which bounced inside her black leotard like rubber balls. She bounded along like a fawn or, rather, like a bespectacled bunny, and it was all he could do to keep up with her, breathing the high mountain air while treading the winding path that circled behind the houses, cowsheds, and chicken coops over the terra rossa earth of the Galilee that turned even the rain puddles red.

Every now and then she stopped to let him catch up, though she failed to return his smile but simply stared at him somberly through her funny glasses. "What's wrong with your father?" he asked, and when she did not understand him, "What's he sick with?" "He's got something in his blood. He was in the hospital," she answered warily, continuing to lead him past old farm tools and rusting plows and cultivators half-buried in earth. They kept turning into new side paths and finally passed through a dark shed under the anxious eyes of a large cow and into the backyard of a little house standing on the hillside, falling straight into an ambush set by the children from school, who burst suddenly out of their hiding place. "We got here first!" they shouted merrily.

The girl ignored them. Proud and reproachful, she ushered Molkho into a kitchen, where dressed in pajamas stood a tall, young, dark-skinned Jew of Indian extraction, wearing glasses just like those worn by the girl, whose height and ebony fineness clearly derived from him. She ran to him and hugged him, while he gently patted her head, and Molkho had the eerie thought, this man is going to die and she doesn't know that she knows. He felt drawn inside the house, as if Death, having parted from him in the autumn and run ahead like a mad dog to the far end of the Galilee, now lay drowsing there beneath a table. "So it's you," he whispered to it warmly, stepping into the kitchen and introducing himself to the lanky Indian, who seemed to blanch slightly, despite his dark skin. "I was told you were the treasurer," he said.

"Treasurer?" The man smiled uncertainly. "Not exactly. I only help Ben-Ya'ish a bit with the accounts. But come in." He whispered something to the girl and disappeared, and quickly clearing a pile of books from a chair, she led Molkho into a small, clean, simply furnished room and asked him to sit down. He did, his eyes glued to her lithe body with its black leotard and pink slippers, and the steel-rimmed glasses on her ebony face, wanting to reach out and touch her, to verify that she was real. "Where's your mother?" he asked, and was told that she worked in a shoe factory in Kiryat Shmonah. "A shoe factory?" he murmured, watching her as, with an unchildlike assurance, she tidied up quietly. "Do you take ballet in school?" "Not everyone," she said, "only me." Just imagine, he thought, right here, in this country, at the far end of nowhere, are people like this, and we don't even know they exist. Why, you never even hear about them.

The father returned to the room, still unshaven but wearing pants and a black sweater that made him look even darker. Like a stranger in his own home, he looked hesitantly around before sitting down stiffly. At once the girl sat protectively nearby him, unconsciously imitating his movements. She was slightly cross-eyed, Molkho realized, once again failing to get a response to his smile. With a glance out the window at the towering mountains, he opened his files and spread them out on a little table, suddenly feeling a great fatigue. "How old is this village?" he asked the thin Indian, who was observing him curiously. "Something tells me I've been here before, maybe on some army bivouac." The village, the Indian told him, was first built for new immigrants back in the early 1950s but had twice been abandoned; the present population dated from several years later, when, in addition to some Jews from North Africa, several Indian families arrived. The girl, Molkho saw, was listening too, straight-backed and flat-chested, her head framed by the window against a background of mountains and clouds. She's certainly a strange one, he thought, unless I just don't know what little girls are like anymore.

"Who lives here now?" he asked the Indian. "Are they still traditional Jews?" Not as much as all that, he was told; on Sabbaths most people still attended synagogue, but some preferred to sleep or work. "And what sort of work," he asked, "do they do?" Most used to raise laying hens, said the Indian, but in the egg glut of 1982 the coops were abandoned, and now the women worked in Kiryat Shmonah, while the men farmed as best they could, though some did nothing at all. In fact, times were so hard that the only thing keeping people in the village was their having nowhere else to go. "And were these financial statements drawn up by you?" inquired Molkho, spreading out his papers and leafing through them impatiently, afraid the man's dirge was simply a cover-up for the faked accounts. No, they weren't, said the Indian; he had only helped Ben Ya'ish with his arithmetic. That is, he was an arithmetic teacher not a treasurer, but since his illness, which had forced him to stop teaching, he had been employed by the council manager in a part-time capacity.

Yet, when Molkho inquired about the man's illness, he answered quite apathetically and knew so little about it that even its name was a mystery. From time to time he went for treatments to Rambam Hospital in Haifa. "In what ward? With what doctors?" asked Molkho, now fully alert. But the Indian was unable to enlighten him: he arrived, he lay down on a bed, he had some blood taken, he was given a shot, and he went home again—that was all he knew. "I know that hospital well," Molkho told him, fishing for more information. "My wife died of cancer six months ago." Yet the Indian said nothing, forcing Molkho to keep talking about his wife, while the girl jiggled her thin, dark leg in wonder. Indeed, he couldn't stop; it had been a while since he'd last shared his wife's illness with anyone, so that he quite enjoyed telling about it now, right down to the drama of those final months and the little field hospital he had set up at home to ensure a comfortable death. "And she really died there?" asked the girl, staring hard at him. "Of course," Molkho said. "It happened early in the morning. She hardly suffered at all." Could he have met this child in the army thirty years ago too, he wondered, feeling the sense of déjà vu again. "How many children do you have?" he asked the Indian. "So far, only one," said the man, hugging his daughter with a smile. "But we hope to give her a little brother or sister soon."

Molkho gazed at them for a moment and asked for some water. "Gladly," said the Indian. "Or would you prefer a glass of juice?" "Juice will be fine," answered Molkho, and the girl glided out with dancelike steps to fetch it. "She's a lovely child," remarked Molkho. "How old is she?" "Eleven," said the Indian. "That's all?" marveled Molkho. "And she needs glasses already?" "Not exactly," said her father. "She wants to wear them, because she is slightly cross-eyed, and thinks they hide it."

The girl returned with a large glass of watery yellow liquid. "You forgot to stir it," said her father. "Never mind," Molkho told him, still wanting to touch her ebony skin, no matter how lightly, though she seemed too grown-up for him to risk a paternal pat. He took a sip of his drink, which was very bitter, and said to the Indian, who was sitting stock-still and ignoring the papers on the table, as if it were just a matter of time before they went away by themselves, "I'm afraid we're going to make things difficult for you. You won't get another penny of government money. We can cut you off without a cent." "But why?" asked the Indian innocently. "Because you haven't done anything right here, that's why," said Molkho, quietly sifting the papers. "What isn't right?" asked the Indian wearily. "Everything," said Molkho. "Nothing is even close to being right. This looks like a criminal case to me, and it will end up with the police." Although he knew he sounded angry, he felt perfectly calm inside. "Who does this Ben-Ya'ish of yours think he is? I came all the way up here to see him today, and he doesn't even bother to show up!" "But he will," said the Indian. "He has to. You can wait for him right here. You can see his house from this window. We'll know the minute he gets home." He pointed further up the rocky hillside to a gardenless hut that had not a single patch of green around it. "Maybe I should go talk to his wife," suggested Molkho. "He doesn't have any," said the Indian. "No wife?" "No, he's still young. He's only twenty-three." "Twenty-four," corrected the girl, who had been listening to every word. "It's his birthday soon."

Her father smiled at her. "He has a way with kids. They're very fond of him," he explained, telling Molkho that the young man had arrived in the village two years ago as a substitute teacher, had taken a liking to the place, and had done such a good job as an organizer and fund-raiser that he was elected council manager. In fact, he obtained all kinds of things for next to nothing, or even for nothing at all, which was a great help, since everyone had debts and times were so hard that no one could have managed without him. "What kind of things?" Molkho asked. "Everything. Seed. Fodder for the animals and chickens. Cheap clothes." "And food too," the girl reminded her father. "Yes," he nodded, "food too." "Food?" queried Molkho. "What sort of food?" "Why, canned goods and meat." "And cake and ice cream too," said the girl, who appeared to love Ben-Ya'ish dearly. "But where does he get it all from?" asked Molkho anxiously. "From all kinds of organizations and agencies in Tel Aviv," said the Indian. "He's there all the time studying, because he's still working on his B.A." "But not a word of that's written down here!" exclaimed Molkho in exasperation. "That's true," explained the Indian. "It isn't, but that's only because it comes from outside funds, not from the village budget." Molkho felt himself losing his temper. "All right, fine," he declared, "outside funds are his own business; but here he lists a road that cost ten million shekels, and here he says he's planted a park. Where is this park of his? I'd like to see it!" And when the Indian said nothing, casting a worried glance at his daughter, he continued sarcastically, "And here it says he bought himself a tractor! Where does he get off buying unauthorized tractors? Doesn't he know he has to go through proper channels? Look here, the reason I'm here is to get your side of the story before we hand this over to the police." But still the Indian was silent, his head bowed languidly. "Where's the road?" demanded Molkho. "Where's the park? Nothing in these accounts makes any sense!" "He'll explain everything," insisted the Indian with dogged obstinacy. "All I did was add up the figures for him. He'll explain them to you himself."

All at once, as if the mountain opposite the window had caved in on the house, the bright sunlight faded and Molkho felt as hungry as if he had not eaten all day. Gathering up his papers, he returned them to his briefcase. In the sudden gloom the girl looked as dark as if a black night were under her skin and he jumped to his feet with a start. "Where are you going?" asked the Indian. "Why don't you wait? He should be here any minute." "I'm going to have a look at the village," said Molkho. "But won't you have lunch with us?" asked the man. "No, thank you," said Molkho, thinking of his expense-account meal. "If you'll be so kind as to show me the bathroom first, I think I'll have a look around."

Yet, when the girl led him to a room that at first glance looked clean and comfortable, he was shocked to discover that it had no door, just a curtain over the entrance. He relieved himself as quietly as he could, his face toward the open window, through which there was a breathtaking view of a snowcapped Mount Hermon. So the snow is still after me, he thought with a smile, washing his hands. Controlling himself, he kept from peeking at the medicine cabinet and emerged with a friendly glance at the Indian, who, as though lost in thought, had not budged from his place. "If you'll just let your daughter show me the way back to my car," Molkho told him, "I'll have myself a little look around."

And so, again he strode behind her, this time along the main street, her body, thin as a rail, growing longer in the soft, grayish light that seemed a throwback to winter. As they passed beneath a huge pylon that hummed electrically, apparently the relay of a regional grid that seemed to come from and continue to nowhere, he asked her for her name and the name of the cow in the shed, after which, his supply of questions exhausted, he continued to trail after her through the ghostly silence, falling a little behind. There was not a sign of human activity anywhere, let alone a paved road or park, not even the sound of a farm vehicle, though three workers were standing by a fire in a distant field, from which the moist scent of burning brush was wafted on the air. His hunger growing, he kept his eyes on the little bottom bouncing firmly in its tight leotard. What, he wondered, did he find so infatuating about her? Why, it was sheer madness! Suddenly, the horrendously funny, frightening, ghastly thought occurred to him that he could quite unsexually eat her like an animal, literally chew her flesh. Fortunately, she did not seem to guess what the wintry man lagging behind her with his briefcase was thinking and went on leading him with proud but fragile determination past the schoolhouse to his car, around which a crowd of children was swarming like flies, touching the shiny paint and sprawling on the ground to peer up at the chassis. Sternly he made his way among them, aided by the girl, who imperiously began driving them away, though soon she vanished in their midst.

Molkho opened the trunk, laid his briefcase in it, started to drive off, realized he did not know to where, and decided to stop in the little shopping center, where perhaps he could buy some expense-account groceries. He circled the square, which housed a wool store, an appliance store, a stationery store, a vegetable store, and a grocery, coming at last to a small café with a sign that featured a spit of shishkebab, his progress followed by every one of the shopkeepers. Apparently they had heard all about him, and the thought of his new prominence rather pleased him as he stepped out of the car.

He made his way past some scattered tables and entered the café, where he was greeted by an Indian even darker than the first. "Do you serve meals or just snacks?" Molkho asked him. "Meals too," said the man. "And you'll give me a receipt?" Molkho asked. "No problem," said the man. "What do you have to eat?" Molkho asked. "What would you like?" asked the man. "But tell me what there is," insisted Molkho, looking around to check if the place was clean. Someone sat in a far corner eating something out of a bowl. "What's that?" Molkho asked. "Organs," said the man. "Whose?" asked Molkho worriedly. "It's a lung-and-liver stew," replied the café owner quietly, looking deferentially at his new customer. "It's real good." "Do you have steak?" Molkho asked. "Whatever you like," said the Indian. "Perhaps then," said Molkho somewhat officiously, "you can show it to me." Leading him into a dirty kitchen that Molkho's wife would have fled from, the man passed a big pot simmering on a burner, opened a refrigerator, and took out a drooping piece of meat clotted with old, purplish blood. Molkho regarded it doubtfully; it was certainly not very hygienic-looking. In the end, they'll poison me here, he told himself, still feeling a craving for meat. "Do you have sausages?" he asked. But the man did not. And so, after thinking it over, he ordered the organ stew, left the kitchen, and sat down irritably at a table, keeping an eye on his car while recalling the times his wife had made him go from restaurant to restaurant until she found one clean enough to suit her. But all that was past history. Now he would eat what and where he wanted. And his car seemed quite safe. Most of the children had gone off somewhere else, and those remaining now sat by the front wheels, among them the Indian girl, who crouched licking a popsicle like a little grasshopper with folded wings.

A pickup truck pulled up in the square and a young man climbed out of it. Could that be Ben-Ya'ish? wondered Molkho—but the young man was an Arab and his thoughts returned to his wife. No, he hadn't killed her—the idea was obscene and insane. He had simply helped her to die when she was ready. And yet, had he not perhaps been too quick to resign himself to her death? From the very beginning, bending down that spring night to kiss the nipple of her white breast and cautiously, tenderly saying, though the words cracked like a whip, "Yes, there's some kind of a lump here," he hadn't believed in her chances. And now here he was, sitting in this unsavory spot in this God-forsaken Galilean village, watching the women shoppers—all of whom, even the young ones, still looked like immigrants—as they came and went, and thinking, How cold they all still leave me. A tractor emerged from an alleyway, tried climbing the steps of the shopping arcade, and came to a sudden halt. Some children passed by. Abandoning himself to the tranquillity, he let the cool breeze fan his appetite. The place did not look as if times were as hard as all that. It was just talk. If you believed half you heard, the whole country had been falling apart for years, and yet everything was still there. In fact, wherever you went, there was a tractor clearing new ground.

The group of children by the car had disappeared. While the café owner set the bare table and brought a plate of pita bread and a small bowl of olives, Molkho queried him about the village. Had any new roads been paved lately? Not that he knew of. How about a park or public garden? He knew nothing about them either. Meanwhile, several men, looking freshly awakened from sleep, approached Molkho in a friendly manner. "Are you the fellow who's waiting for Ben-Ya'ish? He left a message saying he'll be here soon. What did you come to check out—the accounts? There's nothing wrong with them! He'll explain everything. We're all behind him." "I heard your wife died," said one of the men, reaching out to shake Molkho's hand, "I'm very sorry to hear about it." Before he knew it, he was shaking hands with them all, startled by their knowledge, as if the wind had carried the news. He was about to ask them about the road and park, too, when the steaming bowl of stew arrived, full of dark, smooth, slightly rubbery chunks of meat swimming in a bright brown gravy and giving off a funky odor like his father's sweat, and shaking from hunger, he pitched in before it got cold. The meat, when speared with a fork, was of various spongy consistencies, apparently because it came from different organs, and had a strange sweetness that caused him a brief moment of anxiety before he attacked it in earnest, dipping his bread in the gravy between bites. "This mountain air gives a man an appetite," he apologized to the café owner, who sat there watching him eat. "Where's this meat from?" he asked. "It's all kinds of organs," answered the man. "Don't you like it?" "Yes, I do," Molkho said, "it's delicious. I was just wondering if you took it from a cow." "*I* took it from a cow?" The Indian seemed alarmed, though in the end he caught on. "Oh, you mean beef!" "Yes," said Molkho, chewing away, his face lit by the sun, which had come back out of the clouds. All around him was silence, as if the whole village were hiding, except for the café owner sitting nearby, who rose now and then to bring a cold drink or more bread, which

Molkho dipped ravenously in the gravy. "It's this mountain air," he said again with a smile, and this time the man smiled back and said, "Yes, the one thing we've got here is air." Then he cleared the table and made Molkho some coffee to wash down the gamy-tasting stew. "Should I list everything you ate?" he asked when Molkho rose to pay, tearing a page out of a notebook. "No," Molkho said. "Just the date and what it cost."

It was 2 P.M. and the sun was beating down as if in anticipation of summer, the rainy morning a thing of the past. Passing a pay phone, he thought of calling home or maybe his mother, but then changed his mind. So what if I don't? I've got a right to disappear if I want to, he told himself while walking to his car, which stood baking in the sun. If I don't keep it covered, it will fade and lose its value, he thought. Yet, catching sight of the complicated dashboard, his hand resting on the fresh-smelling seat, he was conscious of getting less pleasure from it than from new cars in the past. He took off his jacket and sweater, loosened his tie, settled himself behind the wheel, and opened the window, through which the wind came whooshing down from the mountains, whistling straight toward him as though somewhere in the distance a giant fan were aimed at him. Well, that's that, he thought, that little swindler can look for me, now. But suddenly, as the wind shrieked high overhead, his eagerness to take off faltered, perhaps because the stew was weighing him down. Should he move the car into the shade and rest a bit? But he had lost all sense of direction and wasn't sure which way the sun was heading. In the end, locking the gear shift and flicking the hidden switch disconnecting the ignition, he stepped out of the car and started back toward the girl's house to tell her father he was leaving.

Once more he followed the muddy path among fields stippled with yellow flowers whose name he didn't know. Far-off, the mountains were turning purple. A rusty silence still hung over the village. The natives are taking their siesta, thought Molkho. The field with the fire was empty now, though thin wisps of grayish smoke still spiraled up from it and hot ashes writhed like ribbons of quicksilver on the moist, coppery ground. He noticed to one side a trail running off into a deep, jungly ravine, which lay between high, sawtoothed cliffs looking like ancient cadavers that had died clinging to the hillside. Fierce colors flashed there, green, blue, and claret, cut by the bold brown slash of the path. That's it, then! thought Molkho. It's a place that's hiked in; I must have been here with the Scouts. He stood gazing into it, listening to the wind gather strength, and musing that were he to die in there, no one would discover his traces. "Not that there's anything wrong with that," he told himself out loud. "At least I'd rest in peace then."

He turned and headed on toward the girl's house, passing it, however, and continuing on to Ben-Ya'ish's hut, where he knocked on the door and received no response. Through an open shutter he caught a glimpse of the interior: an unmade bed, a television, a video, a set of speakers, and a pile of dirty dishes on the table, which indicated that the occupant had left not long ago. Circling the dwelling through tall, thorny weeds, he glanced up the hillside and made out an old wooden outhouse that looked like an upended coffin. It still had a door, though, he saw as he approached it, clearing his way through the dense undergrowth. The ceiling was low, no higher than a man's head, and more weeds sprouted from the cesspit. Shutting the door behind him, the wind moaning dully through the dry wooden planks as though through a stifling hand, he unzipped his pants and tried relieving himself, but the trickle that came out only increased his sense of debility. Why, a person might think I was in love with that little dark girl, he thought, that I meant to wait right here for her to grow up! Walking back down the hill, he knocked on the door of her house.

The Indian opened it. "Ben-Ya'ish isn't here yet," said Molkho with a show of calm. "It looks like I've wasted my time, and so I'll be heading back. Just please tell him that I was here and that I'm sore as hell," he continued, not feeling sore in the least. "If he wants to tell me his side of the story—if he has any story to tell—he can try looking for me, because I'm through looking for him."

The Indian listened earnestly, at his back the shadowy room full of books. "But what's the rush?" he demurred. "He'll come. He has to. You can rest here while you wait." "What for?" asked Molkho. "I've waited long enough." "But you have to have patience," said the Indian. "Why don't you come in. I'll give you a bed to lie down in." "Your wife isn't home yet?" asked Molkho. "My wife? She doesn't come home until five." And when Molkho said nothing, he set about persuading him again. "Why don't you come in? He'll feel bad if he knows you didn't wait."

Molkho felt himself waver, wondering where the girl was. Hopelessly he looked around the room full of books and at the kitchen table with its unwashed lunch dishes, hearing the wind whistle behind him. "I don't want to impose," he said. "But it's no imposition at all," said the Indian. "I'll be keeping you from your work," explained Molkho, still in the doorway. "You won't be keeping me from anything," insisted the Indian. "Perhaps I could lie down in another room," suggested Molkho; it could even be the girl's. "Right here in the living room will be fine," said the Indian. "I was just arranging some books I brought home." But seeing that Molkho was unyielding, he said, "All right, come on in. I'll find you someplace else." Entering the girl's room, he emerged a minute later with her, still in her leotard and big glasses, her books and homework in her arms. "Come this way. You'll have all the quiet you want," he cajoled, pointing to the girl's bedroom, though Molkho was disappointed to see that it did not look like a schoolgirl's room at all and was full of heavy old furniture, even a fourposter bed.

The Indian laid a gentle hand on his arm, as one might do to a tired old man. "But I don't want to impose on your daughter either," murmured Molkho weakly, already sinking into the soft bed. Dismissing the objection out of hand, the Indian brought a pillow and a blanket, lowered the blinds, and declared, "Now you wait for him here. He'll feel bad if you don't," as if making clear that what mattered most was not the accounts or even the pains taken by Molkho, but rather the tender feelings of the young council manager. "But it's totally inconsiderate of him," said Molkho, smiling wryly from the bed, on which he sat with an air of noblesse oblige, though in fact it surprised him how happy and peaceful he felt. "He had an appointment with me!" "Why don't you take your shoes off," said the Indian.

But Molkho left them on, remaining seated on the bed until the man had left and shut the door behind him. She wouldn't have liked this one bit, he reflected, thinking of his wife, who was always careful to observe the proprieties, of which imposing on strangers was not one. Taking a volume of a children's encyclopedia from the girl's desk, he placed it on the blanket, lay down with his shoes on it, and shut his eyes, abandoning himself to the wind that shrieked and stopped, shrieked and stopped, like some infernal machine. It's a rockaby-baby wind, he thought happily, dozing off, only to awake with a start ten minutes later to discover that he had been in a deep sleep. The only sound in the house was the purr of the refrigerator through the kitchen wall. He rose, went to the window, raised the blinds, and stood looking out at the mountains and the cowshed, inhaling the clean country air. What am I doing here? he wondered. You'd think I had no house or children of my own. But his tiredness welled irresistibly inside him, like a firm but gentle hand that wrestled him down, and taking off his shoes, he plumped the pillow and lay deliciously down again on the honey-sweet bed. Just look where you've landed me this time, he whispered mournfully to his wife, falling asleep in an instant.

Several times he sought to rouse himself, yet each time he only plunged deeper into sleep, wetting the pillow slightly with his drool, so that when he awoke at last, the room was dark. Water was dripping somewhere in the house, and the reddish tongues of the sunset licked at the slats of the blinds. It was six o'clock; he had been sleeping for over three hours. Aghast, he sat up, yet at once sank exhaustedly back onto the pillow. Then, more slowly, he sat up again, put on his shoes, folded the blanket, returned the book to the desk, donned his jacket, smoothed his hair, and cautiously opened the door.

There, crouched at his feet and mopping the floor with a rag, was a young and very pregnant woman of Middle Eastern appearance —the mother who worked in the shoe factory. Molkho reddened. She looked up at him suspiciously, almost hostilely, as if his sleep were an act of impertinence. Behind her, in the kitchen, the Indian was cooking in an apron, while the girl knelt on the living room rug doing homework with ink-stained fingers, her glasses tinted a smoky color as if by virtue of the effort she was making. All three of them had apparently been doing their best to let him sleep. But before he could apologize for his thoughtlessly long nap or blame it on the mountain air, the Indian announced dolefully, "He still isn't back from Tel Aviv, he wasn't on the last bus, and we don't know where he is. Maybe he got the date wrong." "More likely he's just scared of me," said Molkho, standing there grumpily unkempt, as if his sleep had been a particularly strenuous form of exercise. "And I don't blame him either." The girl's mouth dropped and suddenly it struck him that these people were scared of him too. "If you could just wait a little longer," said the Indian. "He may have caught a ride with someone." Molkho smiled at him sardonically. "Only the Messiah is worth waiting that long for. But it's not your fault, and I see your wife's tired," he said, "so I won't disturb you anymore." In fact, the woman, who was standing in a corner, seemed less tired than alarmed; despite her youth, she looked rather worn and remote from her husband and daughter. "I'll be off, then," said Molkho. "It's dark out already, and I'm running in a new car and can't drive fast." "All right, I'll walk you to it," said the Indian, wiping his hands on his apron.

The girl jumped up from the rug like a dog following its master and the three of them stepped outside. There was a sharp, dawnlike chill in the air, so that Molkho, setting out for his car with his two escorts following him, imagined for a moment that the dying evening light would soon begin to grow brighter. The cow mooed sadly in its shed, and he remembered hearing the same sound in his sleep. It was a perfect spring evening, free of all dross of day. Refreshed and rested, he arrived in the shopping center, which was now full of life; in fact, such a crowd was gathered around his car, in its midst many children, that it almost seemed as if the whole village had been waiting for him to awake from his prodigious slumber, which had produced in them an uneasy, though by no means unhopeful, expectancy. "What, you're going?" they asked, pressing around him. "Of course," he smiled. "But he's coming! We'll find him! If you've already gone to the trouble . . ." Yet Molkho just went on smiling at the crowd, which did all it could to detain him, afraid of what he might say about the council manager, whom it wanted so badly to protect. "It's not as bad as all that," he promised. "I'll put off writing the report a little longer. Tell him to call me for an appointment in the morning." And stepping into his car, he unlocked the gear shift, reconnected the ignition, fastened the seat belt, started the engine, and sat there letting it warm up, the beam of the headlights sweeping over the mass of children, among them the strange, tall girl. Can I really be in love with her? wondered Molkho.

He was given directions to reach the main road and drove off. After a few kilometers he stopped to wipe the front windshield. Back in the driver's seat, with the ceiling light switched off, he suddenly imagined his wife sitting next to him in her seat belt, leaning against the headrest as she had done last spring, when the vertebrae in her neck were already rotted by her illness and he had to drive with great care to keep from jarring her. It can't go on like this, he told himself, not daring to glance at her, laying his head hopelessly on the steering wheel. It's not my fault. This loneliness will be the death of me.

10

T HE TRIP HOME took less time than he thought, because he knew the way and drove quickly on the empty roads without stopping. Within forty minutes he was on the Safed-Acre highway with the lights of Haifa Bay twinkling in the distance, speeding by the Karmiel turnoff without giving a lift to the lone soldier who tried desperately to flag him down, for he had not yet bought seat covers and was afraid the man's rifle might poke a hole in the upholstery. For a change, he arrived home to find his youngest son doing homework rather than sprawled in a stupor before the television. The boy, so it seemed, was getting used to spending long hours at home by himself. Better yet, not a single new can had been opened in the kitchen and the leftovers had been eaten from the pots. He's beginning to shape up, Molkho thought; he even talked freely to his father about school and friends, and later got out of bed because he had forgotten to give him the message that his grandmother had called. "What about?" asked Molkho anxiously. About whether Molkho knew anyone in the immigration department of the Jewish Agency, his son told him. "The immigration department?" repeated Molkho in a puzzled voice. "What on earth does she want with them?"

He walked about the dark, quiet house, patiently carrying his wakefulness around with him. The stew he had eaten for lunch was a distant memory now, but the delicious afternoon nap tingled on in the cells of his body, which felt as if rubbed down with liniment. Going to bed was out of the question. He drew up a list of the day's expenses to present to the office in the morning and then began leafing through the family albums, looking at pictures of his children when they were little, at his wedding pictures, at pictures of himself as a young man, at pictures of his parents and cousins, and finally, with a sense of incredulity, at himself as a baby lying on a white sheet. It was 1 A.M. when he got into bed, and even then, he lay for a long while without shutting his eyes before falling asleep.

Upon arriving in the office the next morning, he was told by his secretary that the council manager of Zeru'a had called and wished to speak to him. Swearing under his breath, he called back and once again heard children singing to the strains of an accordion at the other end of the line, over which the quickly summoned music teacher informed him that Mr. Ben-Ya'ish had arrived half an hour after his departure and had been very sorry to miss him. "I'm very sorry too," said Molkho quietly. "He wants to explain everything," said the music teacher. "Then he can do it right here in my office," answered Molkho dryly. "No, he can't," said the music teacher. "He wants to show you what the money has been spent on. You have to see it yourself." "Where is he?" asked Molkho after a moment's hesitation. "Let me speak to him." The council manager, however, was not available just then, though the music teacher promised that he would be there whenever Molkho wished to come, and would even send a car for him. "He'll send a car for me?" "Yes, that's a promise!" "In that case," said Molkho over the phone, calculating the profit he could make by still claiming car expenses, "call me again tomorrow."

He hung up and put the file aside. Later that morning he was buzzed by the director's office. Had he gone to the village? What was the story there? He phrased his answer carefully. The case indeed looked suspicious, just as they had thought: the council manager, a young student of questionable experience, had apparently diverted funds earmarked for public projects to the inhabitants of the village, using the money to buy them food and clothing at wholesale prices. There was no indication that he had bothered collecting taxes either. But the fellow himself hadn't been there, and perhaps he deserved a chance to clear himself.

Several days went by without a call from the village. That weekend, daylight saving time began, and the days seemed suddenly endless. One evening, just as Molkho had decided to hand the file over to the legal department, the music teacher called him at home. She was sorry for the late hour, but could he tell her what his answer was? "You know what?" said Molkho. "If he wants me up there so badly, let him send that car for me." And so it was decided that on Thursday, between 10 and 11 A.M., the car would pick him up at home. He had already hung up and was wandering distractedly about the house, excited by the thought of revisiting the village, when he realized that he had forgotten to ask if there would be a ride back to Haifa too.

11

THE NEXT DAY he informed the office that he was making one more trip to the Galilee and received permission and authorization for expenses. On Thursday morning, which proved to be muggy and overcast, he went to do some shopping, returning home to find the cleaning woman, whom he had not encountered in weeks. At first, he tried keeping out of her way by shutting himself in his room, but she seemed in a particularly gay mood, singing while she beat the rugs and coming in to talk to him, pleased to find him at home. "You're looking better, Mr. Molkho," she said in the end. "Much better." When she finally departed, leaving a silent, sparkling house, it was already twelve o'clock. The promised car had not arrived. At one he went to the kitchen to make himself something to eat. If I want to claim lunch expenses, he thought gloomily, I'll have to write myself out my own receipt. As soon as he finished eating, he decided, he would summarize the file and get rid of it.

At two the doorbell rang. It was the driver, a burly Arab of about Molkho's age who came from a village near Zeru'a. "How come you're so late?" Molkho scolded him. Despite the man's explanation that he had lost his way for two hours and couldn't find the address, he debated whether to go; but in the end, the thought of the girl and the car expenses prevailed. "You'll have to bring me back, though," he warned the driver, who, however, disclaimed all knowledge of any such responsibility. His job was to drive Molkho to Zeru'a; perhaps someone else would return him. Again Molkho hesitated; then he went to get the file, put it in his briefcase, added a pair of pajamas and some slippers wrapped in a newspaper just in case, and put on some old, heavy shoes. "Let's go," he grumpily said to the Arab, locking the door of the house.

The car turned out to be an old pickup with a load in the back and the Arab's wife, a large peasant woman dressed in black, in the front. Before Molkho could protest, he was made to sit between them, and they started out, driving slowly and with a great clatter of the engine in the heat of the day. Every now and then, they turned off the main road to make a delivery to some remote Arab village that Molkho had never even heard of. Sweatily squeezed between the driver and his wife and dismally cursing his fate, he watched the road go by while throwing hostile glances at the man shifting gears, an operation that was conducted each time with great caution but little sign of expertise. After asking where the man knew Ben-Ya'ish from and being told that the council manager had close ties with the

nearby Arab villages and even helped them with their books, there
was nothing left to talk about and they drove on in silence, the
Arab's wife dozing with her head resting lightly on Molkho's shoulder. By the time they began the climb into the mountains, his eyes,
too, began to close; periodically he nodded off, found himself tilting
against the peasant woman's heavy breasts, and sat up again with a
start. The trip took three hours and included a stop in the driver's
village—which looked like something from the wilds of Anatolia—
where the woman got out, took off her shoes, and slipped into her
house while her husband unloaded the remaining crates and invited
Molkho, still rubbing the sleep from his eyes, to come in for a cup of
coffee. He went to the bathroom, which surprised him by its cleanliness, and returned to the sitting room to find the coffee waiting there.
"I understand you lost your wife," said the Arab. Molkho was non-
plussed. Was it written all over his face? But no, the man had heard
of it in Zeru'a. What else had he heard there? Molkho asked. Nothing. They just told him to bring Molkho in his truck.

It was 5 P.M. when he reached the school building. Though he
saw at once in the mild afternoon light that it was locked and deserted, he did not feel at all surprised; on the contrary, something
had told him all along that Ben-Ya'ish would not be there. The fields
had yellowed a bit in the ten days that had passed, but here and
there he saw summer flowers he hadn't noticed the last time, and on
the whole, the place seemed more livable. He walked between the
houses, feeling watched by dark silhouettes of Indians. "It's that
man from the ministry again," he heard someone say. Slowly he
crossed the shopping center, where this time, as though out of compassion, people avoided his eyes.

He walked on to the little house on the hillside, passing under
the tall, humming pylon and once again experiencing the sense of
déjà vu, though this time it was possible that his previous visit was
the cause of it. Ben-Ya'ish's house was locked and silent, the lowered
blinds preventing a glimpse inside, but when he knocked on the
door, he thought he heard a sound there. "Mr. Ben-Ya'ish?" he
called out. "Mr. Ben-Ya'ish?" But the sound stopped, and Molkho,
all but trembling with anticipation, walked back down the hill to the

house of the treasurer, whose daughter opened the door. "Where's your father?" he asked, feeling himself turn as red as her polka-dot dress. She seemed to have grown smaller since last he had seen her, but her gaze was as pure and earnest as ever. Her father, she said, was in the hospital. "In the hospital? How long has he been there?" he asked, his heart sinking. But he had gone only that morning and would soon be back, she informed him, her thin, finely wrought hand on the door, uncertain whether Molkho wished to enter, perhaps even concerned that he might sleep in her bed again. Nor was he at all sure himself how proper it was to be alone with her in the house. He felt unsteady, as if squatting inside him were a sexless little gnome who had fallen in love with a nymph. Behind her he could see her bedroom with one end of her antique bed, its blanket thrown off, and the heavy furniture. She followed his gaze earnestly, a joyless, humorless, somber little Indian, just like her father. "Do you want to wait here for him?" she asked. "No," Molkho said, "I've come to see Ya-ir Ben-Ya'ish. Do you have any idea where he is?" "He was waiting for you all morning at the school," said the girl, raising an arm as if to fend Molkho off. "You should look for him there." "But the school is locked," he said patiently, "I just came from there," and when she said nothing he continued, "Why don't you show me where the secretary lives, that music teacher." She glided outdoors in her bare feet, explaining to him how to get there; yet touching her so lightly that he barely felt her, as though she were made out of air, he said, "Take me there yourself, please. Just put on some shoes first." And so again he followed her between the houses, looking at her matchstick legs in their sneakers while trying to carry on a conversation, first asking her about her mother and when the new baby was expected, then about the cow, and finally about the wild ravine, the name of which he had forgotten. But she did not know it either and was not even certain that it had one. All she could tell him was that if you walked a ways down it, you came to a waterfall. "What waterfall is that?" Molkho asked. "Oh, just a waterfall."

The music teacher turned pale when Molkho arrived with the girl. "It's you? You came after all? But when? We'd already given up on you." "*You'd* given up?" he snickered. "Yes, we waited for you

all morning. Ya'ir was beside himself. An hour ago he took the bus to
Fasuta to look for the driver." While Molkho related what had happened, she hurried to give him a chair and a drink, and told the girl
she could go. Molkho, though, did not want to stay in her house
either, for it was noisy with children and too full of cheap bric-a-brac
and glassware. He had a deep urge to stroll in the honeyed spring
light, vigilant though forbearing in the knowledge, which both
pleased and touched him, that the council manager was afraid of
him, but determined to meet the young man and do what he could to
console him. "Never mind. I'll take a walk around and wait for him
at their house," he said to the music teacher with a nod toward the
girl, who stood frozen for some reason in a corner. "Is your father
back?" the music teacher asked her. "He will be soon," said the girl.
"Then find Mr. Molkho a place to rest," said the teacher, happy to
get rid of him.

And so once more Molkho walked behind the girl along the
path between the houses, aware of the surreptitious stares cast his
way. "Where's the trail leading to that waterfall?" he asked her. She
guided him to it, leading him across a field to a broad dirt track.
"Well, then," he said, "I'll go down and have a look and come right
back." She was reluctant to leave him there, though. "You'd better
let me show you the way." "There's really no need to," answered
Molkho, not trusting himself alone with her in the ravine. "I'll find it
by myself. Just please take my briefcase back to your house." And
indeed, the request reassured her, so that she stood there watching
him set out, squinting through her comic glasses with a sudden,
sweet flutter of her eyes. The broad trail soon narrowed and grew
rocky, bushes and boulders blocked the way, and moisture from an
unseen source softened the earth beneath his feet, which glistened a
turfy green. And yet the more tangled and difficult the path became,
the more lustrously vibrant grew the light. The far side of the ravine
was hidden by the thick bushes, and from time to time he had to
slide down a steep rock on his bottom. Should he stop and turn
back? But the winding trail lured him on, the damp earth giving off
new smells, joined now by a metal pipe, no doubt for sewage or
irrigation, which snaked downward through the lush undergrowth, in

which it seemed strangely out of place. Molkho followed it, treading on it now and then to make sure he could find his way back through the thickening brush. He skirted little puddles of water and crossed other paths joining this one, trodden grassless by hikers. It grew darker, there was a pungent smell of dust and rushing water, the walls of a little canyon rose on either side of him, and then all at once he was standing in a clearing of golden light and there was the waterfall.

It was not nearly as small as he had thought it would be. Falling gilded by the sunlight into a gray-green pool that trickled off in an unseen direction, the water burst forth from mosses that concealed a lipped groove in a boulder. He sat on a rock facing it, enjoying the coolness of the air and gazing at some unfamiliar purple flowers and at a weeping willow whose little leaves were like delicate ferns, the sharp scent of artemisia riveting his senses. Here was a place of eternal wakefulness, and though he failed to remember it, he felt sure he had been here as a boy, for the Scouts would never have missed it. How his wife would have liked it too! Places like this made her fall profoundly silent, her judgmental nagging briefly stilled. How sad to think of the lost peace this cascade would have given her! And yet it was years since they last had taken a pleasure trip, and then, too, they never went on foot. Even before she fell ill, she had always been too tired to go anywhere on Saturdays and had passed the time irritably glancing at the weekend papers and uttering her jeremiads. "Stop reading all that junk," he would say to her. "It's all a lot of lies and exaggerations. Why let it get to you." But she simply saw in this one more sign of the dangerously Levantine, apolitical naïveté that was leading the country to catastrophe. Now she was rotting slowly, decomposing in the earth, and he was by himself, squatting comfortably on his heels in Levantine fashion across from the marvelous waterfall, overcome by sorrow and longing. He picked up a pebble and chucked it into the pool.

Just then he heard a rustle of branches and the sound of children, and a minute later the children themselves appeared, staring down at him from further up the ravine, having followed him apparently from the village. He beckoned to them. At first, they hesitated·

then, the bigger ones first and the smaller ones after them, they descended like a herd of dark goats and stood with an unwashed smell in a circle around him while he chatted with them easily and patted their heads and backs, until suddenly, green with envy, the girl appeared and drove them away, her father having returned and sent her to look for him, afraid he might be lost. Molkho laughed. "Has Ben-Ya'ish come back too?" he asked. But the girl hadn't seen him.

And so, yet another time, he found himself walking behind her, his eyes on her thin, skimming legs as he climbed arduously up the steep path with the children scrambling in his wake like a pack of nimble monkeys. At the entrance to the ravine, he found her father waiting in the company of two or three other anxious men, all apparently afraid he had taken leave of his senses. "What were you looking for down there?" they asked. "Nothing," said Molkho, brushing off his clothes, "just the waterfall. Your daughter told me about it, so I went down to have a look." "You walked all the way to the waterfall?" they marveled, making him wonder how old a man they took him for. "Yes, is that so unusual?" he replied before asking them about Ben-Ya'ish. But Ben-Ya'ish, it appeared, was still being looked for. "Never has a bureaucrat been given such a runaround by a citizen," sighed Molkho pensively with something like inner satisfaction, basking in the mild, clear light that made the whole world look transparent. "Well, I suppose there's nothing to do but wait for him," he added, turning to go to the Indian's house.

Though the Indian seemed unprepared, he had little choice but to join Molkho, who was already striding purposefully toward the house, in front of which he found his briefcase. Perhaps they'll offer me the girl's bed again, he thought, but instead he was ushered into the familiar living room and asked if he wanted some coffee. He accepted and sat drinking it, trying once more to elicit the details of the man's illness, at least the names of the drugs that he took. But the Indian was no more forthcoming than before, and perhaps he really knew nothing about it, as if his illness were someone else's that he had merely borrowed for a while. Remembering with longing his sleep of ten days ago, Molkho stole a tender glance at the girl's room. "He's playing a game with me, this Ben-Ya'ish of yours," he sighed, tired from the trip and his hike in the ravine but doubtful whether he could fall asleep so late in the afternoon, especially since the soporific wind was no longer blowing. "Maybe he's just afraid of me, but he's playing with fire," he continued, trying to make the Indian feel a measure of guilt or, at least, responsibility. But the Indian too, so it seemed, had despaired of understanding the council manager; sitting straight-backed on the edge of his chair beside his daughter, who appeared, with the light glinting off her glasses, to imitate his movements with unconscious precision, he said sulkily, "I told him he had nothing to be afraid of, that you were a reasonable man and would give folks like us a fair hearing. But I guess he's afraid you won't understand his method of bookkeeping and there'll be trouble."

There was a long silence in the room. The cow mooed longingly in her shed, and Molkho sat back in the little armchair, surprised at his inner serenity, which the Indian, perhaps because he feared another session of sleep, appeared to regard with apprehension. "So you really think he won't show up?" asked Molkho. "I honestly don't know," said the Indian. "But where is he now?" asked Molkho. The council manager, replied the Indian, was last seen departing for the Arab driver's village; since then, he hadn't been heard from and the music teacher had gone to look for him. "He promised me a ride back to Haifa too," Molkho said. The Indian, however, had no idea how such a promise might be kept. "When is the last bus out of here?" Molkho asked. In fifteen minutes, was the answer. Yet he made no move to rise from his chair, too entranced by the silent aura of the girl to tear himself away. I must be going crazy, he thought, gazing at her bare arms and legs, on which, near the ankle, there was a fresh, thin scratch. "Your daughter cut herself," he told the Indian. "Perhaps you should put on a Band-Aid." "It's from the ravine," explained the girl, rubbing the dried blood off with some saliva. "Well, then," said Molkho, reaching for his briefcase, "I guess I'll be on my way." He stepped out into the charmed evening, cut behind the house, paused to regard the big cow in her shed, and continued along the path that skirted the village, which he now

seemed to see for the first time in all its pathetic decay: the un-
watered fields, the untended hothouses, the abandoned chicken coops, the half-empty cowsheds, the tractors rusting beneath their tattered tarpaulins, the forlorn wildflowers in a sea of yellowing thistles.
The whole place, he thought, was like a dying patient who lets the
doctor do what he wants with him. The villagers he passed looked at
him unseeingly, sometimes keeping in step with him awhile before
falling behind or forging ahead. The dead keep giving us orders, he
thought, not without satisfaction, recalling, while continuing his tour
of the village, how his wife would send him out for such walks to
perk him up from the long hours of sitting by her bed, mechanically
making small talk—but just then he froze, for there, in the little
shopping center, a bus had just pulled in and was disgorging weary-
looking passengers returning from work, among them the Indian's
pregnant wife, who started out for home on her short, knobby legs.
Why, it's the last bus, he realized with a panicky yet oddly happy
sensation, watching it pull out past the perimeter fence while feeling
how, bright but invisible in the lingering light, someone was shadow-
ing him, perhaps Ya-ir Ben-Ya'ish himself, who, in the most childish
case of corruption Molkho had ever encountered, had used government money as a slush fund for the local inhabitants.

He continued to describe a large circle, following the perimeter
fence from point to point, leaving nowhere unexplored, not even the
distant spot on the hillside where another huge pylon shunted its
lines into town. Though the sun had already set, it was still bright
out, as if, by fiat of the Ministry of the Interior, for which he worked,
daylight saving time had stopped the earth in its tracks and kept the
long, glimmering twilight afloat. How his wife would have loved this
slow, light-drenched evening, she who was always so afraid of the
oncoming night! He had now reached the northern limits of the
settlement, where the fence began doubling back, still without finding the least trace of a park or paved road that might allow him to file
a less incriminating report, and so he turned and headed southeast,
watching his shadow grow longer and thinner in the dimming reddish light until it became a faint specter. A large, heavy woman, none
other than a very red-faced and out-of-breath music teacher, was

running after him, shouting and waving her hands. He stopped and regarded her sternly while listening to her news, uncertain whether the catch in her voice was from heartbreak or hilarity. Ben-Ya'ish, it seemed, had just called. "Where is he?" Molkho asked. "You won't believe this," said the music teacher, "but he's in Haifa. He never went to Fasuta at all. He went straight to Haifa, because he was sure that the Arab had never picked you up. He just called from somewhere on the Carmel. Isn't that where you live? Then he must be right near your house! But he's already started back, so you may as well wait for him here."

"Wait for him?" whispered Molkho, almost amused by the infinite impudence of the man. "You want *me* to wait some more?" he asked, staring at her half-menacingly and half-comically while the light behind her went on dying, flattening the children in the playground near the shopping center into black paper cutouts. The music teacher, however, did not seem to see the irony of it. "Yes," she said, matching him stare for stare, "that's what he told me to tell you. He'll feel terrible if you leave now." Once again Ben-Ya'ish's feelings were being flaunted as though they were those of an innocent child who must be prevented from suffering at all costs! "First of all," said Molkho sharply, with the smile of a man who has seen everything, "first of all, I want a telephone. A real one on which I can talk. After that, I'll tell you my decision." Apparently the music teacher had had just such a contingency in mind, because jingling in her hands were the keys not only to the office but to Ben-Ya'ish's house, which was now offered to him as a sanctuary. And so together they walked back to the school, by which children were still playing soccer; there she unlocked the front gate and the office, switched on the light, and hurried off with the excuse that she had left something cooking at home, flinging the keys on the desk of the disorderly room like a title deed.

His first call was to his younger son, whom he informed that he might not be coming home that night, grateful that his children were already grown up and no longer dependent on him. Then he phoned his mother in Jerusalem to say hello, and was asked where he was calling from and why he sounded so distant. "I'm in the Galilee," he said. "The Galilee? What are you doing there?" "I'm here on business," he told her. "But it's already night," she remonstrated. "So what?" he asked. "So be careful." "All right, I'll be careful," promised Molkho, wondering whom to call next. Perhaps his cousin in Paris, to whom he had not spoken or even written a thank-you note since he got back? It was a tempting thought, but fearful the call might be traced to him, he refrained. He glanced again at his files, which seemed suddenly quite pointless, locked the office door behind him, and wandered down the dark corridor, wondering whether compositions were still hung on the walls as they were when he was a boy and even entering several classrooms, turning on the light in each; but there were no compositions, just pictures of flowers and animals. Which class was the girl in? Unless she had skipped a grade, he guessed, she must be a fifth-grader, and finding her classroom, he spent a long while there and even sat in one of the seats. In general, the school surprised him by being so clean and orderly that he considered praising it in his report as the single bright spot in the village. Even the bathrooms were well kept, and he was especially impressed by the little child-size toilets. Now there's creative thinking, he mused, sitting on one of them and trying to imagine how a child would feel on it.

At last he locked the front gate of the school and put the keys in his pocket. Many eyes, he felt, were on him in the darkness, wondering about the long-suffering but persistent ministry whose loyal representative he was. He walked back to the shopping center, which was now crowded with people and brightly lit by neon lights. In the café, which was doing a brisk business, small children ran back and forth between the tables. People looked at him warmly now, their former reserve gone, as if by virtue of the keys he was no longer the outside inspector but a local, if still temporary, resident, and he sat down at a table, nodding to people he knew, while the dark-skinned café owner, as unshaven and unkempt as ever (did he ever wash his hands? Molkho wondered), hovered silently behind him like a shade. If he wants to serve me more cannibal stew, thought Molkho, I'm afraid I don't have an appetite. In fact, his hike to the waterfall and his evening walk had so satisfied him that he didn't feel like eating anything, not for all the receipts in the world, and all he asked for was a cup of tea, unsweetened, please. Meanwhile, a small crowd had gathered approvingly around him, praising his patience in waiting for Ben-Ya'ish, who was sure to arrive and set everything to rights, since he had only their good in mind. Why, if Molkho hadn't stayed, Ben-Ya'ish would have been disappointed—they all would have been!

From that, they passed to other things. What did Molkho think about the situation in Lebanon? And what did he believe would happen now that the army was withdrawing? He should know that just because they lived near the border and had suffered from PLO attacks was no reason to blame them for the frightful war. They felt for the soldiers who were killed in it, yet there was no denying it had given them three years of peace, without a single shot or shell fired at them. What would happen now? Would they have to go back to living in shelters? They talked on and on, about the present prime minister and the former prime minister and the prime ministers before him and who was better and what was good and bad about each and life in general, and even asked Molkho about himself. Why, these people are folks just like me! he thought. When the television news came on, they all fell silent, watching the pullout from Lebanon with its loaded trucks and tank carriers. Just then a flame-faced boy came running up to him: Ben-Ya'ish had phoned! He was already in Acre and hoped that Molkho would wait.

The report was received with satisfaction, and when the news was over the café dimmed its lights and the customers rose and drifted out. "There's a movie now. Why don't you come?" they said to Molkho, who decided to join them, wondering whether he could put in for overtime. He was led to a part of the village he hadn't been in before and shown into the local cinema, apparently a renovated chicken run, which was soon packed with more people than he would have guessed lived in the place, many of them young couples. The natives are stirring, he thought, looking up at the high corrugated-tin ceiling on its wooden rafters and down at the seats, which seemed to be ordinary house chairs spread in a semicircle on the dirt floor, which still smelled of chicken manure. A large sheet hung at one end of the hall and a projector occupied a table in the middle, while in a far corner mint tea and sunflower seeds were being served to the audience, which stood around joking and laughing at the children who were caught sneaking in. The Indian girl's mother was there too, seated with a peaceful look on her face, wet wisps of freshly washed hair sticking out from under a black kerchief, her large belly protruding and her eyes already glued to the makeshift screen. Molkho sat near her and waved a friendly hello, which she returned with a smile after a brief hesitation. All in all, he now felt welcomed by the villagers, who seemed content with him as well as curious.

The lights had gone out and the reel was being wound when he felt a hand on his arm. It was the music teacher. "I've got good news," she said. "Ben-Ya'ish just called from Karmiel. He's halfway here!" By now, Molkho had the feeling that Ben-Ya'ish was less an actual person than a collective identity passed from one villager to another, but making no comment, he stretched out in his chair, sipping slowly from his mint tea. The movie, which was in Turkish or Greek, was amateurishly made and promised from the outset to be a rather erotic, if not out-and-out pornographic, film about high-society sex in a luxury hotel on some Mediterranean coast. The female lead was a dark-haired, buxom woman, not pretty but vivacious and bold, even oddly maternal, to whom the audience responded with a buzz of whispers and a cracking of sunflower seeds while Molkho scooped up some dirt from the floor and let it trickle through his fingers until only a few crumbs were left, raising them to his nose and inhaling the aroma of chicken dung flavored with poultry feed. Meanwhile, the actors on the screen having dramatically stripped and begun making love, the audience fell quiet, its every breath audible, its eyes narrowed as though with somnolence—Molkho's, too, though he was also beginning to feel hungry. Idly he sat watching the passionate embraces, wondering whether they were real or shammed, his head lolling heavily; but suddenly, as if a rusty old motor inside him had suddenly turned over, he felt his member grow stiff, and he frowned deeply, sickened and titillated at once.

The lights were kept dimmed when it was time for the reel to be changed, leaving people to whisper unseen in the dark. Someone knelt in front of Molkho. It was a young woman who said, "Ben-Ya'ish called again! He caught a ride to Kiryat Shmonah." "Kiryat Shmonah?" echoed Molkho mirthfully, for the council manager, it seemed, had overshot his mark and now had to travel back the other way. "Yes, but he'll try to get back here tonight. You may as well stay." As if by now he had anywhere to go!

The movie ended at eleven. Heavily the audience rose and stretched itself, yawning disappointedly. Molkho exited behind the Indian's pregnant wife, who waddled on her short, crooked legs like a big duck; she was, he noticed when she smiled at him, slightly cross-eyed, like her daughter. The moon was just rising in the starry sky, and it was very cold. Briefcase in hand he walked silently by her side, adjusting himself to her slow pace. The audience began to disperse, and she, too, chose a path and struck out on it, quickening her tiny steps as if pursuing the stomach that preceded her. It takes guts to go to the movies when you're so close to giving birth, Molkho thought. Not that there was any reason for concern, for even if she were to deliver right here and now, in the middle of the path, there were still lights in many houses and the village showed no signs of going to bed. On the contrary, the later the hour, the livelier things seemed: shadowy figures could be seen carrying work tools, a tractor chugged somewhere nearby, and there was an overall sense of definite, if rather vague, activity.

The lights were on in the Indian's house too. He was waiting up and did not seem surprised to see Molkho appear with his wife, as if it had been clear to him all along that the visitor was fated to sleep there. Did he want to eat anything? asked the man, who was wearing pants and pajama tops, in a low but wakeful tone of voice. Molkho, though, did not want to bother his host—who, surrounded by his piles of books, appeared at this midnight hour to be full of intellectual vigor—and agreed only to drink a glass of wine with him. "Ben-Ya'ish is on his way. Everyone says so," Molkho whispered, and the Indian nodded, though the whereabouts of the council manager did not seem to concern him unduly. While his wife took out fresh sheets and cleared the living room couch, he went to his daughter's room, lifted her in her sleep, and carried her out like a folded ebony bird.

Molkho tried to help, catching hold of the girl's leg and feeling a wave of warmth when her large, sleepy eyes, without their glasses now, opened for a moment to regard him. The woman spread the child's sheets on the couch, and the Indian laid her down and covered her. Then her bed was remade with fresh sheets for Molkho, who was given a towel too. "I'm sorry to be such a nuisance," he said happily, "but what could I do? This Ben-Ya'ish of yours is playing games with us all."

The door shut behind him. Shut, too, were the windows and blinds of the room, which still was warm from the girl's sleep. He put his briefcase on the desk and paused to look at the schoolbooks scattered there, careful not to touch the glasses that lay opened on top of them and stirred his pity in some unclear way. He debated whether to put on the pajamas he had brought or to lie down in his underwear and decided in the end that he needed the pajamas to sleep. Why, he thought, full of wonder at himself, she hated sleeping in other people's houses and this is the second time this week I'm doing it!

There was a knock on the door. It was the woman, who had come to bring him an extra pillow, her eyes on the floor as if embarrassed to see him in pajamas. "I know I'm inconveniencing you," whispered Molkho again, "but it's not my fault. He pulled a fast one on all of us. He's playing games with me." Slowly he stretched out on the child's bed, not feeling at all tired, convinced he would never be able to sleep. In his mind he replayed the scenes of the movie and once more smelled the manure, and then thought of the pregnant woman hurrying on crooked legs down the moonlight-spangled path, of the cow in its shed, and of his sexual desperation, picturing the girl being carried like an ebony bird, the kernel of pure desire hidden in her folded wings. Why here? he began to argue bitterly with his wife. What do you want from me? How can you say that I killed you? But he knew she wouldn't answer and that the silence surrounding him would never be broken, for the days were gone when there was someone to know whatever was on his mind, even at a distance: as soon as he phoned her from the office, she knew just what he was feeling and thinking. Now he was free to do as he pleased, and so he rose barefoot in the dark, carefully lifted the glasses from the desk, held them up, kissed them, fogging the lenses with his lips, wet them slightly, dried them, folded them, and put them back in their place. I've never been so exhausted in my life, he thought, lying down again in preparation for a sleepless night while listening to the crickets and the sound of a tractor.

And yet, despite himself, he fell asleep, waking up five hours later with a feeling of amazement at having gotten through the night. As in his distant days of army service, he rose at once and dressed, made the bed, and put on his shoes in a jiffy. Then, returning his things to the briefcase, he opened the window and leapt straight out into the grainy light of the thick mist swaddling the mountain. Soon the sun would be up. Shivering with cold, he stopped to relieve himself by the cowshed before stepping inside to look at the cow, who stood there alertly as if expecting company. Wondering if cows had feelings, he took a friendly step toward her, tapping her bony forehead with his fist and folding her ears in two like cardboard. No, they didn't, he concluded, stepping back outside with his briefcase. The rim of the sun appeared over the hill, directly above Ben-Ya'ish's house, the windows of which, he noticed, were open. And indeed, hurrying up to it, he found its bed occupied and woke the sleeper at once.

It was Ben-Ya'ish himself, a young man in heavy flannel pajamas who resembled a student more than a politician and lay beneath a pile of quilts surrounded by electrical appliances. "I'm so terribly sorry," he said, smiling at Molkho guiltily, already apologizing before he was awake. "Please, please forgive me. We kept getting our signals crossed. Why, I went all the way to Haifa just to see you, and getting back from there wasn't easy. Why didn't you sleep here? I told my secretary to give you the keys, and all the account books too. You've got me wrong and I'll prove it. I know, I know, you looked for the road and the park and couldn't find them, but I'll show you all the plans. There were just so many out-of-work men who had used up their unemployment checks that I had to dip into the budget to help them, but we'll balance the books yet; everything will add up in the end. Maybe you can show me the best way to do it, because I'm really not very experienced. I mean, I know the money was budgeted for development, but how can you develop a village that's starving to death?"

Molkho sat there listening quietly, incapable of anger, resigned to defeat by this sleepy, stubble-cheeked, bright-eyed young man, toward whom he was feeling increasingly sympathetic. In the end, he knew, he would not even be able to scold him, especially not now, when he had just seen the sun rise in its glory on men in need of mercy. And so he waited for him to dress and drink his coffee, and followed him outside into the still chilly but now clear morning, feeling slightly feverish as he was led to a field with some saplings and bushes that had apparently been planted the night before in lieu of a park and, thence, greeted by cheerful good-mornings, to the other end of the village, where some fresh piles of sand and gravel dumped on a path beside an oil drum full of bubbling tar were meant to signify a road. There was even a steamroller, painted green like a picture from an old children's book. Ben-Ya'ish talked on and on, waving documents and plans. "Just show me the best way to state the facts," he begged Molkho, "the best way to keep us out of trouble, because more trouble is the last thing we need." And in the end, that was just what Molkho did.

12

T HEY WORKED TOGETHER all morning in the office, besieged on all sides by the sound of children practicing Passover songs for a school assembly. The music teacher, Molkho had to admit, was a force to be reckoned with; the singing, coming from all the class-rooms, filled every cranny of the building and inspired him to fill in the missing gaps in the accounts. By eleven, the job was finished and he knew that it was time to leave; but first he asked to see the Indian girl, who was taken out of class for him to remind her to thank her parents. She nodded, darkly solemn behind her big, funny glasses, dressed in her leotard again, and Molkho, who felt sure that hard times were in store for her, was overcome by pity. Damp-eyed, he could not restrain himself from bending down and giving her a kiss. "You're a fine girl," he said to her. "I'll never forget you. Would you like a little brother or a sister?" "Whatever comes," she murmured by rote, as though the answer were rehearsed. By now, it was nearly twelve, and he was being warned not to miss the last bus, which left early on Friday, if he did not want to be stuck in the village again.

The bus took two-and-a-half tiresome hours and seemed to stop in every town in the Galilee, and though evening was still far away when he arrived in Haifa, there was already a Sabbath quiet in the air. At home he was surprised to find his three children happily eating together in the kitchen, his daughter still in her officer's uniform and the college student in high spirits because he had done well on an exam that morning. "You got a nice tan up there," they told him, and he described the village, with all its Indians, for them and even said a few words about the girl. He peered into the pots, emptied food from one to another, ordered the college student to do the dishes, and went to run a bath, shave, and nap, feeling worn out but satisfied, as if after a long but happily ended ordeal.

It was evening when he awoke and found the three of them eating again in the kitchen. "Why didn't you wait?" he scolded them. "It's Sabbath eve!" Even when they explained to him that their grandmother had called to say she wasn't coming, because she had guests of her own, her Russian friend and the friend's daughter, Molkho was not mollified. "So what? That doesn't mean we needn't have a Sabbath dinner! What's the matter with you?" Brooking no objections, he made them stop eating, move their plates to the large table in the dining room, and light the Sabbath candles.

After dinner some friends he had long been out of touch with phoned to invite him over, which pleased him greatly, because he had felt abandoned by their social circle since his wife's death. He had known, of course, that she was more popular than he, for he was considered a dull conversationalist. Still, he had kept telling himself, you would think they'd feel an obligation—toward her, if not toward me.

He dressed his best for the occasion, arrived at his hosts' home to find several couples already there, some of whom he knew, and was seated next to an overweight, heavily bejeweled woman, a divorcée who had come all the way from Tel Aviv and stared at him with liquid, bovine eyes he did not like. Though at first the situation amused him, he soon lapsed into indignant silence. The woman, it seemed, knew a great deal about him and asked him many well-informed questions, to which his answers were short and laconic. Did he ever get to Tel Aviv? she inquired at last. Hardly ever anymore, he replied; the gas simply cost too much. "You could take a bus," she said, blushing. "Yes, I know," answered Molkho. "I took one from the Galilee for three hours today, and I hope I never take another." The guests sitting close to him snickered, and he felt sure that his hostess was offended. Suddenly he feared they might give up on him.

Though he rose early the next morning, it was already very hot. He put on old clothes, did a wash in the machine, and went down to wash his car and hoe his little garden plot. At ten, he called his mother-in-law, but her room did not answer and the information desk did not know where she was, so he sat down to itemize his Galilee expenses, which seemed far too small, no matter how long the list grew. He then hung the wash on the line, cleaned the storeroom, throwing out some old cans of dry paint, and was about to shower when, loath to take off his work clothes so soon, he went about energetically looking for something else to do. Finding nothing, he said to his younger son, "Come on, let's take a walk in the ravine. That's something we haven't done in ages." The boy, however, was too lazy to move, so that Molkho, though reluctant to go by himself, changed his shoes and headed down the familiar path. At first, he had to traverse an obstacle course of building debris, old cement sacks, rusting boilers, and even an intact washing machine, all indisputable evidence of his neighbors' economic progress; but the farther down he walked, the more nature reasserted itself with rank lushness, and a deep silence descended on the path, which wound in and out among bushes. The sea below him vanished from sight, as did the houses above, leaving him as alone as if he were in the heart of a jungle. Conscious of his quickened heartbeat, he stopped and considered turning back, knowing that the climb up would be even harder; but the last few days had given him new strength and he kept on going to the bottom, where the winter rain had unfurled such a carpet of curly grass that he could have lain down and rolled in it were it not for all the detritus, which included the bleached bones of a large animal. The sea was back in sight now, and deciding not to retrace his steps but rather to ascend the opposite slope, where the vegetation was thinner, and from there to telephone his children to pick him up in the car, he set out in that direction, passing three merrily picnicking women drinking tea. He exchanged a few friendly words with them and started up the path, which was less overgrown but very steep, heading toward a row of houses crowning the hill. The sun was beating down now, and the unfamiliar ascent was fatiguing, especially as it ended at a barbed-wire fence surrounding the backyard of the first house. By the time he managed to get through it, he had torn his pants, cut his leg, and come to regret the whole adventure. Dirty and thirsty, he came out on a little street that did not seem to have a pay phone, only a synagogue, from which some men were just emerging. He would be better off, he decided, going to his mother-in-law's nearby old-age home, slipping unnoticed up to her room, and tidying up there.

Head down, he passed quickly through the big glass entrance and crossed the spic-and-span lobby, whose occupants, dressed in their Sabbath best, looked approvingly at the figure in torn work clothes, no doubt a repairman come to fix something. Taking the slow, solid elevator up to the ninth floor, he walked down the dim hallway and knocked on his mother-in-law's door. Though there was no answer, the door opened when he tried the handle. Surprisingly, the room was in a state of great disorder: an open suitcase lay on the floor with a dress half-thrown over it, and pillows and pillowcases had been hung out to air on the railing of the little terrace. He was still bewilderedly taking it in when the sheets rustled on his mother-in-law's bed and up sat a stranger in pajamas, a plump, sturdy woman of about thirty-five with big bright eyes.

Molkho saw at once by her resemblance to her mother that she was the daughter of the little old Russian, the young lady who was unhappy in Israel and wished to return to the Soviet Union. At first, roused from her beauty sleep by an unexpected intruder, she seemed terrified, even hysterical; yet before many seconds had gone by, he began to suspect that she was in fact drunk. And on a summery day like this, he marveled, startled by the strong scent of alcohol. She knew almost no Hebrew, let alone English or French, and the few words she uttered between giggles sounded odd indeed.

Through the open window the sky seemed very blue. He tried explaining who he was while the plump woman tried telling him where his mother-in-law had gone to, laughing over each Hebrew word as if it were a particularly funny joke. Finally, despairing of communicating, she led him out on the terrace and pointed at the lawn below, where, near the rosebush-ringed swimming pool, sat his wife's mother and her Russian friend, sunbathing on flowery blankets. Molkho nodded, weighed going to the bathroom for a drink of water, ruled against it, and strode quickly back out to the elevator. Yet he did not ride it all the way down but got out on the fifth floor, where the usual solemn silence prevailed in the medical ward, though because of the heat the doors of the sickrooms were open, revealing grave oldsters who sat leafing through magazines beside their moribund friends. Molkho thrilled to the sight of the familiar equipment, the white intravenous bottles, the wheelchairs, and the gray tanks of oxygen, and was about to sit down to rest when a nurse blocked his way. Rolling up his ripped pants, he showed her the cut on his leg. "I'm Mrs. Starkman's son-in-law," he explained, "and I thought you might give me first aid." At once he was ushered into a sunny little office, where, after he washed, the cut was disinfected, treated with a yellow, pollenlike powder, and bandaged with gauze. It must be a welcome change for the nurses to deal with something nonterminal, he thought, eagerly examining the apparatus around him and happily concluding that, allowing for his modest budget, the care received by his wife had been quite state-of-the-art.

He descended to the lobby with his bandaged leg. As usual, he reflected, summer had come all at once, bursting through every window. Head high, he made straight for the lawn, where he found his mother-in-law, drugged by the sun, in a state of brazen nirvana, fast asleep in a house frock that bared her veiny old legs, while her Russian friend sat silently guarding her, a bit fearful of the unaccustomedly strong sun, her white hair tinged with a few last strands of gold. Recognizing him at once, she rose and executed her odd little bow, then introduced herself in a pleasant voice as Stasya, and chatted in a Hebrew that wasn't bad at all. Molkho, for his part, speaking in a whisper so as not to wake his mother-in-law, whose profound slumber seemed slightly worrisome to him too, explained why he was there and even displayed his new bandage. He had just asked the Russian woman why her daughter didn't like Israel when his mother-in-law, hearing his voice, awoke and opened her faded gray, sun-softened eyes with surprise and a hint of annoyance. Yet, though Molkho began telling her at once of his adventures, rolling up his pants to show the bandage again, she did not appear to listen. Even when he switched the subject to her grandchildren, she seemed too weak from the sun to respond, barely able to keep her eyes from shutting. Why, in a minute she'll melt away right in front of me! he thought. It grieved him to see her so springlike and peaceful on this blue Saturday afternoon, as if she had already forgotten all about her daughter's death.

13

THE NEXT MORNING, he asked to see the director. At ten o'clock he was summoned, laying his report on the desk with a solemnity that took his easygoing boss by surprise. "I was there twice and even stayed over one night," Molkho told him. "I had a look around and checked things out as best I could. I don't claim to have it figured out down to the bottom line, but I did see quite a lot, and my impression is that there may be a lot of confusion up there, but there's no corruption. There's a road being built and a park being planted, and while the village council doesn't own a tractor, I did see a steam-roller. I helped them put their accounts in order and insisted that they itemize everything and attach receipts. If they do, I think we can pass the file on to the state comptroller's office. Maybe there are still dark secrets to unearth; that's their job. But I think we've done what we could. Of course, it's up to you."

The director leafed through the file, asked a few questions, and thanked Molkho profusely, as if he had done something heroic, after which he inquired about the health of his children and his mother-in-law, whom he remembered well. And that was the end of it. Or, at least, so Molkho thought until later that day he was again called to the director's office, where, to his alarm, he found the legal adviser sitting in a sleeveless knit dress, her high-heeled shoes crossed, turn-ing the Xeroxed pages of the file. She looked pale, and he suddenly feared that she was about to exact her pound of flesh for his failure to go to bed with her. Why, oh why, couldn't he at least have kissed those lily-white arms, which certainly deserved some consideration? Greeting him with a faint smile, she made no attempt to conceal the coolness with which she had already written him off. She had been invited, explained the director, to ask Molkho a few questions, which he proceeded to answer as best he could. Yes, work on the road had begun; he had seen it himself. And the park, too; the trees and bushes had already been planted. Not that he knew what they needed a park for with all that natural magnificence around them, but of course, it was their prerogative to have one. As for the tractor, yes, it was in his report—that is, it was not exactly a tractor: it was a secondhand steamroller, but it did exist and a copy of its registration was included. And though there was no denying that Ben-Ya'ish was a rather muddled young man who had taken administrative liberties with unemployment checks, this was not the first such case come across by their office, which had always looked the other way in the past. After all, times were hard up there.

The legal adviser stared at him intently, her freckles pale in the afternoon sunlight. Did she still roam the world for opera? wondered Molkho, who had himself given music short shrift in recent months. Looking down at the desk, he phrased his defense of Ben-Ya'ish carefully while the director sat listening in silence. "So you think everything is just fine up there?" the legal adviser interrupted mockingly, as though he were a clearly hopeless case. "You found no problems? No irregularities?" I didn't say that, answered Molkho patiently. "I was there twice and even stayed over one night, but I can't say I went into it thoroughly." "That's obvious," she laughed snidely, continuing to leaf through the file. But the director, though noncommittal, seemed to be on Molkho's side; with a kind look in his direction he picked up the original file and began to thumb through it too. All at once Molkho's fears vanished. Casually, as though the rest no longer mattered, he rose and crossed the large room to the open window, from where he watched the two of them studying the file. For a moment he just stood there. Then, feeling the need to make some overture to her, or perhaps to them both, he declared, "Why, it's really summer!" Startled by the sound of his voice, he pointed out the window by way of illustration. "It's always the same," he explained. "Spring is over before you even know it."

PART IV SUMMER

1

BUT THAT FIRST SUMMER gave birth to a supersummer, so brutally torrid that even the nights were blistering. It started halfway through July; a firm but invisible hand blocked the sea with a wall of grimy white haze, turning the temperately hot Mediterranean coast into a brutal miasma. No matter how early you rose in the morning, a scorching wind was already blowing. The thermometer zoomed upward and stuck there. The weather was often the lead item on the news, the forecasters being called upon to explain the inexplicable in half-menacing, half-apologetic tones. Worse yet, the travel tax was suddenly doubled, forcing mass cancellations by those planning to seek relief abroad. Despairingly people flocked to the beaches, among them Molkho, who hadn't been to the seashore for years and was only halfway through a diet meant to enhance his romantic prospects. For days on end, he ate nothing but blotchy, seedless watermelons, staring angrily every morning at the stubborn scales that registered his weight loss with agonizing slowness. The thought of all the good food that he was missing or sometimes reluctantly left on his plate enveloped him in a thin web of gloom. He was still not used to the shy promptings of sex that, having first stirred faintly in the spring, now accompanied him with gingerly steps like a stray but thoroughbred cat that had adopted him, its stiff, velvety tail sometimes brushing his thighs.

It's high time, he thought, making his way among the bodies scattered in the sand and scrutinizing some that he hardly would have glanced at until recently. Rarely did they interest him, for nearly all seemed badly flawed and limp with the humidity, though now and then he caught a glimpse of some almost painfully attractive feature. Best of all, he liked the young mothers, who had a harried-looking glow, so different from the better-groomed singles, with their hard-bitten lust to be tanned. Stepping into the water, which toward evening resembled a salty, tepid bath, he thought, if only I could make a collage—a leg from here, a head from there, a shoulder or smile from somewhere else—I might construct someone lovable. Wading through the breaking surf, which pounded so hard at this time of year that he swallowed whole mouthfuls of it, he pushed on into deeper, calmer water, where he swam beside lone figures like himself, mostly brawny old women with helmetlike bathing caps, sometimes peeing silently while staring innocently up at a sun that seemed never to set but simply to dissipate in a white curtain of haze, after which he swam slowly back, letting the breakers cast him ashore like a corpse. Resurrected and still dripping water, he strolled through the crowd feeling like a sandwich board: See for Yourself! This Is My Body! Untouched by Death! Find Me a Woman! Often he ran into people he knew—colleagues from work, former neighbors, friends of his wife's, doctors and staff from the hospital—and stood over them, patting his chest and chatting about the crazy weather, this second, superhot summer begotten by the first. Whether smiling or serious, they lay looking up at him as though conscious that it was not the weather but his uncontrollable lust that had brought him down to the beach, and then inquired about his children and mother-in-law, shaking their heads upon hearing how well the old woman was doing, as if amazed that her daughter's death hadn't done her in too. Sometimes, to cheer him, they would tell him the latest news about who else was dying of cancer, which was often no news at all, since he had already seen the victim in the hospital, slipping with a frightened look through the doors of the oncology ward, so that he stood there inattentively glancing at the mountains, from which the gray smoke of forest fires had been rising all summer long, aware of their trying to guess whether he had gotten over his wife's death—since which, incredibly enough, less than a year had gone by. At last, feeling them weary of him, he unobtrusively went off to dry himself and dress, returning home to a cruelly long and too brightly lit evening of Volume I of *Anna Karenina*, which he would have put down long ago, were it not for the pleas of his daughter, now discharged from the army and vacationing in Europe. "Don't give up, Dad. It's a really good book. Why don't you try to finish it?"

And then, in the first week of August, the supersummer begat a superbaby of its own, the whitest and most devilish of them all: the air rolled over and died, the sun approached meltdown, and a livid sky shut out the world while hordes of newly arrived black Jews from Ethiopia staged protest marches on the roads that sent the mercury shooting even higher. You're lucky to be out of this hellhole, Molkho whispered through parched lips to his dead wife upon rising each morning. There was talk of mysterious sunspots, yet Europe was deluged by rain, and most likely the culprit was a stubborn high-pressure front that refused to budge from the Turkish-Iranian frontier. Shown on television, it resembled a shapeless, odorless, irregularly formed amoeba, and for a moment, thinking that it might be connected to her too, that it was perhaps her last signal from galactic space before streaking to her final annihilation, Molkho was gripped by the transcendent fear that this strange, abstract blob was all that was left of his wife.

2

H E SAT UP in the middle of the night, unable to sleep comfortably. In the neighboring houses lights were on too, for the heat kept everyone awake. He stepped out on the terrace and gazed up at the yellow halo around the moon, musing—no longer fearfully, but with a deep sorrow—on how his wife was pared down to a last, nameless cell that still fought to preserve its identity. The thought that it, too, would soon be snuffed out in some vast, dark emptiness made him shiver. I must fall in love, he told himself before climbing back into bed, because otherwise this longing will destroy me.

In the morning he spoke as usual to his mother, who complained bitterly about the heat, which was even worse in Jerusalem. Suppose, she asked suddenly, that she came to stay with him for a while and spent some time on the beach? Horrified, he tried to talk her out of it. "The humidity here is ghastly," he explained. "You'll never fall asleep at night. At least in Jerusalem there's a breeze. Why don't you buy yourself an air conditioner? I'll even come and pick it out for you." But his mother did not want an air conditioner. She wanted to stay with him, and there was nothing he could do about it.

And so, that Friday, he pulled her, damp and sweating, out of the taxi that brought her to his house, helped her hang her dresses in the college student's old room, and sat silently across from her on the terrace facing the sea. In the evening, playing host to two old women, he muttered the blessing over the Sabbath wine and ate the meat loaf brought by his mother, who talked nonstop, taking advantage of his mother-in-law's patience, behind whose expression of eager interest lay concealed a thin mockery like his wife's. At last, sapped by the humidity, his mother trundled off to bed, from where he heard her snoring lightly.

On Sunday, after work, he took the little beach chair and went with her to the seashore, making sure to find an isolated spot where no one was likely to see her. Depositing her there, a large, heavy, funny-looking woman with bared fat legs, he went for a swim and a walk, heading first up the beach and then down, until finally, toward sunset, when the shore was nearly deserted, he ventured to sit beside her in the wet sand, absentmindedly digging a trench by her chair while letting her ramble on about her financial worries and his father and her childhood in Jerusalem and her neighbors and her friends and their children and their grandchildren and everyone who asked about him, happy to hear that his praises were being sung in his hometown, where ghostly figures from his past kept running into her, old friends and not-even-friends from school and the army, all eager to know how he was faring. And it was there, by the sea, a molten sun grazing the horizon, that Molkho first heard about his old youth-movement counselor, Uri, who together with his wife, Ya'ara, seemed to take an avid interest in him.

3

"BUT WE'VE BEEN THINKING and talking of you ever since last summer!" said his old counselor to him, lightly resting a hand on his shoulder. "Since last summer?" Molkho asked, touched to be so unexpectedly thought of after so many years, even if it did seem rather odd. "But why since last summer? My wife was still alive then." "Yes, I know," said his old counselor, "but all of Jerusalem already knew that it was terminal." "It did?" asked Molkho with a shiver of excitement. "Yes," replied his counselor. "There are always people who make it their business to spread bad news; even if they don't know who it's about, it makes them feel better. There were all sorts of rumors about you, and your mother talked a lot too; she had to tell everyone all the medical details, even when she didn't understand them. You have no idea how well informed we were, especially about how you took the whole long, hard death on yourself. So that when we heard that it was over, I said to Ya'ara, 'Who knows, perhaps this is the very man God has in mind for us. What actually do we remember about him, though? Was he really once in love with you?' "

They were standing on the long stone steps of the Jerusalem Theater on a broiling Saturday afternoon, hugging the thin line of shade by the closed box offices. A fiery silence reigned all around. Not a soul was to be seen in the empty white plaza. The shutters of the aristocratic old houses of the neighborhood were all shut. Further up the hill they could see the stone wall of the Presidential Mansion, and further down, where the street slanted steeply, the mysterious building of the old Turkish leper colony in its dusty copse of trees. As soon as he had stepped out of his car in the parking lot, Molkho had spied his former counselor's tall, thin figure walking back and forth in the shade along the top step, a wide-brimmed black hat clutched in one hand, looking down like a lone actor waiting impatiently onstage for his supporting cast. Solemnly Molkho had ascended the steps and greeted him with a timorous smile, heartened by the confidence radiating from the strong, bony frame in the black pants and sweaty white shirt of an Orthodox Jew, his dusty, broadbrimmed hat rather reassuringly resembling a cowboy's, for Molkho had been afraid of this reunion after nearly thirty years and was relieved to find he still liked the man. The old-fashioned garb; the heavy, slightly graying beard; even the ritual fringes of the undershirt sticking untidily out from the shirt—to Molkho these seemed but the latest disguise of this eternal Kierkegaardian-Buberian truthseeker who had come to them in those days from some left-wing kibbutz and was now (as he had informed his ex-youth-grouper the week before on the telephone) an observant Jew. Molkho had remembered him well, had in fact always admired him, though he himself had never been a "Schechterite," as his counselor's group of sensitive, if sometimes strange, friends were called, after the Haifa Bible teacher who was their guru. Indeed, it had never occurred to him to join them, having no interest in their way of life, which involved drifting from one kibbutz to another, only to be expelled from each in the end for what was considered their elitist factionalism, not to mention their mysticism and talent for attracting the prettiest girls while disdaining socialist goals, preferring to search their navels for the Meaning of Life while composing odd hymns and prayers. Ultimately they had founded a kibbutz of their own called Yodfat in the Lower Galilee, where some settled down but most eventually left, scattering in all directions, though a few, like Uri Adler, who had been one of their leaders, continued their religious quest.

Thus, Molkho was not totally surprised by the strange telephone call he had received, the purpose of which he had guessed at once. Why, he thought, warmly shaking the hand held out to greet him, it's kind but only natural that someone should want to cook me up a woman in this bake-house of a summer. And yet he blushed with embarrassment, as though it were undignified to have agreed so readily to such a rendezvous. "How did you hear about me?" he asked. "From whom?" "But we've been thinking and talking about you ever since last summer!" answered his old counselor, heartily returning his handshake.

4

MOLKHO LET OUT A LITTLE LAUGH and blushed again, feeling an odd happiness. It was still too much to absorb. Had he really once been in love with her? he asked himself candidly, trying his best to remember. Thirty-four years had gone by, and even then Ya'ara and he hadn't been in one class for long; that is, she had been a grade ahead of him until their junior year, which she was forced to repeat—a tall, blonde, quietly attractive, academically unsuccessful girl who drifted back to her old classmates during recess. Had he really been in love with her? The fact of the matter was that he was constantly falling in love in those days, each time with a vague and secretive passion that he strove to inflame, in order to break free from his dominating mother, whose only child he was.

Clearly, though, he couldn't leave it at that. "Did she ever finish high school?" he asked his old counselor, whose every gesture, smile, intonation, and burst of enthusiasm seemed to erase the lapsed years, despite Molkho's suspicion that the love in question was purely imaginary. "Was I actually in love with her?" he wondered aloud again, afraid of the deterrent effect of too staunch a denial, so that, standing there in the torrid sun with the Sabbath peace all around them, he was quite prepared to fall in love retroactively if only it would prove helpful. "It's been so long," he laughed. "Maybe I was a bit, but she was older than I was." "Just by a year," his counselor hurried to correct him. "In fact, not even. She's August and you're May. It's only a few months' difference, and after all, you were in the same class, you sat next to each other, you even once

wrote her a love letter. That was the year I was your counselor—or
have you forgotten that too?"

"Of course not," protested Molkho. "How could I forget you?
You were the best thing to happen to us, even if there was all kinds
of gossip about you." "Yes," said his counselor, as though recalling
it with relish, "and not all of it was pure gossip, let me tell you. But
you yourself were never really one of us. Ideas didn't interest you—
not just ours, but anyone's. I can still remember you sitting quietly
through our meetings like a well-brought-up little boy." "Yes, I've
never been an intellectual," confessed Molkho, trying to make the
best of it. "I was always too realistic." "And in the end you dropped
out of the movement without even trying life on a kibbutz, didn't
you?" asked his counselor. "Yes," admitted Molkho, marveling how
this ancient transgression could still be held against him. "And what
did you do in the army?" inquired Uri. "I was a medic," Molkho
said. "That's where I met my wife."

They walked back and forth in the fringe of shade by the box
office, Molkho first speaking about himself, amazed that Uri already
knew so much about him, and then listening to the story of his old
counselor's life with Ya'ara, over which hung the misfortune of a
childless marriage. "That's been our great tragedy," said Uri,
"though it took us a long time to accept it." There had been, he told
Molkho, a long series of painful miscarriages, terminated pregnancies, and endless treatments, during which they had gone from place
to place in search of better luck: from the kibbutz in the Galilee to a
farming village, and then to the city, and then to South America
(where Uri worked as an agricultural adviser, saving money for more
visits to the doctors), and then to the Far East for a fling at medita-
tion and Oriental healing. Finally, ten years ago, they had returned
to Israel with the realization that they had gotten nowhere.

It was his despair of having children that made Molkho's old
counselor turn to Judaism and become a disciple of an Orthodox
rabbi. At first, he thought of this, too, as merely a stage; yet gradually he came to see that the process was a long one, and indeed, there
was still no end to it in sight, because the wisdom he was seeking

could not be found in books but only through contact with those who lived it. True, he refused to be labeled "a penitent Jew," a fundamentalist expression he abhorred; in the last elections he had actually voted for a left-wing candidate. But the fact remained that if he was to make any spiritual progress at all he had to be accepted by the rabbi and his followers, which was far from easy, since an outsider like himself was always under suspicion. They were difficult people, and for several years they had been urging him to remarry and have children, a childless man being religiously incomplete. At first, he hadn't wanted to hear of it; yet the longer he spent with them, the more he saw the inner logic of the demand, spiritually if not psychologically. He felt torn in two, because his love for his wife, whom it wasn't simple to live with under such circumstances, was as great as ever; but the years were going by, he wasn't getting any younger, and his craving for children, which was only aggravated by his situation, kept growing. In fact, he had even been offered a match, and Ya'ara was ready to divorce him. "It's my fate to be childless," she had told him, "but you can still have a family. Just don't imagine that I can go on living with you and watching you suffer." He had been agonizing about it for a year now, for how could a professionless woman of over fifty (her life having passed in travel and trying to become pregnant, so that to this day she was only an assistant in a kindergarten) get along on her own, especially as he himself earned precious little from his job as a public-school teacher, most of his time being devoted to study? Naturally, the rabbi's followers were willing to find a match for her too; but she had no desire to join their community, while he refused even to consider a divorce before her future was taken care of. Yet whom could they find for her when they were socially so out of touch? The only old friends they ever saw were those they ran into by chance, from one of whom they had heard about Molkho. They had actually looked him up in an old photograph from the movement, a chubby, friendly-looking boy. "But what do we remember about him?" Molkho's old counselor had asked his wife. "Was he really in love with you?"

Molkho walked beside him in the shrinking line of shade, listening in a turmoil. "So you want me to marry your wife?" he asked at last, looking at his old counselor, who stood staring palely into space. "Yes," replied Uri, returning an anxious glance. "It would be a way of keeping it in the family. After all, we were once all so close."

5

T HAT EVENING, when it was already dark and the sky was strewn with clear summer stars above a city flapping in the hot desert wind like a woman awakened from her afternoon nap and crossly dragging her bedclothes, Molkho stood waiting for his counselor by the entrance to the Edison Cinema on the corner of Isaiah and Rabbi Isaac of Prague streets, along which ran the unofficial border between observant and nonobservant Jerusalem, watching some moviegoers decide whether to buy tickets for the first show. Although he hadn't been in this spot for years, everything was as he remembered it from his childhood, which had passed unhappily a few blocks away. The large white building, a teenage haunt of his, was unchanged too; nostalgically he surveyed its three marble steps and long vitrines, with their pictures of movie stars, while recalling the many hours he had spent in its front rows, the cheapest seats available, his eyes tearing from the flickering screen and the sad fate of Vivien Leigh in *Gone With the Wind,* with whom he had fallen so madly in love that he had spent weeks imagining how, despite his tender age, he might become her beau.

The last undecideds outside the theater made up their minds at last and vanished into its darkened hall while the old ticket-taker locked the glass doors, switched off the lights in the lobby, and retired to a comfortable corner. His counselor's lateness, by now considerable, was beginning to annoy Molkho. Was he waiting in the wrong place? Could he have been such a flop that morning that the whole thing had been called off? And I still have to drive all the way back to Haifa, he grumbled to himself, striding moodily down the dark street that led to the Orthodox North Side, which lay spread out before him in a great puddle of light. He should at least have thought of taking down their address, since they hadn't any telephone. But, just then, up the street swung a nearly empty, brightly lit bus, inside of which he made out his old counselor, dressed the same except for the black hat, which now rested on his head, though tilted back with a jaunty defiance. Angry at having been kept waiting, he remained standing on the dark street, but his counselor, stepping quickly off the bus at the stop opposite the theater and spotting Molkho at once, was already striding toward him apologetically; the rabbi's weekly sermon, he explained, had run on past the end of the Sabbath and there had been a long wait for the bus. "I was afraid we had gotten our signals crossed," confessed Molkho, the words scarcely out of his mouth before he regretted sounding overeager. Uri made no reply. His breezy manner of the morning gone, he regarded Molkho with a worried look. Both felt the awkwardness of the situation. "I should have gone straight to your house," Molkho said. "You never would have found it," said his counselor. "You may have grown up in this city, but in the neighborhood I live in, even a native could get lost."

They walked to Molkho's car, which seemed to arouse his counselor's interest. "It's considered quite feminine," Molkho chuckled, pointing out its special features. "A feminine car?" marveled Uri. "Do cars have sexes, then?" "Only if you want them to," answered Molkho, pleased with his witty rejoinder. "It's amazing," declared his counselor, removing his hat and settling into the front seat, "how refined the anatomy of human pleasure has become." At the first corner, they turned left toward a neighborhood where Molkho's grandfather had lived years ago, in whose empty streets the desert heat of the day seemed transmuted into a sad solitude. "I was born near here," Molkho said, stopping for four black-coated Talmudists to cross the street with unreasonable slowness. "I wouldn't recognize the house, though. I haven't been here for ages and everything's changed." "I suppose it would be," said his counselor, guiding them through a maze of streets that were full of dead ends and no-entrances. "The ultra-Orthodox have taken over here too," he added,

telling Molkho to bear right at a traffic light onto a northbound
highway and then right again toward a project that seemed to grow
vaster the further into it they drove, so that Molkho, who had lost his
bearings completely, felt as if they had left dark Jerusalem behind
them and were now in another city lit by thousands of bulbs like a
gigantic power plant. "This is Kiryat Mattersdorf," explained his
counselor while piloting him through a large, full parking lot to an
empty space in a far corner that seemed reserved just for them.

They struck out down a dark alley past some tanks of cooking
gas and emerged in a square where children were running back and
forth among young mothers pushing baby carriages. On one corner
several men in white shirts were engrossed in lively conversation.
Uri walked quickly, his head slightly bowed, looking up now and
then to greet some passing acquaintance, while Molkho trailed behind him, vaguely troubled by the strange surroundings. Suddenly
he stopped, reaching out to touch his counselor's shoulder. "You'd
better know now," he whispered, "that I'm not a believer at all. Far
from it." But his counselor was undaunted. "Nothing is far from it,"
he answered sharply, the hint of a rebuke in his voice. "It's enough
to say you don't believe. Neither do I. Come, let's cut through here."
They passed a row of garbage pails and climbed a few steps to a
building, inside of which some tots and pregnant women were waiting for two elevators. "What, you have elevators?" asked Molkho in
surprise. "And why not?" smiled Uri, weaving his way through the
crowd of toddlers with a respectful glance at his neighbors, who all
wished him a good new week. The elevators seemed to be stopping at
every floor, where more crowds of children were no doubt waiting,
and indeed, when one finally arrived, a horde of merry youngsters
burst out of it. Though scratched and battered, it was large enough
for a department store and everyone fitted easily into it. In no time,
pressed by eager little hands, every button was lit, and they were
stopping at floor after floor, on each of which more children got on
and off under the eyes of the good-naturedly chiding adults, and
Molkho, slightly alarmed by so much teeming life, glimpsed men and
women lounging outside their apartments.

They got out on a top floor and walked down a long hallway, at the end of which Molkho's counselor knocked rhythmically on a door, opening it himself when there was no answer. The apartment was dark and warm, the only light coming from a crescent moon, which shone unhindered through a window. Apparently as surprised by this state of affairs as Molkho, Uri dropped his hat on the living room table and hurried to a back room, through the doorway of which Molkho made out the lower half of a woman's body covered by a thin blanket. Still adjusting his eyes to the darkness, he heard a whisper, no doubt a plea to get up, followed by a soft, sleepy murmur, and reminded of the times he had fought to arouse his deathward-slumbering wife, he felt a dreamy rush of desire. He shut his eyes to hear better, taking a small, weary step in their direction; but at once he caught himself and stood looking around the room, from the shadows of which now emerged some straw chairs with embroidered pillows and several hangings on the walls. On the large table were a folded tablecloth, a set of tall pewter candlesticks, a bottle of wine, an open book, and an ivory comb, each object an erotic gleam in the darkness, as though destined, like herself, for his possession.

A light was switched on in the bedroom, casting new shadows on the walls, and there was a brief laugh; then, shutting the door behind him, Molkho's counselor returned to the living room, beaming brightly, if still a bit uncomfortably. Quickly he turned on a light there too, which fell on some more furniture stacked in a little hallway, and cleared an armchair of some books. "Sit down," he urged Molkho. "Ya'ara went to sleep early because she decided we weren't coming. It's all my fault for being late. Please sit down." He moved some books from a second chair too, hurrying to make order, but Molkho remained awkwardly standing, trying to stay calm while gazing out the window at the lights dotting the hillside across from him. You'd think this were my idea! he thought indignantly, hearing the sound of running water and of something that sounded like the beating of wings. You'd think I were some salesman who had come knocking on their door! Just then, though, the bedroom door opened and Ya'ara stepped out. Tense with expectation, he cast a soft, weary glance at her, his heart missing a beat, only to realize at once that he had confused her with someone else or, rather, combined in his memory two different people who now immediately split up again. Of course, he thought astonishedly, that's who she was! Why, I really was in love with her; I may even have written her that love letter, he told himself, feeling a pang at the sight of the gray, though still lavish, hair gathered at the nape of her neck in an old-fashioned braid.

She was tall and long-legged, though her body, while still lissome, bulged slightly at the belly beneath a terry-cloth robe, as if all her failed pregnancies were gathered there in the form of a question mark. He shook her hand and glanced at her makeupless face, which, whether from sleep or excitement, was flushed like his own. Her skin was dry but smooth, except for the crow's-feet by her small, pearly eyes, their strange, greenish beige color highlighted by her gray hair. "Why, you haven't changed one bit," she said in a husky drawl. "I'd have recognized you anywhere, I swear!" "I haven't?" he asked self-consciously, feeling almost slighted. "But how can that be?" It was as if they wanted to keep him a boy forever, to deny that he had grown up. "Ya'ara has a wonderful memory for faces," explained her husband, pulling up a chair for her as if she, too, were a guest. Slowly she sank into it, while Molkho sat down with an understanding nod, his covertly male glance running quickly down to her bare, snow-white feet, their small, perfect toenails as clear as if made of cut glass. He caught his breath, overwhelmed by the heat and her presence, which seemed to promise untold pleasures that he was not at all sure he could cope with. In any case, he promised himself, I'll go to bed with her at least once.

Her husband stood beside her, affably listening to him explain his mistake. "To tell you the truth, it just now dawned on me that I was under a wrong impression. You see, I partly confused you with someone else from our class," he stammered, mentioning a name that neither of them knew. "I pictured you differently, but it's all come back to me now." He made his confession gladly, though feeling parched and fatigued, and she flashed him a crimson smile, reaching into the pocket of her robe for a crumpled yellow pack, from which she blindly took a cigarette, stuck it in her mouth, lit it with a lighter in her hand, and inhaled deeply, only then remembering to offer the pack to Molkho. On it was a picture of some gaunt black horsemen who seemed to have ridden out of the pages of history. "And we really did share a desk for several months!" he added excitedly.

His counselor offered to make him some coffee to perk him up for the drive back to Haifa. "Are you sure you won't sleep over?" he asked. "Yes," replied Molkho, "I have to be at the office at eight." While Uri went to the kitchen, Ya'ara asked Molkho about his work. He did his best to explain it, trying to be precise without too much dull detail, though mentioning by way of illustration his recent trips to the Galilee. "Do you travel a lot?" she asked, sucking greedily on her cigarette. "No," he replied, feeling her bright sympathy. "During my wife's illness I hardly went anywhere." Through the walls of the apartment came various noises mingled with the voices of children, wide awake despite the late hour. Evidently Saturday nights were a time when the building came alive.

"We heard you had a hard year," said his counselor's wife huskily, her small eyes taking his measure. "Just one?" he scoffed, feeling the right to sound resentful, his own eyes resting briefly on her bulging belly before returning to her feet. "There were seven of them, all awful! It wasn't so much the physical part; that was never the worst of it. It was the constant fear, starting with the first operation. It never left us for a moment."

He glanced out the open window, seeking to catch a whiff of the Jerusalem air of his childhood, conscious of having betrayed his dead wife with this woman he hardly knew. Her husband brought Turkish coffee and a plate of cookies on a tray, and she rose to bring Molkho a little table to put it on. "No cookies for me, thank you," he said, "I happen to be on a diet." "You, on a diet! What ever for?" she asked with a laugh. "But just look at me!" he exclaimed, gladdened by this sign of her approval, though with such vehemence that his counselor, seated in a rocking chair, changed the subject to the guest's children, especially his younger son, who appeared to be something of a problem, because the boy was doing so badly in school that there was again talk of leaving him back. "Did you ever think of sending him to a boarding school," inquired Uri, "or aren't there any good ones in your area? Say what you will about the Orthodox, their boarding schools are first-rate."

The conversation now shifted to Orthodox Jews, whom Molkho was careful not to criticize, unlike his wife, who grew apoplectic at the mere mention of them. But his caution, he soon saw, was unnecessary, for Uri, rocking wildly, gave vent to such violently anti-Orthodox opinions himself that for a moment his long beard seemed no more than the badge of a bohemian kibbutznik. Ya'ara sat puffing attentively on her cigarette, the smoke swirling in little clouds out the window and into the vast night; she had, Molkho noticed sadly, several varicose veins in her legs. They must be real night owls, he thought, for they did not seem to be tired at all, and remembering the long drive ahead of him, he took advantage of the first lull to rise from his seat. "Do you ever get to Haifa?" he asked offhandedly, as if hardly expecting to see them again. "Rarely," said his counselor, rising too, "but now we will. Perhaps Ya'ara will come visit you," he added, putting an arm around his wife. She rose lazily from her chair, causing Molkho a moment's worry that she might be too tall for him; but the firmness of her handshake banished all his fears, for they had already, so it seemed, decided in his favor and nothing he could say or do could make them change their minds. They were strong, self-willed people, joined by the powerful bond that only childless couples have, world travelers for whom all things were possible. Now, at this midnight hour, he felt glad to be in their hands.

"Do you own this apartment or lease it?" he asked on his way to the front door, looking with interest at the walls. The question surprised them. Neither, they replied; they simply paid a monthly rental, which was not very high. "And you don't own a home anywhere?" Molkho asked. No, they said; they had never saved the money to buy one. He took her hand again, feeling it soft and smooth in his palm. "Well, then, I hope we'll meet again," he declared, tensing at the sight of her dead gray hair. "Perhaps on my next visit to Jerusalem."

Her husband walked him to the elevator, in which children were still riding up and down, no doubt to make up for the forced

inactivity of the long summer Sabbath. "You live in a busy building," Molkho said, trying to pat the head of a little boy, who jumped
back so fearfully that his companions burst out laughing.

Despite the late hour, the street was full of cars and pedestrians. The passersby regarded him curiously, but his counselor merely
nodded to them without offering to introduce him, so that Molkho
thought, I suppose I've disappointed him after all. Yet when he unlocked the car door, something kept him rooted to the spot. "It's
damn queer, what you're doing," he said, swallowing hard. "My wife
has been dead for ten months, and I still can't get over it, can't
connect with anyone. It's like having a phantom limb. For years I
suffered in silence, and now I have to be careful. Why, two months
ago I fell in love with a little girl in some village in the Galilee, just a
black little Indian! It was the strangest thing."

His counselor listened with bowed head. "Let her think about
it," Molkho added blackly. "You do that too, and then we might give
it a try, only slowly. Don't be so sure that I'm the right man for you.
After all, what would you have done if my wife were still alive?" His
counselor didn't answer. Eyes shut and only half-listening, he
seemed loath to talk, perhaps because three black-hatted youths were
eavesdropping from their perch on a nearby fence. "Drive carefully," he said. "I'll be in touch." Slowly Molkho backed out of the
parking lot, the lights of the project in his rearview mirror like
hundreds of questioning eyes.

6

FEELING HIS TIREDNESS lurking inside him he drove slowly,
heading north along the coast, happy to see from the cars on the
road and the campfires on the beach that he was not alone in the
night. On the outskirts of Haifa he decided to park and walk by the
sea for a breath of the humid night air. He wanted to cry, to conjure

up his old high school love and relive it. Even if I never marry her, he thought. Even if she's mine just long enough to start the sap running again.

It was after one when he came home. To his surprise, he found the living room light on. No doubt the high school boy, who was sleeping at a friend's house, had returned for something and forgotten to turn it off. Drawers were open too, the television had been moved, and a strap was torn on one of the blinds. What on earth had gotten into the boy? Perhaps boarding school was not such a bad idea. But Molkho was too tired to pursue the thought and went to bed without showering, crawling naked between the sheets as though loath to wash off Ya'ara's touch. Not until he was already lying in the dark did he notice the ugly white patch on the wall where a picture had been. Suddenly realizing that he had been burgled, he jumped out of bed and ran turning on the lights from room to room. The expensive tape recorder with the stereo earphones was gone. As was the electric kettle. And the alarm clock. All the closets and cabinets had been rifled too, though it was hard to tell what had been taken. Apparently the thief had started to make off with the television also, changing his mind at the last moment. Stunned, Molkho slipped on his pants and went to call the police, noticing on his way that other paintings were missing from the walls. "Call back in the morning," the desk sergeant told him, "and meanwhile, don't touch a thing." "But I've already touched everything," he groaned in despair. He went out to the terrace and stared down into the ravine, where a campfire was glowing. Was the burglar still down there in the bushes? Was he looking back up at him right now? Turning out the lights, he stood there for a long while in the darkness.

Early in the morning a neighbor rang the doorbell. Draped over his arm was Molkho's wife's big fur coat, slightly torn and wet with dew; he had found it hanging on the fence and was sure it must have fallen by mistake. Molkho was thunderstruck. "What, they even took this old coat?" he asked aggrievedly, handling it with care, he explained, so as not to leave false fingerprints for the police, who were due to arrive any minute. "Fingerprints?" snorted the neighbor. "Before you know it, they'll be accusing me!" Molkho, however, did not hear him, for he was already hurrying into the ravine, vainly searching for additional belongings.

The burglary was so on his mind all day long that he forgot about his visit to Jerusalem. The police did not show up until the afternoon, when they lackadaisically wrote everything down. "Do you think it was just a chance hit or an inside job by someone after your paintings?" they asked, pointing out to Molkho the bedroom window through which the thief had entered and proceeding to lose all interest in the case as soon as they were told that the paintings' value was purely sentimental. Then he waited for the insurance agent, who came that evening, examined the apartment at length, haggled over the worth of each stolen item, and insisted that bars be put on the guilty window.

No less worried than the agent, the neighbors suggested that he install an alarm. The next morning, he went downtown to look for one, but he soon gave up the idea, for the thought of having to tiptoe to the bathroom at night for fear of setting it off seemed thoroughly absurd. Bars were the best solution—though by no means a simple one, he realized, discovering the great price differences among them. Nor was there anyone to consult, since his sons made light of the whole business and he did not wish to worry his mother-in-law. His wife had always made such decisions herself, and this was the first one left up to him. Yet, while he was tempted to put it off until his daughter's return from abroad, he was fearful of another burglary.

7

I T STAYED HOT, and Molkho waited to hear from Jerusalem, jumping up whenever the telephone rang, though relieved each time it proved to be someone else. On Tuesday night, however, Uri called at last, sounding muffled over the wires, which crackled with other voices. "I've been burgled," Molkho informed him at once. "It happened the same night I saw you." His counselor was unimpressed. When did Molkho plan to be in Jerusalem again? he asked. "I don't know," Molkho answered. "I really haven't made any plans. I thought you might want to come to Haifa." "Fine," replied Uri at once. "When would be the best time for you—morning, afternoon, or evening?" And when Molkho, taken aback, had trouble deciding, he added, "What time do you get home from work? Or do you take a nap then?" "As a matter of fact, I do," admitted Molkho, straining to hear the voice on the phone, which seemed tired and tentative, "But I don't mind missing it." "How about four or five o'clock, then?" asked his counselor. "That's perfect," replied Molkho. "I'll pick you up at the bus station. Just call me before you leave." But when, his counselor wanted to know, was the last bus back to Jerusalem? "I couldn't tell you," Molkho said. "I'll have to check. I never go to Jerusalem by bus, but I'll find out."

There was silence at the other end of the line. Was his counselor offended? "But why not sleep over here?" he offered weakly. "There's plenty of room." "No, that isn't possible," replied Uri. "Although maybe Ya'ara would like to spend a few days with you by herself." "That's an excellent idea," responded Molkho. "Really, it is!" But his counselor chose to backtrack, asking Molkho whether he couldn't perhaps come to Jerusalem after all. "Well, I suppose I could," conceded Molkho. "Maybe this Saturday." *"Saturday?"* The voice on the phone sounded more doubtful than ever. "On Saturday someone's liable to throw a rock at your car; let's make it Saturday night." "What, Saturday night again?" objected Molkho. "What's the point of spending another Saturday night at your place?" Once more there was silence while the interference on the line grew worse. "You're right," admitted his counselor, his voice fading in the distance. "That won't get us anywhere. You know what? Let me think about it. I'm a bit tired now. I'll be in touch."

The torrid weather continued, and Molkho, picturing Ya'ara's bare feet sticking out of her old housedress and her gray hair done up in its adolescent braid, felt the need to see her again. But his counselor did not call back. By Friday morning he was so impatient that he decided to drive to Jerusalem, and so, phoning his mother-in-law, he canceled her standing invitation to the Friday night meal. "Are you planning to visit your mother again?" she asked. "Yes," he answered tersely. "Isn't she feeling well?" asked his mother-in-law. "She's feeling fine," he told her, anxious to forestall further questioning—and indeed, there was none. After lunch, he packed a small suitcase and set out. Less than halfway there, however, he stopped the car and turned around. I need more patience, he thought, heading back to Haifa. I'll just scare them off this way. I'd better give them more time.

8

A FEW DAYS LATER some men came to install the bars, and Molkho left work early to be on hand when they arrived. In the middle of all their hammering and drilling, he suddenly spied Uri, tall, pale, and bony, standing in the doorway with his black cowboy hat in one hand. "I thought I'd come see where you lived," said his counselor matter-of-factly, stepping inside. "It's an awfully nice area. Is anyone else here?" "Just some workers," replied Molkho, offering him a drink. His counselor declined. "No thank you, I'm fasting today," he said, entering the living room and glancing at the books on the shelves. "They're putting up some bars," explained Molkho. "Bars?" asked the visitor, vaguely interested. "I told you I had a burglary," Molkho reminded him, bringing him to the bedroom to see where the thief had broken in. "What a view!" marveled Uri, saying hello to the two workers, who were drilling holes in the wall by the window. "And the air is so fresh up here. Does that wadi down below have a name?" "I wouldn't know," Molkho said, feeling proud of the splendid green ravine. "But it must," said his counselor. "Not necessarily," reasoned Molkho. "This neighborhood isn't very old. It was only developed in the last twenty years or so."

His counselor said nothing and looked curiously around him,

his glance falling on Volume I of *Anna Karenina*, which lay on the bed that the workers had moved from the window. "Are you reading that?" he asked. "Yes," Molkho said. "For the first time?" asked his counselor warmly, picking up the book and leafing through it caressingly with his long, thin fingers. "Yes," Molkho confessed. "I never got around to it before. Back in school, if you remember, all they ever gave us to read was a bunch of boring Hebrew authors." His counselor looked at him curiously. "Do you like it?" "Yes," replied Molkho, "as a matter of fact, I do. Sometimes it's a bit on the dull side, but it's really quite moving, all that business about Anna leaving her husband and child for love. I wonder how it ends. I don't suppose very happily." "No," said his counselor gently. "In the end she kills herself." "She does?" cried Molkho distraughtly. Uri nodded. "She does?" he repeated. And seeing that the visitor was not about to change Anna's fate just for him, he added, "I wish you hadn't told me that. But why? Does Vronsky leave her?" "Oh no," said Uri. "He stays with her, but she loses all sense of freedom. Since her husband won't divorce her, her affair remains a scandal, only now she's no longer at liberty to break it off. And being an unusually independent woman, she feels trapped."

Molkho nodded, even though he didn't quite follow. The drilling started deafeningly up again. "When did you read it?" he shouted over the noise. "Oh, years ago," smiled Uri, "but I never forget a book." Carefully he laid the open volume down on the bed. "And how's Ya'ara?" shouted Molkho, reddening. "She's fine," said his counselor. "What did she have to say about my visit?" asked Molkho. "What did she think of me?" "She thought a great deal of you," replied Uri. "She said you hadn't changed at all, that you're exactly the same." "I am?" laughed Molkho, feeling injured all over again. "But how can that be?" "She meant the kind of person you were," explained Uri. "That you were just as she remembered you— quiet, patient, and a bit depressed." "Depressed?" Molkho gave a start. "How?" But his counselor simply stood looking at the room. "Is this where your wife died?" he asked. "Yes, right here," said Molkho mournfully. "In this bed?" "Oh no," Molkho explained. "She had a special hospital bed with a water mattress to prevent bed sores." And while his counselor played absentmindedly with his hat, he proceeded to describe how the room had been arranged and what other apparatuses had been in it. "There was a rabbi in Jerusalem who had the same thing," said Uri when Molkho was finished. "But he recovered." "But that's impossible!" exclaimed Molkho resentfully. "It couldn't have been the same thing! Everyone makes the same mistake. They think one cancer is just like another, but there are hundreds of different varieties. Believe me," he said, his head bobbing up and down excitedly, "that's one thing I know something about."

Uri looked at him expressionlessly, preferring not to argue. Slowly he passed out of the bedroom and through the living room toward the still open front door, in which, dressed only in a bathing suit, red-skinned and caked with salt, appeared the high school boy, just returned from the beach. "This is Gabi, my younger son," Molkho introduced him to the visitor, who shook his hand heartily. "Just imagine, Uri was once my counselor in a youth movement!" "Why, he's a big fellow already. He must be nearly army age!" said Molkho's counselor with satisfaction. "You know," he added once the boy, who did not seem thrilled by the meeting, had gone off to his room, "when I see such big children, I actually feel jealous. Where at my age will I find the patience to stand rocking cradles in the middle of the night?"

The workers announced that they were finished and asked Molkho to come look. His heart sank when he did, for the window facing the ravine was now barred by an ugly silver grid that was blackened by solder at the edges and seemed to disfigure the whole house. Angry without knowing at whom, he paid the two men, and they left.

His counselor had now reached the kitchen in his slow tour of the house and was so impressed with its neatness that Molkho had to tell him all about the cleaning woman, who came three times a week. Barely listening, however, Uri simply nodded. "Are you sure you don't want something to drink?" Molkho asked. "No," said Uri, "I already told you I'm fasting today." "But why?" asked Molkho. "For my sins," replied his counselor with a wry laugh at Molkho, who followed him hypnotically to the door. They shook hands in silence. "Well, what do you think?" asked the visitor. "We may as well try," whispered Molkho anxiously. "What's there to lose?"

9

T HE SUN WAS STILL ABLAZE in the west that Friday evening when Omri, the college student, arriving for dinner with his grandmother, saw the new bars and let out a howl of protest. The old woman, too, though refraining from comment, was clearly displeased with the change. "You could at least have left room for a few flower-pots," exclaimed the student angrily. "It would have looked less like a jail window then!" Molkho hurried to admit his mistake: "You're right, I didn't think. I had no one to ask. I'm sorry. It doesn't matter —I'll have it changed, I promise they'll replace it, I don't care what it costs, I'm not even going to paint it." So ardent were his apologies that it took all of them together to calm him down.

Later, when he and Omri stood on the terrace watching the sun dissolve in the evening heat, he told him about Ya'ara—the whole story ("Her husband wants to give her to me; he was once a counselor of mine") now seeming distinctly odd to him. Yet, the more his son listened, the more his initial skepticism gave way to sympathy, his face softening especially when told that the woman was several months his father's senior. "What's there to lose?" Molkho almost pleaded, with which his son agreed. "Maybe she'll come tomorrow night and stay for a few days. Gabi is going off on some hike in the morning, which is just as well, because he may not like the idea. Do you think I should tell him tonight or wait until he gets back?" "But why shouldn't he like the idea?" asked the college student. "If you'd like, I'll talk to him now." "No, you'll just spoil his hike for him," said Molkho, unconvinced. "We'd better wait. Let me be the one to tell him."

Though he considered asking his mother-in-law's opinion when he brought her back to the home after dinner, he was reluctant to involve her. Because of the heat she was wearing a light, almost transparent white blouse that made him feel he could see right through her body, which struck him as being the color of green soap. "I'm off to Jerusalem again tomorrow," he told her as she slowly opened the door of the car. "I'm glad you're seeing so much of your mother," she replied sympathetically. "I know how lonely she must be." "It's not just to see her," he said cautiously. "That is, it's her too, but mainly I'm going to meet some old school friends who have gotten religion." Were they friends of her daughter's too? the old woman wanted to know. "No," Molkho said. "I hadn't seen them for years and then suddenly they turned up." "Has religion gotten you also?" she asked. Sometimes he couldn't tell if she was being cunning or simply slipping up in her Hebrew, which had gotten worse in the past year, her German accent becoming more pronounced. "No," he told her, "not at all," though sitting there worriedly by the open car door, she did not seem reassured. "Maybe they think they can influence you because of your wife's death?" she asked. "But they don't," he replied, irritably regretting having told her. "It has nothing to do with religion. It's something else entirely." He could feel his pulse quicken. "What kind of something else?" he was sure she would ask, but she simply sat there while the passing headlights of a car threw her face into bright relief. Suddenly, though he felt guilty for thinking it, he wished she would die. She'll just get in my way, even if she never says a word, he thought bitterly, waiting for her to disappear through the large glass door of the home.

There was no chance to talk the next morning to the high school boy, who awoke as usual at the last minute, collected his things frantically, and vanished with the brief announcement that he would be back Monday night. Not that it matters, thought Molkho; in fact, by then Ya'ara will most likely be gone. Though at first he thought of giving her the college student's room, which had the best view of the ravine, its walls looked so naked that he decided on his daughter's room instead. Removing some of her clothes from the closet and chest of drawers, he found an old pair of fossilized-looking slippers that had belonged to his wife and, after sniffing them lightly, tossed them in the garbage pail. Then he stripped the sheets from the bed, put them in the washing machine, and opened all the windows to air out the house before leaving for Jerusalem.

He set out in midmorning, happy that his vulnerable window was protected by heavy bars, and drove straight to his mother's, where lunch was waiting for him. First, though, he went to wash, taking a cold shower because the boiler was out of order, so that he yowled and beat his chest and rushed into the arms of a dry towel, feeling like a new man. Peering into the medicine cabinet, he found an appealingly scented old bottle of his mother's perfume and dabbed himself with it. Now was the time to break the news to her.

She listened in heavy silence, neither for nor against, though clearly disapproving of Ya'ara's lack of economic independence. "If you expect it to work," she declared at last, "you'll have to become a little bit religious yourself, at least enough to suit her." "But they don't care about that at all," he replied scornfully. "Why, she doesn't even believe in God. It's just something she goes along with!" And yet all at once he felt certain that nothing would come of it and that his counselor would never give her up. But I'll go to bed with her anyway, he promised himself, because after all, I did love her once. "I need to rest," he told his mother. "I have a long night ahead of me." Yet, once in his old room, he couldn't fall asleep.

Toward evening the Jerusalem skies clouded over unseasonably. Checking the calendar, he was astounded to see how late the Sabbath ended. It's no wonder the religious are up in arms about daylight saving time, he thought as he drove at nine-thirty to the project, which seemed dark and quiet, as if the Day of Rest were being held prisoner. The elevator, too, was nearly empty, its only other passenger a small boy with blond earlocks who stood peeling off the chrome paint of the buttons with his fingernails. Getting off at the wrong floor, Molkho wandered down a long, dark corridor in search of the stairs, passing curious tenants until he nervously arrived at the right apartment.

His counselor opened the door. "So you're here," he smiled glumly, a saturnine flush in his cheeks. "You really are going

through with it!" "I am?" gulped Molkho guiltily. "How is that?"
His counselor laid a light hand on him. "I was afraid you'd get cold
feet. But come in, come on in."

Yet, when he entered, there was only darkness and an open
suitcase on the bed where Ya'ara had lain the last time. The apartment was chilly, perhaps because the windows and shutters had been
closed against the sun all day long, and smelled as if the Sabbath,
trapped between its walls for over twenty-four hours, had begun to go
bad. "I'll get her," declared Uri, reaching for his hat and explaining
that Ya'ara had gone to visit a sick friend in the next building. "No,
don't go yet," requested Molkho, blocking the way. "I have to tell
you that I still don't know what to make of all this, that I feel like
I'm in a strange dream. Not that I'm against arranged matches. If
they were good enough for the Middle Ages, they're good enough for
me. But I'm asking you again, why me? Why not someone else?"

"It happened by pure chance," whispered his counselor to
Molkho, who replied, feeling weak as if with stage fright, "Where do
you get the strength for all this? I feel that I'm completely in your
hands, that this whole thing is humanly incredible, that it will be a
miracle if it works. I've already told my mother and elder son and
was amazed it didn't shock them, because I'm still in shock myself.
Are you sure you've thought it through?" His counselor was listening with his eyes shut, as if to a musical theme. "You say I once
loved her, but what difference does that make now? And there's
something else I don't get either: does your divorcing her just depend on me?"

"No," said his counselor, opening his eyes, "it depends on me
too." He smiled faintly and patted Molkho's back. "And on her,"
Molkho pointed out logically. "She's already agreed," smiled his
counselor again. "But what does she know about me?" asked
Molkho in alarm. "I'm not so easy to get along with. In fact, I was
even accused by someone of causing my wife's death." "Forget it,"
said Uri unconcernedly. "Don't listen to what other people say. Listen to yourself. Your life is your own now." He glanced at his watch.
"It's getting late," Molkho said. "I'd like to get an early start." "I'll

go get her," said his counselor. "I really don't know what can be keeping her."

Molkho walked about the small apartment, in which he now took an almost proprietary interest, even entering the little bedroom to inspect the open suitcase. In it were some dresses and a pair of slippers, the thought of whose arrival in his Haifa home made him tingle expectantly. Packed away, too, was a large, mysterious package of absorbent cotton and a small jar of red pills bearing the label of a local pharmacy. Was she still bleeding from her miscarriages? Would she be penetrable or blocked by debris? Was he meant to heal her or put her out of her misery? For he did want to heal her, he thought.

Through the bedroom window, the only one open in the house, a mild scent of pine trees was borne on the cool breeze that drifted in from the Jerusalem night. Staring at the carelessly made bed, he suddenly felt that everything about it—the pillows, the blankets, even the scattered books—reeked of endless fornication. For a moment he froze; yet hearing the rumble of the elevator in the hallway, he hurried back to the living room just as the front door opened. She was alone, dressed in a checked jumper that stressed her little belly, loafers with white bobbysocks folded schoolgirlishly over them, and a tight kerchief that she removed and tossed on the table while shaking out her gray hair. "I see Uri found you," he said, still not sure how he felt about her. Should he offer to shake hands? Not that it matters, he thought—yet he gave her his hand and she took it in her own as if not quite knowing what to do with it. "I was paying a sick call, but I'm already packed," she explained, stepping into the bathroom to collect her toilet articles as her husband entered the apartment. "All right," said Molkho's counselor, "let's go. We don't want to take all night. Are you sure you have everything?" he asked, shutting the suitcase and carrying it outside. "Yes," said Ya'ara after a moment's thought. "What about toothpaste?" he asked. "She's not going to the wilderness," put in Molkho, who had been listening nervously. "But your book, you forgot your book," exclaimed Uri, and she returned to the little bedroom and slipped it into her bag before putting her kerchief back on. They turned off the lights. "Wait a minute," said Molkho's counselor, opening the windows to let in the cool air while Molkho, dazzled by the great clusters of lights on the hillsides, remarked, "I don't know a single one of all those new neighborhoods. I couldn't even tell you which are Jewish and which are Arab." Neither Uri nor Ya'ara responded. As though suddenly gripped by a powerful emotion, their attention seemed focused elsewhere.

They slipped through the building in their religious garb, which looked half like a disguise and half like an exotic costume. Opening the baggage compartment of his car, Molkho laid the suitcase in it while his counselor, who had decided to drive with them to the city limits, sat in the front seat with his wife behind him. With a sinking feeling, Molkho glanced at her in the mirror, her kerchiefed face small, lined, and gray, framed by the dusky night. It's what I get for not looking harder, he thought bitterly, for expecting others to do it for me. Slowly he backed out of the parking lot and drove to the outskirts of town, stopping by a yellow filling station at the point where the road began its long plunge to the coast. "Do you need gas?" asked his counselor, getting slowly out of the car as if loath to part with them. "No, I have plenty," said Molkho impatiently. "And where should Ya'ara sit?" inquired Uri, "in the front or in the back?" "In the front," answered Molkho. "It's more comfortable and safer, because of the seat belt." His counselor opened the front door for her, and the two men helped belt her in. "Are you all right?" asked Uri nervously. She nodded with a dutiful smile. "Just a minute," declared Molkho, noticing how cramped she was, "let's give you some more legroom." He bent toward her to pull her seat handle while his counselor pushed her back, the smell of her sweat making her seem very real. "How about taking a soldier?" asked Uri as several hitchhikers in uniform began crowding around the car. "I'd rather not," said Molkho. "You never give lifts to soldiers?" Ya'ara asked. "Yes, I do, but not now," he answered crossly. "Maybe later, when we reach the coast."

Uri seemed satisfied, suggesting only that they clean the windshield, which was smeared with dust and dead bugs. "Otherwise you won't see a thing," he told Molkho, who got out of the car, wiped the front window, got back in again, refastened his seat belt, and drove off into the night. His last glimpse of his tall counselor was in the rearview mirror, standing in the cold yellow light by the air pump. Has he really signed her away to me? he wondered, his heart going out to the man.

10

S HE CERTAINLY DOES what she's told, he marveled as she sat there in her seat belt, wide awake and content to watch the night go by outside the window. Perhaps they would make a happy couple after all. Meanwhile, he had to be on his best behavior and, above all, to avoid awkward silences. On his way to Jerusalem he had already thought of a few things to talk about apart from his wife and her illness, which he would leave for the next day, when Ya'ara would be better able to concentrate. The best thing was to get her to tell him about herself: thirty-two years had passed since their schooldays, so that at a rate of no more than four minutes per year they could reach Haifa without his having to make small talk or carry on intellectually like her husband—although just to be on the safe side, he had a tape of *The Magic Flute* playing softly in the deck, its volume ready to be turned up the moment the conversation faltered. Indeed, Ya'ara was no more talkative than he was, being evidently used to letting Uri hold the stage, so that already by the first sharp downhill turns he had to start drawing her out. Who, he cautiously asked her, a bit uncomfortable for her sake, was the match that Uri was thinking of? The woman, she replied, was a young widow, the mother of a small child, whose husband, a follower of the rabbi, was killed a year ago in a car accident. "Have you ever met her?" he asked, intrigued. "No," she said. "Neither has Uri. He doesn't see the point of it before there's an arrangement for me." Molkho winced. It might simplify matters, he thought wryly, if he would take the young widow for himself and leave his friends' marriage intact.

But young widows attracted him less than this woman beside him, who made him feel so full of life. She had removed her kerchief again, making her face look broader, and now sat with her legs crossed comfortably, smoking her first cigarette after having found the ashtray by herself, her pearllike eyes darting from the dashboard to the gear shift with an impressive if somewhat frightening intensity. In the darkness broken by the flicker of headlights her face had softened above the slim shoulders that belied the bulge below. Even when someone like her fell ill, the prognosis was bound to be good. And perhaps he could get her to dye her hair, use makeup, and dress more smartly. And to learn to drive so that she might find a better job. Again he stole a glance at her, afraid to look away for too long from the serpentine curves; one hand resting on the open window and a cigarette glowing in her mouth, she was calmly observing the thinly wooded hills by the roadside. They can't have been waiting just for me, he told himself, the odd thought crossing his mind that this mightn't be the first time, that perhaps they had tried it before. Was I really in love with her? he struggled to recall. Or was it just an adolescent crush; after all, who hadn't had one on her back then, such a strikingly well-developed girl?

He kept turning the conversation back to her husband, as if regretting having abandoned him at the gas station. Clearly, she adored the man: hadn't she, his faithful fellow wanderer, always followed him blindly wherever he went? They were out of the mountains now, and Molkho wondered whether to take the old road by the airport, which was shorter but slower, or to go by the coast. In the end, he chose the inland route, switching on the radio to drown out her adulation, though when he made some comment on the news bulletin, he saw that she either hadn't been listening or didn't know who the foreign minister was—a fact, however, that he found rather pleasing, indeed even titillating. As she was lighting up a fresh cigarette by the entrance to the airport, he turned the radio off and delicately broached the subject of her childlessness. "You know," he said, a catch in his voice, "my wife had a miscarriage too. We wanted a fourth child, but after a few weeks she lost it. Maybe that was the first sign of her illness, though we couldn't have guessed it at the time." Ya'ara bowed a sorrowful head. She herself, she told Molkho, had had seven miscarriages, all the same. "The same as what?" he asked. "I mean, what month did it happen in?" "The fifth or sixth," she answered quietly. "The sixth?" he exclaimed with an involuntary grimace. "How awful!" She smiled appreciatively but said nothing. "You must have suffered terribly," he went on. "Why, it can be dangerous then!" She listened to him uncertainly, the yellow light from the terminals falling on her face, while he thought of soft, dead fetuses. On the cabinet of the nature room in high school had stood a jar of formaldehyde in which was preserved an upside-down embryo, its arms and legs folded. The girls had been scared of it, and the boys had joked and even given it a pet name; but Molkho sometimes looked at it sympathetically, trying to make out its tiny limbs in the cloudy solution. Now, however, he had better curb his desire to know more about her medical history. It wouldn't do to show his fascination with the details of her pregnancies, of the long months spent bedridden in all the cheap rooms they had rented in their travels. Had his counselor taken good care of her? Had he been able to change the sheets without hurting her, or was he too busy searching for the Meaning of Life? And her poor, bleeding uterus—did she still have it or had it been removed? He felt sure it had not been and wanted nothing more than to kneel with his head pressed against it. If I don't scare her off, he thought, she'll let me do that too.

And indeed, sitting there contentedly in the steamy coastal humidity while staring at the moon rising over the mountains and shimmering on the distant white foam of the sea, she did not seem scared in the least. It's good she's so relaxed, he thought, too weary to remember the names of the old classmates about whom he had planned to reminisce with her. It was past midnight when he drove through the empty streets of Haifa, giddy with the promise of happiness. She's a real option, he told himself, carrying her suitcase, which he rather wished were heavier, up the stairs. And she wouldn't die on him either, that was for sure. He wished it were earlier so that the neighbors might see her. They would be relieved to hear that the first woman he brought home wasn't young, because widowers who took up with young women were disapproved of. Afterward, he might start reducing the age. Meanwhile, here he was with the autumn and mild winter and summery spring behind him, already halfway through this cruelly hot summer that had begotten two hotter summers than itself.

He switched on the hallway light and opened the front door for her, again noticing her girlish loafers with their white bobbysocks. He could fall in love with her easily, he thought, turning on lights everywhere and showing her the apartment like a moonlighting real estate agent; it was simply a matter of getting to know her. "It's nice here," she said, looking cheerily around her. "Yes, we tried to make it that way," he replied with a smile that thanked her while reminding her of the woman who preceded her. Dead tired, he brought in her suitcase. "This is my daughter Enat's room," he said. "She's in Europe now." "By herself?" asked Ya'ara. "Yes," Molkho said, "she's very independent." They returned to the living room, where Ya'ara sat in the armchair and took another cigarette from her pack, wide awake and every inch a night bird. "Would you like something to eat or drink?" he asked none too eagerly, already missing his lost privacy. "If you're having a bite, I'll join you," she replied. He led her to the kitchen, took out bread, cheese, and cake, and put some water up to boil. At least she isn't spoiled, he thought, amazedly watching her eat everything he put before her, even a piece of old cheese. Although I wish she had a better-paying job.

11

H E RATHER LIKED her lazy way of doing things: of eating, for instance, or making her bed, which he had purposely left bare with the folded sheets on top of it to let her see that they were fresh. By now her religious facade had peeled away completely, leaving

only the girlish Young Pioneer who had turned gray overnight. Tired
though he was, he was soon giving her an account of his wife's
illness, to which she listened so intently that he felt he was telling
about it for the first time.

Just then the telephone rang. "Don't worry, it's Uri," she told
him, once again making him wonder whether she hadn't done this
before. "Hello," he said when he picked up the receiver. "Yes, we
had a good trip and now we're sitting and talking. My only complaint," he joked, feeling a need to sound critical, "is that she
doesn't stop smoking. Would you like to talk with her? She's right
here."

She picked up the phone, speaking into it in a whisper while
Molkho went tactfully to his room, from where he watched her question-mark figure through the doorway. Perhaps I'll keep her, he
thought. But she must dye her hair. There's no reason why she
shouldn't, or use a bit of makeup for my sake.

12

"I F YOU NEED ANYTHING, just ask," he told her, wanting to turn
in. "Feel at home. If you'd like to read in bed, there are plenty of
books. I even have Volume I of *Anna Karenina,* which I finished
yesterday. You can take it back to Jerusalem with you. Good night,"
he added, retiring to his room, where he decided that it would be
unfair to use the air conditioner while she had to sleep without it. He
undressed and got into bed, but though it was nearly 2 A.M., he
couldn't fall asleep. Eight months had gone by since the death of his
wife and now another woman was in the house at last—not in the
same room, to be sure, but at least in the same apartment. That's
certainly progress, he told himself, rising to switch on the air conditioner, its familiar purr lulling him into a dim slumber in which he
dreamed that his son the high school boy had turned into a girl.

Good for him, he thought in the dream, as if the boy's problems were solved.

At four, unable to keep warm beneath the thin blanket, he rose and switched off the air conditioner. Suddenly, remembering Ya'ara in the next room, he felt a glow like that which he had felt as a child when his mother once surprised him with a new puppy and he awoke in the middle of the night to find it on the kitchen porch wagging its tail in the dark, as if it had been waiting just for him, little Molkho. Now, wanting to see her no less badly, he slipped into his pants, leaving on his pajama tops, and stepped into the darkened living room, from which he saw a crack of light beneath her door. Was she still reading, or had she fallen asleep with the light on? He froze, menaced by her wakefulness. Was the light meant for him? He turned around. I mustn't be so aggressive, he thought, crawling back into bed, his head feeling infinitely heavier than his body. That's never been my strong suit.

13

IT WAS AFTER SEVEN when he awoke again, amazed at how he had slept, for he usually rose by six. Certain she must be up, he dressed, made his bed, washed and shaved quickly, and came out to say good morning. She was gone, her bed made too, though less neatly than his, her suitcase on the floor with all her clothes still in it. Nor, when he went downstairs to look for her, was she anywhere to be seen. Glad to be alone, he sliced bread, set the table for breakfast, and, feeling ravenous, sat down to eat, making little piles of the crumbs while reading the morning paper until he heard a light knock on the door and rose to open it. She was wearing the same faded jumper, her pearly eyes squinting in the morning light, which ruddily tinted her cheeks and streaked her gray hair with gold. "I was worried about you," he said. "When did you get up? I was afraid you might have run away." But she had merely risen at dawn and gone out for a walk, even starting down the tempting ravine. In fact, she had proceeded quite a distance, though not to the very bottom, and had lost her way coming back, which was why her shoes were caked with dirt. He poured her coffee and served her breakfast, of which she obediently ate every bit. Yet, when he cleared the table, she made no move to wash or dry the dishes. Chin in hand, she remained seated at the table, thoughtfully smoking while watching him at the sink, after which she asked for a glass of water, took two aspirins from her pocket, and swallowed them. "Do you have a headache?" he asked. "No," she said, "it's just in case."

Since they were ready to go out now, he proposed that she clean her shoes, even producing a brush and polish and spreading a newspaper on the terrace. Standing beside her while prying open the can of polish that she had fumbled with unsuccessfully, he saw there was hardly an inch difference between them—which was still enough, however, to annoy him. She took off her shoes and stood in her white socks, her legs downy in the morning light, and removing his too, he suggested that she apply the polish while he wield the brush. She had hardly begun, however, when the telephone rang. "You get it; it may be for you," he said, wanting the unknown caller to hear a woman's voice. Dutifully she went and picked up the receiver, clutching it with both hands as if afraid of dropping it, her question-mark figure turned to him in profile. It was Uri again, and while Molkho waited for her to finish, he impatiently polished his shoes, put them back on, and then polished hers while trying to guess their age. She'll have to dye her hair and take the fuzz off her legs and buy new shoes and use makeup, he grumbled to himself. And if she says it's a matter of principle, she can choose between her principles and me. He put away the rags and brush, and brought her shoes to her, the two of them now the same height, waiting to see if his counselor wished to speak to him. But soon she hung up. "He sends regards," she said, putting on her shoes with a grateful look.

14

I'LL NEVER DO ANYTHING like this again, thought Molkho
crossly, though he was glad that her husband kept calling. At least
he hasn't just dumped her on me, he told himself; I can always
return her with a clean conscience. He had already planned the day,
and now he told her about it. In the morning they would do some
shopping, visit the mountaintop campus of the university, and lunch
at an outdoor restaurant; in the afternoon, after resting up, they
would go to the beach; and in the evening, if she liked, there was a
concert in unusual surroundings, the subterranean Knights Hall in
old Acre, which hosted chamber-music groups all summer long.
"Chamber music?" she asked doubtfully. He brought her an old
program, which she thumbed through unenthusiastically; yet the
tickets were expensive and he was determined to use them, especially
as they were unlikely to be sellable at the performance. His wife had
had a passion for such concerts, which often struck him as monotonous, indeed as one of the punishments of Culture, although sometimes, near the end of them, either because his liberation was near or
because the music had finally penetrated, he felt a euphoric serenity.

"Tomorrow, though, we can go see a movie," he added intimately. "I'd like that," she smiled. "And perhaps," he suggested,
"we'll go to the beach again." She nodded her gray head. "The
beach sounds nice. I haven't been to it for ages." "Did you bring a
bathing suit?" he asked rhetorically, being thoroughly acquainted
with the contents of her suitcase. "No," she said. "But why not?" he
asked. "Are you afraid that one of your religious friends from Jerusalem will see you?" "Maybe next time," she blushed, as if baffled or
overwhelmed by all his questions. If there is a next time, he almost

said out loud. But he didn't. After all, he thought, I really loved her once, and after a day or two I may remember why.

Though he had hoped she would change into another, livelier dress, she clearly did not share his taste and wore her jumper to the nearby shopping center, where they entered a small optometrist's shop, the owners of which Molkho knew from the Philharmonic series. Facing her in a seat that looked like a barber's chair, he tried on frames of glasses to see which went best with his new bifocals, which he had gotten because his once-perfect distance vision now called for correction too. The optometrist regarded Ya'ara curiously, appraising her odd combination of jumper, bobbysocks, gray hair, and wedding ring while gallantly asking for her opinion, as if it alone had any value. Lighting up a cigarette, she fumbled for words and seemed relieved when they all agreed on a pair of gold frames, on which Molkho put a deposit.

They made their way along the busy street. She had, Molkho noticed, a hapless way of falling behind that might once have appealed to him but simply annoyed him now. Abruptly he entered a building and climbed to a second-floor apartment that had been converted into a boutique, in the soft light of which local matrons in bright bathing suits circulated among curtained shelves. Only when they were approached by a salesgirl and Molkho gestured toward Ya'ara, however, did she realize what he had in mind. "I can't!" she pleaded, turning crimson and stiffening. "But I'll pay for it," he whispered. "It's so we can go to the beach." Yet still she balked, taking a feeble step backward, so that in the soft light, surrounded by partially dressed ladies, he was struck again by her old beauty. He tried to persuade her while the salesgirl stood by politely smiling, even giving her hand a squeeze, though quickly letting go of it.

15

T HEN AT LEAST A DRESS, he thought. If she would only buy one
of those summery dresses in the show windows, something styl-
ish and fresh-looking, because her faded old jumper, on which there
was already a light stain of sweat, was making him more and more
unhappy. She was unhealthily attached to it, which made him fear
she might wear it to the concert that evening too. Not wanting to
upset her even more, though, he decided to walk with her to Pan-
orama Road for a scenic view of the harbor and bay, but arriving
there, they found the visibility poor. A heavy mist lay over the bay,
while to the north, the mountains of the Galilee lay shrouded in a
grayish haze, the only clear landmark being the golden dome of the
Bahai Temple down the mountainside. "In autumn," he assured her
disappointedly, "you can see for miles around. The houses in Acre
look like toy blocks, and the mountains seem close enough to touch."
He suggested having coffee in an elegant café inside a big new department store, through which he led her past racks of dresses,
pants, and shirts, stopping now and then to check fabrics and prices
in the hope of arousing her interest. "The 'in' look today is the wide
look," he said, sounding more mystified than informed. "Anything
goes—and usually with anything else!" Yet lagging behind again,
she did not even glance at the clothes, perhaps afraid of being forced
to buy something, so that they were both relieved to reach the men's
department, where she gladly looked with him at the new collarless
shirts, one of which appealed to him especially. "What do you
think?" he asked her, holding it up in front of him just as a young
salesman approached and urged him to try it on for size. "Tell your
husband not to mind the missing collar," Molkho heard him say

beyond the dressing curtain as he buttoned up the shirt. "He'll get used to it. It's the new look." "But what do I want with the new look," Ya'ara replied, her answer pleasing him greatly, "when his old look suited me fine?"

In the café he tried discussing politics, but the subject failed to interest her. Nor, when asked about her husband's views, did she seem to think it interested him. "What does, then?" inquired Molkho. She looked at him in bewilderment, unused to having to explain the man who was always there by her side to explain himself. "He's looking for the Meaning," she murmured, drawing on her cigarette. "For the Purpose of it all. Not just to live with as much pleasure and as little pain as possible." "What Purpose is that?" inquired Molkho. "But that's what he's looking for!" she answered. "Yes, I know," he said a bit sarcastically. "He told us that in the movement thirty years ago—but what has he found since then?" "It's not like discovering some Big Idea," she tried to explain. "It's something you have to live." "But isn't life itself the Purpose?" he asked. "To get through it as best you can before Death comes for you?" "But Death doesn't mean a thing to him!" she retorted admiringly. "He doesn't believe in it!" "Oh, he doesn't!" Molkho grinned at her painfully. "Do you think Death cares whether he believes in it or not?" Frightened by his vehemence, she tried changing the subject. "But I want to know!" he insisted, just getting more worked up. "What does he believe in?" "Don't ask me, ask him," she answered softly. "And you? How about you?" he queried. "I'd rather not think about Death," she said. "I feel more like you do about it. Even when I had all those miscarriages, I never thought of them as deaths, just as failures, because how can you die if you haven't been born?"

Once again he was reminded of her old directness, of the naive honesty she had answered all their teachers with. So it wasn't just her looks that made me love her, he mused, trying to remember more. Left back a grade, she had sat there not caring about her studies, wanting only to get through the year. She hadn't even pretended to care. And though all her friends were seniors, she made a strong impression on the junior class she was banished to. "Sitting here with you," Molkho told her, "I feel that I'm back in high school again, only this time without homework or exams and with spending money in my pocket." She flashed him an intimate smile. How can we keep the feeling of closeness? he wondered just as he spotted the two little Russians, mother and daughter, heading for the exit of the café, followed by an old woman with a cane who stopped to pay the cashier. For a moment, sure he had been noticed, he caught his breath; then, turning to Ya'ara, he whispered, "Look over there, that woman in the white peasant blouse—she's my mother-in-law. Just wait until you get to know her. She's eighty-two and clear as a bell. Would you believe how she looks? And she does everything! She doesn't even need that cane; it's just something she carries around with her. It's incredible how lucid she is."

Ya'ara looked curiously at the old woman, who was counting her change over the counter. Satisfied it was correct, she scooped it up and made her way slowly toward the exit, listing slightly like a ship. "Was your wife like her?" asked Ya'ara. "I never used to think so," said Molkho. "Recently, though, perhaps because I'm forgetting, I've begun to see a resemblance."

16

H E CHANGED PLANS and took her to the Bahai Temple, where they joined a group of Dutch tourists in a manicured garden full of flowering bushes, led down a paved path by their guide to the golden dome of the sanctuary. "It reminds me so of Europe," marveled Molkho. "I've been living in Haifa for thirty years—twice a day I drive right past this place, and yet I've never been here before. It's something I've always meant to do."

By the door of the golden-domed structure, they were asked to take off their shoes, after which they entered a small room with thick Persian carpets on the floor, Persian and English inscriptions on the walls, and several decorative lamps and objets d'art behind a lace curtain. Molkho assumed they would next be taken to view the interior of the sanctuary itself, but presently they were told that their visit was over and that no one, not even Bahais, ever saw the dome from within. "But what's in it?" he asked disappointedly. "Nothing," replied the guide. *"Nothing?"* Laughing with disbelief, he put on his shoes and took a free brochure about the Bahais and their faith.

From there, they drove downtown for lunch in an Arab restaurant, where Ya'ara hungrily fell upon the bread even before the appetizers arrived, her voraciousness once again amazing him. Is that where I'll first kiss her? he wondered, looking at her smooth forehead, or will I find someplace better? She ate quickly, enjoying the meal, while he told her about his mother and her tedious complaints over the telephone each morning. Her own mother, she said, had died a few years ago, and the two of them had never been close. But the heat and noise in the crowded restaurant made it difficult to talk, and eventually they lapsed into silence, waiting for their Turkish coffee. Why, she's even duller than I am, he thought, suddenly recalling how in public school, not wanting to hurt the feelings of a fat girl with pigtails who had been foisted on him as a girlfriend, he had put up with her for a whole year while eagerly waiting for the summer vacation to free him.

A muggy hour later, on the stairs to his apartment, they encountered his elderly downstairs neighbor, who, dressed in an undershirt, stopped to inspect the new woman while asking some question about the hallway light. Upstairs in the apartment the telephone was ringing, and feeling Ya'ara stiffen, Molkho handed her the key and said, "Go see who it is. Maybe it's for you again." She ran up the stairs while his neighbor, never taking his eyes off her, kept on about the light. "Do we have a new tenant, then?" he asked slyly. Molkho patted his shoulder. "I really couldn't tell you," he said.

He found her gripping the telephone, her belly bulging softly as if the last of her dead babies were still trapped there. She was talking to her husband, whose concern for her seemed boundless. Or perhaps he was coaching her from the sidelines in ways unclear to Molkho, who slowly lowered the blinds of the sun-baked apartment, plunging it into darkness. Maybe he wants to know if we've made love yet, he thought. Anything is possible with them. He opened the refrigerator, took out a pitcher of cold water, poured himself a glass, drank it, poured her one too, and set it on the table in front of her. Is that really his plan for us? he wondered. And here I am, playing the tourist guide! Though if that's what's expected of me, what better time than now?

"Uri would like to have a word with you," Ya'ara said, handing him the telephone and walking away. "Are you having problems?" asked his counselor. He sounded nervous and rushed, and Molkho was surprised by his directness. "If you'd like, I can come for her tomorrow." "But why?" protested Molkho. "There's no need. I've already told the office that I'm taking two days off. Everything is fine here. We're still getting acquainted," he chuckled. But his counselor sounded somber. "Talk to her!" he urged. "Talk to her! She's used to it and is a good listener. Talk to her!" "It's all right," whispered Molkho tensely into the receiver. "You don't have to worry."

He went to his room, turned on the air conditioner to dry off his sweaty body, and asked Ya'ara if she might like to nap there. "No, thank you," she replied, preferring to sit in the easy chair facing the TV. "I never sleep in the afternoon. I've spent too much of my life in bed as it is." He showered and put on fresh clothes instead of a bathrobe, regretting his lost privacy again. A fresh cigarette in her mouth, she was staring at the unlit screen of the television as though waiting for an important message. "Wouldn't you like to shower too?" he asked. "No, why?" she answered puzzledly, as if, sitting there as fresh as a daisy in her old jumper, showers were not for her. "Then perhaps you'd like to watch TV," he said. "The educational channel is on now." She gladly agreed, settling back in her chair with her legs crossed, while he switched on the set and sat down beside her to watch some program about insects in the jungle. The wasted humming of the air conditioner kept making him want to shut his eyes. "Are you sure you don't want to lie down in my room?" he asked, getting to his feet. She shook her head, her eyes glued to the screen, and so he brought a fan and aimed it at her, its current of air playing with her silvery hair. "Do you mind if I go lie down, then?"

he asked. "I've become so dependent on my afternoon nap that I'm a wreck at night if I don't get it." "Of course," she blushed. "Go right ahead. Don't let me bother you."

He brought her the newspaper, showed her how to switch off the set, shut the door of his room, undressed, and climbed into the cool bed in his underpants, feeling as though his head weighed a ton. How can I make love to her, he wondered, if I have to talk to her all the time? The television droned on in the living room, but the purr of the air conditioner drowned it out and soon put him to sleep.

He awoke shivering from cold an hour later and went to turn off the machine, hearing the voices of many children in the apartment next door, which suddenly sounded like a schoolroom. Dressing quickly, he stepped into the living room, where striped light fell through the slatted blinds. She was still in the same chair, which his wife had liked to sit in, too, before becoming bedridden, so that for a moment, not yet brought back to reality by the head of gray hair, he thought that's who it was. The folded newspaper was where he had left it on the table. Was Ya'ara asleep? She didn't stir or seem to notice him. Stepping closer, however, he saw that she was watching a children's program that featured a bowlegged green hedgehog that spoke in a funny voice. The room felt like a furnace. "You didn't sleep?" he asked, laying a hand on her startled shoulder. "There are some really good children's programs," he added, not wanting to sound disapproving of the drivel on the screen. "Don't you have TV at home?" "No," she said, enthralled by the hedgehog, which was trying out a new stunt. "But sometimes I stop to watch it in the store windows." The fan had dried her skin a waxen color. "Come, let's have coffee," he said, "and then I'll show you the university."

She didn't offer to help this time, either. Only when he switched off the TV and told her the coffee was ready did she rise from her chair in her faded old jumper, which looked like a woman prisoner's, girlishly stretching her limbs while a wave of warm desire swept over him. First we'll dye her hair, he thought. There's no reason not to. And get her to use makeup. And to buy some new clothes. And then maybe I'll marry her. After all, the neighbors seem to like her, and I really did love her once.

17

O N THE HIGH CAMPUS of the university the air was as sultry as elsewhere; the spectacular view was swaddled in the same blue haze they had stared at that morning, and the observation tower was closed. Ya'ara was disappointed, for though she had hoped to catch a glimpse of the mountain range near Yodfat, perhaps even of Yodfat itself, where she had spent the happiest years of her life, it was hidden by a great bank of mist. Nearer to them the brutal summer had burned red blotches in the landscape and the vivid green of the Carmel was smeared a streaky gray. "Did you ever finish high school?" asked Molkho, steering her to what he hoped might be a better vantage point. No, Ya'ara answered, she never did. "And you're not sorry?" he asked softly. No, she said, and neither, for that matter, was Uri. Molkho pointed out a few sights to her, telling her how much better he liked Haifa than Jerusalem. "Even if it is a bit boring here," he confessed—although if she was bored, she gave no sign of it. What now? he wondered, feeling he had run out of topics. Nothing would seem natural until they had gone to bed.

On their way back to the apartment, they stopped off at a supermarket. "You push and I'll fill," he joked, giving her a cart, "but feel free to take what you want." She took nothing, however, merely blushing each time he inquired whether she liked, ate, or ever had tried this or that item on a shelf. Well, he thought, tossing it into the cart anyway, she'll have a lifetime with me to get used to it.

Back home he suggested once more that she shower, but again she preferred the television. This time, however, determined to involve her in supper, which he had decided to eat on the terrace facing the sunset, he asked her to slice vegetables for a salad. She did, washing them well and carefully peeling the tomatoes in a special way she had learned in South America. It's a good thing the children aren't home, Molkho thought, sitting opposite her on the terrace while looking now and then at the bright arrows of sunlight shooting through the clouds. Though his children did not seem to interest her, he began discussing them anyway. All of them, he told her, worried him: the college student, who had started going out with an older woman; his daughter, who had never had a boyfriend and seemed strangely hardened by her mother's death; and most of all, the high school boy, who went about in a daze and was likely to be left back in school. But he loved them, felt close to them, and considered himself responsible for their future. Needless to say, everything he owned would be theirs one day. He listed this for her, stating the value of the apartment and all his bank accounts, while she listened without comment, eating heartily and smoking between bites of food or else glancing westward, where the sun had burned a blazing hole in the sky through which purple rays glinted off their plates and glasses. Could she still be on the same pack of cigarettes or had she brought more from Jerusalem?

Finally she rose and went to wash, leaving him again to do the dishes, though he was relieved to note that she returned with a new dress on, a jumper, too, yet brighter and more flowery. Nighttime became her, he thought, smoothing out the wrinkles on her old beauty. "Don't you ever use makeup?" he asked offhandedly with a look at the long-strapped black handbag slung over her shoulder. "No," she said. "The thought of smearing all that junk on my face revolts me." It was late, and they drove hurriedly to the old Crusader fortress in Acre, descending a flight of stairs to the Knights' Hall, whose thick stone walls were damp with humidity. Though the hall wasn't full, several people there knew him and came over to say hello and have a look at his new partner. "This is Ya'ara," he introduced her casually, glad she made a good impression. His old friends the doctor and his wife were there too, apologetic for having been out of touch. "This is Ya'ara," he said as they scrutinized her, puzzled by the plain old dress, which seemed like a throwback to their teens, though Molkho soon sidetracked their efforts to place her by inquir-

ing about their son, who was a classmate of Gabi's. "Did he tell you
about that hike of theirs?" he asked. The doctor and his wife,
though, hadn't heard of any hike. Their son, they said, had gone to
Tel Aviv to spend a few days with a friend.

"I have a feeling we're in for some dry music tonight," whispered Molkho to Ya'ara as they settled into their wooden chairs and
watched a violinist, a cellist, and a violist mount the stage, proud to
be initiating her into a world of values no less stringent than her
husband's. She nodded apprehensively, her body straight as a rod.
Why, with a posture like that she'll be indestructible! he thought.
Indeed, the music was harsh and cerebral: no sooner did the violin
play a lyric bar than the cello and the viola overcame it, attacking the
theme and breaking it down analytically. At first, he could see she
was following, her eyes fixed on the musicians, yet soon her attention
wandered. He smiled at her mournfully, glancing down at her dusty
shoes with their still neatly folded bobbysocks on the sunken old
stone floor. Once more he noticed the curly blond down on her legs.
How can I kiss a woman with so much fuzz? he wondered gloomily.
And her black handbag would have to go too. Her bulge of a belly
rose and fell as though an unborn child kept getting up and sitting
down there, each time about to walk out on the avant-garde trio that
chose to play such highbrow music on so heat-struck a summer night.
"How's your head?" he asked in a whisper. "It hurts," she confided,
impressed by his diagnostic powers. "I've had a headache for a
while."

During the intermission he took her out to the garden and led
her to a stone bench beneath a leafy tree, where she sat wanly with
her head back while he went to fetch some water. She was smoking
when he returned. Were her migraines chronic, he inquired, or were
they something new? "I've had them for several years," she said.
"In that case," he reassured her, "you have nothing to worry about.
Just to be on the safe side, though, you might want to have a brain
scan. It's a perfectly painless procedure."

The doctor and his wife appeared in the garden, no doubt looking for them, and he clung to the shadow of the tree to avoid detec-
tion. The warning bell rang. "You go on in," Ya'ara said. "I'll wait

out here until it's over." Alarmed by her sudden rebellion, he sat down beside her. "Then let's go home now," he said. "No," she protested. "If you like it, I don't want you to miss it. It's not a question of liking it," he explained. "I don't care for it much myself, but sometimes, if you sit it out to the end, you feel something has rubbed off on you." "Then why deprive yourself?" she said. "My head hurts too much for me to go back, but that's no reason why you shouldn't." "No, never mind," said Molkho. "I'm sorry I brought you to such a dull concert without asking you. It was my mistake. It was entirely my mistake." It pleased him to repeat the phrase; he would not abandon her now. They sat in silence beneath the dark tree, waiting for the last of the audience to disappear inside, after which he brought her some more water and waited for her to smoke another cigarette before they left.

They did not go straight home, though. Taking a detour by the port, he drove through the downtown streets with their empty office buildings and peroxided whores outside smoky bars and emerged at the city's southern end, where he made a right turn toward the beach. "Come," he said. "Let's go down to the water and cool off a bit."

The dark night smoldered in its prison of air, the sea struggling to break free of the enchaining vapors of day. Slowly they walked along the water's edge, listening to the simple, monotonous boom of the surf. Beyond it, out among the breakers, youths in dark swimsuits rested on boards, waiting for a wave to ride to shore. Shoulder to shoulder Molkho and Ya'ara watched the silent scene, the surfers like a school of gray dolphins on the dim breast of the sea. He glanced at her, still unsure how much taller she was. She smiled and looked seaward, greedily gulping the salt tang of the thick air while automatically groping in her bag for a cigarette, which she lit at once. That's all her freedom amounts to, he thought: a private little revolt against her lungs that will poison her in the end. "If you hadn't made such a fuss about that bathing suit this morning, we could have gone for a swim now," he said, his voice full of unsuspected malice. She gave him a startled look. "Come on," he said, not knowing what made him so angry, "let's at least get our feet wet." He knelt to take off his shoes and socks, rolling up the cuffs of his pants. "Come," he said more softly. Hesitantly, her cigarette still in her mouth, she removed her shoes and white socks, laying them next to his. He caught his breath, glimpsing the delicate blur of white legs in the darkness, and strode ahead of her into the warm, oily water, rolling his pants up still further. The hem of her jumper, he saw, was wet, yet she made no effort to raise it.

He headed for some rocks and climbed atop one, suddenly towering above her. She laughed, finding it comic, and then climbed on a rock of her own, the smoke from her cigarette drifting fragrantly past him. "Watch out, it's slippery," he called, though there was really no danger. Now she rose above him, her gray hair loose about her neck as she stood staring landward. A thin, emblematic moon clung to the tower of the university. She took a last greedy puff of her cigarette and threw it into the sea. Molkho sighed softly. "I suppose he's trying to phone us now," he mused. "No, he's not," she replied. "His Talmud class never lets out before eleven." "Well," Molkho said, "it's his problem anyway, because this whole crazy business was his idea."

She threw him a quick smile. For an ambiguous moment a light flared on the horizon, like the blue flame of a burner that someone had forgotten to turn off. Then it went out. "He told me to keep talking to you," smiled Molkho slyly, "because you're such a quiet type." Shocked, she jumped off her rock. "He told you *that?*" she asked in a hurt voice. "Yes," he said uncontritely, "he did. I'm not very good at small talk either," he added more gently. "My wife did most of the talking; generally I just answered her." Ya'ara jumped back on her rock and then leapt to another, a bitter smile on her suddenly hard face. "I don't know why he said that," she said. "You don't have to talk to me at all. I really don't know what made him say that. As far as I'm concerned, you needn't talk at all." He laid a soothing hand on her shoulder. "Forget it," he said. "I shouldn't have told you that. Let's go home."

18

B ACK IN THE APARTMENT, still gritty with sand, she went right to the television. Slowly she sank into her chair, riveted to the end of some thriller. Molkho went to the kitchen, prepared two bowls of ice cream, and handed her one of them, which she polished off at once. There was a splotch of tar on the blonde down of her shin and the tan she had acquired during the day had softened the lines of her face. The late-night movie over, a passage from the Bible was being read in a preachery voice. He rose, took the empty bowls to the kitchen, from which he heard the concluding news bulletin, and returned with some napkins and a plate of fruit. "Don't you get Jordan?" she asked, staring at a blank screenful of snow while reaching out for an apple. "Good lord," he laughed, switching off the set, "you *are* an addict!" She nodded happily. "Doesn't anyone in that community of yours have a TV?" he asked. "Oh no," she said. "The rabbi wouldn't stand for it." "What's his name?" asked Molkho. "Reb Yudl," said Ya'ara. "Reb Yudl?" The name tickled his funny bone. *"Reb Yudl?"* She seemed amused by it too. "I'd like to meet the man," said Molkho, sitting beside her.

It's now or never, he thought. If we're going to make love, what are we waiting for? He could always make a final decision later, he told himself, feeling a sweet tingle of anxiety. This was it. Tomorrow his son would return from his hike, complicating everything. And if she turned out to be a screamer or a sobber, better late at night in an empty apartment. He tried staring at her telepathically. A cricket chirped in the ravine. Then there was quiet. One by one, she was plucking grapes from the plate and popping them into her mouth, not looking sleepy at all.

"Well, what shall we do tomorrow?" he asked her wearily. "We've just about seen Haifa. That is, there's some kind of museum here somewhere, but I don't even know where it is. How about a day trip to the Galilee? I was up there a few months ago, and it was lovely. We can even visit Yodfat. You haven't been there for ages, and I'm sure you'd like to see it."

The idea appealed to her. The one problem was that she would have liked Uri to come too. Couldn't they put it off until Tuesday? "Absolutely not," replied Molkho indignantly. On Tuesday he had to be at work. Even taking two days off had been difficult, because half the office was away on vacation and he still owed a great deal of back leave. Through the open door of his bedroom, he could see the dark, velvety night beyond the new bars on the window. The telephone rang. It was not his counselor but the parents of a classmate of Gabi's, frantically calling to ask about their son. Was he by any chance with Gabi? "Gabi's not here," Molkho told them. "He went off on a hike two days ago." "What kind of a hike?" they asked. But Molkho couldn't remember. Had Gabi even bothered to tell him? "I think it's the Scouts," he said uncertainly. But they had called every boy in the class, the worried parents said, and no one had mentioned any hike. "How can that be?" asked Molkho. "I know for a fact that there is one!"

He had barely hung up when the phone rang again. It was his counselor, wide awake and eager to know what had been played at the concert. "Bach," said Molkho, not recalling the names of the pieces. "I mean, not the real Bach. The other one, his son." "Philip Emanuel!" exclaimed his counselor, disappointed not to be there to share his musical knowledge with them. "We didn't stay until the end," Molkho told him. "Ya'ara had a migraine and we left after the intermission." Encouraged by the sympathetic silence at the other end of the line, which was presumably more for his misspent evening than for Ya'ara's headache, he began complaining good-humoredly about her smoking, her uncommunicativeness, and her lack of interest in music, while she sat passively by his side as though someone else were being talked about. "We're going to Yodfat tomorrow," he told Uri. "Whose idea was that?" marveled his counselor, approving of the initiative while regretting he couldn't take part in it. "It's been years since we've been there. I suppose I've been afraid to go back, but I'm glad Ya'ara is going." Ya'ara herself was moodily leafing through the newspaper, half-listening to the conversation. She would rather he hung up, Molkho felt; however, placing the receiver gently on the table with a nod in her direction, he went off to brush his teeth in the bathroom.

The first day with her, though something of a standoff, had at least not been too strained, he reflected, the white foam of the toothpaste bubbling on his lips. Damn that boy's parents, though, for making him worry about the hike, which was beginning to seem like something he had imagined! He decided to shave the five o'clock shadow from his chin, which he dabbed with a spicy scent that his wife had liked. But, when he returned to the living room, Ya'ara wasn't there and the door of her bedroom was shut. And without so much as saying good night! he grieved, going off to bed himself. Why, you'd think I was running a hotel here!

Still, it seemed unfair to use the air conditioner while abandoning her to the humidity, and so he undressed and stood cooling off by the window, staring at the forbidding bars. How could they have made anything so ugly, he wondered, calculating what it would cost to replace them. Switching on the bed lamp, he took out a road map and studied it; then, putting on fresh pajamas, he went to her room, knocked softly on the door, and entered. "Can I bring you anything?" he asked. "I see you're having trouble sleeping." "I haven't been trying to sleep," she snapped with unaccustomed sharpness, her head on the pillow and the newspaper still in her hand. The radio was on and she was smoking, her gray hair loose around her shoulders. "Does Reb Yudl allow you to smoke in bed?" he joked, joining her surprised burst of laughter. He liked her flannel nightgown, despite its wintry look, perhaps because it made her look more solid. "It's all right. I hardly sleep at home either," she said, grinding out her cigarette in a little ashtray she had found. Yellow grains of sand gleamed on the white socks folded neatly in her shoes. Would she wear them again tomorrow? "There's something I've been wanting to ask you," he said, taking a step toward the bed. "Did you ever think of adopting?" Yes, they did, she replied. In fact, they had even filed an application several years ago and been rejected. "But why?" Molkho asked. Apparently, explained Ya'ara, because Uri's instability and her own lack of a diploma hadn't made a good impression. "What a pity," Molkho said. "Here, let me turn out the overhead light so that you needn't get up to do it later." He flicked the switch, leaving her in brown shadow. "Don't let me sleep late tomorrow," he said. "Wake me when you get up. And no more vanishing acts!"

19

AND WAKE HIM SHE DID. Why, obedient isn't the word for her! he thought, pretending to be still asleep. He let her knock, open the door, step inside, and call to him, hoping all the time that she would touch him. But she didn't. She simply called his name again and contrived to make some noise until he sat up and thanked her, though in fact it was so early that he soon fell back upon the pillow, from where he went on thinking about her while looking out the window at an overcast, prematurely autumnal day.

A few minutes later she knocked and called again. "Just a minute!" he called back. It's no wonder she never finished high school, he thought. She's fifty-two years old and never sleeps—and neither will I if I marry her! Defiantly he sank back into bed, curling up in a ball beneath the sheet and dozing off again, only to feel even sleepier upon awakening. He washed and dressed hurriedly to the muffled sound of the radio in her room, where he pictured her hungrily waiting for her breakfast, but when he looked for her there after noting with satisfaction that the kitchen table had been set (she was finally beginning to feel at home, then!), he found only her suitcase beneath her hastily made bed and three dresses hanging in the closet. Didn't she have any dirty laundry? he wondered, tempted to look for it in the suitcase.

He returned to the living room. No doubt she had gone for another walk in the ravine, and he went down to look for her, only to see her coming up the street with a bag of milk, her large sunglasses flattering her small eyes. The milk in the refrigerator was sour, she announced with an edge in her voice, starting up the stairs ahead of him as he took the morning paper from the mailbox. Before he could apologize, a friendly neighbor wished them a good morning, and Molkho, glancing at her neatly folded bobbysocks, decided that their relationship had a future. I can't afford to be choosy, he told himself, carefully taking the milk as though it weighed a great deal and remarking that the day would be another scorcher once the clouds burned off. I'm sure I once loved her, he thought, following her up the stairs. That's something we can build on. If only she'll dye her hair and use makeup. She can even keep the same wedding ring. What do I care who she got it from?

They sat down to breakfast. He was glad he had given the cleaning woman the day off, and Ya'ara washed the dishes without prompting, though she forgot to clean the sink and left suds and soggy food in the drain. She was looking forward to Yodfat. "We've thought of visiting there so many times," she told him, "but the place meant so much to us that we were always afraid to go back." Before leaving, Molkho phoned his mother-in-law, who asked when he planned to be in his office, because she wanted to consult him about her Russian friends. "As a matter of fact, I'm taking the day off," he said, "but I'll be in tomorrow. I hope it's not urgent." Apparently it was, though, for he felt her hesitate, though typically she didn't press the matter. "Well, then, perhaps tomorrow," she said, remembering to ask about the children. Pleased to hear that the high school boy was off on a hike, she asked where it was to. "To the Galilee," replied Molkho after a moment's pause. "Yes, I believe it's to the Galilee." "Is it a school hike?" she asked. He paused again. "No, it's a Scout hike." How could it be a school hike when school was out for the summer?

20

T HEY ARRIVED in Yodfat shortly before noon. The roads leading
out of the city were clogged, and on one he took a wrong turn
and had to backtrack, yet once on the new highway to the Lower
Galilee, they sped along unobstructed and Molkho praised everything he saw: the well-engineered road, the fresh green forests, the
new settlements on the hilltops, the large, clearly lettered road signs.
Belted in beside him and looking good in her sunglasses, Ya'ara, too,
kept oohing and aahing. The silence as they climbed the last curves
to Yodfat reminded him of the approach to Zeru'a, but here the
houses were well built and attractive, surrounded by trees and neat
lawns. Hardly able to wait, Ya'ara undid her seat belt and guided him
to a parking lot by a large, red stone building, jumping youthfully
out of the car the moment it came to a stop. "Does it still look the
same to you?" he asked, pleased to see her so excited. "Yes and no,"
she answered, looking eagerly around her. "I guess more no than
yes, though." She was already starting up a narrow path toward
several prominent houses standing amid the gray rocks of the hillside. "You go ahead," he told her, sensing her wish to be alone with
her memories. "I'll catch up with you."

He circled the large red building, no doubt a public structure of
some sort, looking for an open door. But there was none, and so he
walked up the paved street searching for a place to relieve himself,
encountering only closely spaced houses with gardens featuring the
same gray rock. He had despaired of finding even a suitable tree
when he spied an old prefab that apparently served for office space,
inside of which, at the end of a short corridor, he came to a small,
dirty washroom. Extracting a warm and somewhat distended penis,

he tenderly aimed it with both hands at the toilet bowl, dissuaded
from talking to it only by the sound of an electric calculator on the
other side of the wall, where an unseen bookkeeper was at work. He
flushed the toilet, washed at the soapless, towelless little sink, and
returned to the corridor, shaking drops of water from his hands,
where he was intercepted by the bookkeeper, a short, burly man with
thick, steel-rimmed glasses and a head of blond curls. Who, the
bookkeeper wanted to know, was he looking for? "I'm just accompanying someone who once lived here," Molkho told him, mentioning
Ya'ara by name. "What, they're here?" asked the short man excitedly. "Just she is," answered Molkho. "By herself?" The man
seemed mystified, as if it made no sense. "But where is he?" "In
Jerusalem," Molkho said. "And is it true what they say about him?"
asked the man tensely. "Yes," replied Molkho, who could only guess
at the meaning of the question. The bookkeeper gave his head of
boyish curls an angry though not unadmiring shake. "I might have
known!" he said. "An anarchist like him is capable of anything."
Molkho nodded sympathetically. Though he would have liked to
inquire about the village, the man seemed in the grip of such powerful memories that he deemed it best not to. "Is there anything you'd
like me to tell her?" he asked, wiping his wet hands on his pants.
"Never mind," snapped the bookkeeper with inexplicable ire, wheel-
ing to return to his cubicle.

Molkho retraced his steps to the parking lot, from where he
started up the path after Ya'ara. Beneath the overcast sky the air was
hot and dry. Scraggly pine forests covered the hillsides, some of
which were dotted with white houses, the same new settlements ad-
vertised by the road signs. Somewhere off in the distance a machine
buzzed stubbornly, its faint rasp set against the silence. A young
woman emerged from a house with a baby in a blue backpack,
glanced at Molkho slipping past her, and started down the path.
When he reached the top of it, by the uppermost houses, Ya'ara was
still not in sight. He paused for a moment, debating which way to
turn in the rocky terrain, which seemed to grow wilder in the still-
ness. There was a rustle in the bushes. He headed toward it, crossing
a stony field full of weeds, and soon spied her standing beneath a

window. A rusty hoe and some crates of rotting potatoes stood against the wall of a house that was apparently empty. Mysterious-looking in her dark sunglasses, she took several crates, piled them on top of each other, and climbed up to look through the window. "This was my window," she told him, taking off her glasses to peer inside. "I lay in bed beneath it for four months." "Was it winter?" he asked, rather oddly. She didn't turn to look at him. "Yes, it was winter," she answered, as if the question were perfectly natural. "And autumn. And once, for three months, summer. And there was another time too, right before we left. It was every year and every season," she said, standing on tiptoe to get a glimpse of the house she had felt happy and loved in, despite her great anguish, because she still had had hope. "But why not go inside?" he suggested. She threw him a grateful look, stepped down from the crates, circled the house to a locked door, and groped for a rusty key above the lintel. With a squeak it turned in the lock. Pushing the door open with her little belly, she stepped unhesitatingly inside. Molkho remained in the doorway, peering curiously into the house, which looked surprisingly tidy, with its plain furniture, straw mats, and shelves full of books and clay figurines. Who last had lived here? he wondered. Had they had children? Ya'ara stood looking around her, tall against the low ceiling. She looks best in this gray light, he thought as she led him to her old room, though I'll never know her if I don't make love to her. If she would only cry now, it would melt me so fast that sex would be no problem. Yet, though he waited patiently, she did not. Eagerly she prowled about the room, handling things, forgetting she was not in her own house, even opening an old closet as if hoping to find her dead babies there.

There was a crackle of dry grass. Someone was coming up the path. It was the curly little bookkeeper, determined to speak to her after all. Oblivious of Molkho's presence, he began plaintively inquiring about Uri, while Ya'ara fended him off with polite but evasive replies. Now and then she tried asking him about himself, but each time he returned to Molkho's counselor. Why had he never come to visit? How could he have forgotten them? He had to come, he had to, if only to explain himself! Ya'ara nodded, bending down to the little man, apparently a bachelor, who was perhaps once in love with her too. "We'll come again," she promised, looking her most majestic, so that Molkho, half in shadow in the corner, felt comforted too.

21

"IF YOU'D LIKE TO HAVE LUNCH in a really unusual restaurant, let me take you to that little town called Zeru'a that I was telling you about," said Molkho as the car silently took the curves back down to the main road. "It's a bit far but well worth it." He stopped to check the road map, then took the next turnoff, made a right onto the Acre-Safed highway, and turned left soon after at Rama, heading north on the climb toward Peki'in. They drove slowly up the winding mountain road, recalling the hikes taken by their youth group, a new feeling of intimacy between them. Had she ever thought of going back to Yodfat by herself? he asked. "No, I could never live without a man," she answered, her frankness startling him again. "And certainly not there."

It was nearly two o'clock when they reached Zeru'a, which was as quiet as a ghost town. He drove past the shopping center and along the dirt road that led to the Indians' house, telling her whimsically about the dark-skinned girl he had all but fallen in love with. Yes, she said earnestly, you can fall in love even with a child. Wait here, he told her, parking near the house and going to knock on the door. But it was locked and the windows were shuttered, the only sign of life being the cow, which stood sadly chewing her cud in her shed, her face crawling with flies. He went to ask at the house of some neighbors, who recognized him at once. The Indians, they said, had gone to visit some cousins down south; in fact, they were thinking of moving there. "Did they have a boy or a girl?" he asked. "Another girl," they said. "And how is the father?" asked Molkho.

"Oh, he's fine now," they told him, causing him to feel a sudden pang. "He's all better."

They drove back to the shopping center, which was abandoned for the afternoon siesta. The little restaurant was open, however, its tall, dark owner sitting shadelike in a corner. He, too, remembered Molkho and rose to shake his hand warmly, as did the handful of customers; he had made, it seemed, quite an impression. They shook Ya'ara's hand too, though blind, Molkho sensed, to her old beauty and disappointed she wasn't younger. Moreover, the Indian was all out of organ stew. "If only I had known," he lamented upon hearing how far Molkho had come for it. If they didn't mind waiting a few hours, he would be glad to whip up a new batch, but to Molkho's chagrin, they made do instead with dry steaks and soggy french fries, though the friendly crowd that formed around the table was compensation of sorts. Soon Ben-Ya'ish himself arrived, smiling, unshaven, and heavier than Molkho remembered him. "Whatever happened to that report of yours?" he asked, shaking hands with a conspiratorial grin. "It's on the state comptroller's desk," Molkho told him. "We tried putting things in the best light, but it's up to him now." Satisfied that he had come just to show off his new girlfriend, a much-appreciated gesture despite their doubts about her, the locals grew even friendlier. When he rose to ask for the bill, the Indian owner flashed him a dark smile. "Don't worry about it—it's on the house!" called out voices. "The pleasure was ours!" They were offended when Molkho, loath to be suspected of venality, insisted on paying. "You're insulting us," they told him, pointing out that in any case, the Indian having suddenly vanished, there was no one to pay.

On their way back to Haifa, Molkho felt that he and Ya'ara had been together for weeks. She, too, seemed more relaxed, and once out of the mountains, after stopping to buy a watermelon at a roadside stand, she shut her eyes and fell asleep. Just then, though, the engine began to knock, and glancing sideways at her tired face, Molkho felt depressed by the thought of coming home and having to explain her to the high school boy, who, hungry and dirty, would no doubt be back from his hike.

She awoke at the outskirts of Haifa, lit her last cigarette, and asked him to stop for a new pack, reading the movie ads on a sign-board while he entered a grocery. Though his anxiety grew worse as they neared home, he was relieved to discover that the boy wasn't there yet. Ya'ara rushed inside uninhibitedly, beating him to the bathroom, as if she were no longer a guest but a roommate. Had she perhaps really decided to move in with him? Before he knew it, she had gone to the kitchen, taken out the big cutting knife, split the melon in half, sliced each half lengthwise, and put the pieces away in the refrigerator. The miracle is happening, thought Molkho, watch-ing her move freely around the apartment, turn on the television, take out some cake, and put water up to boil. "How's your head?" he asked. "Oh, it's fine," she laughed.

He went to shower and emerged to find her eating melon on the terrace with her dusty shoes and socks off, her toes stuck through the railing of the terrace. How worn and raw they looked, so different from the delicate cut-glass ones he had seen in Jerusalem! It can't be that she's fallen in love with me, he thought, gazing westward at the sun struggling out of the afternoon haze, feeling groggy from his missed nap. All summer long the sun had seemed to rise several times a day, each sunrise hotter and more brutal. The red juice of the watermelon trickled down her chin. She wiped it with the back of her hand and went off to shower and wash her hair, which was wrapped in a red-striped towel when she returned.

It was 6 P.M., though the light still glared fiercely. Suddenly the house seemed full of her: there wasn't a corner where she hadn't left some part of her, some item she had touched or used. Through her thin house frock, her breasts looked small and weak. It would have been different if I'd found her myself, he thought, instead of having her served up to me. She was leafing though the newspaper, drops of water dripping from her hair, still eating slice after slice of water-melon. "That lunch made me terribly thirsty," she apologized, glanc-ing at the movie section. Had he decided what film he wanted to see? Molkho hesitated. If he knew his son, the boy hadn't taken a key; perhaps they should wait for him, after which he would be glad to see *Carmen*. The music, he smiled, would be livelier than last night's chamber concert, although if she wasn't in the mood for opera, *Gandhi* was recommended too.

All at once he found himself telling her about his trip to Berlin. She listened tensely while he described the *Voles Opera,* which were the latest thing in Europe, where the opera houses were as full as the theaters were empty; the performance of *Orpheus and Eurydice,* in which the male lead had astoundingly been sung by a woman; and— but why was he doing this; and with a grin yet!—his conversation in the beer cellar with the legal adviser. What an absurd idea that woman had sprung on him—and yet, as if it made perfect sense, he hadn't stopped thinking of it since! From time to time, Ya'ara turned her bowed head to stare at the sea, which glittered with the rays of the slowly setting sun. "How could she have said such a thing?" he demanded resentfully. "Maybe I could have done more to keep my wife alive. I wouldn't have minded her telling me that. After all, she had a husband who died too. If I killed my wife, then you killed him, I told her. But that didn't faze her one bit. Maybe I did, but not like you, she said to me."

He sniffed glumly. There were sounds outside the apartment. Suddenly fearing that his son might arrive and find Ya'ara in a house frock with his wife's towel like a turban on her head, he rose impulsively. "Come," he said, "let's catch the first show. We'll leave the key with the neighbors and put a note on the door. I honestly can't remember what time he said he'd be back—*if* he said anything, because lately he doesn't say much to me."

22

T HE LAST STRANDS of light were still glimmering in the summer night when they returned after nine. From the stairs, he saw with a sinking feeling that his note was still there, and hurriedly unlocking the door, he found the apartment dark and empty. "But what's the matter with him!'' he cried out in despair, overcome by fresh worry. "Where is he? He said he'd be home tonight! He's been gone since Saturday morning; how long can a hike last?" Going to the boy's room, which looked like a foreign land in the yellow lamplight, he began rummaging among piles of papers on the desk, fumbling through drawers of old notebooks, even turning inside out the pockets of the dirty jeans on the bed, looking for some sign, some Scout circular, some name of a friend, that might be a clue to the boy's whereabouts. "It's ridiculous to have to be doing this," he yelled irately, grabbing the phone book and searching for the number of his son's classmate's parents who had called the night before. "Did your boy turn up in the end?" he asked them over the phone. It took them a while to remember that he had ever been lost. "Now it's my turn to be worried," he said to them. "My son still isn't back from his hike. I thought perhaps you might know the names of some of the boys in the class."

He jotted down some names and numbers and dialed them one by one, yet no one could tell him anything. Wide-eyed, he looked at Ya'ara, who was sitting in front of the silent television, calmly watching him panic. "But I can't have this!" he wailed, pacing frantically. "I want to know where he is and who he went with! Maybe I should go to his Scout den." "Why don't you," said Ya'ara. "I'll wait here." "No, come with me," he insisted. "He'll have the shock of his life if he comes home to find a strange woman in the house. Let's go."

They drove the few blocks to the den, a green cabin that stood at the bottom of some stairs. "Don't bother," he said to her as she opened her car door, "I'll be right back." He all but ran down the dark steps, but the cabin was locked and lifeless. In an empty lot nearby, some children were standing around a small fire, and he went to have a word with them; though they too knew nothing about any hike, they were at least able to give him the name and address of one of the Scout leaders. "That's the best I could do," he told Ya'ara when he rejoined her in the car. "Maybe I'm being hysterical, but I feel I should go there."

Again he told her to wait for him in the car. "I won't be a minute," he said, dashing into the building, where he quickly scanned the mailboxes, bounded up the stairs, and rang a doorbell. The Scout leader was not home.

Although she was waiting obediently in the car when he returned, she gave him a searching look. "I know I'm overdoing it," he apologized, boyishly out of breath, "but I have to clear this up. It doesn't make sense that no one knows anything. Maybe he went off somewhere on his own. Why don't we drop by his school? Of course, it's closed for vacation—but still . . ."

Indeed, the school was dark and abandoned. "Wait here," he said once more to Ya'ara, who clearly hadn't thought of doing anything else. "I'll have a look around and see if there are any notices up. Here, let me turn on the radio for you." He found her a station that played music, unsuccessfully tried the locked gate, and then worked his way along the fence until he came to a hole. It was small and nearly at ground level, but after a moment's indecision, he knelt and wriggled through it into the schoolyard, ducking volleyball nets and dodging backboards until he came to the main building, where he passed a bare bulletin board in a hallway and tried in vain to force the door of the principal's office. Ya'ara was smoking thoughtfully when he came running back. "I couldn't find a thing," he shouted through the fence. "The place is dead. But I think there's a janitor on the premises, and if you'll just wait a while, I'll try to find him." He ran back into the building and down a staircase, passing from wing to wing, through the high school, the junior high school, the elementary school, losing his way in the eerily silent corridors with their inexpungible smells of rotten bananas and old sneakers, and even entering an open classroom, through whose windows the thin moon that shone on the desks stacked with chairs made him feel all over again the stomach-knotted sorrow of youth. Damn him! he thought, weeping inwardly. And I'm to blame, I'm to blame too.

It was nearly ten by the time he returned to the car, pale and anguished. "Let's listen to the ten o'clock news," he said. "If anything happened, we'll hear about it." But there was nothing. "Maybe he's home by now," suggested Ya'ara softly. "Yes," Molkho agreed, "and here we'll have been going out of our minds with worry! There's a pay phone up the street by the post office; we can call from there. Now you see what children are like! Sometimes they're nothing but trouble."

But there was no answer when he called. He laid his head on the steering wheel, feeling his fear get the better of him, and then decided to look for the college student. "I know he's studying for an exam," he told Ya'ara, "but it is his brother." He drove to the campus and parked by the library. "If you don't mind," he said gently yet another time, for it was premature to introduce her to the family, "wait for me here. You can stretch your legs on the lawn if you'd like. I want to see if Omri knows anything." He entered the large reading room with its windows looking out on the lights of the city and its air-conditioned atmosphere, which felt like that of another planet, passing down the rows of students hunched by their lamps until he found the college boy sitting drowsily beside a pile of books and laid a gentle hand on his shoulder. But tall, thin Omri, when told in a whisper what had happened, did not seem at all upset. "He must be delayed somewhere, Dad. What are you so worried about?" "But what hike was he on?" demanded Molkho. "No one knows a thing about it." "Maybe he went with a different Scout pack," drawled Omri. "Why don't you wait for him at home?" "No, I'd better call the police," said Molkho inconsolably. "But it's too early for that," objected his son with a baffled look. "They won't understand what you want from them." "You're right," whispered Molkho, turning the pages of a book. "I'm at my wits' end. It's a good thing your mother is dead. If anything's happened to him, I'll want to die too!" The college student shut his eyes, his head full of formulas and numbers. "Would you like me to sleep at your place tonight?" he asked wearily. "No, there's no need," answered Molkho. "If he's not home by midnight, I'll let you know. I just hope he knows what he's doing."

He rose, leaned over his son's crew-cut head, patted it lightly, and stepped out into the night, where Ya'ara's silhouette through the dark window of the car looked like a smoke-wreathed ghost. He thought of Gandhi and of millions of Indians and then tried picturing the cosmos flipping over and his son falling out of it. "You smoke too much," he said, brushing against Ya'ara as he slipped into the car.

"You're poisoning yourself for no good reason." Annoyed, she huddled in her seat without answering. Naturally, Omri knew nothing, Molkho told her. "Since my wife's death, it's been every man for himself in our family. Let's drive to Carmel Center. Maybe he's waiting for a bus." He cruised slowly past the bus stops in the Center, but the boy wasn't there, and he swung around and started home, driving slowly downhill in low gear. "Maybe he decided to walk. You look on your side and I'll look on mine. If you see a teenager with curly hair just like mine, that's him."

She quickly opened her door when they pulled up by the house, exhausted and eager to get upstairs. "Just a minute, you wait here," he ordered, jumping out first and stopping short when he saw that the apartment was still dark. And the note was still on the door, an air of permanency about it. Unthinkingly he grabbed it and hurried back to the car, where her thin, pale arm was resting in the window. "He's not there," he said. "I can't just sit up waiting for him. He's only sixteen. Suppose something happened? His mother would murder me! We'd better look some more. I know you're tired, but what if he missed the last bus from the Central Station and can't get home? I'm worried," he said with a lump in his throat. "If he's not there, I'll call the police."

This time he insisted that she come with him, leading her through an underground passage and up to the silent ramps that stood between the deserted fast-food stands and the parked rows of dusty buses. She followed him in silence, lagging behind a bit, yellow in the dim, fluorescent light. By some pay phones they watched the last buses whoosh up and discharge a few rumpled passengers— red-eyed soldiers with rifles, yeshiva students with bags of books, young vagabonds with backpacks. All vanished quickly, as if into the thick concrete walls, while Molkho went off to dial his apartment and stood listening to the telephone ringing in the darkness.

They returned to the car and drove past the bus station toward the traffic lights at the corner. But, instead of continuing straight, he instinctively turned left toward Rambam Hospital, in front of which, despite the late hour, there was the usual commotion of shiny ambulances slipping in and out the gate. Security guards stood talking to visitors, including entire families with baskets and pots of food. Over the main entrance shone the green light that meant the emergency room was functioning normally. A car pulled up and out of it stepped a young woman in an advanced state of pregnancy, a gay grimace of pain on her face; plucked away like a large, ripe fruit, she slowly advanced toward the lit entrance without waiting for her husband, who, having parked, was now running after her with a small suitcase. For a moment Molkho sat there transfixed, feeling the old fear rise from his gut and bear him off on a sweet wave of longing. He glanced up at the cloudless midnight sky, in which large, splendid stars stood silent sentinel. "As long as we're here anyway," he almost begged, seeing the disbelief on Ya'ara's face, "why not take a look inside? I know it's irrational, but I'll feel better if I check the emergency room. Won't you come too? There's no point in waiting out here."

23

A LTHOUGH THE APARTMENT was still dark, there was nothing to do but return to it. At the top of the stairs, however, he saw a new note on the door, which bore a message from the neighbor: Molkho's mother-in-law, it said, had called to announce that the high school boy was with her, having arrived home at ten-thirty with no key. His sleeping bag was by the fence behind the house. "Didn't I tell you he'd forget his key?" exclaimed Molkho triumphantly. "What can you do with such a child!" He let Ya'ara inside, switched on the lights, and went down for the sleeping bag, which was dirty and covered with burrs, hugging its campfire smell to his chest with untold relief and exhaustion. She was out on the terrace when he returned, her face turned to the night as if away from him. Should he embrace her gratefully? But no, that might prove awkward—and so he laid a limp hand on her shoulder and stared down with her at the ravine, which lay bright and vital in the moonlight. "Well, we had a nice day," he said. "I'm sorry if Gabi and I spoiled the evening for you." "But you didn't," she answered earnestly. "It's not your fault. I could see how worried you were." "Yes," he said swallowing hard, the waves of tiredness that were breaking within him threatening to carry him away. "He always makes me feel so guilty. I've never had an easy time with him. He's taken everything the hardest in this family, and he still hasn't accepted the fact of his mother's death. But it's awfully late. Go to bed. It's time you got some rest. Go to bed," he repeated with the last of his strength, feeling as if an impersonator within him had taken over to keep him from collapsing.

In the morning he was pleased to find her still obediently sound asleep. He phoned his mother-in-law, who listened to him berate her grandson, speaking up only to ask that he bring the boy some fresh clothes. The house seemed to bask in Ya'ara's slumber, as once it had done when his wife was peacefully sleeping off a hard night, and glad to be by himself, he ate breakfast, washed the dishes, went downstairs for the paper, hung his son's sleeping bag out to air on the terrace, made himself a sandwich for work, and put it in his briefcase. Lastly, he packed some fresh clothes for his son in a shopping bag, taking two of everything just to be on the safe side. He was almost out the door when he recalled his wife's insistence that he always say good-bye to her, no matter how fast asleep she was, and so he knocked lightly on Ya'ara's door and opened it. She did not feel him enter. He sat on the edge of her bed and touched her shoulder, surprised to encounter the soft, round warmth of her breast beneath her flannel nightgown, as if it had changed places during the night. "You really were bushed," he said with a bright smile. Disconcerted by the sight of him, she sat up and apologized for having been up until dawn. "Go back to sleep," he said, gently restraining her, as if her insomnia were medically indicated. "I'm going to the office. If you want to go out, the key is on the kitchen table by the newspaper. Feel at home. Take what you want from the refrigerator and use the stove too if you wish. I think there's a morning movie on TV. I'll be back by one."

He drove with the clothes to the old-age home, where he found his mother-in-law alone by the garden pool, her cane beside her and a crumpled straw hat spangled with glass cherries on her head. Looking pale and drawn, she said she had come downstairs to intercept him before he woke the sleeping boy to scold him. "But I wouldn't have done that at all!" he objected. "I'll give him hell later, but now he can sleep all he wants. You should have seen what he did to us," he added, wondering if she had guessed that he had spent the last few days with a woman. Still, he was sorry not to have warned her about the boy in advance, since they both knew he had a habit of going off without his key. "And without enough money," declared the old lady. "What do you mean?" asked Molkho indignantly. "That's what he told me," she insisted. "He said you didn't give him enough." "But that's ridiculous," protested Molkho. "I always give him exactly what he needs, because he just loses the rest of it anyway."

She nodded curtly when asked how she was. The endless summer, it seemed, was beginning to get to her too. The radio predicted cooler weather, she told him, but could you believe what they said? "Why not?" argued Molkho. "No one's paying them to say it, so it must be true." He handed her the bag of clothes, pointing out the double items. A long silence ensued while he waited for a cleaning woman to finish mopping the lobby in order to walk her back inside. "Until when will you be in the office today?" she asked. "Until noon," he replied. "I'm taking a half-day off." The cherries tinkled thoughtfully on her hat. He could tell there was something she wanted from him but was embarrassed to ask for.

24

THERE WAS GRUMBLING in the office at his lateness. No one gave
him credit anymore. A new generation of secretaries clamored
for his signature and decisions, for he was the only ranking official
not away on vacation. He worked hard all morning, looking up toward noontime to discover that the papers on his desk were flapping
in a sudden, dusty breeze.

His thoughts turned to the woman in his apartment. Later in
the day he would bring her to the bus station, but first he would
embrace her, though not so unequivocally as to keep her from guessing what it meant. He considered how best to deliver a kiss that
would arouse neither resistance nor false hopes, and then he dialed
his mother-in-law. "Has the boy turned over in bed yet?" he inquired, startled to hear that his son was already up, dressed, and on
his way home. He rushed out of the office, stopped to buy a cake at a
bakery, and drove home as fast as he could. Stepping into the apartment, he momentarily feared he had gone blind, for the living room
was dark except for a few motes of light that fell through the lowered
blinds and drawn curtains upon the rug and chairs. Apprehensively
he made out Ya'ara's suitcase in the kitchen door. She was chatting
quietly with Uri and Gabi, who, washed and combed, was sitting in
the easy chair like a defendant in juvenile court. "We waited to say
good-bye to you," said his counselor, rising to shake Molkho's hand,
a melancholy smile on his lips. "But what are you doing here?"
asked Molkho, turning red as if from a reprimand. "I'm sorry I kept
you waiting, but you needn't have come," he said to Uri, stunned by
the thought that Ya'ara had asked him to. She sat in the corner in
her old jumper and white bobbysocks, her little eyes watching him

with fresh interest. "You should have let me know. I couldn't leave
the office sooner, because I'm temporarily in charge of the department." Was I supposed to be making love to her all this time? he
wondered, noticing their depressed look. Was that the secret plan I
spoiled? "Why, I thought you'd sleep at least until tomorrow!" he
said with a brave smile to his son. "How come you're up so bright
and early? And after giving me all those gray hairs last night too!
Did you tell him about it, Ya'ara?" he asked his counselor's wife,
who sat there intently, her hands folded over her little belly. "Did
you tell him he had me worried sick?" He went over to shake the
boy's shoulders and then stood there gripping them. But Uri and
Ya'ara were already on their feet, preparing to depart. "So soon?"
asked Molkho despairingly. "Won't you at least have a bite to eat
first?" But they had eaten and drunk before he came and were eager
to get back to Jerusalem.

But he was not ready to part with them. At least he owed them
a summation, some sort of grade that could be given to his days with
her, which were certainly not uneventful. Hurriedly he began with
their visit to Yodfat, relating his impressions of the place. "Why,
they're still waiting for you there!" he told his tall counselor, who
stood with his head to one side. "They think of you and hope you'll
come back when you're through with the phase you're in." Uri
smiled and shook his head impatiently, gently steering Ya'ara toward
the door while donning his broad, cowboyish hat. And yet on anyone
else it wouldn't look half so classy, thought Molkho admiringly. If
they would wait for him to drink a glass of water, he told them,
seeing their minds were made up, he would gladly drive them to the
bus station: there was a bus to Jerusalem every hour on the hour, and
they could still make the two o'clock one. "But why don't we just
take a cab?" asked his counselor. Molkho's feelings were hurt. "The
hell you will!" he snapped, no less startled by his language than they
were.

In the busy station he was left alone with Uri while Ya'ara went
to buy a ticket. "When shall we meet again?" he asked, feeling his
old counselor softening. "It's terrible not being able to phone you.
How can you live without a phone? Suppose I have to talk to you!"

When, asked his counselor, did he plan to be in Jerusalem again? "Soon," answered Molkho eagerly. "Very soon. In fact, maybe even this Saturday. But how can I let you know?"

Uri stood thinking. "Please phone me," Molkho urged as Ya'ara, tall and stately, approached from the ticket booth. He seized her hand ardently. "I'm counting on a call from you," he said. But their bus was already pulling out and they rushed to board it without answering. As he was unlocking his car in the street outside the station a gust of cool wind announced the end of the heat wave. He thought of his mother-in-law. Had she felt it too? he wondered, proud of having told her that morning to put her trust in the radio.

25

D RIVING HOME, he felt a new wave of worry. Had his counselor come solely to bring Ya'ara back to Jerusalem, or had he also hoped—and failed—to receive a clear answer? In the house, he found Gabi half-naked in the kitchen, eating some yellow stringbeans from a pot. Recognizing them from the vegetable bin of the refrigerator, he realized that Ya'ara must have cooked them that morning and rejoiced that she had left him a memento. "Wait a minute," he said to his son, "why don't you warm them first?" But the boy kept on eating uncontrollably. "Are they that good?" asked Molkho excitedly, breading a cutlet and tossing it into a frying pan. "Didn't Grandma ask you to join her for lunch?" "No," answered Gabi. "That Russian friend of hers came with her daughter and I left." He kept on eating hungrily, stringbeans falling off the fork as he shoveled them into his mouth. "Will you stop eating like an animal!" shouted Molkho, losing his temper. "Here, you can have all you want, but be civilized," he said, bringing a plate and lighting a fire beneath the pot. But the boy, his bean-passion having abated, merely slumped in a chair and stared dully at his father dancing around the stove.

Molkho sat down to eat, from time to time salting the tasty stringbeans and tender cutlet while describing Ya'ara and Uri to Gabi as if they had been his guests together. "When I was your age I even had a crush on her," he said, taking more beans from the bubbling pot. His son looked at him with a gleam of curiosity. "How was your hike?" he asked. Receiving the usual grunt in reply, he resolved not to take it for an answer. "What's wrong with you?" he asked, surprised by the deathly quiet of his voice. "You change Scout packs without telling me, you go off with some kids from another school and don't even let me know—who do you think I am, the doorman? And you have the nerve to complain that I don't give you enough money! When did I ever refuse you money?" "But that's not what I said," protested Gabi hotly. "Yes, it is!" replied Molkho, cut to the quick. "Your Grandma would never make it up. How do you think that makes me look?" He was shouting now and practically in tears. "You, of all people, who lose your school-bus ticket every week, who can't put a pair of pants in the wash without leaving money in the pockets—*you* dare accuse me?" Frightened by the display of temper, the boy rose to leave the house. "And don't forget your key!" cried Molkho running after him, suddenly full of pity for his mortified, curly-headed son. "Where is it?" he demanded. But the boy couldn't find it, and so he slipped his own key off its chain, passed a string through it, knotted it, and hung it around his son's neck as though he were a toddler. At first, Gabi looked for a pocket; then, realizing his sweat suit didn't have one, he sheepishly let the key hang, even returning the bear hug his father gave him.

Only now did Molkho realize how tired he was. He showered, lay down, and fell into a deep sleep, awakening hours later with the feeling that someone was walking silently about the house. Was it his son? But no, the boy had not come back. It was as quiet as could be. Suddenly he was reminded of the end of the week of mourning, with its hollow feeling of freedom that had accompanied him ever since. Still, the house felt less empty now. Which is strange, he thought, considering she was here for all of three days and hardly spoke. He pictured her tall, question-mark figure, which seemed to bear the last of its unborn babies inside it. Grieving as if for yet another death, although this time a small, quick one, he set out in quest of her, going first to the kitchen, where he scraped the last charred, sweet beans from the pot, chewing them sleepily and licking his fingers clean. From there he went to his daughter's room but there, too, there was no trace of her, the sheets so neatly folded and stacked on the bed that he wondered whether to keep them for the next time or to throw them in the wash. Not that she'll ever know the difference, he told himself, putting them away in the closet. He glanced at his watch. By now they were in Jerusalem. Had they made up their minds about him yet? Returning to the kitchen to throw out a scrap of paper, he was surprised to find some half-eaten stringbeans and a crushed pack of cigarettes in the garbage pail. Though he was tempted to salvage the half-empty pack, it was already much too begrimed.

26

T HOUGH HE WASN'T SURE if he really missed her, he thought of her all the next day. Things were simpler without her, yet he was already considering another trip to Jerusalem to see her. Both the loss of her and the thought that she might still be available made him desire her more. Even the legal adviser, when he ran into her now at the office, aroused nothing but warm, friendly feelings. Was she aware that she had grown slightly dumpy since the winter? Not only did he no longer fear her, but he felt strong enough to readmit her to his life.

One blinding, hot noon he felt an urge to see her. He rose from his desk, left his room, and wandered off down the empty corridors of the Ministry of the Interior, most of whose employees were away, though even those who remained seemed on vacation, as if their hearts were not in their work. Inventing some imaginary problem to discuss, he descended the stone steps of the dignified old British building, crossed the courtyard to the opposite wing, climbed two flights of stairs, and knocked on the legal adviser's door. As there was no response, he entered the office of her secretary, an impish young thing who sat doing her nails with red polish. "Is the legal adviser away?" he asked. "Yes," she said, not bothering to look up. "How long has she been gone?" he inquired. "Three weeks," said the secretary. "Three weeks and no one is filling in for her?" marveled Molkho. "No one can," smiled the secretary. "But suppose I have a legal problem?" he demanded. "In the middle of a summer like this?" she teased, amused by his seriousness. "Yes, in the middle of a summer like this," he insisted. "Then it will have to wait," she replied. "But suppose it can't?" he asked. "Then let it solve itself," laughed the secretary.

He laughed too and walked slowly back down the stairs, at the bottom of which he encountered his mother-in-law in her big, crumpled hat, palely clutching some office forms. "Why, what are you doing here?" he asked, the thought crossing his mind that she wasn't long for this world. Among some people determinedly waiting on a bench, he spied the old Russian, who bowed cordially in his direction, while next to her, her plump daughter beamed at him brightly. The office forms were printed on old, yellow paper the likes of which he hadn't seen for years: one was a request for a laissez-passer, the other for a waiver of Israeli citizenship. "But why waive citizenship?" he asked after ushering the three of them into an empty room. Because, explained his mother-in-law, grateful for his help, the Finnish embassy in Tel Aviv, which represented the Soviet Union, thought it the best way to convince the Russians that her friend's daughter really wished to return. It would be even better, of course, for her to regain her refugee status, but that could only be done through the Jewish Agency in Vienna, which had refused to answer her letters. "Then her mind is made up?" asked Molkho impartially, looking curiously at the young woman, who was dressed too warmly for the weather, while his mother-in-law translated. Satisfied that this was the case, he went to another department, received a new set of forms from an unfamiliar clerk, and brought them back to be filled out and stamped before the office closed for the day. The women couldn't thank him enough, and the plump little Russian—laughing, sighing, and turning beet-red as the talk went from Hebrew to German, to Russian, and back again—tried explaining herself in rapid-fire bursts, of which all he understood was that the Israeli bureaucracy was to blame for everything. You might think, he mused with a sense of injury, that there weren't any bureaucrats in Russia—but his mother-in-law seemed so anxious to humor him that he shrugged it off good-naturedly, took the forms to the department head to be stamped, had duplicates made on the office copying machine, and even gave the three women a lift, dropping the two Russians off at a bus stop and driving his mother-in-law to the home.

Their shared hour of paperwork had renewed the old bond between them, and she looked so pale, old, and tired in the blinding afternoon light that he went to open her car door and walked her to the lobby while she continued to thank him for his efforts. "Don't mention it," he said. "I admire your energy, but if you had just bothered to explain it to me on the phone, I could have saved you the trouble of coming down in person." Why, though, he asked, advancing with her across the lobby, was her friend's daughter so eager to return to Russia? But he barely listened to her answer, for he was busy peering through the open doors of the dining room, in which at the tables, with their starched white cloths, a mere handful of oldsters sat in silence, as if all their companions had died overnight. "What's happened?" he demanded. "Where is everyone?" Some of the residents, his mother-in-law explained, were vacationing abroad, while others were visiting their children. "And they keep the dining room open for so few of you?" he marveled, watching the waitresses come and go with trays of soup. His mother-in-law countered with a question of her own: Was his housekeeper still on vacation too? "Yes," Molkho said. "I gave her the whole month off. That's what she asked for. As a matter of fact, I think she's pregnant, though I'm not even sure if she's married." The old woman nodded fretfully. "Perhaps you should find someone else," she advised. "But what will you do for a hot meal today?" And before he could tell her that he would open a can, she had invited him to lunch in requital for his pains. "Don't you have to notify the management?" he asked. "Not in summer," she replied, taking off her shapeless hat and leading him to a table at which a little old man was eating soup.

The food was not as good as Molkho had imagined; indeed, it was overdone, saltless, and cooked with almost no oil. Judging by the curious looks he received, the other diners were pleased to have his company, no doubt flattered to be joined by such a youngster. What's happening to me? he asked himself gloomily, politely chewing his meal in the large, quiet hall, with its white tablecloths and polished silver. Instead of finding myself a woman, here I am sitting with my dead wife's mother among a lot of old German Jews, practically ready for an old-age home myself!

27

AFTER A BRIEF NAP at home, he took out some stationery and began to write. "Dear Friends, I'm writing you both together. I'm too confused to know how to feel. You must admit that this whole thing is very strange. I don't know what marks you've given me, but the days together left me with a nice feeling. But I feel that I still need more time and that you must have patience with me. Perhaps we should try again next month. Ya'ara and I could take a trip abroad, because here at home you're always running into the wrong people."

He put down his pen. The word "nice" seemed inadequate and he tried to think of something better while crossing out "abroad" and writing over it, "to some hotel." But after composing a few more sentences he gave up, paced restlessly up and down, and then put on a pair of old work pants and took a can of black paint from the closet. Prying the can open with a screwdriver, he stirred the sticky dark mixture, brought a small ladder, spread some newspapers on the floor, and began painting the bars on the window. "It's just temporary," he explained to the high school boy, who came to watch. "When I get around to it, I'll order new bars like you want, with room for flowerpots, but meanwhile these may as well be painted."

28

H E STILL JUMPED whenever the telephone rang, hoping it might be them. As it never was though, he finished his letter, made a clean copy, and was about to put it in an envelope when he realized that he didn't know their address and had no way of finding it out. And so, deciding to drive to Jerusalem that Saturday, ascertain what it was, and drop the letter in the nearest mailbox, he called his mother to tell her he was coming. "Good," she said. "Come Friday and we'll visit your father's grave. It's about time we did." "But I can't take the day off," he explained. "I'm the only senior person left in the department. After all, think how nice they've been to me."

He arrived in Jerusalem late Saturday morning, just in time for the heavy lunch she had cooked. "Never mind," she said to him, sensing at once that something had gone wrong with his new relationship. "At least you tried, that's all anyone can do." But when she tried pumping him for more details, he suddenly cried out, "For God's sake, leave me alone!"

In his old room he couldn't fall asleep. A new family with a baby that cried all the time had moved in next door, and not even the thick stone walls were able to shut out the noise. Having decided it was safest to visit his counselor's building during the afternoon siesta, he drove there at two-thirty, when the city was deep in Sabbath slumber, parking a distance away from the religious neighborhood to avoid the risk of being stoned. I mustn't get on their wrong side, he told himself.

The housing project seemed larger by day than it had on his

two nighttime visits. Apart from a few children at play, it was indeed
deserted. The day was hot, and the sweat stung his eyes. When he
came to where his counselor lived, there was no house number anywhere, and the building itself, he now noticed, was but part of a
much larger complex. Stopping a young woman on her way out the
front door, he asked for the address. "Which house are you looking
for?" she asked. "For this one," he replied. "Then you've found it,"
she said. "So I have," smiled Molkho, "but suppose I want to send
someone a letter?" She paused to consider and then said, "There is
no address. Just write the name of the project and the family. It will
reach them. We've never use house numbers."

Nevertheless, deciding it was safer to leave the letter underneath his friends' door, he thanked her and slipped inside, hearing
the groan of the elevator as it started and stopped overhead. Finally
it arrived with a creak, smelling of pot roast and boiled carrots. It
was a Sabbath elevator that stopped automatically at each floor; the
door would open and Molkho would remain standing in silence, awkwardly waiting for what seemed forever, until it buzzed and shut
again as slowly as if designed for paraplegics. When at last he
reached his destination, a pregnant woman in a doorway informed
him that the Adlers lived a floor below. He descended the stairs and
was about to slip the letter beneath their door when it struck him
that they might think it a cowardly thing to do. Besides, he missed
their little apartment. If only he could have made love to her there!
In his own home it simply wasn't possible.

He knocked lightly. Someone came to the door. It was a
drowsy-looking Uri, dressed in an undershirt and gym shorts, his
beard shiny in the sunlight. "Oh, it's you," he said drily, looking
neither glad nor annoyed. "You don't have a telephone, you don't
have an address, a person can't even get in touch with you!" exclaimed Molkho defensively as he entered. "I felt we couldn't just
leave things the way they were. I had to talk to you, to know what
you think." "Who is that?" called a husky voice from the bedroom.
"It's me," Molkho called back. "It's me, Ya'ara. I just thought I'd
drop by." Uri went to the bedroom to put on a shirt, and Molkho
heard them whispering, after which they came out together. Ya'ara,

too, must have been sleeping, the last traces of her Galilee suntan still visible on the once beautiful face that was now past its prime. Why does she seem so much more desirable to me here? he wondered.

"We had no idea you were coming," they said in a reserved but not unfriendly tone. "Neither did I," he apologized wanly. "I wrote you a letter but had no address to mail it to, and so I brought it myself. Tell me, though, what exactly is the rationale for that weird Sabbath elevator of yours?" But his attempt at humor only made his counselor frown. "I'm sure you didn't come here to discuss the religious ontology of elevators," said Uri so sharply that Molkho cringed. "Talking to a nonbeliever about such things simply makes them seem ridiculous." They all sat down. Too downcast to talk, Molkho nervously took out his letter and handed it to the two of them. They read it together with a new sense of solidarity, as if the sole purpose of Ya'ara's visit to Haifa had been to return her to this overpopulated Orthodox world more dependent on her husband than ever. Automatically she reached out for the cigarettes on the table, and gently Uri's hand closed over hers to remind her that she musn't smoke on the Sabbath.

"Well?" asked Molkho from the edge of his chair as they silently put the letter down. "Well," said his counselor. "I agree that all this may have been a bit premature for you. We had no idea that you were like this." "Like what?" asked Molkho in a whisper. "Why, so inhibited," said his counselor. "So depressed over your wife's death. You haven't begun to confront your guilt for having killed her." There were steps outside in the hallway. Molkho looked up in puzzlement. Was Uri trying to keep his hopes alive? "Yes," he said. "Yes, it is a bit premature. I'm on the slow side, and you yourselves do everything so quickly, so almost . . . anarchistically. You really are anarchists," he complained. Uri smiled, content with the description. "I don't know myself very well," confessed Molkho, preferring to look out the window rather than meet their eyes. "And suppose I should want to have more children," he continued, pleased and alarmed by the unexpected thought. "It's true my wife warned me not to, but she couldn't have thought that far ahead or known what would be best for me."

They sat in weary silence. A light breeze blew the food smells of the elevator through the open window. In the afternoon light, the white rocks on the hillside were turning copper. He glanced involuntarily at Ya'ara's smooth, bare feet, sorry he hadn't ever kissed them. She and Uri seemed to be growing steadily more distant, as if regretting the involvement and wishing he would go away.

He walked back to his car like a sleepwalker, down streets whose Sabbath silence only made him feel worse. Once behind the wheel, he drove to the Old City, where he strolled through the narrow lanes of the souk until twilight, thinking it was a good thing Jerusalem had Arabs to give it some life on Saturdays. Passing the house where his father was born, he felt weak and wished he were dead. The stars were already out when, hot and tired, he reached his mother's apartment, carrying bags of fruit from the market, grapes and fresh figs and fragrant apples and pomegranates, just like his father used to do. "The weather here is unbearable," he told her. "But look how cool the evenings are," she soothed him. "Summer is over. It's already autumn now."

"No, it isn't," cried Molkho in despair, expertly dividing the fruit between them. "They may call it that, but it isn't any such thing."

PART V AUTUMN

1

AND INDEED it wasn't autumn, just a mellower summer, with days so wonderfully clear that Molkho felt he was looking at the world with new eyes. There were mornings when, driving to work down the Carmel, he could see clear to the white cliffs of the Lebanese border twenty miles away, the shoreline along the soft curve of Haifa Bay traced in precise detail. How little we're aware of what the smogs and mists hide from us, he mused. Why, if one more veil were to fall away, I might see all the way to Turkey! In the evenings the air glimmered like a golden wine, which was perhaps the reason for his hearty appetite, which had caused him to put on a few pounds again. And yet, as guilty as the orgies of food on his terrace made him feel, he kept returning to the refrigerator for more.

He had begun Volume II of *Anna Karenina*, vaguely recalling his counselor's warning that it ended with Anna's suicide, though forgetting the reason why. They were telling the truth, he thought. I was really in love with her my whole junior year. Why couldn't I at least have allowed myself a kiss or two? I'm sure her body is still young. Maybe some people never grow old, because the cells of their bodies keep changing. There were spots, he remembered, where even his wife had remained lusciously youthful to the end—around her hips, for instance, and in the curves of her thighs and insteps. They never gave me a chance, he thought dejectedly. Or had they simply used him to shore up their childless love in their little apartment in fertile Jerusalem?

He felt thankful that his own children had been brought into the world easily and long ago, and that they were no longer small.

The problem was that he was seeing less and less of them. Though his daughter was back from Europe, she had enrolled in the psychology department of the Hebrew University of Jerusalem and rarely came home, even on weekends, while the college student now spent his free time with his older girlfriend. Molkho had once seen her at the movies, a pinched-looking woman with ferrety eyes that aroused his instinctive hostility. "But what does she want from you?" he angrily asked his son, who seemed unable or disinclined to tell him and didn't seem to think it mattered. "She doesn't want anything," he answered uncomprehendingly. "We're just good friends who like to get together." Even the secretly consulted computer of the Ministry of the Interior could supply Molkho with no more than the woman's date of birth, her marital status (she had been divorced ten years ago), and an address that proved incorrect.

One Saturday he emotionally discussed the matter with his daughter, who didn't seem troubled at all. Omri, she told her father straightforwardly, was probably just looking for a mother figure. "A mother figure?" Molkho was dumbstruck. "What is that supposed to mean?" In grim silence he listened to her explanation, suddenly persuaded that the woman in fact resembled his dead wife. "But what an awful thing to happen!" he exclaimed. "The boy needs to see a psychiatrist! Please talk to him! Just the thought of that woman being in this house is too much for me!" "But why, Dad?" smiled Enat. "It's only a superficial relationship." "All right," he said resentfully, trying to smile back. "If you say so."

The child he felt sorriest for was the high school boy, who, after long, soul-searching discussions with his principal and teachers, had been left back a grade. "It's for his own good," explained the principal after patiently listening to Molkho's fears. "It's really not such a tragedy." Molkho nodded, thinking how he too might have liked to be left back, though in a different way.

2

THE SAVAGE SUMMER was still mellowing when the government overcame months of indecision to announce a bold new economic program that called for drastic wage cuts, shortly after which daylight saving time ended and the early darkness brought home the changing seasons. The approaching autumn made Molkho nostalgically recall the anxious days of a year ago. Premature though it was, he took out the calendar, sat staring at it for a long while, and finally circled a date for visiting the cemetery that fell several days before the anniversary of his wife's death. After all, he told himself, if I'm free to remarry, I'm free to move a date around. "Make sure you have no commitments or exams then," he warned his children. "Later it will be too late to change, because I intend to invite that nice rabbi again."

That Friday night, after the usual frozen fish served up with the inevitability of Fate, he told his mother-in-law. "What, you've already decided?" she asked, removing her glasses and bending over to pinpoint the day on the calendar, taken aback by his haste, despite her own penchant for orderliness. Molkho glanced mildly at the old woman, of whom there seemed to be less and less, as if her daughter's death had sprung a leak through which she herself was gradually escaping. Somehow she seemed to him like a burden he had to carry or like a barrier standing in his way. If only she had remarried and had had more children when she first came to this country, he thought, I wouldn't be saddled with her now. Had she ever had a lover after her husband's death? He found it hard to meet her eyes; lately, he felt, she was constantly appraising him, as if taking his measure for something. Before her mother entered the old-age home, his wife had sometimes sent him to her apartment to tighten a screw, change a light bulb, or drive a new nail in the wall, all of which he took his time doing, as if to put her patience to the test; after all, she had already bought the materials at his request and possessed her own little hammer, screwdriver, and box of nails and screws, so that she could easily have done the repair herself instead of waiting for him. Yet the fact was that he liked using her tools, even though he sometimes had to go back for a drill or wrench of his own, which led to yet further delays. "She has more patience than God," he would say with a smile to his wife, who never suspected him of deliberately procrastinating. Now, though the home had a janitor for such things, she sometimes still looked at Molkho as though sizing him up for some job.

So things stood when late one Friday afternoon, after a brief but violent squall that seemed to have come out of nowhere to put an end to the lingering summer, followed by an equally sudden clearing in which the sun emerged alive and well again, she stepped out of the home to greet him in the same heavy winter coat and red woolen cap that she had worn on the night of his wife's death. When he opened the car door for her heavily bundled figure with its brightly sunken eyes, he found himself wondering if she might be getting senile, even before she startled him by asking, "How would you like to take another trip to Europe?"

3

I T WAS TRULY AUTUMN NOW: one rain followed another until he could hardly remember it having ever been otherwise. Leaves that had seemed fated never to fall turned yellow and scudded along the sidewalks before fierce winds. Early one such morning, dressed in a warm coat and with a suitcase at his feet, Molkho stood downstairs peering into a thin fog that made the streetlamps flicker unsteadily, repeatedly feeling his pockets to make sure that the passport, tickets, and money that his mother-in-law had given him were still there. He thought of the protean newspaper deliverer on the morning of his wife's death, and of how, though realizing in the end it was a man, he still preferred to think it was a grimly large woman, wearing glasses and wrapped in a scarf. He would have liked to see her again now, pedaling along with her wavering light.

But his taxi was already coming up the street, its motor audible above the shriek of the wind. Soon it appeared, on its roof rack a low wooden object that it took him a while to identify as a steamer trunk. I don't believe it, he thought resentfully. Of all the luggage in the world, she has to travel with that antique! He quickly put his suitcase in the baggage compartment and slipped into the empty front seat, nodding hello to the three women who sat huddled in the back like a single lump of furry dough, their eyes red from lack of sleep. They nodded back deferentially. Why, those two old biddies actually make me feel young, he thought debonairly, trying to catch the low music on the radio, which sounded like a church choir singing in the vast nave of some cathedral. What kind of station plays music like that at 4 A.M.? he wondered, glancing at the car radio before noticing the cassette that the elderly chauffeur of the old-age home, a retired bus driver in a brimmed cap, had put in the tape deck. When it comes to German Jews, even the cabbies are cultured, he thought with a smile, turning around to exchange glances with the plump young Russian, whose documents were in his pocket. Squeezed between the two old women, only her pretty eyes were clearly her own. And that, I'm sorry to say, is about all there is to her, thought Molkho, remembering the steamer trunk on the roof. In fact, this whole trip is one big wild goose chase, he told himself, loosening his seat belt a bit and turning to ask his mother-in-law how she had passed the night with her two guests. "We're all set, then," he said to her, "although to tell you the truth, I wouldn't pin my hopes too high." He had told her that from the start, from the moment she first had proposed him as an escort, and if he repeated it now, it was not to convince anyone but simply to point out that even a model of common sense like herself was capable of a rash venture. Her only response, however,

was a cough and wan smile. Her Russian friend whispered something
to her daughter, perhaps even a translation of his words, and he
shook a despairing head to confirm that such was indeed his opinion,
though the way the plump young lady smiled back at him left him far
from sure that she agreed.

4

ONLY AT THE AIRPORT, when he had to take it off the roof, did
he realize how heavy the trunk was. Although at first the old
driver tried holding up his end of it, he soon let the full weight fall
on Molkho, who was left to wrestle it to the ground while the women
watched unconcernedly, not feeling the slightest compunction, not
even his mother-in-law, who stood silently clutching her worn handbag. "Oh yes, it has a handle, we just had one put on," she remembered to tell him once the trunk was safely down, pointing to a gilded
appurtenance screwed into the dark wood. "They must think I'm
their native porter," he thought with a new sense of grievance. The
plump little Russian, too, he noticed, was standing idly by without
even looking for a baggage cart, curiously regarding the travelers
coming and going in the dawn light. Well, you can't blame her, he
told himself, going off to fetch two carts, in Russia they haven't
invented the wheel yet. But why a steamer trunk when two or three
plain suitcases would do just as well? "You see," said his mother-in-
law as though reading his mind, "she couldn't bear to part with it,"
and indeed, it was a handsome piece, a narrow oak chest with an old
wrought-iron lock. Molkho knew that he, too, would have done all he
could to keep it.

The four of them stood silently in line at the baggage counter,
already exhausted, though the journey had barely begun. To
Molkho's surprise and somewhat to his disappointment, for he had
hoped for a glimpse of its contents, the steamer trunk passed security

with a cursory check and rode quickly off on a conveyor belt, disappearing via a portal through which an overcast morning was visible. Linking arms, the three women walked to the departure gate, where a sleepy policeman checked the boarding passes. "Well, then," Molkho told his mother-in-law, "this is as far as you go. From here on, it's just the two of us." The old woman said something in German to her friend, who halted, let out a sudden wail, distraughtly grabbed hold of the oddly passive little Russian, and hugged her in a deathly embrace while Molkho quickly maneuvered them out of the gateway and stepped back to let them part, half tempted to cry himself, though his mother-in-law, he noticed, stood there dry-eyed, her soft face looking out of focus. I suppose that at the age of eighty-three all this emotion must seem pointless, he thought. While the two Russians went on sobbing, he removed his new bifocals, folded them carefully, and put them away in his pocket. Why, he recalled, I didn't even cry when my wife died and neither did her mother. The illness dried up all our tears. I'd cry now if she would, but what good would it do, because I'm not going to get my wife back.

"If you ask me, this is all a wild goose chase," he said with a smile to his mother-in-law, who didn't appear to understand the expression. "No one is going to take her back. I'm only doing this to help her make peace with the fact that this is where she'll have to live."

5

A ND THEN they were by themselves. Though he had prepared himself for this moment, no sooner did they mount the escalator leading to passport control than the silence between them grew onerous. Even as his wife lay dying, he had spoken to her and understood her, whereas now, setting out with this funny little Russian, there was little hope of communication between them (Hebrew, their only common language, being by no means a reliable medium), which was why he had decided to keep her new laissez-passer in his pocket; indeed, his mother-in-law had as much as told him that her friend's daughter had a tendency to lose things and should not be trusted with important papers. And yet, unlike Molkho's wife, who wouldn't hear of his carrying her passport, the little Russian did not seem to mind, whether because she lacked the words to object or because she didn't care about a document from a country she had already renounced. Silently they watched their hand luggage pass through electronic surveillance, first her large red handbag, than her green umbrella, and finally his own faithful briefcase, which contained, besides his correspondence on her behalf with the Jewish Agency in Vienna, Volume II of *Anna Karenina*, the weekend supplement of the Friday newspaper, and several apples that he was loath to let rot in the refrigerator.

In the large waiting room they still had an hour until takeoff. The little Russian's tears had dried, leaving only a thin scar in her makeup, and once more she was looking curiously about her with her baby blue eyes. Like a little white rabbit, thought Molkho, observing her plump body, the fleshy folds of which exuded pampered innocence. And stubborn too—for since she looked far from stupid, what else but stubbornness could account for her having sat for months in an immigrants' Hebrew class while barely learning a word? No, she was not stupid, he decided as she anxiously appealed to him for permission to visit the duty-free shop, which she had nosed out with an animal instinct, despite the fact that this was her first commercial flight. Eagerly scurrying off to it, she snatched a shopping basket and headed for the well-stocked shelves with Molkho on her heels checking prices. Once he would have gone straight to the tobacco department, but one of the first sacrifices he had made to his wife's illness had been smoking, and in any case, what interested the little Russian was not cigarettes: apart from some chocolate bars, her basket already contained two bottles of Scotch, to which, with a nervous glance in his direction, she now added a fifth of vodka. Could she still be a virgin? wondered Molkho, mentally adding up the bill. His mother-in-law had given him eight hundred dollars for expenses, and he had to make the money last; yet, as though it were meant to flow through his fingers, he now counted it out with a smile. Unsuccessfully trying out a few words of beginner's Hebrew, he led her gently to a seat by the boarding gate, where she sat for a while, blissful with her purchases, until she suddenly popped up again and dashed off to the bathroom, leaving him with her things.

So far, so good, thought Molkho, who was only now beginning to feel his fatigue, having hardly slept a wink all night. Slouched in his seat, he scanned the faces of the other passengers, looking especially for Arabs who might hijack him. But Arabs, it seemed, did not fly El Al to Europe and, in fact, probably did not fly to Europe at all, being by nature thriftier than Jews. Why, just look at me, he thought: my wife isn't dead a year yet and I'm taking my second trip abroad, although, of course, I'm not doing it for pleasure. In the plate-glass window that looked out on the gray morning he saw the reflection of his own silver curls and his dark eyes, which brimmed with liquid melancholy. Though the clouds looked thick as concrete, their plane would find a way through them.

He shut his eyes, listening to the quiet murmur around him. Once it would have been louder, but Israelis were becoming more civilized: the more they failed in war and politics, the politer they became, he mused, dozing off for a moment to be awakened by a loudspeaker announcing their flight. His fellow passengers rose to queue up by the gate, but the little Russian was nowhere in sight, and Molkho, who hated being late, impatiently grabbed her things and ran to the women's bathroom. For a moment he stood helplessly outside, recalling the special whistle he and his wife had had for such contingencies; then, giving the door a slight push, he furtively stuck in his head. An eerie silence greeted him from the deserted row of white sinks, broken only by a thin trickle of water, as if an underground spring were bubbling up in one of the toilet booths. Could she have locked herself in there? he wondered, not daring to enter. The first order of business in Europe would be to teach her to whistle. At least we can communicate that way, he decided, anticipating a difficult trip. But meanwhile there must be a way of luring her out of the bathroom. How would it look if he couldn't even get off the ground with her? Out in the waiting room their flight was being announced again. Trying not to panic, he ran back to the duty-free shop. After all, he told himself, if worse comes to worst and I've lost her, I can always go home and catch up on my sleep. In fact, she wasn't there, and he hurried to the boarding gate, arriving just in time to see the last stewardess vanish through the door. But this is madness, he thought bitterly, hearing the two of them paged on the loudspeaker, a white-rabbit hunter whose quarry had eluded him. Just then, however, she waddled out of the bathroom on her high heels, freshly made up and bright with excitement. "We'd better hurry," he exclaimed, wagging a finger at her, a resort to words being pointless. Could his mother-in-law be plotting to marry her off to him out of pity—for her, for him, or for both?

6

WITHOUT THINKING TWICE about it, he gallantly offered her the window seat. She had hardly flown before and might never fly again, so why not let her enjoy it? He explained the seating arrangements to her in sign language, making sure to fasten her belt while considering how to convey to the other passengers, who were staring at him curiously, that she was neither his wife, cousin, nor mistress but rather someone he was escorting to Europe for a fee and a free weekend in Paris. Perhaps her broken Hebrew would suffice to make that clear; indeed, he now regretted not having brought along a pocket Hebrew-Russian dictionary. Meanwhile, he spoke as simply as possible, omitting adverbs and adjectives and sticking mainly to nouns, with an occasional verb thrown in. She listened to the Hebrew words with amusement, giggling at being treated like a retarded child as she had done when discovered by him that summer in his mother-in-law's bed.

Unawed by the takeoff, she turned away from the window once

the plane gained altitude over the sea. Yet again, her savoir faire surprised him, for as soon as the stewardess came down the aisle with drinks, she asked for a glass of Scotch and downed it before breakfast, merely picking at her food while he finished his and hungrily eyed her full tray, which his wife, had it been hers, would have been thoughtful enough to offer him. They were over the Greek islands by now, and since she still seemed wide awake and he was tired of looking up all the time from his magazine to smile at her, he rented her a pair of earphones, helped adjust them on her head, and ordered her another whiskey, though this time letting her pay for it, which she anxiously did from a little purse stuffed with one-dollar bills. Then, to help pass the time, he reached for his *Anna Karenina*, showing her the title page. "Ah, Tolstoy, Tolstoy," she exclaimed with a tragic sigh, though he rather doubted she had ever read a word of it. Before he had gotten very far in Part Seven the plane was already descending through the clouds, bouncing and shuddering in the gray fog, and she was on her third Scotch. He shut the book and glanced at the contents of his briefcase, annoyed to discover that his mother-in-law, who had promised to see to everything, had forgotten to take out medical insurance for him. I should never have trusted her, he thought, already worrying about what might happen if he fell ill.

7

A T THE AIRPORT in Vienna the wooden trunk was the first piece of luggage to appear on the conveyor belt, sailing proudly into the arrival hall as if it had come all the way from Tel Aviv under its own steam. Molkho let it circle, grabbed it by its new handle, and struggled to stand it upright on a cart, convinced that either it had grown heavier or he had grown weaker during the flight. Soon their two suitcases came, and they wheeled the cart out into a muggy afternoon over sidewalks strewn with autumn leaves. But here, too, the trunk proved a problem, for the Austrian capital did not boast many cabs with baggage racks. Moreover, the little Russian, who, smelling faintly of alcohol, seemed as happy as a puppy, suddenly discovered that she had lost her umbrella, which not only strength- ened Molkho's resolve to hold onto her documents but made him wonder whether to confiscate her personal effects and money too. It was nearly four o'clock, and all at once the brief day was fighting for its life as the light ebbed out of it. Impatiently he scanned the traffic for the right kind of cab, hoping he might still manage to call the Jewish Agency before closing time to confirm their next day's ap- pointment. He had never spoken to his wife about Austria. Would she have objected to his coming here too? Most likely she had never thought of it. She had thought of most things, but not all.

Their hotel, in which his mother-in-law had made reservations through a travel agent on the recommendation of someone in her old- age home, turned out to be a large, centrally located, overpriced, slightly rundown, decadently grand establishment, in which the old steamer trunk, dragged into the lobby by Molkho, nearly created an anti-Semitic incident. "What's in it?" demanded the Austrians, evi- dently concerned for their reputation, first surrounding it with sev- eral bellhops and then bundling it off into an elevator as quickly as possible. Though not as fancy as the lobby, the little Russian's room was large and faced out on a broad boulevard. At first, the bellhops tried sliding the trunk beneath the big double bed, but it was several inches too high. Nor did it fit into the closets, and so they pushed it into a corner and draped it with a cloth while Molkho stood stonily watching from the doorway. His own room, though on the same floor, was off a dark corridor and faced in a different direction. Too late did the profuse thank-yous of the bellhops, who put down his light suit- case with an expression of relief, inform him that he had overtipped them.

8

A T LEAST THIS TIME there aren't any stairs to climb, Molkho thought, still sorrowing over the size of the tip. His first task, he decided, was to learn the value of the Austrian currency that his mother-in-law had handed him in an envelope. Spreading out the bills and coins on his bed, he studied their colors and pictures, turning them this way and that. How big had the tip been? Why, they might think he was a gangster with a corpse in his trunk! Finally, satisfied it wasn't that much, only about seven dollars, he hung up his pants and jackets, put away his shirts and underwear, and shoved the empty suitcase underneath the bed, feeling immediately less transient. There was no New Testament in the room, nor for that matter any Old, just a brochure about Vienna, and so he went to have a look at the large, multimirrored bathroom, which offered all the modern conveniences, despite its period appearance. Stashing away the extra bars of soap in his toilet kit, he decided to leave the container of blue bath bubbles by the tub and proceeded to check the plumbing, whose bent, rusty pipes testified to its age. Still, there was no denying that the place was kept up well.

He returned to the bedroom and theatrically flung open the velvet curtain on the large window, which unfortunately faced a drab side street lined by gray buildings that made him think of the wings of a hospital. Had his mother-in-law forgotten the little Russian's medical insurance too? Drawing the curtain, he read the fire regulations that hung on the wall beside the authorized room price, whose exorbitance dawned on him only now. As if having to spend the next few days with a plump rabbit he couldn't talk to was not bad enough, there would be, he suddenly realized, almost no money left for his

planned weekend in Paris. He would have to operate on a shoestring:
if he could not arrange her return to Russia within a day or two, he
would simply transfer her to a cheaper hotel and let her and her
trunk get back to Israel by themselves.

He took off his shoes and undressed, preparing to take a bath.
It was one of the pleasures of good hotels that there was plenty of hot
water, just as there had been in Jerusalem during his childhood,
when he bathed once a week on Thursday night. His wife had been
so shocked by this revelation that she had all but called off their
marriage. "But you have to shower daily!" she had told him. "In
bathtubs you just sit in your own filth!" Indeed, even as she lay
dying thirty years later, she still didn't trust him, sometimes sitting
up deliriously in bed to ask if he had washed yet. The surest way to
her heart was by showering twice a day, a measure guaranteed to win
a loving look. Only in hotels was he granted a special dispensation to
take baths.

He had already opened both faucets of the tub when he remembered his phone call to the Jewish Agency. After all, he thought, I
didn't come to Vienna to bathe. Still in his underpants, he turned off
the water and went to dial the number given him of a certain Mr.
Shimoni, whose Israeli secretary answered the phone. Molkho introduced himself, explained that he was representing a Miss Nina Zand,
referred to the letters sent on her behalf and to the answers received,
and asked to confirm the appointment he had made for the next day
in order to obtain the assistance and missing documents still re-
quired. "I'm afraid," said the secretary, "that your appointment has
been canceled because Mr. Shimoni is indisposed. He hasn't come to
work for several days." "You mean he's sick?" asked Molkho in
dismay. He hadn't taken such a possibility into account. "But we've
come all the way from Israel just to see him!" "Yes, indeed," the
secretary assured him. She knew all about it. Mr. Shimoni hadn't
forgotten the appointment. In fact, he had taken the file home with
him and even telephoned her that morning to ask that Mr. Molkho
call him there.

Molkho breathed a sigh of relief, and the secretary gave him
the phone number, requesting only that he call later in the day, since

Mr. Shimoni liked to take a long afternoon nap. "As one public servant to another," Molkho told her, "I want to thank you for being so helpful. I must say we don't deserve our bad name." "No, we don't, do we?" answered the secretary vivaciously. "If it's not too much to ask," continued Molkho, "what exactly ails Mr. Shimoni?" The secretary wasn't sure. "It's probably a diplomatic illness," she laughed, "because he's terribly bored being an immigration official without immigrants." Molkho laughed too and started to hang up, but now it was her turn to question him. When did he arrive in Vienna? And how was his flight? And what was new in Israel? "Nothing is new," he said. "And how's the weather?" she asked to make conversation, as bored by her job as was her boss. "It's been rainy," said Molkho, "but not very cold, although, of course, not as hot as the summer." Apparently, however, she hadn't heard of the hellish summer. How long was he staying in Vienna, she wanted to know. "Oh, just a day or two," Molkho said. "As long as it takes to find out if the Soviets will repatriate Miss Zand." "Just a day or two?" She seemed disappointed. "Why not stay longer and enjoy yourself? There's lots to do here that doesn't call for any German, all kinds of operas and concerts. Would you like me to suggest something?" Molkho guffawed. "No, thank you," he said, "I've been to enough operas and concerts to last me for a while. But perhaps you could recommend some good ballet." At once, as if she worked for a ticket office, she listed several performances, even spelling them out for him in Hebrew letters. Clearly, she didn't want to hang up, and Molkho listened patiently, distressed to see in the large wall mirror that he had indeed put on weight and had even sprouted little breasts.

When he finally got into the bath, he lay for a long while in the deliciously sudsy water with his eyes closed. Then he dried himself, shaved, applied some lotion, ate the last apple in his briefcase, dressed, stepped out into the corridor, and knocked on the little Russian's door. There was no answer. He knocked harder, but there was still no response. Good grief, he wondered, do I have another Sleeping Beauty on my hands?

9

H E DIALED HER ROOM, but no one answered the telephone either. I shouldn't have spent so long in the bathtub, he fretted,
descending to the lobby to look for her. But she was not there either,
nor had she left any message or key at the desk. He searched in vain
in the large dining room, where a gypsy band was playing, and
stepped out into the broad boulevard, which was now bathed in
twilight, peering into shops as he passed them, though the chances of
finding her were slim. Could she have gone off to see the sights
without telling him? Not that she was under any formal obligation,
but it was a matter of simple courtesy. He asked again at the desk,
knocked once more on her door, tried phoning her room a second
time—but she had vanished into thin air. Could she, he wondered,
racking his brain, have unknown friends in Vienna? It was getting
dark out. Bright lights came on in the lobby. He sank grouchily into
a leather chair that commanded a view of the entrance, ordered some
coffee, and was about to ask for a slice of the cream pie on the pastry
cart when he remembered his little breasts in the mirror and decided
to wait for dinner.

Three veiled young ladies with their arms full of shopping bags
entered the lobby with a man who could have been either their father
or their husband, a large, swarthy Arab with the mien of a desert
prince, no doubt from the Persian Gulf, dressed in a white kaffiyeh
and an expensive European suit. Chattering in rapid Arabic, they
deposited him and their parcels in a seat next to Molkho's and darted
excitedly out again, off on another spree. The prince, in a state of
shock from his purchases, or perhaps from the Western clothes he
had been made to wear, tilted his sun-bronzed face toward an invisi-

ble horizon and soon sank into such a trance that he did not even notice the cup of coffee brought him by a sedulous waiter. Suddenly, however, sitting up amid the bags of women's wear and glancing desperately around him, he noticed Molkho, who was sitting a few feet away, and beamed with recognition, as though spying a fellow tribesman. Molkho looked uncomfortably away, yet the big Arab was already leaning toward him with a grin, his dark eyes lighting up. Not wanting to disappoint him, Molkho fled to the telephone booths by the reception desk and dialed Mr. Shimoni's home number. Mr. Shimoni answered the phone. "Yes, I'm not well," he declared in an overrefined voice, "but if time is of the essence, perhaps I could receive you at home this evening and see what I can do." Dictating his address, he insisted that Molkho write it down.

The little Russian's disappearance was getting to be serious. Molkho hurried to her room and knocked loudly on the door, though not so loud as to attract the attention of the guests descending for dinner, and then went to look for her again in the dining room, sidestepping tray-laden waiters, passing a small, dimly lit bar whose customers were lining up for their first cocktails, and emerging in a garden where some staff was folding chairs. This is no joke, he thought worriedly, stepping back into the street. Might she be in trouble somewhere and in need of help? I shouldn't have been so standoffish on the plane, he chided himself, returning to the lobby, which he decided to explore in greater depth. Descending some stairs, he opened an apparently locked door and soon came to a floor of large conference rooms, smoke-filled billiard parlors, a gymnasium, and even an empty swimming pool still smelling of chlorine. Peering into dark washrooms, he headed for some lights at the end of a passageway and found himself in an underground shopping center full of little boutiques and cafés, a subterranean world that was shutting down for the night. A few last customers were leaving the shops, in which the personnel was wiping counters and mopping floors before closing. A sixth sense telling him that his white rabbit was near, he quickened his stride. We must have a whistle, he resolved just as he saw her through the window of a small beauty parlor, happily seated beneath a dryer with curlers in her hair. He was about to burst angrily inside when he spied a large, pasty woman in a corner, staring balefully with her arms crossed at the obstinate client whose hair had to be done at the last minute, when the lights were already dimmed and the scissors and combs put away for the day. Relieved to have found her, he stood watching from a safe distance. Though it was comic to think that a fresh permanent would matter to Mr. Shimoni, he slowly felt his ridicule yield to an odd compassion.

10

A T NINE THAT EVENING a taxi brought them to a baroque apartment building in a middle-class suburb, where a stocky guard met them at the door and took them up to the second floor in a dark elevator. Stepping into a vestibule wallpapered with a forest of gold trees and faded green leaves, they waited for their guide to unlock a door and usher them into an ornate drawing room in which stood a grand piano covered with musical scores. Large windows looked out on a dimly lit park; on the leather chairs and sofa lay piles of newspapers, magazines, and office files; shelves of books and Judaica lined the walls; and the overall jumble was such that Molkho cast a worried glance at his plump Goldilocks while their guide vanished down a hallway to look for Mr. Shimoni, who proved to be a tall, thin, sallow, bald man in his sixties, dressed in a silk bathrobe and high slippers and with a cultivated air. Sucking on a cough drop, he shook their hands formally, the blue veins bulging in his broad, intellectual brow. Yes, he's even sicker than I thought, decided Molkho, begging pardon for the late-hour intrusion. Mr. Shimoni waved off the apology and sank into a leather armchair, imperiously dismissing the silent guard while inviting his guests to sit down. "Well, then, this is the Miss Zand that I wrote you about," began Molkho, removing some Hebrew newspapers from a chair and pointing to his rabbit, who teetered on her high heels in a dress slightly creased from her suitcase. "She was processed by you in Vienna nearly a year ago on her way from Russia to Israel. I understand you don't see many new faces these days, so perhaps you even remember her."

If he took umbrage, the official gave no sign. Smiling faintly at Miss Zand, who, bright with excitement, was settling into a chair, he began questioning her in a fluent Russian that he evidently kept handy for such occasions. She answered him solemnly, her stiff curls shaking with each emphatic bob of her head. "Then you don't remember her?" interrupted Molkho, feeling left out. "What difference does it make?" replied Mr. Shimoni brusquely, barely glancing in his direction. "They're only here for a day or two; their train pulls in from Russia in the morning, and by the next evening they're on a plane to Israel." "Well," said Molkho, discouraged by the patronizing tone, "she wants to go back. She's been in Israel nine months and doesn't like it. You don't like it, do you?" he asked her while Mr. Shimoni stared ironically at the floor. Suspicious at the sudden switch to Hebrew, which no longer seemed quite so amusing, she looked from one man to the other. "Where in Israel did she live?" asked Shimoni, using his divide-and-conquer technique to repeat the question in Russian without waiting for Molkho to answer. Sitting on the edge of her chair, Miss Zand replied to all his queries, pulling out a packet of letters from her handbag and even showing him one from her old place of employment in the Soviet Union declaring its readiness to take her back.

"In Israel she was unemployed," put in Molkho, refusing to be excluded. It was his duty, he felt, if only to his mother-in-law, to serve as the little Russian's counsel. "She was enrolled in an intensive Hebrew course, though you can see that she didn't learn a word." "But no one at the embassy will take her back," snapped Mr. Shimoni with sudden irritation. "You're just wasting your time!" Molkho knew this was true, but startled to hear it put so baldly, he began zealously defending a faith he didn't share—namely, that if the Jewish Agency would return Miss Zand's exit visa and give her a letter stating that she had only left the Soviet Union to accompany her old mother to Vienna, all would be well. "But what good will that do?" scoffed Shimoni. "The Finns say it will give her back her refugee status," answered Molkho. "A lot the Finns know!" jeered the official, putting on his glasses to read the Russian's letters while continuing his interrogation.

Why argue? reasoned Molkho, growing calmer. The man is right. Why take all her problems on myself? He glanced out the paneled window at the bright lights of Vienna, glimpsing the electric spark of a trolley along the tree line of the park. Mr. Shimoni's sickly pallor made him appreciate his own good health. Despite his fears that his wife's illness would turn on him once she died, a year had gone by without a single visit to the doctor. Not even to the dentist, he thought contentedly, reaching into his jacket pocket for his bifocals in order to glance at a newspaper. Yet the little Russian's musical voice held his attention. Happy to be speaking her own language, she was excitedly explaining something, now pointing to her letters and now to Molkho, as though telling the official all about him. Perhaps there's more to her than just those pretty eyes after all, he thought, resolving not to be unkind. Though he didn't understand a word, he felt he knew what she was saying. "After all," he interrupted, eager to rejoin the conversation, "why shouldn't they take Miss Zand back? Think of the publicity it will give them." "They don't need our publicity," sniffed Mr. Shimoni, sucking on his cough drop like an elderly infant, his condescending expression unchanged. "And besides, even if they wanted to take her back, it's not bureaucratically possible." He grinned, baring decayed teeth. "But why must it be Russia? If Miss Zand is prepared to go to America or Canada, that's something that might be arranged." Molkho had no objections, but when the idea was broached to the little Russian, she so tearfully shook her head and heaved her ample bosom that her mettle rather pleased him, though it only made Shimoni crosser.

"Have you ever had such a case before?" Molkho asked. His mouth was dry from the central heating and it was beginning to dawn on him that the official, who apparently lived by himself, was not going to offer them refreshment. "One or two," Shimoni replied. "They all come to me with their complaints as if it were my fault that they didn't like Israel." "You see," said Molkho with a sympathetic nod at his client, who perhaps understood more Hebrew than she let on, "she couldn't take the climate either. This past summer was an especially bad one." And when the official merely snorted, he went on, "Why, she's more Russian than Jewish. Just look at her! The idea of her having to go through all this is absurd! And don't talk to me about a common Jewish destiny," he added heatedly, though Mr. Shimoni had done nothing of the sort, "because there is no such thing! That's only the slogan of unhappy Jews like us who want more Jews to be unhappy with them." Sucking bemusedly on his cough drop, Mr. Shimoni rested his long buttery fingers on the leather arms of his chair. Molkho felt unbearably thirsty. "Could you please tell me where the bathroom is?" he asked hoarsely, and Shimoni led him down a long corridor and switched on a light at the end of it.

"You have a big place here," Molkho said. "Big?" echoed Mr. Shimoni defensively. "Why, it's huge, to say nothing of far too old! It's too much for a single person like me, but it was a bequest to the Agency from some rich Jew, and there's nothing to do about it. Tell me," he asked Molkho, who wanted only to get into the bathroom, "did you really come all the way to Vienna just for Miss Zand?" "Yes," Molkho said. "Her mother is an old friend of my mother-in-law's, and I'm the only other person they could turn to. I didn't want her to have to come alone, especially since she has heavy luggage, and so I offered to escort her." "But you can't even talk to her!" objected Mr. Shimoni. "No, I can't," conceded Molkho. "She doesn't know any English or French either. It's all terribly uncivilized, but what can I do?" "And you really think the Russians will take her?" asked Shimoni. "To tell you the truth," answered Molkho honestly, "I don't. I told my mother-in-law that too. But we thought it best to leave no stone unturned. It was really the Finns who put her up to it."

Mr. Shimoni's lips curled in a smile, and Molkho escaped into the bathroom, leaving the door slightly ajar. Taking off his bifocals, he turned on the faucet, bent over the sink, and gulped handfuls of cold water until he had had enough. Then, afraid to risk infection from the towels, he waited for his face to dry, threw a desultory glance at the toilet, and regarded the mirror of the medicine cabinet, his bloodshot eyes staring back at him. He had barely begun to explore the cabinet's contents when he heard the little Russian gasp. I have to help her, he shuddered, thinking warmly of her snowy throat, whose double chin was perhaps only an illusion. I mustn't be so critical. Every woman has something lovable. He turned out the light and groped his way back up the hallway, peering into the rooms leading off it, in one of which he was startled to glimpse a tiny old woman in a nightgown, crouched on a bed with her bare feet clawing the air.

He was barely noticed when he returned to the drawing room, where Shimoni, his bald, pale head between his hands, was listening intriguedly to Miss Zand, now and then grinning broadly. I must be missing a good story, mourned Molkho, collapsing into his chair, from which he took advantage of the first lull to inquire if Shimoni could lend him a Hebrew-Russian dictionary. "Hebrew-Russian?" marveled the official. "I doubt if we even have one in the office. But you can find English-Russian or French-Russian in any bookstore. Do you want to talk to her or understand her?" "Both," answered Molkho. "It's enough to drive a person crazy. Today she disappeared without telling me, and it took me an hour to find her in some beauty parlor." Shimoni laughed. "It's no joke," declared Molkho, laughing too. "Please tell her to let me know where she goes." The official translated, Molkho wagged an admonishing finger, and the little Russian giggled hotly. "Is that a promise?" he asked, smiling angrily. "Promise," she agreed, latching on to the Hebrew word. "Promise, promise, promise."

As they were leaving Molkho asked again if Mr. Shimoni couldn't give them a letter to the Russian embassy certifying that Miss Zand was still a refugee. But the official was adamant. "Believe me," he said, "any letter from me would only make things worse. She'll just have to take her chances. And what are your own plans?" "Oh, I'll stick around for a while to see what happens," Molkho said. Shimoni nodded, loath to part with such an entertaining couple. "Well, let me know how it turns out," he told them, first in Hebrew and then in Russian. "I feel responsible in spite of everything."

Molkho gratefully shook his hand, and Shimoni put a friendly arm around Miss Zand and steered them both toward the elevator. "What's there to do mornings in Vienna?" asked Molkho as the red arrow lit up. "All sorts of things," said Shimoni. "What are you interested in?" "Oh, some museum or historical site," Molkho answered. "Even one of Jewish interest," he added patriotically. "Some old synagogue, for instance, or maybe Herzl's grave." "Herzl's grave?" chuckled the Jewish Agency official. "Herzl's grave is in Jerusalem. Perhaps you mean Herzl's house. There's nothing but a plaque there though, and it's hardly worth the effort." He looked smugly at Molkho, who smiled in embarrassment. "If tomorrow is as nice as today, and I don't see why it shouldn't be, I suggest you take a walk in the Vienna Woods and go to the zoo." "The *zoo?*" Molkho was mortified. "Yes," said Mr. Shimoni, "why not? The zoo here is marvelous, and you probably haven't been to one in ages. Take the number 6 or 8 trolley, and you won't regret it. Sometimes there's a military band there too. I'm sure you'll enjoy every minute." Graciously opening the door of the groaning elevator, he saw them on their way.

11

I N THE MIDDLE OF THE NIGHT Molkho was awoken by a muffled shout and angry voices. He dragged himself out of bed to the sink, gulped more water while wondering why Vienna made him so thirsty, and went over to the dark window, where he drew the heavy curtain and stared down at the street below. By the locked gate of the building that he had taken for a hospital, two guards were arguing with the driver of a white car. In that case, he thought groggily, it can't be a hospital, because it wouldn't turn away an ambulance. Suddenly he remembered having dreamt about his wife. Although he had dreamt of her before, this time she was in company, sitting off to one side in a room with familiar wallpaper. The others did not know, or pretended not to know, that she was dead, so that, unaware of Molkho's presence, as if he, not she, were the ghost, she sat there perfectly content. Meanwhile, down below, the argument finally ended with the opening of the gate and the disappearance of the white car. Much to Molkho's relief, the night grew silent again.

In the morning he found his little rabbit in the lobby, pale and baggy-eyed in a conservative red woolen suit with stiff, padded shoulders. Her new curls had softened agreeably overnight, making her look rather cuddly. "How did you sleep?" he asked concernedly, repeating the question a second time in even more basic Hebrew. "Terrible," she replied with a glum smile, the wealth of her vocabulary surprising him. "Much terrible." Smelling alcohol as he led her to the dining room, he sat her at a table, took out a map, and showed her the location of the Soviet Embassy. As simply, though in as many ways as possible, because even if she understood only a fifth of what he said it was worth it, he reviewed their meeting with Mr. Shimoni, trying his best to sound hopeful. As a government official himself, he said, he had one bit of advice to give her: tell the Russians the truth and nothing but. Though the fact of the matter is, he thought, watching her tubbily bounce off to the buffet for another fresh roll, that if I believed they might take her, I would have made love to her last night as a parting gift from Israel. It's not as if that could have been taken as a commitment. But the chin above her white, shapely throat was double after all, and he couldn't be blamed if his wife's illness had made him suspicious of swellings. Besides which, he told himself, I happen to have high standards. In fact, they're only getting higher, which is why I'm wasting precious time on these oddballs instead of going to some dance hall and grabbing the first woman on the floor.

It was eight o'clock, and since the embassies didn't open until nine and the weather was nice and the distance not great, Molkho suggested that they walk. They strolled through the awakening streets of the city, soon coming to a colorful farmers' market that was just being set up. Making their way past mounds of fruits and vegetables, they lingered by stands of seafood sparkling with crushed ice, looking at the little black mussels, the large gray fossil-like clams, the piles of purplish shrimp and ruddy lobsters fanning slow antennae, the wicked coils of eels and lampreys. "Why, it's just like Paris," exclaimed Molkho enthusiastically, "it's exactly the same!" Shoulder to shoulder, for he didn't care what people here took them for, they followed the map through a clean, pleasant quarter, stopping now and then to window-shop while he translated prices into shekels and dollars.

A cordon of armed Austrian policemen indicated the site of the Soviet embassy from afar. Molkho halted and handed the little Russian her laissez-passer, which she deftly slipped into her handbag, after which they carefully circled the building, checking its various entrances and the visiting hours posted outside them. Even if nothing comes of it, he thought, even if it was only a gesture, I'll have done my human duty. "I'll wait here for an hour or two," he said, pointing to a little cafe on the corner, "and after that we'll meet back at the hotel. Just no more disappearing acts, please!" She nodded, and since they still had time, they entered the café together. From everywhere came the melody of Russian voices, for the place was full of embassy officials who had dropped in for a hot drink or something stronger. Aglow at the sight of so many compatriots, the little Russian followed Molkho to an empty table in a corner and ordered brandy, while he asked for coffee, wondering if he should be seen with her here, where he might be mistaken for a Western intelligence officer running a secret agent. She, too, it seemed, had the same thought, because as soon as she downed her drink, she went off to the rest room, leaving him by himself. Watching the embassy workers come and go with friendly greetings, he felt more optimistic. After all, they're human beings just like us, he thought, why shouldn't they agree to take her? What do they stand to lose? It's natural to feel homesick. What's one more Jew to them when they already have millions? If she stays in Israel, I'll be the one to suffer, because I'll just have to marry her in the end. Surreptitiously slipping one of the hotel's cards into her handbag, he took his coffee to a distant table, from which he watched her leave the rest room. She looked for him, caught sight of his furtive wave, and showed she understood it by exiting to join the line already forming by the gate of the embassy, through which the Russians now streamed from the café, brandishing their ID cards at a new shift of burly guards.

He let the café empty out and went to pay the waiter, asking for a receipt. Not, he mused, that his mother-in-law would check his expenses, but he should be able to give her a general account of where her money had gone. Perhaps she would even want to send him abroad again; it was certainly more likely than a junket from work like the legal adviser's. He jotted down what other outlays he remembered on the back of the receipt, counted his change carefully, stuck it in his pocket, and looked out at the busy street. The little Russian had vanished through the gate of the embassy, and when after a while she failed to return, his hopes soared even higher.

12

A T LAST, he stepped outside himself, surprised at how warm the clear autumn air had become. Fallen leaves crackling underfoot, he strode by the lavish storefronts determined to withstand temptation and not waste the morning shopping. And so, though still smarting from Mr. Shimoni's advice, as if museums and galleries were beyond the ken of a mere Levantine like himself, he found a number-6 trolley stop, made sure he was headed in the right direction, and boarded the next car for the Vienna Woods with a contingent of old ladies, young mothers, and noisy children. At last, with a great clatter and clang of bells, the trolley came to the end of the line. It was indeed right next to the zoo, which Molkho, despite a moment's uncertainty, decided he was too old for, opting instead to go for a walk among the tall trees of the park, its well-trodden paths being full of local hikers. Eventually he reached a large outdoor café with a fountain adorned by statues of animals, beside one of which, a skillful figure of a deer with blind, stony eyes, he sat down in a shady spot. After looking around at the crowd, which was composed mostly of old people enjoying the warm fall day, he glanced at an article about abused women in the weekend supplement of his Hebrew newspaper and then took out Volume II of *Anna Karenina*, turned to Part Seven, and began to read. Quickly he grew absorbed in the story, turning page after page until at last the beautiful Anna threw herself in despair beneath the wheels of a train and he shut the book with shaking hands. Though his old counselor had warned him of Anna's fate months ago, the actual description of it, so precise and yet so simple, left him numb with a grief that yielded only slowly to a warm feeling of appreciation. Wanting somehow to express his gratitude to the dead author, he rose, walked stretching himself among the tables until he came to a glass case full of cakes, and ordered one that he ate hungrily. And yet, reopening the book to Part Eight, in which he had expected to be told of Vronsky's reaction to Anna's death, he was disappointed to discover that the novel took another turn entirely, so that after reading with flagging interest for several more pages he shut it dispiritedly.

It was nearly noon, and schoolchildren began arriving in the park, in which bright parasols against the sun now made their appearance too. Molkho took the trolley back into town, looked for his little Russian in the hotel, and then returned to their café, where there was no trace of her among the handful of customers. In front of the embassy all was quiet. Why, they must have agreed to take her after all, he told himself, smiling at the thought of Mr. Shimoni's surprise.

13

M EANWHILE, HE THOUGHT, I had better put my time to good use, and so, though hungry again, he decided to find out the cheapest route to the Soviet Union. On a street they had walked on that morning, he recalled, there had been a travel agency whose window was designed to look like a train compartment, complete with a white-sheeted Pullman bed and a female mannequin looking out at the passing landscape while her hair whipped in the breeze. *"Ne manquez pas la route,"* had said a poster in French, and another in English, "Go by Rail and Know Where You've Been." Retracing his steps to the place, on whose wall was a map of railroad lines reaching all the way to Peking, he was plied with so much helpful information that by the time he stepped back out into the street the sky had clouded over and the humid air brushed his face like a damp cloth.

He hurried back to the hotel to see if his little Russian had returned, but her key was still behind the desk, though he imagined for a moment that it swung back and forth as though it had just been hung up. Fraulein Zand, the desk clerk told him knowingly, had neither been back since the morning nor left any message, so that, though the sky was growing more threatening, Molkho had no choice but grumpily to set out again for the café in the hope that she was mistakenly waiting there. But she was not, and so he ordered a club sandwich and thought, She's run out on me again and who's fault is it but my own? I grew soft looking after a wife whose effective range shrank to zero and now I'm paying for it. To calm himself, he took out *Anna Karenina* and resumed reading Part Eight, but soon he put it down unhappily. Indeed, it was so obvious that nothing more was going to happen that he wondered what made Tolstoy keep writing.

Only one guard remained by the gate of the embassy, all the traffic through which was now outward. Could they really have taken her off his hands and left him with his mission accomplished? He paid for his sandwich, left the café, waited for the guard's view to be blocked by some Russians leaving work, and boldly passed through the gate and into the building, down the corridors of which he walked with a pounding heart, reminded of the times he had come to take his wife home from her chemotherapy, which had always ended as the oncology ward was emptying out for the day, so that he would find her alone in a silent room, exhausted yet glowing with hope in her hospital frock. How, he had wanted to ask, did the isotope injected into her veins find the spreading cancer, which he imagined as a reddish lode in a dark mine? Controlling his fear, he glanced cautiously into rooms whose tired officials were cleaning their desks before quitting time, wondering whether, had he taught the little Russian a secret whistle, he would dare use it now. Outside the barred windows a noiseless rain began to fall, drowned out by the chorus of Russian voices in the building. A curly-headed stranger in their midst, he turned and headed back for the entrance, careful not to lose his way.

14

B RIEF THOUGH IT WAS, the fresh-smelling downpour cleared the muggy air, which turned a luminous velvet beneath the prodigal streetlights. After all, thought Molkho on his way back to the hotel, satisfied that his little rabbit wasn't being held prisoner, not even the Russians would torture her in some dungeon just because she's homesick. Taking a shortcut through a busy arcade, he let himself be swept into a large department store, where he decided to look for presents, considered buying a fat English-Russian dictionary in the book department on a top floor, and thought better of it. Why waste the money, even if it wasn't his, when the little Russian would soon be gone anyway? Replacing the book on its rack, he wandered off to the classical music section, which had an especially rich collection of Viennese composers, and soon bought a cassette of Mahler's *The Song of the Earth* for his mother-in-law. This time, rather than another embarrassing blouse or scarf, he would bring her something cultural.

As he was riding the escalator back down he suddenly spied the plump figure of Miss Nina Zand trying on hats before a little mirror. Droplets of rain still clung to her clothing and hair, whose curls had shriveled forlornly, and the makeup was streaked on her worn face. So the answer was no after all, he thought even before laying a pitying hand on her shoulder and smelling the liquor on her breath. She smiled sheepishly, not at all surprised he had found her there drowning her sorrows in shopping, as if it were only natural for him to dog her faithfully everywhere. "What happened?" he asked quietly. "They say no," she replied, slowly removing another hat and throwing it into a pile of discards with a grimace of resignation. "No visa. No nothing. *Byurokratya.* Very too much *byurokratya.* They say no can take me." Her big blue eyes filled with guilt for letting him down. Resignedly he led her to a corner and tried getting more information, but all he could find out was that she had been made to run from one office to another all day long. The bastards, he thought, plying her with more questions that she didn't understand while steering her through the throng of shoppers, furious at the Russians for not helping, perhaps because she looked so crestfallen in her rumpled suit and white blouse, the open collar of which revealed the perspiring whites of her breasts. "Byurokratya," she repeated, as if her encounter had been with some supernatural force. Suddenly he felt a flash of violence. Damn her! he thought, almost shoving her across the boulevard past clanging, orange-lit trolleys and into the regal lobby of the hotel, with its crowd of guests and wild strains of gypsy music from the dining room. Should he go straight to his room and telephone the bad news to Israel or should he wait a little longer?

15

A FTER DINNER they went to see Mr. Shimoni, who was curious to hear the little Russian's story, even if the outcome, which Molkho had told him about on the phone, did not come as a surprise. No doubt he wanted to know about her contacts in the embassy, and perhaps, too, he felt guilty for having denied her the letter she had asked for. This time, they found other guests in the antique drawing room, two Viennese Jews who had come to pay a sick call. Mr. Shimoni, however, seemed much better, for he was now fully dressed in a dark suit and tie, although his face, the ascetic intellectuality of which had so impressed Molkho the night before, was as pale as ever. The tiny old woman from the back room was present too, wearing a black silk dress like a delicate mummy. She was Mr. Shimoni's mother, and after introducing the new arrivals she sat Molkho by her side, while her son moved the piano stool over to Miss Zand's armchair and began a brisk interrogation. Happy to be the center of attention, the little Russian related her adventures in her musical voice, gesturing broadly to help describe the Soviet officials and their offices.

Meanwhile, old Mrs. Shimoni, who didn't know any Russian, commenced an interrogation of her own to find out what sort of Molkho Molkho was, quickly determining that she knew his grandmother and paternal aunt in Jerusalem, from which she had arrived several weeks ago to spend some time with her son. "Doesn't he have children?" Molkho asked. "Of course he does," said his mother, "and very successful ones too, but they're all married with children of their own." "And where is his wife?" inquired Molkho.

"Ah," exclaimed the old woman, "she passed away several years ago." "And he never remarried?" asked Molkho with concern. "I'm afraid," said Mrs. Shimoni with a poignant look, "that finding a new wife isn't easy as you think." Molkho nodded so vigorously that his teacup rattled on its saucer. "You're quite right," he declared. "Everyone thinks it's easy, but it's not. You see," he added with a suffering smile, "I too lost my wife nearly a year ago. It was cancer." He persisted plaintively, even though to his surprise the old woman knew all about it, as if it were written on his face, "An incurable cancer that started in one breast, then spread to the other, and then . . ." But Mrs. Shimoni knew all about that too. The little Russian, it seemed, had told the old woman's son everything the night before.

Molkho fell silent in frustration and turned his attention to the men, who were hanging on the little Russian's words, which Mr. Shimoni summarized for his guests in German, with a running commentary of his own. Slighted to find his presence treated as a mere technicality, Molkho demanded a translation into Hebrew, and so received a summary of the summary. At first, apparently, one of the Soviets had asked Miss Zand to sign an anti-Israel declaration, which she was perfectly willing to do, but at the last minute he changed his mind. Then someone else began to question her abut her absorption center in Israel—especially about immigrants from Ethiopia, who seemed to arouse great interest—only to go on to something else. And so she had been passed from official to official, each of whom, she reported, had been friendly and eager to help, indeed even proud of her, yet unable to do a thing. "What did I tell you!" said Mr. Shimoni, jumping up and walking about. "They can't make unroutine decisions. They're paralyzed by their own bureaucracy!" Smiling in agreement, his two guests added something in German.

And yet, though Molkho tried hard to follow the conversation, even to participate in it, he soon found himself excluded and had to content himself with staring at his Russian, who sat glumly gripping her second glass of Scotch, a twice-failed émigrée. Finally, tired and feeling the need to take some action, he put down his cup of tea and rose to go. "But why so soon?" asked Mr. Shimoni, who seemed sorry to see them leave. "We've imposed on you quite enough," insisted Molkho, adding something about the unseasonably warm weather while beckoning to Miss Zand and nodding good-bye to old Mrs. Shimoni and her guests. By the open door of the elevator, to which he clung as if refusing to part with them, Mr. Shimoni asked Molkho about his day. "I went to the Vienna Woods," Molkho told him. "In fact, I enjoyed it, though I never got to see the zoo." "What a pity," said Mr. Shimoni. "Will the two of you be staying in Vienna or are you going straight back to Israel?" "No, we're not," replied Molkho, annoyed to be permanently coupled with the little Russian. "If I've come this far to get her into Russia, I'll look for another way —one that's less bureaucratic."

16

A T THE CRACK OF DAWN, Molkho left his room with his suit-case and rapped nervously on the little Russian's door. She was fully dressed, packed, and ready. Why, I just had to put my foot down like a man and she's my slave! he congratulated himself, seizing the steamer trunk by its handle and dragging it to the elevator. If only someone had told me about this damn thing, I could have put some wheels on it, he thought. Two is all it would have needed.

Now, however, there was no time even for one. In fact, he was in such a hurry that he skipped breakfast, though it was included in the price of the room, and paid the bill without question, asking only that the desk clerk order a taxi with a roof rack. In the train station, an immense, bustling place still chill with the vapors of dawn, he had a moment's panic that his little Russian might vanish again; but when he warned her not to, her eyes filled with tears, and indeed, she clung to him anxiously, tagging after him as he looked for their train while glancing back now and then as instructed to make sure that their porter was following.

They found their train, car, and compartment and managed to hoist the trunk onto the overhead rack, where it miraculously fitted right in. But of course, it's an old railroad trunk! thought Molkho in amazement just as an elderly conductor passing down the aisle insisted that they take it back down again. Unable to convince him that it wasn't a public menace, Molkho tried pushing it under a seat, attempted to put it on top of one, and finally dragged it to the baggage car behind the locomotive, where it was given a yellow tag, for which he paid a schilling and was handed a receipt.

He hurried worriedly back to his compartment, but the little Russian was sitting dutifully where he had left her, her face bathed in morning light. Has she gotten prettier or have I just gotten used to her? he wondered, gazing out the window at the arriving passengers. Distant music reached him from the train or station, and he shut his eyes, tired but pleased despite his sleepless night. You can't say I haven't tried, he said mentally to his mother-in-law, for whose sake he was doing all this. The air breaks hissed underneath him, and the train glided out of the station. But, throwing an arm across his face, he refused to watch or even glance at his companion, whose eyes, he felt sure, were on him. There's time for that, he told himself, the ever-louder rattle of the wheels and car joints lullabying him to sleep, even as he sensed her slipping out of the compartment. Let her roam, he thought with a smile. This is one place she can't run away from.

She was in the buffet when he awoke, chatting with a Russian soldier. Pretending not to recognize her, he ordered a container of coffee, returned with it to his seat, and reached into his briefcase for *Anna Karenina*, which he was determined to finish once and for all. So far, so good, he thought, checking to see how many pages were left. It's still eight hours to Berlin. Five pages an hour is all that it will take.

17

W ORDS WERE UNNECESSARY, the visiting card of the little hotel being all the taxi driver needed. But he could not drive up
to it, for a large trench barring the street forced them to unload their
luggage a block away despite the cold, rainy night. "Wait here, I'll be
right back," said Molkho softly, leaping carefully over the trench
with a suitcase in each hand and heading for the hotel, the little
lobby of which, he was happy to see, was as neatly crammed with
bric-a-brac as ever. Standing in a dignified black suit behind the
small bar, where he was arranging bottles and glasses, the owner
recognized Molkho at once, and Molkho shook his hand warmly,
pleased to be remembered after so many months, if only because of
his sleeper and a borrowed thermometer. In any event, here he was
again with two suitcases, a trunk up the street that he needed some
help with, and a new companion who would no doubt sleep well too.
At once, someone dashed off to fetch the trunk and the little Russian,
while someone else opened the register to look for Molkho's name
and room number. Alas, neither was there—the reason being,
Molkho explained, that he hadn't made a reservation, having just
arrived unexpectedly from Vienna. Anxiously the register was consulted again before it was triumphantly announced that there was a
room available and that if the guests would hurry up to it and
change, they might still be in time for the opera.

But there remained a small hitch. "I don't want one room; I
want two rooms," declared Molkho with a worried look at his little
Russian, who had just arrived with her trunk and collapsed into a
chair, her eyelids drooping with fatigue, oblivious of the swords and
old maritime maps hanging over her. *"Two roomps?"* echoed the

Germans sadly. *"Two roomps* again?" Doubtfully they rechecked the register, but there were no *two roomps,* only *van roomps,* and that, too, by a stroke of luck. "Only *van roomps?"* asked Molkho softly with a despairing glance at the little dining room that was already set for breakfast. He crossed the lobby, which seemed to have grown even tinier, and peered through the open door of the kitchen behind the reception desk. Everything looked dearly familiar. By the elevator the trunk and suitcases were impatiently waiting. "Can't you find another room?" he pleaded with the proprietor. "But how?" asked the German with an ironic look at his puritanical guest who traveled around the world *two-roomps*ing different women. "All right," sighed Molkho, giving in and handing them his passport, for it was getting dark outside and the little Russian was exhausted. "We'll start with *van roomps* and see."

The grandfather of the family was summoned from the kitchen to celebrate the capitulation. He, too, recognized the newcomer at once and even made some German joke that led to peals of laughter. I certainly made an impression, thought Molkho, taking the elevator with his Russian to the second floor, where they were given a room next to the legal adviser's—in fact, so like it, apart from the picture on the wall, that Molkho was flooded with warm memories. Soon they were joined by the suitcases and the trunk (which Prussian ingenuity fitted into a closet that would have defeated the Austrians) and were left to unpack, the little Russian laying her coat and jacket on the bed that she would have to share with him. How, he wondered, should he tell her? "I'll be back in a jiffy," he announced, hoping she might realize by herself. Then, her Hebrew vocabulary having reached the vanishing point as it always did when she was tired, he repeated, "I will be back soon."

18

H E BYPASSED THE ELEVATOR and bounded down the narrow, familiar stairs two at a time, though once in the lobby he couldn't say what the rush had been. Perhaps he simply wished to chat with the proprietor, who was already pouring a drink for his first customer, a dark, quiet Indian in evening dress. Were there any other reasonably priced hotels in the vicinity? Molkho asked, still looking for a way to find *two roomps.* Not that he knew of, frowned the German. That is, there was an establishment a few blocks away, but it didn't cater to the best clientele and wasn't clean; indeed, he couldn't recommend it at all for a foreign woman. "I see," nodded Molkho, eyeing the chairs in the lobby, from which perhaps a makeshift bed might be rigged.

Meanwhile, shaking drops of rain from his battered jacket, the tall student arrived with his books for the night shift and smiled a friendly hello. Whatever you say about her, thought Molkho of the legal adviser, she knew how to pick a place with the human touch. "Are the old prices still in effect?" he asked the student, who was organizing himself at the desk. They were indeed. And would his room be available the following night too? It most certainly would be. And how about the night after that? The night after that was a problem. "Well, then," declared Molkho, his anxiety abating, "hold it for tomorrow anyway."

Through the open door of the kitchen, he could see the family getting ready for dinner. The grandfather clock on the wall struck eight, and more courtly Indians began descending from above, some with white, sacerdotal turbans. Off to the opera, they filed past the desk to hand their keys to the student, who deftly hung each dove-shaped holder over its cubbyhole until there were eleven little pendulums in a row, all swinging slowly to a stop, so that Molkho, who held the twelfth in his hand and didn't feel at all tired after napping on the train, had an urge to hand it in too, go dine on wurst and fries in his working-class restaurant, and take in an opera himself, perhaps even his lost *Don Giovanni*. But, instead, he climbed slowly back up the stairs, passed his old number *Sechs,* now inhabited by turbaned Sikhs, and knocked lightly on the little Russian's door.

There was no answer. He knocked again. Still no answer. If she's fallen asleep, so much the better, he thought—but just then he heard a barefoot patter and she came to the door, a little woman barely taller than a child. "We have a problem," he smiled glumly. "This is the only room there is, which means I'll have to sleep in it too." Far from sounding despairing, however, the gusty sigh he sat down with seemed to say that this was but a minor setback in a boldly conceived plan that not only had brought them safely in a matter of hours from Vienna to Berlin but had deposited them unerringly on the doorstep of a hotel that actually had a free room, though unfortunately only one. No, he thought as she gaped at him with her big and slightly bleary eyes, I have nothing against those baby blues at all, but they definitely do not turn me on. Still, concerned for her faith in the honorable intentions of the middle-aged widower she was entrusted to, he began to pace up and down, trying to overlook the clothing she had flung all over the room. Suppose she had some organic deformity that a night with her would reveal? After all, there must be some reason she was single, some hidden flaw that might not come to light in airports and department stores but only in more intimate circumstances. Could she be missing a breast? He would have liked to stroke her curly head paternally, but unsure if the gesture would meet with her approval, he tried thinking more practically, for time was passing and they still had to eat and get to sleep if they were to rise refreshed in the morning, when they would try to find a hole in the Iron Curtain big enough for her to slip through.

He began unpacking his things, for which as usual there were not enough hangers. (The reason hotel hangers were always in short supply, his wife had once explained to him, was the management's fear that desperate guests might hang themselves on them, a theory perhaps less farfetched than it seemed.) Opening the closet, he removed the steamer trunk, which left no space for anything else, carried it as gently as a baby's casket to the side of the bed, and made of it a table for his suitcase, from which he took out his toilet articles and the clothes for Paris that he wished to keep from getting creased. Had the double bed had two mattresses, he could have laid one on the floor, but he was not about to sleep on the bare rug, nor for that matter in a chair. With a smile at the barefoot Russian, who stood mesmerized by his flurry of activity, he entered the bathroom and locked the door behind him. The sink was full of soaking laundry, pairs of underpants and bras whose suds aroused in him a flicker of hope. Should he take them out and hang them up? In the end he used the faucet in the bathtub, where he washed and brushed his teeth before placing his toothbrush beside hers in its cup on a basis of perfect equality. Silently he peed into the toilet bowl, surprised at how clearheaded he felt. Should he phone his mother-in-law that he was back in Berlin or keep it as a surprise.

19

I F YOU'D LIKE TO CHANGE into fresh clothes, I'll wait for you in the lobby," said Molkho, translating each word into sign language. Still aghast at having her porter for a bedmate, the little Russian sat slumped on the messy bed with her plump legs spread outward and stared at him in a trance. "We'll have a bite to eat," said Molkho, "and then I'll show you around and perhaps even take you to the wall. Just dress warmly, because the autumn nights here are freezing, though that's something I needn't tell a Russian."

He put on his coat, reached for the key, and then left it for her in the door, hoping she didn't blame him for their predicament, which could have befallen any two travelers. Having seen their guests off to the opera, the friendly Germans were dining in their kitchen, and Molkho put on his bifocals for a better view of them. Time passed. Had the little Russian gotten her signals crossed again? At last, the elevator opened and out she stepped in an old gray raincoat with a funny, matching beret. She had begun to understand him so much better without improving her Hebrew one bit that he was beginning to wonder if language was humanly necessary.

20

THE SAME DRIZZLE that had greeted them at the railroad station was still falling in the reddish haze of the streetlamps. They crossed some boards laid over the trench (the dirt from which, Molkho noticed, pleased to see that the city was built on its own ruins, was full of smashed brick, rotted sacking, rusty iron, and bits of broken glass) and walked to the restaurant. It was practically empty, its low prices unchanged, as were its greasy menus. While waiting for the two beers he ordered, he thought of breaking the ice with a joke about Russian politics making strange bedfellows but was discouraged by her timid look.

After supper he took her to window-shop in the little streets of the quarter, but she seemed so exhausted that he decided she had best go to bed. It was ten o'clock when they returned to the hotel. "If you're tired, go to sleep," he said, letting her into the room and going downstairs to telephone his mother-in-law from the lobby, where he asked the student to place a collect call to Israel. The old lady, however, was not in. Smiling at the thought of an eighty-three-year-old woman being out on the town at such an hour, he sat down to wait and try again. The lobby was pleasantly quiet: the Indians were still at the opera, the student was engrossed in his books, and one of his sisters was setting the breakfast tables in the dining room. I just pray we get through the night, Molkho thought, leafing through some German magazines. Not that there's any reason not to. Whatever happens, if it happens at all, is up to her. He sat there for almost an hour, missing his wife, who would have liked such a civilized place, until the Indians began drifting in, contentedly chock-full of music. What opera had they seen? he wondered, watching them collect their keys and go upstairs. He rose and asked the sleepy student to place another call, but again there was no answer. Now he was beginning to worry. Why, he thought, casting a glance at the swords in their cabinets which seemed smaller than he had remembered them, they're nothing but overgrown daggers! If I had come here with Ya'ara, everything might have been different. The student spread a mattress for himself in a corner and began to turn out the lights.

It was midnight when Molkho took the trusty elevator up to the second floor and opened the door of the room, relieved to find it dark and pungent with innocent sleep. Breathing softly and moving like a cat, he slipped off his shoes and took out his pajamas while casting a wary look at the woman in bed. Had she kept to her side of it or would she have to be rolled back? Though it was hard to tell in the dark, he saw no signs of trespassing. Just then however, scotching his optimism, her young body tossed restlessly. Hurrying to the bathroom, he shut the door and switched on the light. The little room had been the scene of intense activity and was so full of steam that he had to wipe the mirror to see himself. The laundry from the sink had been draped over the radiator with a frank lack of inhibition, and he fingered a pair of panties to see if they would be dry by the morning. Indeed, they would be. He was already undressed when he recalled that he hadn't taken his daily shower. Afraid to wake his sleeping companion, he considered skipping it; but loyalty to his dead wife prevailed and he turned on the water, hoping the sound would blend with her dreams. As he was about to put on his pajamas he noticed they were missing several buttons. My God, he thought bitterly, I should never have agreed to *van roomps!* But it was too late for needle and thread, and so he switched off the bathroom light and groped his way toward the bed, sensing the little Russian's eyes opening in the darkness. Though his side of the sheet was warm about the ankles, a sure sign that her feet had crossed the border, she had left him plenty of room. Turning his back to her, he curled up in a fetal ball. The night will pass quickly after all, he told himself, relaxing in the restful silence. It's a good thing the hotel is full of Indians and not Italians or Greeks. Just then, however, he noticed her breathing, a faint suck of air like a whistle, almost a light snore. Though it was not at all loud or rasping, he felt stunned. I've been sleeping alone for too long, he thought, but I'll get used to it right away.

21

B UT HE DID NOT. He remained wide awake, listening to her breathe. For a while he tried guessing where his mother-in-law might have gone. Then he thought of a newspaper article he once had read about how sleeping with a partner decreased one's chances of heart disease. Indeed, for years he and his wife had slept closely entwined, and her heart had held out to the end. Only during her illness did his embrace become painful, while later, when she was moved to her hospital bed, they no longer slept on one level. Now he had risen again in the world, and were he not such a worrier, it would be natural to cuddle up to the pale form by his side, whose warmth might help him fall asleep. If he managed to return her to Russia, she would no doubt remember him fondly. Yet suppose he didn't? A night like this could be misinterpreted; in fact, there was something quite animal about sleeping in one bed without a common language. Why didn't she know Hebrew, grieved Molkho, rubbing his bare feet together, or at least a little English? Though the room was hot, the soles of his feet couldn't seem to get warm.

Where was his mother-in-law? Was she, too, a secret vanisher? He thought of the summer day seven years ago when she disappeared outside the operating room, where they were waiting for the result of the first biopsy. Just then, much sooner than expected, the green-smocked surgeon appeared to report that it was positive and that the breast would have to be removed. He retired to a little office while Molkho, thunderstruck, ran off to tell his wife's mother. But she was nowhere to be seen, and so he ran back to the office, where the surgeon was nursing a cup of coffee while studying some X rays spread out on a newspaper. Was he waiting for Molkho's consent or just resting before the operation? Molkho never found out, though knocking lightly on the open door, he began to plead with the man. "If there isn't any choice. I have complete faith in you. She's in your hands. The main thing is to get it all out." The surgeon listened quizzically, finished his coffee, and strode wordlessly back to the operating room, leaving Molkho standing by a wall as white as his wife's breast, thinking of all the times he had kissed it and of how he would have liked to say good-bye, after which he went despairingly off to look once more for his mother-in-law, the only person who could comfort him, searching everywhere until he found her on a bench in another ward, chatting with a sick friend. Her smile disappeared as soon as she saw him, but at a loss for words, feeling angry at her for the first time in his life, the only way he could think of breaking the news was to slash the air with his hand.

He lay trying to still the feeling of perpetual motion inside him. Does it have some goal, he wondered, or will it just keep going round and round? Something told him the little Russian was awake: her smooth breathing had stopped and her wholesomely warm body was stiff with tension. Yes, she was awake, there was no doubt of it; he knew the signs well enough even in the dark. During the last weeks of his wife's illness, he had known before she did when she was about to open her eyes. Suppose the little Russian were to touch him now, he wondered, his back still fetally curved to her. What would he do? Their three days together had not encouraged him to think that she was attracted to him. Again he quietly rubbed his cold feet, which were keeping him awake. Though the civil thing to do was to turn and make some gesture, if only to whisper good night, he didn't want to excite her, for she had a long day ahead of her and would need all the sleep she could get. Suddenly he realized that it was raining outside. Was that what had awoken her? Then she would soon fall asleep again, for it was just a soft, windless patter. And yet she kept tossing and turning. There was a sign, followed by a tug and release of the blanket. Perhaps she, too, would sleep better cuddled up to him, he thought, worrying whether it wasn't his duty to help her in any way he could. He opened his eyelids a crack to peek at the dark steamer trunk on which he had put his bifocals. All at once the little Russian sighed again and sat up, as if trying to see beyond his curved back.

She can touch me, he thought. I won't stop her. After all, she knows I'm not sleeping, because I just got into bed. She knows I'm listening to the rain just like she is. She can touch me all she wants. And just then she did, her warm little hand making him ache queerly. I won't stop her, he thought. She can go ahead. Or does she think I'm asleep? He lay with his eyes shut tight, no longer a live fetus rocked by motion but a dead one in the grip of a fateful womb. The warm, plump hand stole up his neck and stroked the back of his head as it might a sick child. Suddenly she slipped out of bed. I'll let her come to me, he thought. But she did not. She went to the bathroom, turned on the light, and shut herself silently up there.

He listened for the gurgle of water, but there was no sound at all, just the ceaseless dripping of the rain—no paper being torn, no bottle being opened, no comb or nightgown or pill, as if she were a hunted little animal afraid to give itself away. Long minutes passed, and he realized that she was waiting too, waiting for him to fall asleep. Then I will, he thought, curling up even tighter and feeling his feet grow warm, so that sleep finally seemed possible. I'm drifting with the current, drifting, drifting, drifting, he thought, wondering whether to coax his little rabbit back under the blankets before sleep enveloped him completely. But where was she? As consciousness faded, so did his sense of direction. Was she nearby or gone for good? But no, she couldn't be. Not even the dead were ever gone for good.

22

A T NINE the next morning, carrying two large handbags that
were packed with the little Russian's clothes, the two of them
stood in a dim underground passage leading to East Berlin, Molkho
with his bifocals on in case he should have to read or sign some
document. Woozy from his night of insufficient if determined sleep,
he tried gauging the halting flow of border crossers ahead of him—
most of them subdued West Germans—like a boatsman nearing
rapids, careful not to crowd the little Russian, who had been so
taciturn all morning that even her few words of Hebrew seemed
forgotten. Not that he minded her silence. On the contrary, it was so
welcome that he all but forgave the ugly woolen suit she was wearing
again, her rigidly retouched curls, and her overdone makeup. Was he
really about to part with her or was this just one more illusion? In
either case, he thought, no one can say I haven't done my best. He
was sorry he hadn't brought his camera, for a visit to the East was
worth recording. Though he had heard reassuring reports about the
day trip behind the Iron Curtain (in fact, had the legal adviser not
slipped and gone to sleep on him, he might have taken it with her), it
was only natural to feel a tingle of fear as he stood facing the metallic
gray doors of Communism and the khaki-clad policeman guarding
them. You would think, he reflected, that if we in the free world are
willing to risk it, the least they could do is paint the entrance something cheerier.

Having demonstrated her independence of him by allowing a
German woman with some shopping baskets to push ahead in line
and stand between them, the plump little Russian stood aloofly waiting her turn, holding the laissez-passer that he had returned to her

that morning after breakfast. If they arrest her, he thought, I can always pretend not to know her. But no one was arrested or even questioned. The two of them were given their visas and directed to some stairs at the far end of the passageway, from which they emerged into a quite ordinary street no different from the one they had left: the same cobblestones, the same people, the same strips of grass and flowers, the same stubborn drizzle that failed to distinguish between East and West. He opened the new umbrella he had bought, and she teetered sulkily beneath it on her high heels as far as the first corner, where they paused to ask someone directions to the Anti-Fascist War Memorial. Though the man knew no English or Russian, he understood them well enough to guide them to a wide boulevard, along which he briefly accompanied them until satisfied they were headed the right way.

Sharing the umbrella, they came to a large, somber edifice covered with scaffolding and sheets of gray plastic and stood staring up at it disappointedly until another passerby took them in hand and pointed across the boulevard, where several tourist buses stood parked before a square, neoclassical structure with a colonnaded facade. Crossing over, they soon found themselves surrounded by tourists speaking a babble of languages, among which the little Russian, her face lighting up, made out her own musical tongue. Eagerly she looked for the source of it, for the first time almost believing that Molkho's wild scheme might yet work.

The group progressed slowly into a large, dim interior, in which, flanked by two East German honor guards standing at attention with bayoneted rifles, an eternal flame burned in a glass chamber. No one spoke. All eyes, including Molkho's, were on the bluish tongues of fire that burst from a sooty opening in the floor, spellbound by their primitive magic. Slowly he shuffled forward with his companion, who, however, was staring not at the flames but at the German soldiers, as though to catch their attention. She stopped to read a Russian inscription on the floor and then, refusing to move on with the crowd, stood reading it again, sighing with such anguish that he instinctively edged away, as if she had some communicable disease.

All at once she uttered something out loud that drew curious stares in her direction. Molkho kept heading for the exit, where he stopped and waited for her to join him. But she did not. Instead, approaching a middle-aged couple, she began speaking to them like old friends, reaching into her handbag for her papers while they stared at her with puzzled sympathy, as if searching within themselves for the code to her distress signal. Yes, she can take care of herself, Molkho observed with sudden admiration, struck by how her poorly cut clothes seemed perfectly in place here, as if everyone else had employed the same tailor. Still, he was worried that her rapid-fire Russian might get him into trouble. Before I know it, they'll repatriate me too, he thought, backing off to the safety of a dark niche in a wall.

23

H AD HE REALIZED those were to be their last moments together, he might not have acted so furtively but rather said a fond good-bye, perhaps even kissing her on both cheeks like a Frenchman. As it was, though, fearful of being incriminated in something he couldn't explain, he waited half in hiding for the tourists to disperse and clear a space around her.

But the crowd simply grew thicker until nothing remained of her but a few flashes of red fabric. Of course, they're curious, he thought. Everyone else wants out of here and she wants in—why, she's making history! Although several men in uniform were approaching and he knew that now was the time to slip out to the boulevard and back to the West, her shrill voice made him cling to his corner. After all, he reasoned, I can always say I'm a decadent tourist who's afraid of the rain.

Suddenly he heard her sob. At last, he thought with relief, listening in the ensuing hush to the traffic in the boulevard. It's about time she let it all out. She sobbed again and then broke once more into speech, her melodic voice rising and falling as though a tightly wound spring were slowly unwinding inside her. Good for her, he thought, noticing an inscription on the stone wall: "Karl Friedrich Schinkel, 1816–1818." Was she crying, too, for her humiliating night with him? But it was all for the best.

And indeed, the crowd around her now asked a pale little officer with a broad-brimmed cap and red lapels, who made Molkho think of a Turkish railroad conductor, to see what he could do. Accompanied by a policeman, he cleared a path to the little Russian and brought her to a sentry booth, in front of which two fresh soldiers with rifles stood ready for the changing of the guard. Assured she was in good hands, Molkho darted from his dark corner, opened his umbrella, and stepped back into the street. The gloomy edifice covered in plastic—which, his map told him, was the old Berlin Opera House—seemed a good vantage point from which to watch for her.

24

T RUE, THAT MORNING he had larded her handbag and coat pockets with a few more of the hotel's visiting cards to ensure her safe return, but his responsibilities, he believed, included keeping up morale in case of failure, and so he remained loyally by the opera house, trying not to lose sight of the memorial, which was continually being blocked by more tourist buses. When after a while she failed to appear, he recrossed the boulevard and joined a group of noisy Spaniards who swept him back past the honor guard, which was beginning, so he thought, to be a bit unsteady on its feet. Though the sentry booth was open, neither his Russian nor the pale officer were in it. Had she gone looking for him? Surely she must have realized that she should wait for him where they had parted. Circling the building, he joined some more tourists of unknown nationality and filed past the blue flame again. "When does the guard change?" he asked a policeman in English, and was answered with a tap of the East German's watch that seemed to mean a quarter of an hour. He went back out to the boulevard, bought a bun to appease his hunger, and returned for the changing of the guard, which took place quite simply, the two replacements stepping smartly up, barking a command in unison, and receiving custody of the flame. Just then the sun peeked out from behind the clouds, and despite the light drizzle, he resolved to go for a walk on the boulevard, which struck him as being more authentically Berlinish than the fashionable streets of the Western zone.

Stopping to ask directions, he was told that the boulevard led to the Brandenburg Gate. Soon he was there, gazing up at the Berlin Wall and its watchtowers from the East. Now, too, an ugly scar reminding the forgetful of the retribution visited upon the Nazi horror, he found it a welcome sight. Walking back up the boulevard, which was called Unter den Linden, he innocently followed a group of Dutch tourists into the memorial, the flame, perhaps because of the sunshine, now looking rather faded. He stood through a lecture in Dutch, passed the sentry booth, where two guards were having lunch, and set out to look for the little Russian in the tourist shops of the Alexanderplatz. But she was not there either, and lured back by the magical flame, he returned to the memorial. Finding it empty, he entered and strolled past the honor guard, head down to avoid recognition, since by now he had been there a suspicious number of times.

It's time to start back, he told himself, noticing the darkening sky. Indeed, the little Russian was most probably waiting in the hotel. He returned to the checkpoint, first stopping by a candy and souvenir stand that was meant to help relieve the visitor of his remaining East German marks, where, under the stern eyes of the kiosk operator, he did some complicated sums to decide how best to spend the money. It was something he was good at. More than once, while waiting for a flight back to Israel, he had exasperated his wife

by running back and forth in the airport to buy souvenirs and choco-
lates, emptying his pockets of every last coin as if he meant never to
travel again.

25

T HE TRENCH HAD RETREATED up the busy street, which was
bathed in the first rays of twilight when Molkho returned to the
hotel. At the desk the schoolgirl was doing her homework, and everything seemed so familiar that he almost expected to see the legal
adviser too. Disappointingly, though, his and the little Russian's key
was still in its cubbyhole. Loath to admit by asking about her that he
couldn't keep track of his women, he took the key with a smile, said
a few words in German, and went up to the room, in which no one
had been but the chambermaid. He considered a nap but chose to
shower instead, thus easing pressure on the bathroom later on when
they might want to go to the opera. While he was under the water,
the telephone rang. Dripping wet, he ran to get it, but it was only the
proprietor, happily informing him that there had been a cancellation
and that another room was available. "On which floor?" asked
Molkho doubtfully. "On the first," said the German. "On the first?
Don't you have anything on the second?" No, replied the German
slyly, he did not, though who knew better than his guest how few
stairs there were between them. "All right," mumbled Molkho into
the phone, "I'll let you know soon."

He went to dry himself, wondering why he felt so put out. Was
it simply his hating to waste the money? After all, the two of them
had reached an understanding that was certainly good for one more
night. Nevertheless, he went downstairs to see the room, which
turned out to be tiny, almost prisonlike in its dimensions, as though
it were the original cell from which the rest of the hotel had grown.
Molkho hesitated. "There's no air here," he complained to the

schoolgirl, who, meaning well, opened a small window. Unappeased, he went off to see the proprietor. Yet, though aware of the room's deficiencies, the German urged Molkho to take it, since his present room was only good for one more night and he didn't want to be left out in the cold.

Molkho agreed and was given a new registration form.

26

HAD HE NOT FELT SO SURE she would be back by midnight, he would never have rented the second room, but despite her talent for disappearing, he was certain that sooner or later she would have to return. He scribbled a note that said, "I'm here"; tore it up because she would be unable to read it; printed another note, which said "I've gone for a walk"; tore that up because she would be unable to understand it; and finally settled on a third note, which said, "I will be back." Then he went out to have a look around and to shop for more presents.

Though it was dark outside and the construction, which was apparently going to be a new shopping mall, gave the quaint streets a harsh look, he still felt perfectly at home: every corner, shop, and restaurant reminded him of his previous stay, which he now saw in a magical light. Could I really have been happier then, he wondered, or was it just the combination of snow, sleep, and music? He felt a sudden urge to revisit the beer cellar where he and the legal adviser had spent their last night, found it easily, and descended to the large hall, which was even more hideous when empty, its cold walls smelling of stale tobacco. Paying no attention to the dozen or so waiters eating at a long table in a corner, he strode silently among the tables set with fresh red cloths. "You killed her," she had said to him with a squirrelly look, sitting over there. "Yes," he had answered suavely, keeping his wits about him, "but in that case, so did you." "Perhaps, but not in the same way," she had reported. He should have had a comeback for that too. She never gave me a chance, he thought. It was much too soon after my wife's death. Today I'd think of something that would put her in her place. "No, thank you," he said to an approaching waiter who was about to show him to a table, "I'm only looking for a friend."

He returned to the hotel, hoping to find his little Russian. But the key was still in its cubbyhole, his note a white feather sticking out of the dove-shaped holder. He tore it up, took the keys to both rooms, debated which to make his own, and climbed to the second floor, passing his first opera-bound Indian of the evening. From the room he tried placing a long-distance call to his mother-in-law, who was out again, after which he called his Haifa apartment. The high school boy answered, his voice indistinct. "It's Dad," shouted Molkho. "It's Dad. How is everything?" The boy ran to turn off the television and returned. "Where are you?" he asked. "I'm in Berlin, Gabi, in West Berlin," Molkho said. "I'm trying to cross her over from here. Why isn't there any answer at Grandma's? I've been trying to get her for days."

The boy didn't know why there wasn't any answer, because his brother and sister were with their sick grandmother right now. "Sick?" Why couldn't he be less vague! "Yes," said Gabi. "She broke her arm and caught a bad cold." "She broke her arm? Which? When? How?" asked Molkho excitedly. But the boy only knew that his grandmother was in a cast and had been in bed for several days —how many he couldn't say. Afraid to run up the bill, Molkho hung up and paced worriedly about the room; then, hastily putting some things in his suitcase, he went down with it to the little room on the first floor and proceeded from there to the lobby. The gaily lit bar was deserted. Exhaustedly he leaned against the counter, sorry he hadn't gone to the opera instead of waiting on tenterhooks here.

Through the open door of the kitchen he watched the German family eat dinner, ladling some sort of dumpling soup out of a large bowl. In a corner flickered the spectral blue light of a television, on which an announcer was reading a weather forecast from a map crisscrossed with arrows. Would he like to join them for a bowl of

Schwemmele? asked the proprietor, noticing him and pointing to the doughy gray dumplings. Tempted, Molkho declined. "Thank you," he replied warmly. Everything looked delicious, but he did not wish to spoil his appetite, for his lady friend would soon arrive and go out with him to eat. He had simply been trying to make out the forecast. "It could be worse," said the German. "Lots of rain." "But no snow?" smiled Molkho. "No snow," the German laughed, remembering Molkho's last visit. He translated for his family, which broke out laughing too. Oh no! No snow! Not yet! They must think I'm some sort of eccentric, Molkho thought as he stepped out into the street. First I bring them a sleeper and then a vanisher, although the truth is that the sleeper brought me.

A thin rain was falling again, and he walked down the block through the yellow fog, hoping his Russian might appear. Could she be lost in it somewhere, wandering between East and West? He recalled his last glimpse of her, sobbing childishly while a crowd formed around her as the pale East German officer arrived. Or was she perhaps crying for joy? Not everyone keeps his emotions under wraps like me, he thought, stepping into his working-class restaurant. Though he considered ordering *Schwemmele*, he dutifully asked for wurst and fries, as if determined to make up for all the sausage meat denied him as a child by his mother, who claimed it was made from offal. He returned to the hotel, wrote a new note that said, "I am in Room 1," and entered his dwarflike cell. Leaving his suitcase unopened, he took off his shoes and lay down to wait in his clothes with the light on.

27

H E MUST HAVE switched off the light in his sleep, because it was dark when he awoke hours later. At first, he couldn't remember where he was. When he did, his first thought was of his mother-in-law. So now she's broken her arm, he thought. That's a bad business. At her age the bones don't knit, which means I'll have a cripple on my hands. Thank God it's just an arm. Or is it? His son had sounded as if he were hiding something. His wife had been right to insist the old woman move to the home. Not that there couldn't be problems there too. Why, just look how she had gone and fallen the minute his back was turned!

He could feel his anger at her growing. She had bitten off more than she could chew this time, and he was the one who would pay for it. He rose and descended to the lobby, where the only light came from the little bulbs lighting the cabinets of swords and maps. The clock showed after two. Behind the desk the student was asleep on his mattress. A lone dove nested in its cubbyhole. Beside it was his note, which he took and read. "I am in Room 1." Then they must have taken her after all! Could it really have gone so smoothly? Or had they simply locked her up for disorderly conduct? And I didn't even say good-bye, he mused sadly, missing his little rabbit. Why hadn't he touched or kissed her plump breasts, which now seemed such an overture to pleasure? Returning to his room, he switched on the night-light and sat guiltily on the edge of the bed. It was irresponsible, even cowardly, to have left her, he thought, studying his passport, which the East Germans hadn't bothered to stamp. Why couldn't he have waited to see what happened to her, the two old women would ask, not fathoming his fear of being trapped in the

East himself. The tiny room made him feel claustrophobic. He returned to the lobby, took the last key, went back to Room 1, packed a few things, and ascended with them to Room 9. If I'm paying for two rooms, I may as well sleep in both, he thought.

28

H E SLEPT LATE and saw by the luggage in the lobby when he came down for breakfast that most of the guests were checking out. A young girl was waxing the furniture and a thorough cleaning was under way.

He spent the morning buying a few last presents, sticking close to the hotel in the hope that his little Russian might give some sign of life, and then returned to the checkpost after lunch. "I crossed yesterday," he told the East German policeman he handed his passport to, "and I liked it so much I've come back. Is that all right?" "Of course," said the policeman without looking up. "Come back all you like. There's no problem as long as you cross back before midnight." He received his visa, ascended to the street, and strolled down Unter den Linden to the old opera house, from which he surveyed the War Memorial across the street. Then, joining a group of tourists, he filed past the glass-enclosed flame and the honor guard. Who knows, he thought, perhaps it really worked. Back on the boulevard he asked some East Germans for the Soviet embassy, but no one seemed to know where it was, and so he proceeded to the Alexanderplatz and walked about among the shops, watching some carefree teenagers who looked like youngsters anywhere. We project our fears and fantasies on the world, he thought, but the world just shrugs them off. He glanced at his map, in the margin of which his mother-in-law's old address was still written, trying to orient himself.

Perhaps he should ask directions, he thought, debating whether to strike out for some low buildings to the east on which the autumn sun shone mildly. In the end he turned to an elderly woman, showing her the writing on the map. "Taxi?" he asked. She stopped to think. "No taxi," she replied, pointing toward an entrance to the underground. "Metro?" inquired Molkho. "Metro," she agreed, happy to find a word in common. He looked at her closely. She had a trustworthy, proletarian face with gray hair pulled straight back and glasses that she removed to study the map. "Magdalenastrasse," she said, pointing to the underground again and ticking off seven stations on her fingers. He nodded gratefully, trying to memorize the name, but seeing it was hard for him, she took a pen and wrote it on the map. Then, as if assisting a foreigner were a privilege that she was determined to make the most of, she turned and climbed down the stairs to the underground, motioning to him to follow.

He did. After all, he smiled to himself, even if she was once a secret agent, she's past retirement age. They came to a gate with a machine that sold tickets and a smaller one that stamped them, though in the absence of guards or ticket takers anyone could have walked right in. Fancy an underground honor system! thought Molkho, who nevertheless feared losing his way in the subterranean labyrinth. But it was too late to change his mind, for his elderly guide had already bought him a ticket and was leading him onto the platform.

Once aboard, he sat beside her and counted the stations, feeling one with the motion of the train, which was quite modern and not at all noisy, though the tunnel it sped through seemed rather crudely hacked out. Bad finish, that's the trouble with Communism, he thought, postponing further consideration of the subject until his return to Israel, because meanwhile here he was in East Berlin, traveling the underground with ordinary people like himself. At the fifth stop his guide got off, holding up two fingers to indicate the stations that were left as if unsure whether foreigners could count. The other passengers now watched him for her. He wondered what they would think if they knew he was looking for his dead wife's first home.

He got off at Magdalenastrasse, the whole car making sure that he didn't miss his stop. Climbing some stairs to ground level, he saw that he was in an old residential area, far from the tourist sites and shops. He had barely taken a few steps when he noticed a sign with the name of his wife's street, which a quick glance revealed to be only a few shabby blocks long. He smiled wryly, thinking of his mother-in-law. So you were right after all. There was nothing here to come back to. Nothing that has to do with you or her.

29

A ND YET, suppose, Molkho thought, that his wife had wanted to come back—suppose she had—would she have recognized anything in this dreary street or only imagined that she had? That playground, for instance, with its little green gate made for children that led to a battered seesaw and some old trees with metal guards that stood sullenly stripped of their leaves. And yet it was here that her mother must have wheeled her in her carriage and here that she first began to crawl, memories that should have moved her as the thought of them moved him. Or that grocery over there—was it as drab before the War too, the few unappetizing tins of crackers, bottles of bilious oil, and bars of soap in its window suggestive of a trading post in some provincial backwater? Slowly he walked down the street, fingering his passport with its East German visa in his pocket. I've seen so many spy movies that I can't help thinking I'm being followed, he thought, though turning around to look will just make me seem more suspicious. I'd better walk slowly enough for any tail to have to pass me, though not so slowly as to be conspicuous. Not as though I were looking for something, but more like someone out for a stroll, someone who isn't quite well. Yes, that's it, he thought eagerly—like someone who hasn't been well and is just getting over it!

His mother-in-law hadn't told him the house number, nor had he thought of asking her, never imagining he would return to Berlin so soon, a notion that would have seemed preposterous; yet now, trying to guess which house had been hers, he felt sure his wife would have approved of him despite all her principles. Yes, sometimes she had wanted him to resist her, not to be so afraid. Because I was afraid of you, he murmured.

A fine, lacy rain had begun to fall and Molkho quickened his steps until he came to a fish store that seemed in such an unlikely location that the only explanation for its being there was that it always had been. Somber gray swordfish lay on beds of crushed ice, and a woman sitting by a large tiled tub stared out the window at him, perhaps hoping he might buy a fish. Did she share in the store's profits or was she simply a state employee who didn't care if there were any? Once more regretting his mother-in-law's vagueness, he walked as far as a large apartment building at the street's end, crossed to its other side, and headed back at a convalescent pace, passing the fish store again and noticing old bullet holes in the walls of some of the houses. Enough! he scolded himself, worried that his leisurely promenade would be noticed from a window. Be glad you found the street. What does the house matter? Don't be a worse perfectionist than she was! And yet the desire to know where she had lived persisted. For a whole year she's run my life by remote control, he thought bitterly. It's as though I've gone right on looking after her. How can I stop now?

He started back toward the underground, yet something in him would not admit defeat, and turning into another gray side street that was full of children on their way home from school, he stepped into a small stationery store with an old-fashioned bell that tinkled each time someone entered. Here, he felt sure, his wife had once bought her school supplies. There was no display window, all the merchandise being ranged behind the counter, and Molkho took out a ten-mark note, mentally chose a pencil and a notebook as mementos, and awaited his turn in the line of quiet children. Behind him the bell tinkled again and a new band of youngsters entered the store, among them a tall blond girl with large glasses and a wistful stare.

Molkho pointed in silence to the items on a shelf, smiling sagely to confirm the storeowner's selection. He received a handful of change, stepped back out into the street, waited for the girl to emerge, and set out after her at a safe distance with a quicker though still ruminative gait. The girl, who had on an old gray raincoat, walked as far as the corner and turned familiarly into his wife's deserted street. This is as far as I go, he told himself, a shiver running down his spine. I've done all I could, I cared for her to the end, and even if she still expects me to follow her, it's time I thought of myself. I have children who need me, an old mother in Jerusalem, and a mother-in-law with a broken arm. Even in a free country a middle-aged man trailing a strange girl down an empty, rainy street would seem suspicious. And, indeed, the girl now turned around to look, her glasses glinting in the gray light. With a show of unconcern, he watched her disappear through a doorway. Suppose I say that's the house, then, he told himself. Suppose I do. Isn't that enough?

30

A FTER ALL, he thought, it's not me who lived there or lay there having dead babies. It's no concern of mine—why stand here with my heart in my throat? And yet he kept on toward it down the unpronounceable street, which swerved oddly at that point, as if badly rebuilt from a wartime bombing. Barely half an hour had passed since his descent into the underground, yet he was so wet to the bones from the driving rain that he felt he had to get out of it and so took shelter in the entrance to the house, a prewar apartment building that appeared to have seen better days. Several mailboxes lined a small vestibule that was too dark for him to read the names on them, and he opened a door that led to a dimly lit staircase, beside which stood the small red cage of an elevator. Then this really is it! he exulted, staring at the ancient box, which suddenly rose with an animal wheeze in response to a call from above, malignantly dragging its dark tail of cables behind it.

He waited in vain for it to return, its caller having apparently vanished. At last, he pressed the button himself. With a jerk and a wheeze the gray tail slid past, followed by the red cage. Molkho opened the two doors of ancient grillwork, entered the malignant cell, and pressed a button, watching the apartment slip by. Once, long ago, her faith in life already shattered, a young girl had stepped forth from one of those doors on her way to Jerusalem. But did I really kill her? he wondered. The elevator stopped, letting him out in a hallway, where he first looked for a door without a name and then knocked on one that had several. There was silence, followed by the scrape of a chair across a floor. A child clambered up to reach the high lock and opened the door a crack, peering earnestly out at the stranger. "Doctor Starkmann?" Molkho asked the wide-eyed little boy, who was apparently all alone. "Doctor Starkmann?" The boy frowned adorably, as if trying to recall the man who had killed himself here fifty years ago, and made a move to shut the door. For a second Molkho tried stopping him, flattening himself sideways as if to slip through the crack; then, with a quick backward step, he turned and dashed down the stairs and into the rainy street to the underground, by which he returned to the Alexanderplatz, which now seemed safely familiar, despite the falling night.

31

I F YOU'RE NOT OUT TO CHANGE THE WORLD, even East Berlin can be home, Molkho thought, passing the War Memorial again, where the tongues of flame flared up in the darkness with a stark beauty. Maybe I should take one last look inside so that I can say I tried everything. Attaching himself to some tourists, he was delighted to discover that they were French and that he finally could understand what the guide was saying. Karl Friedrich Schinkel, it appeared, was the name of the architect of the building, a neoclassical structure with Doric steps and columns that was built in 1816–1818. A guardhouse during the nineteenth century, it was converted into a war memorial after World War I and rededicated to the Victims of militarism and fascism after World War II. Molkho listened with interest to the lively questions of the French tourists and then followed them across the boulevard to the old Berlin Opera House, which they were allowed to enter, despite the renovation underway.

He climbed the steps, which were even steeper than those of the West Berlin opera house. If the legal adviser had fallen here, he thought, she would have broken her neck. Beneath a high portico with grimy ecclesiastical walls, their guide lectured them about the building's architecture. What a pity there's no performance tonight, thought Molkho, whose musical reputation in Haifa would soar if he could see an opera in East Berlin. Meanwhile, impressed by the Frenchmen's curiosity, their guide found a way to usher them into the plastic-wrapped auditorium, where some old paintings on the ceiling were being restored. From a side door came the sound of music and singing. "What's that?" asked the Frenchmen. Unable to answer, their guide opened the door to reveal a small recital hall, where onstage several singers were rehearsing around a table. Could they watch for a while? he asked in German. "But of course!" said the opera singers. It would give them great pleasure for the visitors from France to see them work.

The stage was bare except for a piano and the singers kept repeating a single ensemble, which the short, dark conductor frequently interrupted to comment on. And yet though after a while the French tourists began to fidget, Molkho remained attentive. Even when they left, he stayed behind in his dark corner, particularly enthralled by one of the sopranos, whom he couldn't take his eyes off. He had never been to a rehearsal before, and while he knew he never would see the finished product, watching an opera come into being seemed to him a rare experience.

The music was unfamiliar, and he hadn't the vaguest idea if it was modern, romantic, or even classical. Indeed, sometimes it sounded so primitive that it could have been medieval, though he seemed to remember that opera did not exist then. Gradually his interest centered on the conductor, a furiously energetic little man who hopped about the stage waving his hands, breaking into snatches of song, rushing over to correct the pianist, even snatching the score from the hands of the performers and penciling in new notations, as if he were not only conducting the opera but composing it. The more exhausted the singers grew from his efforts, the more possessed he seemed to become.

Suddenly, noticing a sphinxlike figure in a corner of the stage, Molkho was gripped by the fear that the man was a musical commissar who might give an order to detain him and prevent his return to the West. Rising stealthily, he began to grope his way out. The music stopped. A hush descended on the stage. The little conductor called out to him in German. Stumbling down the aisles, Molkho ignored him. They'll accuse me of musical espionage yet, he thought, making quickly for the door. The commissar rose from his seat. Someone called out again, and this time Molkho turned to look.

Though the singers could not see him clearly, the stage being lit and the hall in darkness, they seemed to think they knew him. "Siegfried?" called one of them in a friendly voice. "Siegfried?" Molkho spun around, but there was no one behind him, and he remained standing with his shoulders hunched forward, one hand over his eyes as if staring off into space. *"Pardon?"* he answered hoarsely, convinced the French word, half a question and half an apology, would be understood. *"Pardon?"* Stumbling on to the door, which to his relief was unlocked, he passed down a hallway full of more scaffolds and tools, exited into the broad boulevard, and hurried back to the checkpoint. Without bothering to rid himself of his East German marks, he stood in line with his passport, handed a policeman his visa, and returned to the West in the very best of moods.

32

T HE TRENCH NEAR THE HOTEL had been filled in during the
day, making the going in the street much easier. The lobby itself,
however, was in an uproar: a noisy new group of Italians had arrived
and all hands were busy with their reception. A merry fire crackled
in the corner, and in cubbyhole number 1 were three messages in
German that were immediately translated into English. The first message was from Fraulein Zand, who had telephoned that afternoon
from East Berlin to tell Molkho not to worry because they had taken
her, although who had taken her where was far from clear. The
second message was from his daughter, Enat, who wished him to
know that she would pick him up at the airport tomorrow night. As
for the third message, it was from the hotel itself, informing him that
Room 9 was now occupied as per prior warning, all its contents
having been moved to Room 1.

He ascended to the first-floor room. Though great pains had
been taken to find space for the little Russian's belongings, the
trunk, having proved an insurmountable challenge, had simply been
laid on the bed as if Molkho were expected to sleep on it. At once he
returned to the lobby to discuss the matter with the proprietress, who
smiled at him charmingly from her post behind the bar, which had
already opened for the evening. He himself, Molkho explained, was
checking out in the morning, but the trunk belonged to Fraulein
Zand, who had moved to East Berlin, though she might yet come
back for it. The owner's wife was sorry to hear about the *Fraulein,*
but regarding the trunk, there was no problem: it was not the first
piece of luggage to be left behind, and there was a special storage
space for such items in the basement. She summoned the grandfa-

ther, who took the wooden trunk down with Molkho in the elevator, from which they dragged it across the lobby past a tumult of Italians, into the kitchen, through a small trapdoor, and down the basement stairs. Indeed, the old man was so gymnastic that it seemed to move by itself, bumping and bouncing along while Molkho apologized in English for the trouble and was answered with a friendly but uncomprehending nod.

The basement itself was warm, dry, and well kept. Firewood and racks of wine bottles stood against two walls, some tools and an old shotgun hung from a third, and the abandoned pieces of luggage were ranged along a fourth, each with its owner's name written on it in large letters. As they pushed the trunk into place the old German stood looking at it thoughtfully, and Molkho realized that he wished to know what was in it. A not unreasonable request, he decided, miming that he didn't have the key and that the lock would have to be pried off. At once the old man brought a flashlight and pliers, and they set to work, wrenching off the lock, opening the trunk, and rummaging through its contents, which predictably contained nothing but clothes and a few boxes of Israel sanitary napkins, whose square Hebrew lettering here, beneath the surface of Berlin, made Molkho feel suddenly homesick. Satisfied, the old German replaced the lock so expertly that no one could see it had been tampered with, and they climbed back up to the kitchen and went off together to wash. Once more the proprietor urged Molkho to join the family for dinner, and this time he agreed, thinking of the steaming *Schwemmele* he had been so curious to taste.

He was seated at the head of the table, by the grandmother. Why hadn't he gone to the opera, everyone wanted to know. And so, in an English that was translated into German, he told them about his little Russian and her adventures in East Berlin, while they listened in astonishment, incredulous that anyone might wish to return to a place all wanted to flee from—indeed, briefly even suspecting him of being a secret agent, perhaps of having attempted to smuggle the legal adviser into East Germany too. Molkho turned red. Oh no, he laughed awkwardly, this was strictly a one-time affair. But why? they demanded. I believe she has a lover there, he told them, thinking of the first plausible excuse. There was no way of getting him out, so she decided to go back. Aha, they nodded, understanding at last, though still finding it hard to accept.

33

W HO WOULD HAVE BELIEVED two trips to Berlin in one year? Molkho asked himself, strapping himself into his El Al seat on the Saturday night flight from Munich. There was a full moon, and the sky was so clear that the captain kept directing the passengers to look at some magic sight below. Once his dinner tray was removed above the already snowy Alps, Molkho took out a sheet of paper and itemized his expenses, which fell far short of the eight hundred dollars given him. I must have forgotten some meals in Vienna or on the train to Berlin, he thought distractedly; this couldn't be all I spent on her. At last he tore up the paper. His mother-in-law was unlikely to ask for an accounting, and even if she did, he could always add a service charge. Despite her condition, he looked forward to seeing her. He rose and strolled about the plane, searching the passengers for a familiar face, peering into the stewards' quarters, and going to the bathroom, where he dabbed himself with some lotion left in a bottle on the sink. Over the Aegean he conversed with a fellow passenger about the latter's aromatic cigar, which a stewardess, much to Molkho's sorrow, had insisted he put out. When the man offered him one to take home, Molkho hesitated and then stuck it in his pocket. He had given up tobacco years ago, he said, but he would smoke the cigar at home and remember its generous bestower.

Standing in line at passport control, he caught sight of his daughter on the other side of the barrier and felt his heart skip a beat, for something must have happened for her to get permission to proceed beyond the arrival gate. "It's Grandma," she wept, throwing her arms around him. "She's in a bad way, she keeps losing consciousness." He clung to her in silence. "We've got to hurry if you want to speak to her," said Enat. "She's been so worried about you." He hugged her hard and asked about her two brothers. "They're fine," she replied.

It was 10 P.M. when they emerged from the terminal into the cool, crisp air. One hand gripping his suitcase and the other resting on Enat, he let her relate the events of the past week. His mother-in-law, it seemed, feeling rather guilty for sending him off to Europe, had come straight back from the airport to make lunch for the high school boy, who was alone, and had slipped and broken her arm on the garden stairs, where she lay painfully in the cold until a neighbor happened by and called a taxi to bring her back to her home. That was on Monday, but the children heard nothing until Wednesday, when her Russian friend called to tell them she had pneumonia. On Thursday she was moved to the fifth-floor medical ward, where her condition was serious. "Now you see," Molkho said, "why your mother and I made her enter a home. We were thinking of emergencies like this."

Enat asked her father to drive. "Why don't you," he said, admiring the ease with which she handled the car. They reached Haifa before midnight and drove straight to the home. The night guard recognized them and opened the big glass door, and Molkho's daughter guided him across the lobby and into the elevator to the fifth floor, where the nurse on duty rose deferentially to greet them. "This is my father," said Enat in low tones. The nurse shook his hand warmly. "How was your flight, Mr. Molkho?" she inquired. "It was fine," he replied, "very smooth." "But you must be exhausted," she said worriedly. "Not at all," Molkho smiled. "I'm still on European time, and it's an hour earlier there. How are things here?" The nurse shook a despairing head and led them to a dimly lit room in which, softly etched in the moonlight, Omri was dozing by the window. Gently Molkho went over and put his hand on him. The poor kids, he grieved, afraid to glance at the large bed, though he already knew everything, for Death, his old friend from last autumn, was waiting here in the room. They still aren't over their mother and now this. It's just a matter of hours.

She lay there gauntly with her broken left arm in a cast and her wiry hair in disarray on the pillow, so small and nakedly frail that it gave him a start. Her eyelids fluttered and she breathed with difficulty. Suddenly Death was real again, eliding the year that had passed. Enat took her grandmother's hand. "Here's Dad," she said. The old woman opened her eyes. But did they see him? Molkho leaned over her. No, they didn't know who he was. Their clever gleam was gone forever.

34

B UT HE WISHED to give her an accounting. He had carried out his mission against all odds, and he wanted her to know it. After all, she had been worried about him, and if he hadn't lived up to her secret hopes for him and her friend's daughter, it wasn't for lack of good intentions. Yet, though Death was still waiting in the wings, this was no time to talk about his trip, for he knew from her fluttering eyes and labored breath that, her lips moving slightly, she was engaged in a more primal dialogue with herself.

He felt proud of his two elder children, especially of Enat, who had taken such good care of her grandmother, despite the trauma of her mother's death. "Has Gabi been here too?" he asked. Yes, he was told. In fact, the boy had spent such long hours in the hospital that the nurses had forced him to go home. Molkho was satisfied. "You see," he said to the nurse with a wry smile, "I'm not exactly a stranger to all this." "Yes, I know," she answered gently, and happy to see he was appreciated, he proceeded to inquire about his mother-in-law's blood pressure, her pulse, her X rays, her temperature, her medicines, and the machines she was hooked up to.

Watching his daughter wet her grandmother's lips with a Q-tip, he felt a wistful resentment. How afraid she had been even to approach her dying mother, and now she sat up with her grandmother as devotedly as if it were her mother instead. "Why don't you go home now," he said, putting an arm around her. "Why don't you both go home and let me stay. Perhaps she'll come to and we'll be able to talk. Go on home. It's later for you than for me, because I'm still on European time. I'll call you if I need you. Just give me money for a taxi and take my suitcase. There's chocolate in it for you, and tomorrow I'll tell you everything."

He inspected the night table by his mother-in-law's bed. There was no tape machine in the drawer, not even a radio. "Why couldn't you have played her some music like I did for your mother?" he asked his two eldest children. "Why didn't you think of it?" But they had, they told him. Their grandmother hadn't wanted it.

35

THEN LET IT BE WITHOUT, Molkho thought. What makes me so sure that dying is easier with music? Maybe it's just harder. He went to wash and then telephoned his mother, gravely waking her in the middle of the night to inform her that he was home. "I don't think she has long now," he glumly told her, alarming her with the news, as if she were certain that Death, once finished in Haifa, would make a beeline for Jerusalem. "Don't wake her," she pleaded. "Let her rest." He hung up and walked down the corridor, peering into the other rooms. Was Death waiting in them too? In one lay two old men hooked up to tubes and instruments. In another was a surprisingly young-looking woman and a private nurse reading a newspaper. In a third was yet another man who groaned in his sleep.

He returned to his mother-in-law's room. She was having trouble breathing, and he opened a window to let in some air. The mild night was cool and clear, the sky studded with big stars, the invisible sea a velvety blur in the background. We in this country don't appreciate what a human climate we have, he reflected, feeling a tap on his shoulder. It was the nurse, come to change the intravenous and bring him some coffee. He sipped it in his chair, no longer Death's humble apprentice but its seasoned overseer, watching her attach the fresh solution. His mother-in-law opened her eyes. He gave her a tragic smile, the coffee mug unsteady in his hand. But already her eyes were blank, the moment of recognition, if such it was, passing at once. Let her wake when she's ready, he thought, it's up to her. Indeed, he could not help but suspect that she might be avoiding him. Had she really intended to fix him up with the little Russian? His wife had often accused him of harboring unconscious motives, and in retaliation, he had tried to find them in her too; but since her death he had rarely thought about such things, the Unconscious sinking into oblivion.

36

AT MIDNIGHT he was awakened from a light sleep by the laughter of the new shift, two young nurses in starched blue uniforms and white bonnets who looked like they still were students. He and his mother-in-law were delivered to their care with a report on the previous eight hours that included a few words about him. "This is her son-in-law. He just flew in from Berlin." "Especially?" asked the new nurses in surprise. "No," Molkho said, "I was planning to come anyway." "But you must be exhausted," they said. "Why don't you let us fix you up a bed?" Molkho thanked them but explained it wasn't necessary: he lived nearby and was hoping his mother-in-law might regain consciousness long enough for him to have a few words with her. "And anyway," he added with a self-deprecating smile, "I'm an hour up on you because I'm still on European time." They took his empty mug, darkened the room a bit, and shut the door, leaving him cozily alone with the old woman and Death, though he still could hear them talking on the other side of the wall. They were louder but better-looking than the day shift, especially one of them, a vivacious, ivory-skinned brunette that something in him found irresistible. In recent years the girls had gotten prettier, that much was for sure.

37

I F SHE'S REALLY DYING, he thought after dozing off again and waking up with a start, imagining for a moment that she had disappeared from the bed, at least she's doing it easily. I should only die as easily myself. It was 2 A.M. and he felt stiff and tired. Going to the door, he looked out at the quiet ward. Only the dark-haired nurse was visible, her graceful white neck arched like a swan's above a book, a transistor radio beside her playing soft Arab music. Passing behind her as softly as a shadow, he did a sudden double take, for the book was in Arabic too. But how could I have mistaken her for a Jew? he wondered, appalled by the blindness of desire, he who had always prided himself on telling the two peoples apart. Was the other nurse also an Arab? He sought her in the hallway, failed to find her, looked in on the two old men, and noticed that an intravenous needle had slipped from its bag and was beginning to take in air. Nervously he readjusted it and returned to his mother-in-law's room, pleased with himself and swearing at the nurses, who, aware that he was up and about, soon came to ask if he meant to stay the night. "Yes," said Molkho, "if I can." "Then why not lie down?" they suggested again. "If she wakes, we'll wake you too." "No, thanks," he declined after a moment's thought. He was fine as he was, though he wouldn't object to another cup of coffee and a pillow. Intrigued by his stout, loyal figure, they brought him the coffee, a pillow, and a blanket, and he covered himself and settled back in his chair to watch the old woman fight for breath in her corner. Now and then, she opened unseeing eyes, as if deliberately snubbing him.

Suddenly he jumped to his feet, called for the nurses, and demanded that the bed be moved. "She has no air," he told them indignantly. "Move her nearer to the window, with her face toward the sunrise. Move her!" he insisted. "The bed has wheels, move it!" They looked at each other in bewilderment, not knowing what to do, but his adamance was such that at last they gave in, first moving the chairs to make room. Drunk with fatigue he stood watching, remembering his wife with her earphones in the large hospital bed, like a radio operator going into battle. Now her mother was off to the front lines too, wheeled eastward toward a sun that soon would rise. Yes, he knew how every window in this hospital faced.

It was 3 A.M. It's only 2 A.M. in Europe, Molkho thought, but so what? I'm not on their time anymore.

38

T HE OLD WOMAN did not awaken when moved. He leaned over to speak to her, calling her name, praying for five minutes of consciousness. Why, she can't leave me like this, he thought, desperate for a word with her. Yet, though her eyes kept fluttering open, even resting on him with seeming approval, she refused to come to. Did she know he was there? Could she hear him? He didn't want to talk to the wall. Her thin arm helpless in its cast, like a schoolgirl's hurt at play, filled him with pity and grief. Would she be buried like that? He wet her lips with the Q-tip, watching her hand fanning in Death. "Maybe we should call a doctor," he pleaded with the nurses, who saw no point in it. "The doctor was here in the evening and will be back at eight," they said. "Why make him come now?" "It's an easy death," added the brunette. "Why make it worse?" Yes, mine should be no harder, thought Molkho, sitting by the open window and wondering about the estate, of whose extent he had no idea. I'll divide it up among the children right away, he decided. I'll split it into three different savings plans for each, or maybe even six, or maybe nine to be on the safe side.

A shadow flitted across the wall. He turned to look. It was the little Russian's mother, who had apparently spent the night in her friend's room and now had come to see how she was. Startled, he half-waited for her droll bow, but she simply stood there, a golden butterball, her shy, exotic wonder all but gone. Though he quickly began to tell her about his trip, she already knew all about it, for her daughter had phoned from the Soviet Union that afternoon; indeed, there were several details that she now filled Molkho in on. "But why was the bed moved?" she asked. "Because I wanted it to be," he answered crossly, determined to show her who was boss. Still, he told himself, I needn't wait to the bitter end. There are people who are being paid for it, and I've already been through it. Twice in one year is too much even for me.

39

A T 3:30 A.M., not looking at all like a man just returned from abroad, he paid and tipped the driver and stepped lightly onto the sidewalk, exhausted yet floating on air. For a moment he lingered in the doorway of his house. Though his daughter had promised to leave the key in the electric box, he doubted whether she had remembered. It's been nearly a year, he thought sadly. One I was sure would be full of women, freedom, adventure—and in the end nothing came of it. Why, I didn't even make love; it's as though I were left back a grade too. And it all comes from being so passive, from expecting others to find someone for me. Lovingly, he tried thinking of his wife, but for the first time he felt that his thoughts grasped at nothing, that each time he cast their hook into the water it bobbed up light as a feather. Am I really free, then? he wondered. And if I am, what good is it? Somewhere there must be other, realer women, but for that a man has to be in love. Otherwise it's pointless, he fretted. A man has to be in love.